The Witch of the Devastation

Not far from the chasm, another dead spot spread through the Devastation. Corrupted strands still writhed, lining a…a gash. That was the only word Ashwyn could use to describe the hole that lay before them. The tear slashed across the forest, a pool of Malady lining an endless black void. Beyond the edges, flashes of silver lightning flickered across the space.

Like the gate to Obitullas depicted on the temple wall.

Ash's mouth went dry. "Where does it go?" she asked.

"A realm of death," Morlinna said. "This is what is left when the Malady takes a Saint. After days of suffering, they become a gap in the world."

Ash couldn't look away.

Morlinna drew herself up. "This is what you are agreeing to fight if you stay here. This is what I have done to myself. It is not pretty nor heroic. It is monstrous. But it serves its purpose. And one day I will turn into a gap. It will be your job to kill me before that happens. Before I tear a hole in the world."

Also by Kendra Merritt

<u>Mishap's Heroes Series</u>

Magic and Misrule

Death and Devotion

Trust and Treason

Illusions and Infamy

Sparks and Scales

Wastelands and War

<u>Mark of the Least Series</u>

By Wingéd Chair

Skin Deep

Catching Cinders

Shroud for a Bride

A Matter of Blood

Unmasked

After the Darkness

The King in the Tower Collection

<u>Daybreak Colony Duology</u>

Surviving Daybreak

Daybreak Sentinel

<u>Eldros Legacy</u>

The Pain Bearer

The Truth Stealer

The Death Bringer

<u>Godwaker Duology</u>

Godwaker

GOD WAKER

BOOK ONE

KENDRA MERRITT

BLUE FYRE PRESS

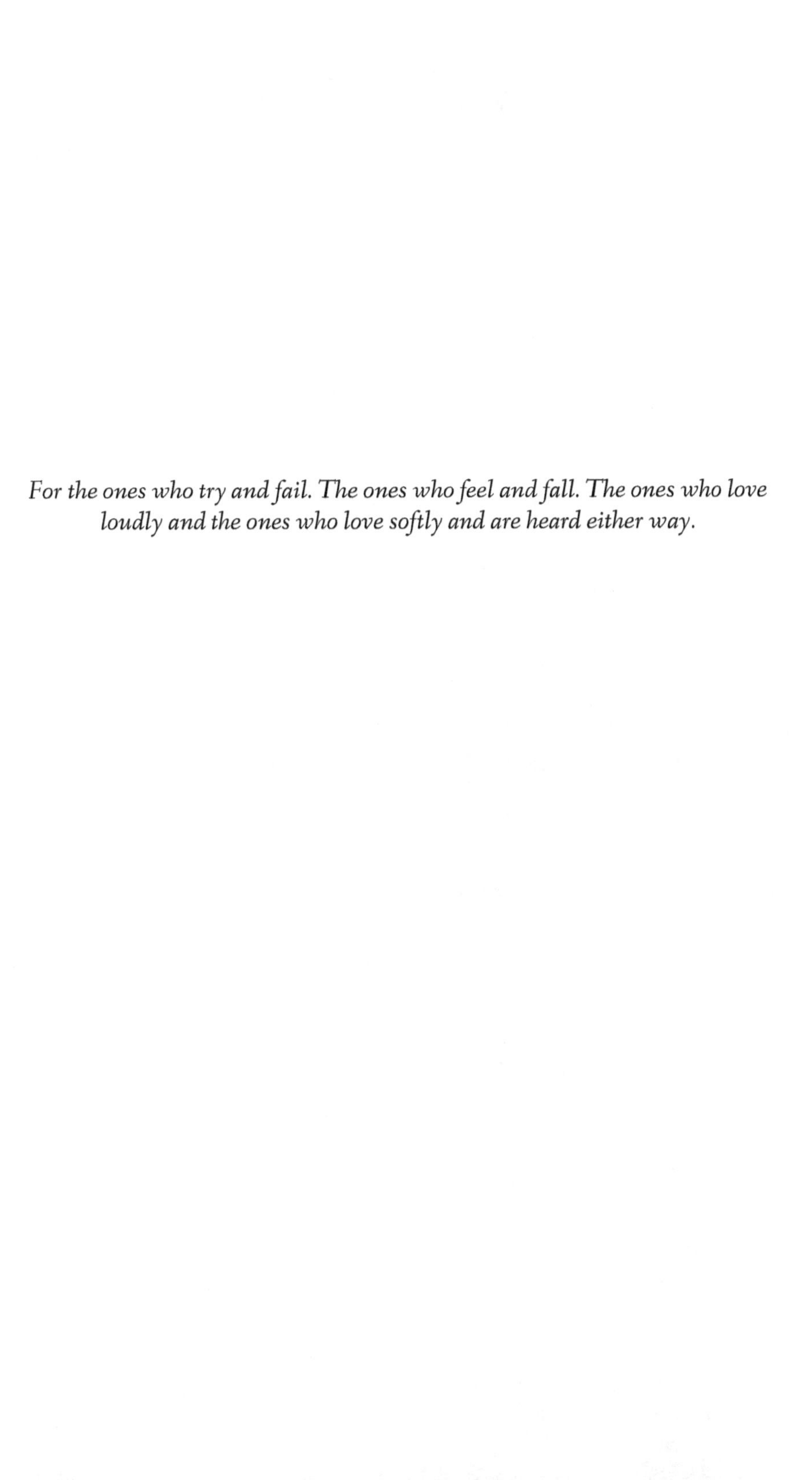

For the ones who try and fail. The ones who feel and fall. The ones who love loudly and the ones who love softly and are heard either way.

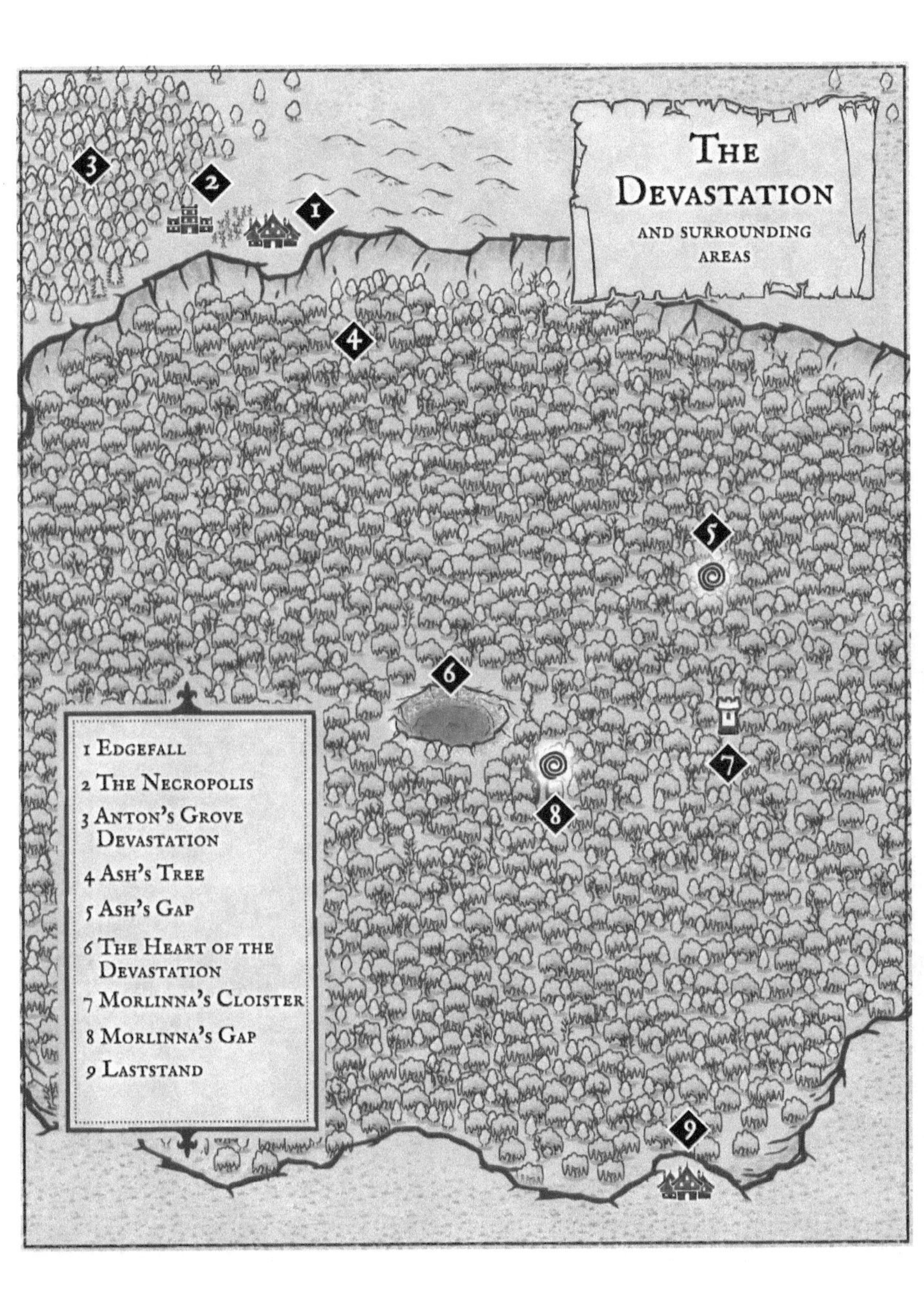

THE
DEVASTATION
AND SURROUNDING
AREAS

1 EDGEFALL
2 THE NECROPOLIS
3 ANTON'S GROVE
DEVASTATION
4 ASH'S TREE
5 ASH'S GAP
6 THE HEART OF THE
DEVASTATION
7 MORLINNA'S CLOISTER
8 MORLINNA'S GAP
9 LASTSTAND

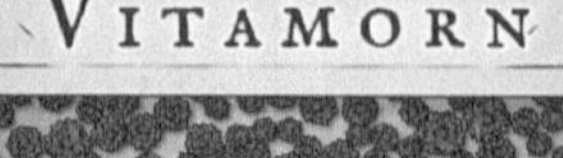

VITAMORN

1 Abdicant's Court
2 Palace of Divines
3 Saints' Hold
4 Greater Temple
5 Pallia's Laundry
6 Wesley Ranimas's House

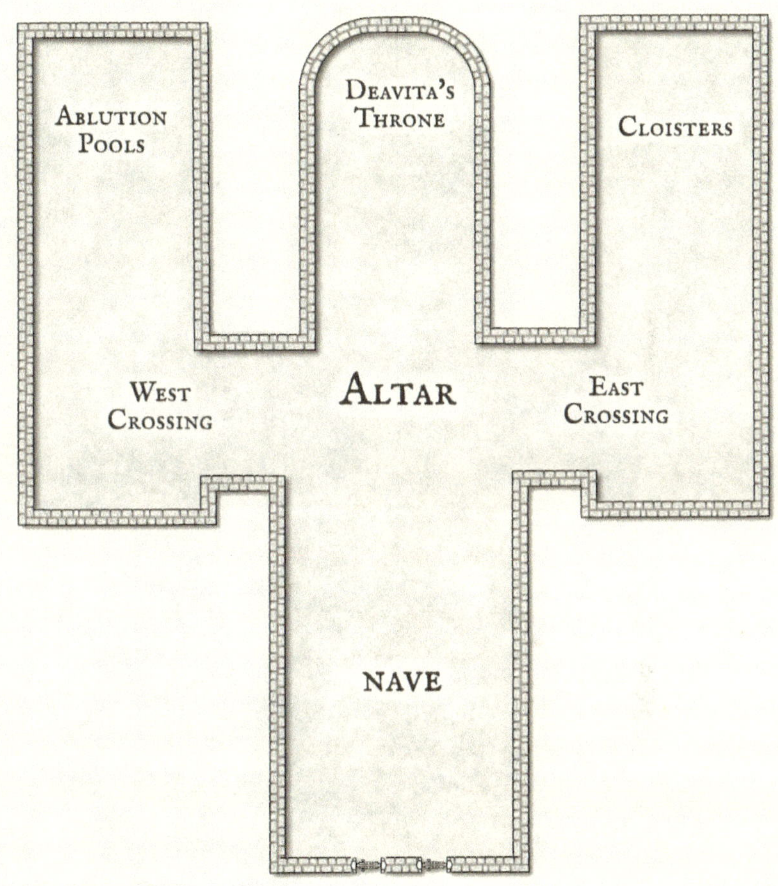

Diagram of a
Vitian Temple

Part One

Chapter 1
Concordim

Ashwyn was six when she learned their forest ate people.

On a bright spring morning, she clutched the splintered railing as Selah stood at the edge of the village and screamed.

The woman's weeping drew a crowd, and later Ashwyn would remember the wall of bodies that blocked her view from the warped porch of the orphan house.

Ash stepped onto the bottom rung of the railing and craned her neck to see. The village herbwoman put her arm around Selah, but Selah stood with her hands over her mouth, and something in her eyes made Ash's insides clench.

Beside her, Cass reached out to twine their small fingers together, and Ash held tight because as long as Cass was there, nothing bad could happen.

"I locked the door," Selah whispered, but the crowd stood quiet enough that her words reached the orphan house. "I know I locked the door."

Her husband, Mikel, sleepwalked. His nightly forays around their house had been Selah's favorite tale to tell the others at the well.

"Last night he opened all the cupboards." Or, "He put the washing away. Why can't I get him to do that when he's awake?"

But this morning they'd all woken to find Selah's door hanging open and Mikel gone. The elderman had found his slipper at the edge of the village where the street disappeared into the tangle of gray vines and black roots that marked the end of the world.

"What happened?" Ash asked Bayna. Cass's mother leaned on the railing beside them, her knuckles going white under their grime. "Where's Mikel?"

Bayna glanced down at them, her mouth pulled tight so the creases disappeared. But it didn't make her look younger. It just made her look haggard.

"He's lost," Bayna said. "Poor soul wandered into the Devastation."

They'd been warned about the place. *Of course,* they'd been warned. "Don't walk near the forest. It will take you."

But the words had always felt like the ones that had warned them away from a hot stove. Or the cupboard where Bayna hid the sweets. "It will burn." Or, "They're not good for you." Important words. But not deadly words.

A flock of magpies erupted from the edge of the forest, and every villager in the crowd flicked their fingers at the corners of their eyes to ward off the bad luck brought by the birds.

But it was too late for Mikel.

Across the road, Edgefall's herbwoman drew on Selah's arm and steered her away from the shadows that crept from the forest's edge. The housewife still clutched Mikel's slipper in her hands.

Bells rang from the Lower Temple, calling for the first shift, and the crowd dispersed. A couple of men shook their heads as they passed beside the orphan house, headed for the far edge of the Devastation with their saws and axes slung over their shoulders.

"It's a shame," one muttered to the other. "Poor Selah."

"She'll heal," the other said. "In time. We always do. Life is hard."

"But Edgefall is harder."

Ash had heard the phrase before, always spoken with that bit of steel under the words. But it didn't make her feel better this time.

"Why don't they go after him?" she asked. Her hand trembled in Cass's grip, as if she could hop off the porch and plunge into the Devastation herself just to look for Mikel.

Bayna snorted and pushed upright. In the morning light, her thin hair seemed more gray than blonde.

"Don't be stupid. No one goes into the Devastation. It kills anyone who sets foot inside. It sees no difference between the missing and the rescuers. Everyone is a meal."

She fixed Ash with a glance that told her it was time to shut up.

Ash had seen the look many times over the years of her short life, but that didn't mean she was any good at heeding it.

"Why do we live here, then?" she said. "If it's so dangerous."

"Because it is *our* danger," Bayna said fiercely. Then she shooed back the other children who had gathered in the doorway. They scattered away from the opening, disappearing inside the cramped orphan house.

"I'd rather have *no* danger," Ashwyn said with all the arrogance of a six-year-old.

Bayna gave her a sour look and crossed her arms. "Hush, girl. You don't know what you're talking about. *Life* is danger. And the Devastation is better than the alternative."

"What does that mean?" Ashwyn said.

"Come inside. We have enough time to attend prayers before you do your chores," Bayna said. "Everyone pulls their weight in Edgefall. If we're to survive."

Ashwyn made a face. "But what does it mean?"

"It's not appropriate for children." Bayna disappeared inside the orphan house, pushing a couple of the others in front of her. "Cassarah? Come along."

Ashwyn huffed and stamped her foot. "That's not an answer," she muttered.

"You don't always get answers. It's the way the world works," Cass said, as if she was quoting her mother.

"Well, it shouldn't." Ashwyn let go of Cass's hand long enough to peer into the house and make sure Bayna was occupied handing out assignments. Then she leaned over the railing to check that no one was paying attention to the two little girls on the porch.

"Come on," she said and grabbed Cass's hand again. There was at least one person who would answer her questions. Rafe was never afraid to tell her things. Even things that other adults thought children shouldn't know.

Cass threw one look back at her mother, where she managed the other war orphans. Then she bit her lip and let Ashwyn tug her along in her wake.

The two girls scampered between workers carrying axes and cauldrons of pitch and farmers with bags of seed slung over their shoulders. The first shift headed for work. In the afternoon, they'd switch with the others and head to the temple for prayers.

Bayna kept telling Ash that as soon as she was big enough to hold an axe, she'd join the workers who cleared the overgrowth. Because Edgefall needed every hand. Even the littles had jobs, and everyone took turns hacking at the vines that threatened the fields.

Ashwyn and Cass wove their way through the hamlet. Sturdy stone buildings with thatched roofs stood along the straight main road. The peaked roof of the Lower Temple presided over the square and the central well, but Ash avoided it just in case someone thought to send them back home.

Just before they reached the fields, a squat, square building rose, framed by the knots of vines and dense thickets of the Devastation. The thick scent of freshly-turned dirt filled the air.

A man pushed through the door of the Saints' barracks, the bright silver buttons catching the sun against his black uniform. He tilted his head, his normally cheerful face subdued for once.

"You shouldn't be about alone, girls," Ingrim said. "Not on a morning like this."

"We're not alone," Ash said quickly. "We have each other." And they were still in the village proper, where it was boring and safe. The only time they had to worry here was during an incursion.

Ashwyn pushed her dark hair back. Bayna always yelled at her to tie it away from her face, but the strands never stayed where she put them.

"Where's Rafe?" she asked.

Ingrim gave them an indulgent smile and rested his hand on the hilt of his sword. "Around back. I'm on duty, so I have to get going."

Ash didn't wait to watch Ingrim join the workers in the fields. She led Cass around the corner of the building. The Saints' barracks was even bigger than the elderman's house. Maybe there had once been more Saints stationed here, and they'd needed the room. But now Rafe often complained that he and Ingrim rattled.

Around the back, facing the fields, stood a practice dummy, a straw archery target, and a forge. Rafe sat at the grindstone, deftly sharpening his long blade against the spinning stone. He wore his overlong hair in a spiky tail at the nape of his neck. Several strands had fallen into his face, but his uniform was crisp and pressed.

Ashwyn finally dropped Cass's hand and trotted up beside the man.

"Ash," he said without looking up. "Have you run away from your chores again?"

"No. I didn't get any." It wasn't a lie. They'd left before Bayna could assign any.

Rafe tilted his head enough to eye her, as if he knew she was stretching the truth. "Really?" he said, drawing the word out.

She shifted her feet. "Yes. Can I talk to you?"

"Oh, Dea, this should be good. What do you want to ask?" he said, but he didn't stop his work.

"Why is the Devastation better than the alternative?" she said, making sure she got all the words right, just as Bayna had said them.

Rafe drew in a breath. Then he let the grindstone fall still and laid his sword carefully beside him before turning to face her. "All right. I'm listening. What all do you want to know?"

"Why won't anyone go after Mikel? They could still find him. Why is everyone so afraid of the forest? Why is it better than the alternative? What's an alternative?"

Rafe's eyes had gone deep and sad, but he gave her a little smile. "That's a lot of questions."

"No one else will answer them."

He patted his knee, and she hopped up to sit on his lap and snuggle close. Cass stepped forward, and he tucked his other arm around her.

"They're right, even if they won't explain it all," he said. "The Devastation is sacred to the Goddess. It is Her domain. And it is as deadly as She is. We do our best to keep people from going in by accident or because they don't know any better. But when an accident does happen..." He grimaced. "We can't throw away more lives looking for someone who is already gone."

He leaned back enough to meet each of their eyes seriously. Like they were grown-ups. "Anyone who goes into the Devastation is lost. We can't get their bodies back, and if we can't get their bodies back, then..." He trailed off like Bayna did during lessons when she was waiting for an answer.

"Then they can't go to the necropolis," Cass said.

Ash wasn't sure why that was so bad. Who wanted to live in a dusty old city after they were Absent?

"Exactly. If we can't find their bodies, then they can't Return."

Oh. And that meant the living would never see them again. The thought made her chest tighten, but she took a deep breath and reminded herself that her mother was already safe in the necropolis.

"So the forest really does eat them," she said.

"Like an animal trying to survive." Rafe extended his arm to indicate the villagers bent over in the fields, the clearers beating away at the knots of vines creeping toward the workers. "But what used to be there was even worse."

His voice grew lower, and the girls leaned closer.

Even at six, Ash knew how ghost stories worked. Some of the older children in the orphan house liked to scare the littles when the lights went out at night. Ash loved the shiver it gave her.

"What used to be there?" she said.

Rafe stood, hoisting Ashwyn in his arms so they could stare out at the tangles of the Devastation and the sweeping spread of it across the land as far as they could see. "The Malady," he said.

Cass sucked in a breath, clutching Rafe's legs.

Ashwyn made a face. The priest loved to talk about the Malady and the Little Wars, but he didn't love telling them what it was.

"Our Devastation," Rafe said, pointing south. "Is where the Malady started."

"What is it?"

"An infection that corrupts all the life it touches. Plants, animals, even people. It spreads and spreads. And then it kills them."

Ash didn't know that word. "It...makes them Absent?"

Rafe met her eyes seriously, and she made sure to listen with her entire body.

"No, Ash," he said. "Absent can Return. The ones who go through the Last Death fall to dust and are gone forever." He hesitated and then added. "Your mother went Absent while fighting the Malady in the Little Wars."

Ash's mouth snapped shut on her next question. She didn't remember much about the fighting that had left so many war orphans, but she did know that if her mother had left to fight the Malady, then it was something to be feared.

Rafe's arms tightened. "You don't have to be afraid. We beat the Malady here long ago. And now we just have the Devastation."

"Why?"

"It's the Goddess's protection. She grew the Devastation to keep us away from the areas that might still be dangerous."

Ash glanced over his shoulder at the Lower Temple in the middle of the village.

"And She and the Order sent the Saints to make sure everyone is safe and stays out of the forest."

"Like you," Ash said quietly. "And Mom." Her fingers touched the thick wool of his black uniform.

His smile went deeper even as his eyes filled with an emotion more complicated than sadness. "Yes. Like your mom. She was the bravest, most selfless person I've ever known. And the best partner." He pulled her closer to whisper. "But don't tell Ingrim I said that."

Ashwyn giggled. "I like Ingrim. He gives us sweets when Bayna's not looking."

Rafe widened his eyes. "Does he now?"

"Ash," Cass said, tugging on the edge of her smock. "Let's go. We're supposed to be going to prayers."

Rafe put Ashwyn down, and she followed Cass to the edge of the Saints' barracks. The flock of magpies had alighted along the crest of the roof, flashing their black and white feathers at each other.

Ash paused at the corner of the building and looked back at Rafe.

She opened her mouth to ask why the Bladesaints hadn't kept Mikel safe. Or her mother. But she knew that would deepen the sad lines around his eyes.

Maybe it had something to do with the big Saints' barracks and all the empty beds lined up inside. Ingrim and Rafe were the most amazing people in her life. But even they couldn't be everywhere at once.

As she followed Cass around the corner, a lump settled under her breastbone.

If the most amazing people said that Mikel was lost, then he really was lost.

After that morning, any time they stole away to play, Ashwyn watched the edge of the Devastation, searching for signs of Mikel. Waiting to see if he'd reappear.

But he never came out again.

Chapter 2
Concordim

Escaping their chores became its own game over the years. If Ashwyn couldn't sneak off before Bayna handed out their daily assignments, then she'd find a way to turn the work into an escape.

She didn't remember the exact day it all changed, but it started when Bayna handed her a couple of swishy branches from a sentinel tree and told her to scare the magpies from the fields. The birds dipped and dove over the village, making the adults flinch and curse, and if they settled for too long in one place, people whispered about bad luck.

The branch rested, light and perfect in her hand, and Ash sprinted away from Bayna, barely hearing her shout to "stay by the fields."

Ash meant to. She really did. She swung her stick as she leaped across the furrows and ducked between towering stalks of corn.

But the birds all took flight, leaving her without an adversary, and a quick scan of the fields revealed Cass's bright hair shining in the sunlight as she followed behind the clearers. There'd been an incursion the day before, and bits of vines and roots littered the ground between here and the forest, waiting for burning.

"Cass," Ashwyn called. "Cass, let's play Swords and Saints!"

Cass bit her lip and glanced at Pauler, the clearer she'd been assigned to that day. He opened his mouth, probably to protest, then shook his head with an indulgent sigh.

Ashwyn took that as tacit permission and grabbed Cass's hand. "Come on."

Cass laughed and dropped her rake to follow her.

Ash meant to stay by the fields and swing her pretend sword at the magpies brave enough to swoop in, but it was so much more fun to jump off the rocks around the village and lunge at each other as they played. She loved the way the switch whistled through the air. In her head, she was a Bladesaint fighting off the nebulous Malady or keeping the village safe from Devastation monsters.

But as she fled Cass's attack and darted between the houses, Bayna's hand shot out and grabbed her arm hard enough to hurt.

"Ow," she cried.

Bayna's palm cracked against her cheek, making her gasp. "Little shirker," she hissed in Ash's ear as Cass looked on, eyes wide. "You don't even understand how much you're costing everyone, do you?"

The words were the same as always, blended together to form a torrent of hate. Ash was always in trouble, but right now the sting in her eyes hurt worse than the sting in her cheek, and it had everything to do with the way Cass was watching.

Bayna took a deep breath and blew it out through her nose before straightening. Her grip stayed firm on Ash's upper arm, fingers digging into the muscle.

"Dea save me from dense little girls," she said, raising her eyes to the heavens. "We don't have enough of anything to be wasting it on children who don't help."

Ash's lips tightened, and she raised her chin. "I—"

"Do you even know that you're different?" Bayna said. "Parents are supposed to feed and clothe their young ones. They take up the slack when they need to and make sure their children are cared for. You don't have that."

"I know," Ash said. They'd even put it in her name. Everyone else got to be from Edgefall. But Ashwyn...she was Ashwyn of Nowhere.

From the look in Bayna's eye she thought she was going to earn another slap. But it didn't come.

Bayna's eyes softened around the edges just a little. "You don't act like it. There's no one for you, Ashwyn. No one and nothing. That means everything you get, someone else had to give up."

Ash's eyes widened. That morning, Cass had shared her bread. Did that mean her friend had gone hungry? The shirt she wore had been a gift from the herbwoman. The Fairhands had given her these shoes after their brood had outgrown them.

"There's no room in this village for someone who hasn't earned what they've been given," Bayna said. "Do you understand now?"

"That's enough, Bayna," Rafe's voice said.

Ash's throat closed up, and she didn't trust herself to speak, but she turned and found the Bladesaint at the corner of the nearest house.

Bayna finally let her arm go and turned to her own daughter, jerking her head at Cass.

No room for her. What did they do to people they didn't have room for? Kick them out? Throw them into the Devastation?

In all of her short life, Ash had never left the village. She'd never dragged Cass farther than the other side of the square where the road disappeared into the hills, and somewhere beyond that it found the city.

Because why would she leave when Cass was here?

Ash shuddered, her switch dropping to the dusty ground.

Rafe stepped across the dusty street and gripped her shoulder. "You all right?"

Ash swallowed the lump in her throat. She looked up at Rafe. He'd always told her the truth. He was the only one who ever did.

But she didn't even get to ask her question.

"Edgefall is a hard place," he said. "You know that."

She turned so he couldn't see the way her eyes filled.

Bayna was right, then. She was costing the village, and no one wanted her here if she didn't help.

She'd have to leave, and she'd never see Cass again.

Unless she worked. Unless she became so valuable, they'd never even think of getting rid of her.

Who was the most important person in the village? The elderman? He made all the rules. Could she do that? But there was only one of him, and Bayna wanted Cass to be the next elderman.

There were others who were important. Even Bayna listened to Rafe because the Bladesaints kept them safe from the Malady and the Devastation.

Had they listened to her mother, too?

"How did Mom become a Bladesaint?" she asked, mind leaping to the next step.

His smile returned. "She was the strongest and cleverest person around," he said. "All Bladesaints have to be."

Strong and clever. The words rang in her head.

A snarl rolled out from the edge of the Devastation followed by a scream. Rafe spared one glance at her before running to guard against whatever came out of the forest. Back to his job that she'd been keeping him from.

She stared down at her empty hands until the sting left her eyes and her cheek.

They hadn't kicked her out yet. There was still time to change. To be someone they wouldn't want to get rid of.

She snatched up her branch again and started for the fields where the magpies gathered along the fence.

Clever wouldn't be hard. Bayna always told her she was so sharp she'd cut herself. And she could be strong if she wanted to be. Her mother's face was a hazy blur in her memory, but she did remember her hands. The way they would toss her high overhead one minute and send her blade through the practice dummy the next. And she remembered the feel of them closing around her small body the last time they'd said goodbye.

She could be a Bladesaint. Then no one would dare make her leave Cass behind.

Chapter 3
Animatim

Vitania stepped through the long grass, keeping her legs bent so her head stayed below the tops of the long stalks. She slid her foot across the ground and transferred her weight toe first, so her boots stayed quiet and didn't disturb the grass.

She was the hunter here, never the prey, but a good hunter never let their quarry know their position.

V stopped and knelt, heedless of the dirt, and ran her small hand over the bent stalk of grass in front of her. She'd nearly missed it. And below the grass, the edge of a boot print, far larger than hers.

V bit her lip and stilled her throat to be sure no noise escaped. But she stood again and moved quickly, her eyes scanning for anything her ears would miss.

A shadow lurked behind the screen of summer-gold grass, and she pounced, wrapping her arms around the startled figure.

Her father grabbed her as she lunged and threw her in the air, laughing. He swung her once more till she was breathless and set her down to free his hands.

"Great work, V," he said, his hands moving in the signs that helped her catch the words he spoke. "I didn't hear you."

She beamed. "I'm quiet," she said. "And I found you. I won!"

"You did. I'm so proud of you. What things did you find?"

She pulled on his hand and led him back through the field at the edge of the estate, pointing out the bent grass and the footprint. In the distance, the roof of the manor rose just on the other side of the hill.

The whole estate belonged to her father's family, and some distant grandparents let them stay there. Because of her. No one had explained why, but somehow, she was important enough that they had all this space to themselves, and they only had to share it with Ben and Jessie and Gell.

Her father gave her another smile. "Great work," he said again. "But you missed this one." He brushed aside a stand of grass to show her the torn strands of his coat hanging on a stalk. "And this one." A bit of blood splattered the dry ground, nearly disappearing into the dust, and she noticed he'd wrapped a bandage around a new cut across his hand.

He gave her a smacking kiss on her forehead, and she grimaced as she wiped the wetness away. "Papa," she signed.

"I know you'll find them next time. You're good at our games."

"I always find you." She tackled him, and although she was only half his height, he tumbled to the ground, giving her the advantage for a second.

She drew her practice sword and sprang over him as he rolled.

He came up swinging, making her dodge back. Her small size let her get close, and she darted past to swipe at the backs of his legs.

He fell to one knee, sword high to take her next blow. So she came in low, sliding the wooden blade across his belly.

His eyes widened in surprise.

"I killed you," she said, her breath huffing out in a triumphant laugh. "You owe me sweets."

He raised a hand to stop her, and she instantly stilled. V swung around to finally see what he'd seen. Jessie and Gell hurried across the meadow.

Jessie wore the worn trousers she always wore when cleaning the house, and she brought with her the faint scent of lavender cakes, which meant her husband, Ben, had to be done readying lunch. V's stomach growled.

Jessie knew the signs V's father used—she was the one who'd taught them to him in the first place—but right now she spoke without them, a sure sign that she wanted to keep whatever was happening from V and Gell.

Unlike Gell, V could hear a lot of what went on around her, but any background noise muddled people's voices until they disappeared into a murky mess. It was much easier to catch what other people said if they used signs.

Her father's smile faded. So many of the lines on his face came from his joy. She hated when anger replaced them.

V glanced at Jessie out of the corner of her eye, gaze on her lips. She couldn't keep up with normal conversations by reading lips. Grown-ups went too fast. But without signs, it was her only option to supplement what she heard.

This time she caught more among the buzzing rise and fall of Jessie's voice, and her heart leapt as the word "Abdicant" surfaced.

"Someone is here to see me," her father signed. "Go play with Gell."

"My mother?" V saw no reason to hide her interest. Whatever the answer, she knew what she would do next.

Her father sighed. "Yes. Stay out of her way and no signing. Right, V-girl?" He held his fingers up in a V and swept them across his chest in her own special sign.

V nodded and let her father push her toward Gell. Jessie's boy was only a couple of years older than V, with long shaggy hair and a dreamy expression behind his blue eyes. But his best feature as far as V was concerned was the way he let her boss him around.

She grabbed his hand and pulled him deeper into the meadow as Jessie and her father turned back toward the house.

Then, at the bottom of the hill, where the grass gave way to a muddy stream bed, now a bare trickle in the summer's heat, she turned to follow its curve back up toward the house. The swell of the hill would hide them until it was too late.

Gell tugged on her hand until she finally turned to see what he signed. His hands were swift and sure, and he didn't even try to voice for her.

"Wait. We have to play out here."

She grinned and shook her head. "I want to see my mom."

"Please don't break the rules."

"Stay here, then," she signed with a huff. "I didn't ask you to come."

She left him with the mud seeping up around his boots.

A trellis outside the kitchen door made a perfect ladder to the second floor, where the open window let in a breeze.

Her heart beat faster as she situated herself below the sill among the thorny roses that grew along the trellis. Her mother was a Nexsaint. One of the best in the world. Which meant she could see the threads of the Nexum. If she glanced toward the window, she'd be able to see V's threads where they shouldn't be. But that was why she'd positioned herself here where her strands would blend with the flowers and the trellis and the wall, and she wouldn't be caught.

At least not immediately. She'd have time to think of an excuse before then.

She nudged the window farther open and peered up over the sill.

There. Her father stood, hands crossed over his chest, as he leaned against the far wall. A woman paced the floor in front of him. Back and forth she strode, her fine robes sweeping out to brush the rug each time she turned. Her hair gleamed long and bright against the black fabric.

V bit her lip and stared. Her mother was usually too busy to check on her progress personally. She'd only been to the manor once a year since V had been born.

No one had told her what the Abdicant did, but V knew it was important.

Really, really important. And it was something only her mother could do. After all, she was always referred to as "*the* Abdicant." Never "*an* Abdicant."

She held her breath so it wouldn't rush in her ears, and she kept her gaze on her father's mouth, hoping to catch some piece of their conversation.

But this wasn't a conversation. It was an argument.

Her mother's face burned red and shiny, like she'd been shouting, and Papa's lips had gone tight. He looked like a completely different person without the smiles or the jokes. Like his face had been carved in stone.

Her mother spoke, but she'd turned from the window so V couldn't hear over the rustle of the vines.

Her father pushed away from the wall, hands falling to his sides, fists clenched. His words at least came slow and intense enough to carry.

"She. Is. Six," he said. "She's not ready for that."

What wasn't she ready for? V bit down the urge to get his attention. To tell him not to embarrass her in front of Mother. She could handle anything her mother wanted.

Her mother turned, hand slashing through the air, as if whatever she said was the final word.

"Make her ready," she said. And then the woman strode for the door.

V sucked in a gasp and skittered down the trellis, hoping to reach the front of the house in time. If she jumped from here, she might make it...

The thorns tore at her clothes and hair, but she launched herself toward the ground and rolled when she struck. Just like in her father's games. Then she sprinted for the door.

She reached the foot of the front steps just as the great double doors opened, and she slid to a halt, sending up a wave of gravel.

V swallowed down her gasps as her mother swept down the stairs. The afternoon sun pulled glints of gold from her honey-colored hair, matching the simple metal circlet that she wore across her brow.

V should leap into the bush. Hide herself. Her father had said to stay out of her way.

But her feet stayed rooted to the spot.

The woman glanced up, and V's mouth went dry.

She didn't sign a thing.

Rule number one in the manor: no signing to anyone outside of Jessie, Ben, Gell, or her father. And for some reason, that included her mother.

Her father had raised her. Her father made sure she was happy. He played games with her, he snuck sweets with her, he came to her in the middle of the night when she woke in muffled darkness.

Her father kept her safe.

She'd never questioned his one rule because then everything else around it would come tumbling down.

So she stared at her mother and didn't sign.

Her mother stared back, then gave her a wide smile that seemed sad at the edges. The Abdicant swept forward, her robes brushing V's scratched arms before V felt a kiss against the top of her head.

Then the woman stepped away and made a pulling gesture with her hand. The black robes swirled, and the Abdicant disappeared into a funnel of whirling colors.

And V was left alone on the step.

A change in the air told her that her father had moved up behind her. She looked up at him.

"What did she say?" she asked.

He carefully fitted a smile over the stony expression he'd used with the Abdicant. And suddenly he was her father again.

"She came to check your progress," he signed. "She's very proud of you."

The words made her belly go warm and squidgy, but V bit her lip and wondered why they also made her want to cry.

The next morning, she woke to a touch on her cheek. It was her father's way of warning her of his presence when he wasn't sure she'd hear him coming. Vitania blinked in the dim light of dawn and sat up to ask, "What is it?"

"Come," was all he said.

Wide awake now, V bounded out of bed. Only the most special of games started before the sun was even up.

But Papa didn't head to the field or the yard with the training dummies. He hefted a pack over his shoulder and led her through the gates at the front of the estate.

V skipped to keep up. The air slipped cool against her skin this early, but Papa hadn't bothered to make her grab her cloak. It would be warm soon enough. She shook her head and let her hair fall down around her shoulders. She normally kept the light strands pulled back while they played, but ever since yesterday she'd wanted it loose. Like Mother's.

Her father veered left off the road just outside the estate walls, and V perked up as she realized where they were going.

The Lower Temple stood at the end of a boulevard lined with trees, its facade covered in carvings of leaves and flowers. One caretaker priest swept the portico and stepped aside with his head bowed as they passed.

Papa led V to the altar, but V knew all about this part and didn't wait for him to bend down before giving her own bow. She craned her neck to see the statue standing over the altar. Her favorite part was the eyes, the way they crinkled at the corners as the Goddess looked down at them. Her father's eyes did that, too, when he smiled.

One day, she'd stand before the Goddess on Her throne in the Greater Temple, and she'd make her offering and become a Nexsaint, just like her mother. She'd see the Goddess for real, not just this stone cast of something that should have been alive and breathing.

V glanced at her father for permission to rise, but he waited, his mouth flat. There were no crinkles at the corners of his eyes this time.

"Why are you sad?" she whispered.

He shook his head. "I'm not sad."

She made a face, and he sighed, his shoulders heaving with it.

"I don't know how to explain. I love our Goddess." He spread his hand up in the sign for Deavita, fingers splayed like a tree or a blooming flower. "But it is our need that holds Her here. That's what makes me sad."

V frowned. If the Goddess hadn't Descended, they wouldn't be able to Return. It was Her greatest gift. And gifts shouldn't make someone sad.

But before she could respond, her father bowed again and ended his internal prayer with the one he'd taught her as a baby.

"Deavita, keep us in goodness, gentleness, and joy. For your freedom we pray."

The Saint's Petition. She'd always thought it was strange for warriors to pray for gentleness and freedom. How were they not free? They only had two rules at home. That wasn't that many compared to other people.

V ducked her head as he stepped down the nave toward the door.

She signed out the prayer, then added her own silently at the end.

Please make him happy. Keep him safe.

She scrambled after her father as they left the temple.

She skipped ahead of him and turned around to walk backward. "Where are we going?"

"You'll see, V-girl," he said, but this time he didn't smile.

That was all right. She could smile for the both of them. And he'd trained patience into her the same way he'd taught her to hold her sword. With care and laughter and games.

They walked for hours, stopping under a spreading tree for lunch. On the horizon, a looming black mountain grew fainter as they moved farther from the estate.

In the late afternoon light, V finally saw something in the distance. A barricade across the road and a line of people standing along the fence. They waited, eyes wary, hands on their swords. Half wore sleek black uniforms with gold-trimmed breastplates glinting in the sun. The other half wore robes, like her mother.

Vitania straightened, trying to look as grown up as a six-year-old could manage. Her eyes scanned the waiting Saints, but she didn't see her mother among them. Still, she kept her hands still. Sometimes, when she was angry or excited, she couldn't keep from signing as she spoke, the words spilling out of her every which way. She always figured it was because she wanted to be heard so badly, her hands forgot the rules.

But it was dangerous with the first rule of her life clinging there, waiting for her to mess up.

As they drew even with the barricades, her father nodded to the Saint blocking the road. The Bladesaint said something that might have been her father's name and saluted him. Then the man glanced at her and bowed before pulling the barricade aside, leaving a gap wide enough to pass.

Her father nodded to him, then gestured her through.

V glanced over her shoulder to see them close the barricade again, blocking off the road.

"Why is it blocked?" she said after she was certain they were far enough away.

Her father's lips thinned. "No one is allowed through," he said. "This place…" He seemed to search for a word she would know and instead said, "Forbidden," and spelled it out for her in sign, but she didn't know that one either.

"It's against the rules," he said instead.

Like leaving the estate or signing to her mother.

She glanced around and gave her dad a deeply quizzical look. "Then why are we here?"

"The rule is for them," he said. "Not us."

V swallowed. "Why not us?"

"You are your mother's daughter," he signed. "And I was important, too."

"How?"

He grinned and gestured back over his shoulder. "I was the commander of the Bladesaints."

"What does that mean?"

"I made the rules."

Her mouth fell open and she struck her chest. "Oh, you're a big man."

He laughed. "Yes. Before."

"Why did we come?"

"Because there is something you must know."

She let her hands fall to her sides, done for now. She wanted to know more, but she could wait. Her father would tell her what she needed when she needed it.

As they walked, the terrain changed. The trees that had grown along the road appeared stunted and fell away entirely into blackened husks that crumbled in the wind. The grass had been seared away from the ground, and puddles of glass formed in places where the ground dipped. Ahead of them, buildings rose, completely intact except for the scorch marks that marred the corners.

V walked close to her father, and he reached to take her hand. Under her palm, she felt him spread his fingers in the sign that meant "I love you." A reassurance when one or the other of them felt scared.

"Was there a fire?" she whispered, not sure why she felt she had to keep her voice down.

Her father shook his head. "Worse. Malady." The sign was a violent breaking motion across the chest.

She sucked in a breath. In all their games, they fought the Malady as if it were a person. Someone who would fall to a sword blow. But this was a place. A place devoid of life.

"You know what your mother does?" her father said.

Her brow furrowed. "She's the Abdicant." She swept an open palm away from her body, as if giving away something important, but she'd never known why that was the sign for her mother.

"Yes," he said. "We don't have kings or queens anymore. Only princes and princesses who give their power to the Primarch Divine so he can rule with the Goddess. We call them Abdicants.

"That is your mother's title. But more than that, she is a Judge. Highest of the Nexsaints. All the royal family become Judges. They are the ones who hunt down heretics and apostates and the ones infected by the Malady. Judges are the ones who give them the Last Death."

He stopped, and she followed his gaze. It took her a minute to pick out what he was actually looking at amid the seared terrain. Her heart thumped when she realized the lump in front of them was a mound of ash in the shape of a body.

Not an Absent. This person had died. Completely. They would never Return.

A sheet of weather-beaten paper was pasted to a flat rock beside it. She sounded out the words in her head.

Infected #12: Executed by Her Eminence, Sahvia Abdicantus.

Now she knew what she was looking at. This village that had been scoured of the Malady until nothing was left. No infection. Nothing.

And this...this had been a person. The person who had spread it. Either on purpose or by accident. It didn't matter. Her mother had stopped it.

She knew why her father had brought her here. She needed to understand what she was supposed to do. One day she would be a Judge, too. Like her mother and the brother she'd never met.

She would hunt those who spread the Malady.

Chapter 4
Concordim

Ash stared up at the soaring stone walls of the Lower Temple while the priest's words droned around them. The echoes of his prayers traveled up and up until they disappeared into the gloom among the rafters.

There was really nothing "lower" about the Lower Temple. Cass had told her it was only called that because the main temple in Vitamorn was the seat of the Goddess's power. A place of worship and Her throne room all in one. But still, the Lower Temple towered over their village and had been here long before Edgefall. No windows relieved the great walls of stone, but candles cast light against the murals and made everything bright.

On Ash's right stood an image of the Goddess, the Gentle Mother and Giver of Life. Bright candlelight lit the lashes of Her closed eyes and struck sparks from the gold leaf that highlighted Her endless red hair. The locks spilled over Her shoulders and framed Her deep green dress before tumbling across the ground. Trees and flowers grew out of the strands as they traveled to the very corners of the temple.

Cass sat on the bench just beneath the Gentle Mother with her own eyes closed. Her hair was the color of sunshine and only brushed the middle of her back, but Ash couldn't help comparing the two. The Goddess might be nice to look at, but Cass was here, and Ash knew that if she called out, Cass would open her eyes and smile.

On the opposite wall, someone long ago had painted the Descent. The Primarch Divine's sleeves flapped like the wings of a white bird and dark clouds boiled around him, making him stand out against the black. He reached to the Goddess, where She floated among the clouds, Her hand outstretched toward him.

But Ash saw tension in Her face, and she wondered if the painter had put it there intentionally. Had it hurt the Goddess to descend and live among them?

Father Liman had laughed when she'd asked him.

"Always so concerned, Little Ash," he'd said. "But don't worry. You cannot hurt a Goddess. And She chose to descend when the Primarch Divine begged Her to. Her presence here in the world means we no longer have to worry about the Last Death. She and the Primarch closed the gates of Obitullas and made it possible for the faithful to Return."

The mural should have been a depiction of triumph, but below them swirled a pool of black shot through with flashes of sickly white lightning. The edges seemed to reach for the Primarch's feet, as if the gate could suck him in.

Ashwyn was old enough now to know it was just an image, but it still gave her shivers and the occasional nightmare she'd never told anyone about. Even Cass.

Silence rang across the temple, and Ash realized the priest's voice had stopped. She glanced down in time to see him lurch to his feet. He braced himself against the altar for a moment before bowing deeply to the statue of the Goddess behind it.

Cass stood and straightened her shirt as the priest turned and started down the nave toward them. He walked with a halting gait, as if one leg wouldn't bend and he had to swing it from his hip.

"Father Liman," Ash said to catch his attention. Cass wouldn't do it. Cass never spoke to adults unless directly spoken to. And even then she'd look at Ash, hoping she'd step in.

The priest glanced up, having missed them where they were tucked against the wall. His hair was still thick and his skin a lustrous brown, and he smiled widely when he saw them.

"Girls," he said. "You're early. Evening prayer isn't for hours yet. Unless you're here for extra lessons. I can always answer more questions."

Ash shook her head. "We're supposed to help you. Bayna said it was our chore for today."

"Oh. Oh, of course." His smile faltered for just an instant, as if he'd really hoped a couple of nine-year-olds had come to him for philosophical discussion, then he brightened again. "Well, there's plenty to do. The weeds need clearing along the road to the necropolis, and after that the candles need replacing."

Ashwyn gulped. "The necropolis?"

Father Liman sighed. "If any of the temple Inspectors stopped by, we would be facing a hefty fine. No one's tended the weeds in a while, and they've gotten to be a bit much."

Because they were all too scared to get close to the necropolis. And if adults were scared of a thing, that usually meant there really was something to be afraid of.

"Do we have to?" Ash said before she'd really thought it through.

The priest gave her a very kind smile, and she flushed.

"I really can't reach the weeds," he said and rubbed his leg. The one that wouldn't bend. "And clearing the growth is one of the most important things we do here in Edgefall. Do you know why?"

"Because the Devastation will take over?" Ash said.

Father Liman tilted his head as if that was half right. "That's true at the edges of the forest. But there's something even older than the Devastation."

Cass bit her lip, and Ash remembered that long ago conversation with Rafe.

"The Malady," she said.

Father Liman nodded. "The Malady. We clear the weeds between the houses and along the roads to keep outbreaks from spreading. To cut it off before it reaches our village, our homes, our neighbors, our Absent. Clearing weeds protects the village and the necropolis. Even now, there is an outbreak to the west. The Saints have been evacuating the area, and we must be extra vigilant."

Ashwyn's shoulders hiked up, as if she could hide behind them. "Okay."

Father Liman put his hand on her shoulder. "The Absent in the necropolis can't hurt you. But the Malady can. Let's protect against the things that are important."

"Yes, Father," Cass said, and Ash nodded.

Cass took her hand, and Ash let her drag her out the door all the while hoping Father Liman wouldn't tell Bayna or the elderman that she'd balked for just that one moment. Just because she was scared didn't mean she wasn't willing to do whatever it took to stay with Cass.

She squeezed her friend's fingers as they trotted down the road toward the black walls that rose beyond the village roofs.

A tiny forest of gnarled gray trees grew between the houses and the gates of the dead city. Most vegetation in the village was ruthlessly cut down or burned back. But as ugly as these were, the feverdusk grew a brilliant pink blossom that the village herbwoman used in so many of her brews. She'd argued to let them stay, and Ash had a feeling that most people were happy with the little bit of separation between the village and the black city.

Cass ducked between the twisted gray trunks just as a gust of wind rattled the dry brittle leaves above them. She laughed and finally let go of Ash's hand in order to skip between the trees.

"What should we play?" she said, hopping onto the wide paving stones of the road.

"We're supposed to be working," Ash said in her best Bayna voice.

Cass snorted. "You always say we can do both. And you have the best games."

She should be paying attention. She should be doing a good job. But the little voice in the back of her head was already coming up with ideas.

"We can be temple Inspectors," she said and pounced on a scraggly weed poking up from between the paving stones. "And every weed we pull means a promotion when we get back to Vitamorn."

She yanked, and the weed came free with a shower of dirt.

Cass found the next one and pulled. "Can temple Inspectors still live in Edgefall?"

Ash shrugged. "I don't think so. But the city's more exciting anyway."

The weeds grew taller and stiffer the farther they got from the village. The worst ones cut into Ash's hands, and she had to plant her feet and wrap her shirt around her fingers to get a good enough grip.

This would have been easier with more people, but Ash had gotten in trouble just that morning for fighting with Lev. Bayna had solved the problem simply by assigning them to opposite ends of the village.

Cass and Ash worked steadily in the heat until the sun passed behind the soulwell and its shadow fell over them.

Ash hadn't even noticed how much they'd done until she looked up in the sudden dark and found the black walls rising in front of her. Her breath caught in her chest, and she gulped.

Smooth stone rose out of the dirt at Ashwyn's feet, and not a single joint or seam marred the obsidian. As if it had grown out of the ground in a single sheet. The only break in the wall was the gate, a thick wooden barrier bound with curling bands of iron, as if the architect had tried to offset the imposing nature of the rest of the wall.

Cass crowded close to her back as Ash forced herself to breathe.

"It's so big." Despite her best efforts, the words came out shaky. "I didn't realize how big it was up close."

"That makes sense," Cass said. "It's where the Absent are kept."

"That's what the adults say." Ash tipped her head back to see the top of the wall, but they were too close. "But what does it actually mean? Is there really a city in there with buildings and stuff?"

"I don't know. The elderman said Keepers from all over the countryside send their Absent here. He said Edgefall is famous for it."

"That doesn't tell me anything."

Beyond the gate, something shuffled.

Ashwyn gasped and hopped back. Cass squeaked.

Her hands shook hard enough that the weeds fell from her fingers. She hated feeling shaky. She hated the way her mouth went dry and her muscles tensed.

Everything in her wanted to run. But that small voice in the back of her head that always had the best ideas whispered that running wouldn't make the fear go away. It would only leave it behind to cause trouble later.

Ash clenched her teeth and threw back her shoulders. If she couldn't outrun the feeling, she'd just have to face it. And fix it.

"Come on," she told Cass and stalked off the road onto the packed dirt that ran along the wall.

Cass scrambled to keep up. "What are you doing?"

"I don't like not knowing what's back there. So, I'm going to find a way to see."

"But—" Cass tripped and righted herself in the grass. "But it's against the rules."

"So is everything fun."

Ash made her way to the corner of the wall and peered around it. The edge of the necropolis marched away to the west, a strip of bare dirt separating it from the grass that grew between sparse trees.

Father Liman said there was an outbreak that way. If that was true, the Saints would be fighting a Little War against the Malady somewhere beyond the necropolis.

But here, a piece of the wall had been sheared away, leaving a jagged scar. The wall was thick enough that it hardly made a difference; plenty of stone still separated the Absent from the rest of the world. But it was enough to climb.

Ash set her foot at the bottom of the gap where it was narrow enough for a girl to wedge herself, and she hauled herself up.

"What would be strong enough to make this?" Cass said, touching the broken edge of stone.

"I don't know, but it's been here a while." Ash picked at the moss that grew in the cracks. Then she pulled it free and tossed it away. Someone should assign clearers to get rid of the greenery.

Ash's foot slipped, and her arms trembled as they took her weight. Rafe had said that Bladesaints were strong and clever. She was going to have to get better at being strong if she was going to be a Saint.

Ash reached the top out of breath and had to pause a moment to let her arms stop burning. Cass caught up, just as winded, and together they peered over the top of the wall.

"It's...just an empty courtyard," Cass said as Ash's shoulders drooped.

She'd been fighting the pit in her stomach this whole time only to look out at a swath of empty flagstones nestled between tall black towers. A statue of the Goddess stood between them, Her hands held out to the viewer, and a couple of benches sat on either side of the courtyard. An alarm bell stood beside the main gate, matching the ones in the village.

"It's not scary," Ash said. "Why are they all frightened of it?"

There was a door set into the base of each tower, nearly big enough to rival the gates in the wall. And grooves cut paths through the flagstones in front of them.

"Where are the Absent?" Cass said.

"They must be in the towers." Ashwyn settled herself a little more comfortably on top of the wall. "Have you ever seen one? An Absent?"

Cass pulled her hair over her shoulder and stroked her fingers through the strands. "Just my gramma. She was old and sick, and one day her heart stopped. She just sat there staring, so they brought her here. But they didn't let me watch."

"I remember the feast," Ash said. Becoming an Absent was as much a chance to celebrate as it was a time to say goodbye to the one leaving. Being Absent meant they could one day come back. One day they might wake up and everything would change for them. They'd be a Divine. Like the Primarch Divine in Vitamorn.

A low groan rolled across the courtyard below, and the big double doors to the nearest tower crept open.

Ash and Cass flattened themselves against the wall so they wouldn't be seen, and Ash held her breath.

A figure slipped through the opening, then turned and bent to put their whole weight into pushing the doors open. The wooden barrier was four inches thick and bound with iron, and it rumbled through the grooves carved into the ground.

"Is that an Absent?" Cass whispered.

Ashwyn screwed up her eyebrows as she squinted. The figure stepped into the light, and Ash recognized Uniah, the Keeper of the necropolis. The woman came into the village once or twice a week but spent most of her time here with her charges.

When the Keeper finished with the door, she turned and gestured, like she coaxed a skittish dog to follow her. Her voice was too low to hear from their perch, but whatever she said worked because the shadows within the tower shifted and stepped forward, and the light finally revealed forms walking into the sunny courtyard. Human forms.

"No," Ash said. "*Those* are the Absent."

Each figure moved with a tired, shuffling gait, and they stared at the ground with vacant eyes. Bodies that had once held bright souls now ambled into the light as if empty.

And they were. Just like Cass's gramma, their souls had departed for the soul well, leaving behind an empty husk that someone had to protect to keep it from being lost or destroyed. A fate far worse than becoming Absent. Without a body, a soul could never Return.

The first few Absent shuffled into the light, each figure wearing a simple gray smock that had been washed and pressed and tied at the waist. They'd been given a simple close-cropped haircut to keep it neat and clean. But it made them all look vaguely similar.

The difference between them and Uniah was stark. The Absent might walk, but they didn't speak. They stayed eerily silent as they crossed the flagstones, guided by the Keeper. And there was no life in their eyes or their movements. No purpose or recognition or thought.

"Why is she letting them outside?" Cass whispered. "They're not...going anywhere.

True. Once they were outside, the Keeper didn't seem anxious to get them anywhere.

"Bayna is always trying to get us to play outside," Ash said. "Especially if we've been pestering her. Maybe they grow stale and smelly in the towers."

Cass snorted and had to muffle her laugh. "Stop. My gramma's down there somewhere. And your mother too, you know."

Ashwyn's stomach lurched.

Of course, her mother would be here. She'd gone Absent in the Little Wars after a blow to the head, but her body had been led here. Or so Rafe said.

Ashwyn had never really thought about it. Never really considered that she might be able to *see* her.

She stood, raising her hand over her eyes to shade them. Trying to make out the faces so far below.

"They really aren't scary," she said. "Just empty."

"Get down!" Cass said, pulling on her arm. "They'll see you."

Ashwyn scoffed, but just then the Keeper tilted back her head to gaze in their direction.

Ashwyn swore and dropped into the gap in the wall. "Go, go!" she told Cass.

The other girl slipped and slithered her way to the ground, and Ash hoped the Keeper couldn't hear the noise. She was the only one to be afraid of within these walls. If Uniah recognized them, she could get them in trouble for spying instead of working.

Hopefully, they'd ducked out of view fast enough.

But just before she'd hopped down, Ashwyn had noticed the Keeper wore a black leather cuirass and carried a sword.

Just like the Bladesaints.

Chapter 5
Animatim

On Vitania's eighth birthday, her father took her to the city. Their estate lay outside of Vitamorn's furthest districts, so V got to watch the black mountain grow closer and closer as they traveled.

The wall of volcanic rock curved around in a huge crescent, the city itself spilling from its open mouth where a long-ago eruption had torn through the side. Necropoli across the countryside had been built with the sacred stone, one of the only things in the world that could stop the spread of the Malady.

V stared up at the buildings as they walked up the main thoroughfare, a street that ran the entire way from the base of the city to the Greater Temple at its heart and the Palace of Divines at its head.

This time her father did not stop to pray, and V gazed at the soaring facade of the temple in disappointment. She'd never seen the Goddess on Her throne.

"Sorry, V-girl," her father said, using her sign across his chest. "No time today. Your mother has called you. We can't keep her waiting."

The Greater Temple stood at the heart of Vitamorn, where the long line of the main street met the cross street. But instead of passing it and continuing to the Palace of Divines, they turned and followed the cross street to its end, then up the fork to the very top of the city. All of Vitamorn spread behind them, laid out along three streets like a spear with three tines.

And the Abdicant's Court sat on the leftmost tine. In their hurry, V got a blurry impression of white walls and pillars giving way to an open foyer and long halls lined with thick rugs and paintings of dour-faced old men and women.

Her excitement bled away. Somehow the enormous spaces felt claustrophobic, like the whole mountain would come down through the ceiling. V felt the weight on her shoulders, completely unlike their cozy home at the estate.

V's fingers clenched on her father's as the servants they passed bowed. And now that she was older, she recognized the word they used when they spoke to her.

"Your Highness." Over and over, as if she didn't have a name besides that.

Her father gripped her hand and then bent his fingers in the sign for "I love you" as he jerked his chin toward one of the portraits. The woman wore a pinched expression, as if the circlet on her head was too tight. He made a face, crossing his eyes and puckering his lips like a fish. The likeness was so remarkable that she laughed and covered her snort with her arm.

She wanted him to tell her not to worry. That they were only here for her mother to check on her progress, but now that they were inside the walls of the court, V stayed silent. She wasn't allowed to sign or let anyone know she could, and with her heart pounding in her ears, she wasn't sure she'd be able to hear or focus on anything he tried to say.

A servant left them in a long hall lined with shelves. Glass vials sat in perfect ordered rows, glinting in the sunlight coming through the window. V's eyes widened as she realized each one held a measure of ash.

The remains of each heretic and apostate that the Judges before her had hunted down and given the Last Death.

Her eyes were drawn to the dais at the end of the hall. It seemed like the perfect place for a throne, but the space sat empty.

Except for her mother.

Her Eminence, Sahvia Abdicantus, stood on the bare dais where a marble crest was laid into the wood floor, waiting for them.

Her eyes caught on V's hand where she clutched her father's fingers.

V swallowed and pulled her hand away, then straightened under her mother's gaze. Her father glanced down at her, eyebrows pulling together. His lips twitched downward before he took a deep breath and smiled at her.

Too many steps stood between them and the dais, so she missed the moment her mother started speaking and she turned back, trying to catch the words that buzzed and blurred. From this distance, the Abdicant's lips weren't clear, and she could only guess at the shapes of the words.

If she'd looked at V, if she'd moved closer, V would have been able to understand her. But Sahvia kept her focus on V's father and didn't even bother to look at her daughter.

So she only caught bits of the conversation.

"...too slow."

"Don't believe..."

"It's time."

Before she'd really interpreted what was being said, her mouth went dry. Something about the way her mother kept gesturing to her made her heart beat faster.

Her father made an effort to keep his face turned toward her, and he spoke slowly so she caught more of his side of the conversation.

"I'm supposed to have two more years," he said.

Her breath hissed through her teeth. Two more years. This was the agreement they'd made when V was born. She was supposed to train with her father until she was ten. Learn to be a Bladesaint. The best Bladesaint. Then, and only then, she would go to her mother to learn how to be a Nexsaint. Even if she couldn't kneel before the Goddess for her gift until she was twenty, she'd still have the training she needed to start her work as a Judge almost immediately.

She wanted to come train with her mother. She wanted to be able to see her every day. To see more than a frown or a sad smile on her face.

But not if it meant leaving her father.

She glanced back in time to catch her mother's expression. And the word that sent terror arcing across V's nerves.

"Now."

She had to live here? In these austere halls with the black mountain coming down to crush her? She'd never see Jessie, or Ben, or Gell again. The only three people in the world she'd had to talk to besides her father.

It wasn't just her father who was supposed to have two more years. *She* was supposed to have two more years with *him*.

She spun to him, crying, "No, no, Papa, no!" Her hands moved in time to the words, desperation overriding sense.

He caught them to his chest, holding them still, but the damage was done. She stared at him as his face went tight and frightened, then smoothed, as if accepting a terrible fate.

She held her breath, glancing at her mother.

Sahvia's brows pulled down over her eyes, dark and heavy. "She signs?" her mother said. This time she spoke loudly enough to breach the distance between them.

The breath went out of her father.

"Yes," he said. He stepped back, letting go of V's hands even though she tried to cling to him. He gestured her toward her mother. "Go ahead," he said and signed the words at the same time.

V's breath stuttered, and she had to swallow against the dryness in her throat, but she gave her mother a little bow and said, "Abdicant" using the sign along with it: a hand reaching out from her chest.

Sahvia's mouth went tight, and her eyes flicked to V's father. "This is not new. She's been learning this for a while."

Her father translated her words, giving V the tiniest space to breathe now that she didn't have to strain to hear.

"Yes," he said.

"You taught her."

That seemed like a good thing to V, but she got the impression that the answer was important. Important enough to change everything.

Her father lifted his chin. "I taught her."

"Against my express wishes?" her mother said. The Abdicant stepped down from the dais, fists clenching at her sides.

"I trained her," V's father said. "As I was supposed to do."

"No." Sahvia's hand slashed through the air. "She must be strong no matter what is going on inside. You made her look weak."

"She was a baby," he said. "She wasn't supposed to be strong."

"We are Judges." Her mother flung out her arms. "We are always strong. The Primarch Divine—no, the Goddess Herself—depends on our strength."

Her father stood still and silent, and her mother let her hands drop. But her chin remained high as she addressed him.

"You promised me you wouldn't make her weak."

"And you promised me ten years." He stared back, his normally joyful expression hidden by a heavy frown.

Sahvia spun away from him and stepped back up onto her dais. "I am still the Abdicant," she said as V's father translated. "I am the final say before the Primarch Divine and our Goddess. Your crime is against me, but it is your daughter who will have to pay for it. The damage is done now. She will just have to make the next twelve years count for double."

A servant came to take V's arm and turn her toward the door. They were taking her out of the room. Without her father.

Her heart jolted, sending a sick feeling to the pit of her stomach, and she lunged for him. But the servants grabbed for her shoulders.

"Papa," she cried and ducked through a pair of arms. She spun and kicked at one of their legs. But she didn't have the weight to take down a full-grown man.

They snatched her and through their arms, she glimpsed her father standing beside the dais, head bowed in defeat.

She screamed as they took her, screamed until her throat ached and she tasted blood.

Sahvia knelt beside V's chair, putting her at eye level. Late afternoon light streamed through the windows, lining her mother's face with pink and gold. Twilight came early this deep in the mountain's bowl.

"You have to eat," Sahvia said, raising her voice to be clear, but V spun so she could keep pretending she didn't understand. That she needed her father to translate.

Sahvia jerked the chair around, forcing V to face her. "Listen."

V laughed, and Sahvia's jaw twitched, a sure sign that her face was going to go red again and maybe this time she'd throw things.

Whatever she said next came garbled, but V was willing to bet it was more of the same.

Sahvia grabbed her jaw to twist her toward the words. "This is your home now."

"Where's Papa?" V cried, yanking her chin away. "Where's Papa? Where's Papa?"

"Speak clearly. You know I can't understand you."

V sobbed. Her father had never mentioned her voice or how blurred her words sounded to everyone else even if V had known the truth deep down. He'd never made her feel like this.

She snatched at the paper and the pen lying on top of it, but her mother's mouth twisted, and she tore the paper in half and flung the pieces away.

"Speak," she said. "You don't need...crutch."

"Sign to me," V said with a gesture. "It helps us understand each other. Where's Papa?"

Sahvia grabbed her hands and thrust them down. V strained to understand her words, understand what was happening, but Sahvia's voice threaded in and out, depending on so many things, and the work to hear her was already making V's hands shake.

"Stop that. Signing...look weak. You...Judge. Strength comes from work, and I need you strong."

V caught the big words but missed the little ones in between as they were snatched away by emotion, and when her mother turned her head, V couldn't even guess them from the shape of her lips.

She thought signing made V look weak? Her voice bothered Sahvia too, obviously. V's breath came ragged through her throat. Clearly, the Abdicant didn't want anyone reminded of V's flaws—especially herself.

And if her mother refused to listen and refused to sign, then V couldn't be heard. She couldn't make her questions—her distress—understood.

"If you're asking about your father, he's been…" She used a word V didn't know. And Sahvia had to guess the confusion from the look on her face.

"De-mo-ted," she said slower. Like V was stupid. "He broke…rules. He did something wrong. And he's…punished. You can't see him."

V turned away, eyes burning.

Her mother gave the chair a little shove before she stood and paced. Five steps to the window. Five steps back.

A man stood beside the door, the pink light from the window reflecting from the same gold hair that he shared with V and their mother. He said something to Sahvia, and her mother shook her head. Then she thrust the platter of cheese and fruit back across toward V. An apple rolled off onto the floor.

Sahvia spoke to the man, her head turned too far and voice too low for V to catch it. She swept out the door, and it slammed shut with a vibration V could feel from her seat.

V's jaw clenched, and she fought down a fresh wave of tears.

The light changed, warning her that the man approached. Instead of kneeling, he swung a chair around the other side of the table, sitting on it backward as he gazed at her.

This was her brother, Tavian. He snatched the apple from the floor and eyed it, his mouth twisting with contemplation. He glanced at the door, then back at her, and lifted his finger to his lips as if to say, shh. Then he took a big bite.

V's stomach rumbled, and she rubbed it.

"I know starving yourself…the only thing you can control right now," he said slowly and carefully, making sure she could see his mouth. "But it won't get you in to see your father."

V gazed at him, weighing the words and the likelihood that he was just trying to get her to do what their mother wanted.

The two of them shared a mother, but Tavian had been born nearly ten years before her from a previous contract. Two different families had petitioned for a chance to meld their bloodlines into the line of Judges and Abdicants and won. And there might be more, eventually. V tried to imagine what it would be like to learn that she would be an older sister and completely failed. Being a sibling meant nothing when she hadn't met Tavian until two days ago.

Her brother took another bite, then held out a piece of cheese to her. A thick yellow slab that smelled like home.

V gulped.

Tavian put his fingers to his lips to mime eating, and it looked so much like her sign for the word that she had to bite her lip against the swell of homesickness. She snatched the cheese from his hand and shoved one end in her mouth, taking big gulping bites.

Tavian watched her, munching his apple.

He made sure she was looking before he spoke again, with more volume and a careful nonchalance. "You're the daughter of Wesley Ranimas, which means you're strong, whatever Mother says." He lifted his arm as if he were flexing. "But you're also the Abdicant's...which means you're smart, too." He tapped his temple. "Smart enough to know not to visit your father in the Greater Temple... where he's been assigned."

His gaze never left hers, and V held her breath.

"Smart enough to know that everyone here is loyal to Her Eminence...will report to her. You'd...have minutes to talk to him. Enough to say goodbye... nothing else." He shrugged and sat back, taking another bite of his apple. "So, it's definitely not worth it."

"Not worth it at all," she said, eyes narrow.

His lip quirked.

"I'll let her know...you to eat. Maybe she'll be satisfied with that for a bit." He turned as he said it, so she had to lean to catch the last part. Then he swung his leg around the chair and stood.

He touched his eye and pointed at her. "See you later, V." He even used her sign, the v sign across his chest. He must have seen it when her father had been here.

V waited until darkness shrouded the city before slipping quietly from her room while she was supposed to be sleeping.

Finding her way out of the court wasn't as easy as stalking her father through the meadows of the estate, but she was used to observing and memorizing details. Eventually she came to the door where they'd entered, and she sprinted down the darkened streets.

This part was much easier. With the entire city built on a grid with the main streets laid out like the wings of a temple, she found her way back to the center where the Greater Temple stood.

V kept her lips clamped shut as she slipped behind the pillars of the great portico and past the guards that waited on the steps. They didn't think to look behind them or to listen for small, slippered feet trained to walk silently.

V raced down the long nave, but a light wobbled in the darkness, and she ducked into the cloisters, her breath coming faster between her teeth as she searched each corner and cubby. Priests slept in their cubicles. Bladesaints stood guard at the corners of the rows. But not her father.

Demoted, her mother had said. A punishment because he'd done something wrong. And V knew she was the something wrong.

He'd taught her to sign when he shouldn't have. And she'd revealed her knowledge to her mother. If she hadn't…If she hadn't broken in that moment of weakness, he would still be with her.

Her breath sobbed in her chest as she hit a dead end. Candlelight glinted in the still pools of water. The hall of ablution, but it stood empty. No one was posted here this late. She spun, the lights blurring in her vision, and she sprinted back the other way to the main hall.

The nave stretched before her, and she checked over her shoulder. The light was back there now. Whoever was patrolling was coming this way again, and she still hadn't found Papa.

She ran past the altar, toward the end of the temple. At the very end rose a dais, just like the one in her mother's room. Only this one wasn't empty.

A woman sat in shadow, her eyes closed as if asleep. Impossibly long hair flowed down nearly black in the darkness, but glints of color sprang out at her from the petals among the strands.

V skidded to a stop, mouth dropping open.

This was Her. The Giver of Life. The Gentle Mother, Deavita.

Maybe *She* knew where Papa was.

V sprang forward, and an arm wrapped around her middle. The light bearer had caught up to her, the glow from his lantern flashing against the walls and the floor as she struggled against him.

She opened her mouth, hoping her cry would bring Papa to her.

A finger touched her cheek, gentle as a whisper of wind, and she went limp, relief rushing through her veins.

He set her on her feet, and she turned, launching herself into his arms, but this time knowing him by his grip and the flash of light across his beloved face.

Her breath sobbed in her chest, and she struggled to calm it, to keep from making any more noise.

He pulled her away before she was ready and set his lantern down so he could kneel.

"Why are you here, V?" he signed quickly, as if something would sneak up on them.

"Papa." For a moment it was the only word she could voice. "Papa, papa."

He stilled her hands in his until she could speak.

"I don't understand," she whispered. "I don't want to live here. I need you. Please. Please."

She saw the way he jerked forward, as if to sweep her into his arms. Then he stopped, his eyes focused behind her.

She was too afraid to turn.

Her father pushed her back gently, one step. Then another. Then he stood and backed away from her.

"Papa."

"You're going to learn from your mother now," he signed, the light of the lantern sending shadows across his face as his hands moved. "It's time."

"No. Two more years. Remember?"

He shook his head, and one hand dropped to his side in a sign that had always meant, "It will be all right." His other raised to form, "I love you."

Sahvia stepped into the light beside her, her silhouette a harsh line. "I had to intervene," she said, nearly shouting in the quiet. As if volume alone would make her understand. "He taught you to embrace your weaknesses. Judges reject them. He knew what he was doing, and he...ruining you."

V sucked in a breath. She glanced at her father, her eyes burning.

A muscle in his neck twitched and after a long moment, he said, "She's right. I was ruining you. On purpose."

The tears poured down her cheeks. Her mother spoke again, her face turned toward her father, but V didn't hear any of it. Everything was blurry now. The light, her parents, the Goddess. Even the inside of her own head.

I'm ruined. The words skittered through her mind. *Why would he...why would he ruin me?*

And the answer came in the silence of the temple. The only thing that made sense. Except it didn't at all.

He'd trained her so well and still had planted this one little flaw.

He wants me to fail.

Her mother reached out and took her hand, and V clung to it like a bird seeking shelter in a storm. She turned with the Abdicant and didn't look back as they walked from the temple. She stifled her sobs, turning them inward where no one could see them or wonder who they were for.

Chapter 6
Animatim

Rain ran down the diamond-paned windows of the Abdicant's Court, catching the light of the candles and sending back a million tiny reflections of V's face. She was used to waking at dawn, but she was also used to dawn at least being visible.

She stared out into the darkness just past the glass. Here at the very head of the city there was nothing between the court and the back of the mountain. The curve of the rock stretched far above them.

How did the rain even reach the windows here? It had such a narrow slice of sky to traverse.

The table under her hand vibrated, making her jump, and she glanced across at her mother and brother, who were staring at her. Her mother's fist rested on the wood as if she'd had to slam it down to get V's attention. She'd been so drawn to the drum of the rain that she hadn't even noticed her mother speaking.

V took a deep breath and shoved down the surprise.

The Abdicant mirrored her sigh and withdrew her hand.

"Mother was asking what you did today," her brother said, using the few signs he'd learned in the last few weeks, keeping his movements low and contained to the space directly in front of him.

"Sorry," V said. "I went to the temple. I prayed."

That had to be an acceptable answer. Her father had always loved to visit the Goddess…

V cut off the thought before she could cry. Maybe that wasn't a good argument after all.

But her mother didn't need to know that she went to pray because she was lonely. Tavian had made a huge effort to learn her hand language in order to talk to her. But he was the only one, and as a Judge, her brother was almost as important and as busy as her mother.

The Abdicant frowned heavily at her.

"Sorry," V signed again, and her mother shook her head. Slashing her hand through the air.

"No signs," she said, facing V clearly. "Not anymore. You're here to learn your own strength, not borrow your father's."

V only understood the words because she was deliberately going slowly. The moment she started going faster, it became nearly impossible.

But the Abdicant had refused to let her use signs or to learn them herself. And writing out a conversation seemed anathema and always ended with her mother stomping off in frustration. Anything that drew attention to her difficulty with hearing made the Abdicant go red and huffy.

V sat on her hands, her chest aching with the things she couldn't say. How was she supposed to prove she was already strong if she couldn't speak? How could she throw away her father's mistake when it made communicating easier?

"Just speak," her mother said. "Clearly."

"But I can't hear you," she said, instead of what she wanted to say.

"Then read my lips."

"That's just guessing!" V would have shoved the chair back to stand, but the heavy thing wouldn't budge against the carpet.

Her brother said something to her mother. He tried to sign it as well, but he didn't have the vocabulary or the speed, and all she caught was that he seemed to be arguing. Something about being cruel. And then when the Abdicant shook her head, he said something about none of them getting what they needed this way.

The Abdicant didn't seem to like this. She stood fast enough to knock her chair over, and she stormed from the room.

V bit her lip and made sure her mother was gone before she turned back to Tavian.

"*What* do we need?" she said.

Tavian stared at the door, his mouth a thin line before he turned back to her. "Another Judge," he said.

V's fingers reached to touch the circlet that dug into her forehead. Hers was a simple band of silver, while her brother's was gold, and her mother's had leaves etched into the metal.

V couldn't be a real Judge until she was at least twenty and a Nexsaint. But she knew how important it was to learn everything that she could before then. So she could start helping immediately.

Her brother reached across the table to touch her hand.

"Don't worry," he said. "She won't stay mad. She's like…" He seemed to search for a word. "Like a volcano. She gets…heat inside, then blows up, and after that, things grow."

He put both hands to his head and blew out his cheeks before spreading his hands like a huge explosion.

V giggled.

Tavian glanced up, and V followed his gaze to see the Abdicant slam through the door again.

V's mother lifted her chin and said, the words clear for once, "I'm fixing this." She must have been responding to Tavian, but V's heart beat faster as the Abdicant gestured to her in a clear "come here" sign.

V swallowed and followed her from the room, leaving Tavian behind, a crease forming between his brows.

The rising sun splashed gold across the buildings of the city as her mother led her through the streets. Few people were out so early, but the ones who were saw them coming and darted out of the way, bowing. V caught several of them whispering things that looked like "Eminence" and "Highness."

Her mother led her to the Saints' Hold on the other side of the city. It sat on the opposite tine of the fork from the Abdicant's Court.

V gulped and looked around her as they passed through the archway into the practice yard. This was where the Saints trained. Bladesaints and Nexsaints alike, and it was where her brother spent most of his time.

His father had trained him when he was little as well, but his family hadn't required that he be isolated. So, he'd been raised here in the cloisters. She envied him that. If she'd lived here for the first eight years of her life, maybe she'd know more and no one would be angry with her now.

Her mother passed the Saints sparring in the yard, and they fell back as they noticed her, bowing from the waist.

A row of buildings lined the back of the yard, and Sahvia led her up the stairs to a wide, airy room lined with beds and basins of clear water.

A woman with long dark hair tied up in a silver net greeted them at the door with a question V didn't catch.

Sahvia said something and gestured to V.

"Hello, Vitania," the woman said and surprisingly, she signed at the same time, spelling her name with crisp, efficient movements. "I've heard a lot about you."

V straightened. Someone else in this city knew her hand language?

"She talks about me?" V said, glancing at the Abdicant.

The woman nodded. "I'm a Mender. You know what that means?"

V nodded. "You heal people."

"I do what I can. Your mother and I talked about your options."

Her mouth went dry. "What options?"

"I know you've learned about the Nexum." She used two fingers tapping to indicate the network of threads in the world. "Difficult to explain in signs. But it's connections between things. I can't fix your ears. But I can connect your ears with the world in order to amplify what's going on around you."

"What would that mean?" she said.

"You would be able to hear. Almost as well as someone born hearing. It's not a miracle. We'll have to adjust the connections to tweak it to you specifically. And even then it will take some getting used to. It will require time and effort."

V's breath came faster. It would be work. Like her mother had said, work would make her strong, and the Abdicant needed her strong. But she'd be able to hear herself speak clearer and more than that. She'd be understood.

Her mother paced to the window to stare down at the Saints practicing in the yard. She must have had this conversation before. But it would have been nice to have someone's hand to hold since V was hearing it for the first time. She missed the feel of an "I love you" sign under her fingers.

The Mender knelt, meeting her eyes, and when she signed, her mouth didn't move. The words were for V alone. Not her mother.

"Vitania, I must have your permission to do this. That's really important. You're the only one who can make this decision."

V's eyes darted to her mother and back. It was her decision, yes, but what would happen to her if she said no? With no one to talk to and a mother who seemed angry every time she looked at her?

The thought made her throat close up.

Her hand language was the only thing she had left of her father, but she should want to leave everything of him behind. Shouldn't she?

"When can we start?" she said.

Chapter 7
Animatim

Mender Misana sat back and stared into V's eyes.

"Is that better?"

V couldn't see the connections the Mender had adjusted. At least not yet. She'd be ready to kneel before the Goddess in just ten years, but for now she could trust that something was happening. Mostly because with each visit, little differences irked her for weeks afterward or the changes made things just a tiny bit easier.

This time the words came clear enough that she could understand, even if there was a weird sort of buzz when she turned her head the wrong way. With practice, the differences would smooth out until she didn't even notice them anymore.

"Yes," she said, making sure to enunciate. Her language tutor said she'd made admirable progress in two years, but V noticed the way her mother still twitched when her words slurred at the end of the day or excitement rounded the edges of her consonants before she'd noticed.

Mender Misana pulled back and placed her tools back in her bag as V sat up and swung her legs over the edge of the bed.

"Do you still have pain in your legs at night, Your Highness?" the Mender asked.

"Sometimes," V said, hopping down.

"It's because you're so tall. I know lots of people who grow so fast their joints ache."

V grinned. Tavian said she was going to catch up to him any day now.

"I can give you something to calm them enough to sleep."

"I'm all right," V said. "How would you even do that? What connections do you make to tell the muscles not to hurt?"

"None, actually." She held up a bottle of dried powder. "Just regular old willow. But if you want to know more about mending, I will be happy to show you."

V bit her lip. She had little time between learning the Nexum with her mother, sparring with her brother, and her lessons in liturgy and language and history. But getting the body to change based on the connections made inside of it made her heart beat a little bit faster.

"I'll fit it in," she said.

Mender Misana chuckled and shook her head. "I'm sure you will. I can't believe the things you've been learning. Most little girls aren't so determined."

Most little girls weren't going to be Judges when they grew up, V thought to herself as she left the infirmary.

She scratched the spot just under the circlet where it always bugged her. It had formed calluses at her temples, so it didn't pinch anymore, but now it itched.

Her mother and Tavian waited at the bottom of the stairs, talking quietly with each other. Even with the amplifying connection, murmured conversations were still muffled, and a lot of times she had to have her head turned exactly right to hear a person's words. Mender Misana said she was still doing a lot of work with the rest of her brain to read lips and body language in order to supplement her hearing, and it was a lot easier to understand a conversation if she could also see what they were saying.

They must have heard her steps because they both turned, Tavian with a smile and her mother with a cross look that bled into something more austere.

V had to practice that. Her mother was always stressed or angry, but the Abdicant couldn't show that sort of thing to normal people. Judges had to be calm and collected.

"Vitania," Sahvia said, opening her hands. But V knew better than to step into them for a hug.

"Mother." She stopped exactly six steps away and bowed from the waist, concentrating on the depth of her movement and the smoothness of her words at the same time.

"You sound much better," her mother said, then stepped forward to kiss her on the forehead. "So sophisticated. I'm proud of you. You've been working so hard."

V practiced the wide smile that said, "I'm happy about this, can't you see?"

"Thank you," she said.

Her mother's fingers trailed down her cheek as she stepped back. "I'm sorry I can't stay. I must meet with the Primarch Divine in half an hour to go over the plans for the Bladesaint celebration. But I believe your sparring session with Tavian is next."

V nodded. That took the sting out of the fact that she'd barely gotten to talk to Sahvia. Sparring was the best.

Her brother pushed off the wall and cast a look at their mother.

Sahvia raised her chin and said, "I will see you when it is done. Dea go with you."

It seemed an odd thing to say when they were just going to the yard to practice with edged sticks, but Tavian nodded solemnly and watched as she walked away.

Then he turned to V. "Ready?" he said.

"To beat you?" she asked, then grinned. "I'm always ready to beat you."

A sharp laugh escaped his chest, and he pushed her ahead of him. She raced to the stand of heavy wooden weapons.

Every now and then, Tavian still signed with her on days when exhaustion stole the words from her mouth and she only had the ones in her hands. But more and more she kept that piece of herself hidden away from her mother—and everyone else. The Abdicant had been right. Anything that drew attention away from her strength was a weakness.

This time of day, several other sets of Saints practiced in the yard, but they cleared room in the middle the moment Tavian took up his wooden blade and swung it back and forth.

V set her feet and went right into a lunge. He knocked her blade away and spun so that she rushed past him. V recovered and swung for his legs, but she didn't even get close.

He stepped forward and clipped her elbow with his blade, sending a shock through her arm. She grunted and stepped back, rubbing the spot.

"You good?" he said.

She let her hand drop and grinned at him. "Fine."

This was the part she loved. He didn't hold back while sparring. She refused to train with any of the other Saint instructors because they all treated her like a child holding a sword too big for her.

Tavian knew why she pushed herself. He knew what lay at the end of her training because he was there already. He was the one teaching her how to be a Judge. And not with stupid games or fake wrestling.

He gave her a second to recover before advancing again.

She'd been faster than this once. She'd never had a problem before she'd come here. Before the one person she'd trusted over everything else had betrayed her.

Every time she gripped her sword, every time her muscles flexed to meet a blow, she hesitated, wondering if she could trust this instinct or if this was another lie she needed to push through to find the truth.

V skipped back a step to give herself a moment and took a deep breath, letting the frustration out with her exhale.

She couldn't be slow. She couldn't hesitate. Hesitation would let the Malady creep up on her, and she'd die in agony.

Tavian swung, noting her pause but not slowing in the slightest.

V's arm raised to block the blow, a tremble echoing through her. Her muscles knew what to do even when her mind fumbled. And it felt good. Blocking, stepping, lunging. It all felt like pieces of a puzzle sliding into place.

So why did she fight it? Because he'd lied to her? Because she couldn't trust him?

She trusted her body. *It* didn't lie.

V took the next breath and skidded into place, ahead of the hesitation that threatened her life and her future.

Her brother's sword cracked across hers, the strike echoing across the yard.

Tavian grinned over their blades. "Very good," he said.

"I know," she whispered, mostly to herself, but his breath huffed in a laugh. V pressed forward in the moment of distraction to lock her leg behind his and pull.

He fell back against the ground with an "oof," his entire length laid out in the dirt.

She just kept herself from leaping on him like she used to do.

He laughed aloud. "Really good, V!" he cried.

She held out her hand, and he even let her take some of his weight as he climbed up out of the dirt.

A cough interrupted them, and V turned to see a pale woman watching them. Her dark hair had been pulled into a waist-length braid and tied with a delicate silver chain that tinkled when she moved. V recognized Tavian's partner, Illyra, the Bladesaint he'd chosen to accompany him when he went out hunting.

"Your Serenity," she said, gaze flicking to Tavian. "I'm sorry to interrupt, but it's time."

Tavian's mouth drew tight, and he gave her a nod. "Right."

V sighed. "You're leaving," she said.

"Yes. I'm sorry. This one's important."

She squared her shoulders. "They're all important. I know that. I'm not a baby."

He gripped her shoulder. "I know. I'll be back within the month."

Probably before that. He left all the time to hunt apostates and heretics and deliver the Last Death to anyone infected by the Malady. But he was always back at the Abdicant's Court before she'd had time to miss him too much.

He tilted his head to catch her eye. "I promise, V."

And he always kept his promises. She darted forward to give him a quick side hug. He never minded them the way their mother did.

"Go then," she said. "Before I dump you on your butt again."

"Dea forbid, I'm going." He hopped away from her with a laugh, and she deliberately didn't watch him walk away to return his practice sword.

Three weeks later V and Sahvia sat at the dining room table in the Abdicant's Court, going over proper techniques to connect the Nexum within sentient creatures to prevent bleed over of their thoughts when the doors burst inward.

Sahvia leaped to her feet, her face red. But Tavian's partner fell through the doorway. Her black leather armor glinted in the candlelight, like it was wet, and it took V a moment to realize blood had soaked through the seams.

"Your Eminence," she gasped out and raised her gaze to Sahvia.

V found herself on her feet without remembering how she got there. Her stomach rolled with a sick feeling that had everything to do with the blood and the look on the woman's face.

"Speak," Sahvia said.

The woman swallowed and shook her head, not in denial but like she couldn't form the words past whatever emotion had gripped her.

"Say it," the Abdicant grated out.

"His...his Serene Highness...Judge Tavian, has succumbed to the Malady. He...he's gone."

V's heart thumped. Tavian...gone?

No, not just gone. If he'd succumbed to the Malady, then he wasn't Absent. He was...dead. The Last Death.

Illyra held out a trembling hand and unfolded her fingers as if they were stiff. A vial of dust lay in her palm.

His dust.

Tavian was never coming back. He'd never Return, never become a Divine. V would never see him again. Or make him laugh or talk in signs behind their mother's back.

She choked, the numbness in her chest rising to her throat.

Tavian's partner reached behind her to unhook something from her belt.

She fumbled it, and metal rang against the stone. A glint of gold made it through the blood caked on its surface.

Her brother's circlet.

Sahvia's gaze swung to her, and V met her eyes.

"Your Serenity," Illyra murmured to V.

Serene Highness. That's what they called the heir. It was her circlet now.

V's teeth clenched, and she raised her chin to acknowledge them both. But inside, she screamed with the pain in her heart.

Besides her mother, she was the only Judge now. And she was the heir to the Abdicancy.

Chapter 8
Concordim

Ashwyn ran the polishing cloth across the bronze plaque one more time and tossed it into the bucket at her feet, then double-checked that each name etched in the metal was legible. The elderman liked to read the names of the Saints out loud on feast days, and his eyesight was getting worse and worse. Ash had had particular trouble with the one that had been scratched through. Someone from Vitamorn had come through a few months ago and taken a chisel to it, and the still rough edges caught on the polishing cloth.

Ash bent to run her fingers over the stricken name.

Morlinna.

She'd wanted to ask the man what the woman had done, but there was only one thing bad enough to get your name stricken from the Saints' record.

She'd embraced the Malady and become an apostate.

Four other names had been slashed through, but their edges had been dulled over time. This one tore at Ash's fingertips, and she pulled back, folding her fingers into a fist.

The elderman's voice rang from the front of the temple, and Ash jumped and straightened beside the Saints' record.

The old man came into sight, leaning on Lev's arm and gesturing some of the other war orphans along behind him.

Ash stepped forward. "Do you have anything else for me, Elderman?"

It wasn't like she liked chores. But it seemed particularly clever to make sure the leader of the village knew she was as hard as Edgefall.

He squinted at her. "I don't, er..."

"Ash," she said very helpfully.

"*We're* working with the council today," Lev said with a sneer.

The elderman waved a hand. "Bayna might have something more for you, child."

Ash blew out her breath. Bayna always had something. The more boring, the better. Ash wasn't looking for boring.

She waited for them to disappear into the council chamber beside the temple and sped away between the houses before anyone else could notice. Ash slipped along the rough stone wall of Cass's house, collecting a handful of flat, round rocks out of the dry grass that rustled under her feet. The area between the village and the Devastation stood clear and freshly tamed. But the grass around the houses grew long and a little neglected, the tops drooping with the heat of the unfettered sun.

Bayna's voice drifted from the open window above Ashwyn, and she froze so the grass wouldn't swish and give her away.

"And when you're done with that, you can check with Haunna, two doors down. She might need another pair of hands to help bring in her washing."

Cass's voice came after, indistinct and subdued. But the intent was clear. She was giving in yet again.

Ashwyn rolled her eyes. At least that meant Cass would welcome an excuse to escape.

Knowing Cass, she'd feel guilty about it afterward, but they got so little time to themselves now they were a little older that they had to snatch every moment they could.

Ashwyn reached up carefully and stacked the flat stones on the windowsill, staying low so Bayna wouldn't catch her in the act. Cass would see them and know what they meant.

She made sure the stack wouldn't fall over and clatter against the side of the house, then she darted away, around the back.

Cass's mom managed the orphan house and ruled the war orphans who lived there, but she'd never moved her family to the rickety building at the edge of the village. She'd kept Cass separate, as if their bad luck would rub off on her.

But Bayna hadn't counted on Cass's kindness or Ash's stubbornness.

The sun glared down, making Ash's skin feel tight and itchy, and she darted between the houses and across the road. She wasn't wasting this rare moment of peace between chores.

The houses fell away, and Ashwyn made a mad dash for the edge of the gnarled trees that divided the village from the necropolis.

Ash breathed a sigh once their twisted gray trunks concealed her, and she picked up her pace, running flat out between the trees. She made sure to run fast enough and long enough to make herself pant because that's what Rafe had said strengthened her heart and lungs as well as her legs. And she didn't stop, even when the black walls loomed large in front of her.

The gray forest thinned and fell away, as if even the trees didn't want to get close to the dead city. And she burst out into the clearing in front of the broad gates.

Ashwyn kept up her pace, racing around to the far side of the necropolis where the gap in the wall made a stairway to the top. A new Devastation clambered close to the walls, where just three years ago there had been rolling hills and scattered trees. A result of the most recent fight with the Malady. The Saints had been triumphant, but the Devastation had swept through afterwards, taking over the area and springing into place nearly overnight.

The ground had been paved in the space between the necropolis and the Devastation to keep the creeping vines back.

Ashwyn ran at the sheer black face and then planted her foot against the surface to launch herself as high as she could. Her fingers caught at the edge of the shattered gap, and she climbed.

She hauled herself up, hand over hand, slipping once in the middle so she skinned her knee against the black surface. Recently, her limbs didn't always want to work together. She would reach and be surprised by the length of her arm, and it threw her off enough to make her clumsy. Rafe said that was just part of being twelve, and she would grow into her length, eventually.

Ashwyn gritted her teeth and found another handhold, her fingers burning with her weight. She had plenty of other exercises to prove she was "strong and clever," just like Rafe had told her years ago, but this one was her favorite. It was her habit to climb the walls of the necropolis once a day now.

She flung her arms over the top and swung her legs so she could roll onto the wide top. The climb still winded her, which just meant she had to keep working at it. But at least she wasn't as bad at it as she'd been three years ago.

Ashwyn lay on her back, breathing hard and enjoying the ache in her muscles. Above her, the soul well churned, a vast cloud of blue shot through with green and purple and gold. The souls of the Absent had gathered where they could look out over the world. Ashwyn always had to fight the urge to wave hello. Were they aware? Could they actually see her? Father Liman always avoided the question when she asked.

Around midday, the sun would finally disappear behind the well for a little over an hour, leaving a shadow to travel over the village. For now, she had to shade her eyes to look directly at it.

"Ash?" Cass's voice called, and Ashwyn rolled so she could peer over the edge of the wall and wave.

"Up here."

Cass stood below, her face upturned so her long blonde braid fell back over her shoulder. Her mouth tipped in a smile, and she stepped back to clamber up the broken side of the wall. She took her time. The other girl didn't have to push herself the same way Ash did, so she arrived at the top breathing normally. Holding her arms out for balance, Cass tiptoed across the narrowest section right above the break.

Then she plopped down beside Ashwyn, letting her feet dangle.

"You got away quick this time," Ashwyn said, rolling so the sun wouldn't be directly behind Cass's head.

Cass sighed and pulled her hair over her shoulder to stroke her fingers through it. "All I have to do is stay quiet, and Ma wears herself out talking."

"If you don't die of old age first. She still wants you to be selected as the next elderman?" Ashwyn said.

"She thinks if I do favors all over the village and make everyone like me, then I'm sure to be selected."

"Everyone has to pull their own weight," Ash said with a snort. "Except when they want you to pull double." She sat up and put her arm around her knee while the other one dangled over the side.

Below them, the Absent ambled across gray flagstones lined with cracks of dark tar designed to keep any foliage out, and with it the Malady.

The Keeper, Uniah, stepped between her charges, eyes steady and hands gentle. Ashwyn had never seen her so much as raise her voice to one of the Absent, though Ash had no doubt she could use the sword strapped to her side if she ever had to defend them.

She caught sight of the girls on the wall and lifted her hand in greeting. In all the years they'd come here to escape, the Keeper had never once ratted them out to Bayna or the other villagers. Maybe she felt like they were keeping her company.

Ashwyn rested her chin on her knee as Uniah passed between the masses of Absent who milled around in the sunshine.

"They look so peaceful," Cass said, voice hushed.

Ashwyn snorted. No one else thought so. The villagers avoided this place. But that meant there was one place where she and Cass could go to be alone.

"Do you actually want to be the next elderman?" Ashwyn asked. "Or is that just Bayna's dream?"

Cass bit her lip. "I don't know."

Ashwyn traced the crumbled edge of the wall. "You'd be good at it, you know."

"Maybe." Cass pressed her lips together and glanced away.

"Better than me," Ashwyn said. "You're quiet, but that just means you listen to people. And you care and you work hard."

"So do you."

"That's just so they'll let me stay."

"Is it?"

"Yes." But Ashwyn sighed and tipped her head back to stare up at the churning soul well. "No. Both, I guess? I...I like when they need me, but I also want to stay."

Some of the other war orphans had talked about going back to their homes once they were grown. It had taken Ashwyn years to figure out why the word home had confused her. It never made her think of the village. Or the orphan house.

Home had always meant Cass. It was nice when the elderman or Father Liman praised her work, but they weren't the ones Ash was staying for.

"You're going to be a Bladesaint," Cass said. "That's more than just useful. The Bladesaints are heroes."

Heat rose in Ashwyn's cheeks, and she glanced at Cass. But Cass was watching the Absent again.

Above them, the shimmering mass of souls let out a spout of blue that lit Cass's face with cerulean light, and they both looked up, breath held. But the swirls and eddies subsided and fell back into each other until Ashwyn couldn't tell which color had been which the moment before.

Cass lay back again, resting her head against Ashwyn's shoulder, and Ashwyn stilled, breath shallow so as not to jostle her.

"Which one do you think will be the next Divine?" Cass said, scanning the milling bodies below.

It was a familiar game, and Ash played along, trying to pick out the oldest, most frayed-looking sash they could see.

"That one." She gestured to an old woman with vacant blue eyes and curling hair as white as a cloud. Her sash looked threadbare, and there weren't nearly as many with the same shade of ochre that indicated the decade she'd been interred.

Cass tipped her head. "Why?"

"Because she deserves it. She's been waiting for so long, so patiently—"

"They're all patient. They can't be anything else; they have no emotions."

"And the Goddess knows that." Ashwyn ignored her interruption. "She must have been some kind of Saint in her life. A Bladesaint or a Nexsaint who gave her life in battle."

"Look at her. She's ancient. Too old to fight battles," Cass protested, but her mouth tilted in a smile.

"That's what makes her so special. Only the greatest warriors make it to old age. The Goddess misses her. That's why She'll bring her back next. She was Her greatest Saint."

Cass laughed as Ashwyn had hoped she would, and she pushed on her shoulder.

"I like the stories you tell," she said.

Ashwyn kept her teeth tight on the admission that most of her stories were designed to make Cass laugh.

"You should tell your stories to the archivist. Get him to write them down for you."

Ashwyn rolled her eyes. "So the whole village can ignore them. I'm pretty sure you're the only one who listens to me."

She never made up stories about her mother. She was down there in one of the sanctums, wearing a teal sash. Waiting for the chance to return as a Divine. But Ashwyn tried not to look for her. It used to be a game to try to recognize her. But it made her heart hurt every time, and now it was better to just imagine she was down there. Not to know it. Not to see her.

A yowl echoed through the nearby Devastation, some sort of animal in anger or pain. The noise sent a flock of birds into flight. They rose in a cloud and turned as one to fly north, and Ashwyn's stomach clenched as the sun flashed from iridescent black wings and the broad white patches underneath them.

Magpies.

She and Cass made the sign against evil, flicking the fingers of both hands on either side of their eyes.

"We should get back," Cass said. "We've been here too long."

Below them, Uniah had frozen at the sound of the primal scream. Now she hurried her charges back into the sanctum, guiding them through the big double doors one by one until they finally got the hint and shambled after each other in a group.

"It's all right," Ashwyn said, as Cass stood and brushed off her backside. "It's just a Devastation beast. Rafe and Ingrim won't let it get far."

Cass shook her head. "Sometimes they can't help it. One got all the way to the road during their patrol last month."

"Really?" Ash surged to her feet, following as Cass climbed down the break in the wall. "Why didn't they say anything?"

"They didn't want to alarm the villagers. But they told the elderman, and the elderman told Ma, and she told me. Said I should know about such things." Cass made a face.

"What did it look like?" Ashwyn jumped the rest of the way down to the ground and straightened, glancing between the edge of the forest and the necropolis.

"It wasn't natural. It was shaped like a bird, but it had scales like a lizard and claws at the tips of its wings." Cass hooked her fingers to demonstrate. "And teeth like a rat."

Ashwyn shivered. "Mortis, that's creepy."

Cass bit her lip to hide a smile. "You're not supposed to swear."

"How can I not swear after hearing something like that? How did it get all the way out here?"

Cass screwed up her nose. "I don't know. And I really don't care as long as it's dead and nothing else comes out of there to kill someone."

Ashwyn winced. "Sorry."

The Devastation was serious. It killed people. Even innocent ones like Mikel. But the danger made it all the more fascinating. Like listening to ghost stories in a dark room.

Cass had never liked ghost stories. She hurried along the narrow clearing between the Devastation and the necropolis with her head down. When she glanced at Ashwyn, it was clear there was still something on her mind.

"It's not just monsters," Cass whispered back to her.

"What?" Ashwyn rushed to catch up.

"It's not just monsters in there. The elderman of Laststand was visiting last week. He said there's a witch."

"What do you mean, a witch?" Ash asked. Then she stopped short and stared through the tangle of vines that blurred the edge of the Devastation. "You mean in there? Someone actually lives in the Devastation?"

Cass tugged on her arm, trying to get her to move. "If you can call it a some-one. She has a white face, and she controls the forest. And they say she kills anyone who strays into the woods."

"So just another monster then."

Cass bit her lip, and her wide eyes flicked to the forest. "Worse. She kills you so you can't come back. Destroys the body and the soul together."

Ashwyn's breath caught and her mouth went dry. "The Last Death."

Cass hauled hard enough to finally get Ash moving again. But Ashwyn couldn't help craning her head, trying to see the flash of a white face through the vines and roots.

It was just a story, like the ones Ash made up. Only Judges could deliver the Last Death. If it were true, the Order would have swarmed the Devastation to eradicate anyone breaking their most sacred laws.

But what would it be like to live fearing death? Knowing that if she died, she'd never be able to come back?

Another shudder wracked her body. It was terrifying. And delicious at the same time.

"Dare me to walk closer to the edge," Ashwyn whispered in Cass's ear.

Cass gasped. "What? No!"

Ash pulled her arm, and Cass came with it as she stepped closer to the mass of vines spilling along the edge.

"Come on, it'll be fun. Maybe we can see her."

Cass squealed and yanked Ashwyn away, dragging her along until they reached the gray trees before the necropolis.

Ashwyn laughed. She'd just wanted to get Cass to react, but a part of her couldn't help glancing over her shoulder, looking for a bit of white between the roots.

There was nothing, and she was content to let Cass lead her away, back toward the village.

Chapter 9
Obitusim

The woman stepped back from the mangled creature on the floor of the forest, its blood seeping into the mess of vines at her feet.

The long, lean body resembled a lizard, but its black fur shimmered in the dim light beneath the branches.

She rested the end of her scythe on the forest floor, giving her shoulders a moment's rest. The weight of it still made her ache, but already she was getting used to the balance of the double-bladed weapon.

The Devastation beast gave one last twitch, and she saw the moment it went from living to Absent, the throes of pain giving way to a morbid sort of peace. It wouldn't be a danger anymore. Its legs were too damaged to carry it further. It could only drag its claws across the vines, leaving ragged furrows in the greenery.

She turned from the creature to the man who lay just beyond the pooling blood. His clothes hung in tatters from the creature's claws, blood and excrement staining them all until they blended into a dark mess.

He gasped for breath as she knelt beside him.

He had moments before he went Absent, his body failing and his soul leaving to join those that swirled above in the soul well.

Unless he got to a Mender.

Impossible. She was the only person desperate enough to brave the Devastation, and she was no Mender.

But she'd seen them work before.

She reached inside him, to the black and gold strands that crisscrossed his body. Too many threads of his Nexum hung loose and broken, their ends shriveling.

She pulled one to try to reconnect it and start his blood flowing back into him instead of onto the vines. But she stopped, her hand freezing just beside his heart.

Deep in his chest, the strands had gone pale. The sickly color of ash crept through the threads.

The man opened his eyes and moaned.

She didn't bother to hide herself from him. So much of her energy went into staying out of sight, so no one could carry stories of her back to the city.

But this man wouldn't be going anywhere now. Even with a hundred Menders on hand.

His eyes widened, and he shifted, trying to lunge away from her. But his arms shook, and he fell back.

She stood, and his eyes followed her, whites showing around the edges. She swung her scythe until the blade came to rest behind his neck.

"No," he whispered.

It was always the worst when they were conscious.

"From Her arms you came; into Her arms I send you."

She pulled, and her blade severed the black and gold heart thread alongside his spine.

He fell back, his head rolling to one side. She stepped away as what remained of his mangled body disintegrated into dust.

A large gray wolf with black horns rising from his brow stepped up next to her. He leaned against her hip, giving her stability as she breathed. The smell of blood still left a tang in the air, but now there was something dry and bitter weaving through it.

Death.

It took her a long moment to recognize the ache in her throat, and she raised her hand to her cheek to find it wet.

You did what you must, the wolf said. *It will not spread now. Because of you.*

"I know."

A voice threaded through the back of her head, much further away than the wolf's. As if someone whispered from a world away.

It will become easier...in time.

Her neck relaxed, easing the ache in her shoulders, and she took one last deep breath.

The Devastation beast's claws flexed against the vines as it tried to stand and found itself too mangled to do so. It might have only been a beast, but she couldn't leave it like this, to face an eternity as a broken thing. She stepped forward and sliced through its heart thread, then watched as it crumbled to dust. Just like the man.

She turned to stare at his remains. It seemed wrong to leave him there, his ashes settling in drifts along the vines, waiting for an errant breeze to erase him. A Judge would know what to do. They were the only ones allowed to deliver the Last Death to humans. But there were no Judges here. She'd made sure of that, whether she'd wanted to or not. Now she was the only one willing to do what had to be done.

Just another sin to add to her tally.

There were many names she'd taken on here among the trees. Sinner. Apostate.

Murderer.

But perhaps executioner was more apt. Her function was monstrous, but necessary. And not without respect. No one was here to deliver the Last Death to the infected. No one even believed her about the infection in the first place. But the voice in her head was not wrong. The proof lay before her feet.

And she would be what she needed to be because she was the only one would.

The executioner wove a net with the threads from her own body with no idea what she would do with it. Only the feeling that this was right. This was a tribute to the life the Goddess held so sacred. The life she had ended.

With a gesture, she sent the net out, sweeping it across the clearing like a wave, and the force of its passing sent the dust flying. The wind carried it, scattered it, until it fell amongst the roots of the Devastation. Old life nourishing new.

It felt right.

She twisted her hands, bringing her threads back to herself, and a flash of white caught her eye. Ashy lines spread through her skin, following the veins in the backs of her hands. The sight filled her stomach with icy dread and something else tangled up inside it that felt more like pride.

She tucked her hand away and stood.

Will anyone miss him and come after you? the wolf asked.

The woman shook her head. "No. Anyone who comes into the Devastation is lost. Everyone knows that."

But the thought sat heavy at the back of her head. If anyone did come, they couldn't know who and what she was.

A shiny, white porcelain mask hung from her belt. She'd found it the second week she'd been in the Devastation, when the Malady had taken a festival merchant. The mess of masks laying on the roots and vines had given her a strange feeling of nostalgia and grief. But this one, with its smooth surface, erased any human features, leaving nothing but dark holes where her eyes should be.

She lifted the mask to her face, then she stepped to the trees, taking up her heavy scythe. The executioner leaped to the branches, letting them close around her, swallowing her until nothing remained of her work but a drift of dust on the breeze.

Chapter 10
Concordim

At fifteen, Ashwyn was strong enough to scale the necropolis wall twice a day. She'd trained her heart and lungs by running between chores and choosing the longest routes around the village. Bayna claimed she did it to waste time.

But when the coughing sickness swept through the babies that spring and the village herbwoman asked for help collecting feverdusk blooms, Ashwyn volunteered first and promised her two full baskets by the end of the day.

Bayna raised an eyebrow before turning to the rest of the orphans.

"Why is she surprised? It's climbing trees," Ash whispered to Cass. "That's so much more fun than anything else."

Cass snorted. "I think you just like looking like a hero to everyone else."

Ash laughed, but couldn't quite hide the pleased flush that crept up her cheeks.

The gray feverdusk trees grew between the village and the necropolis, rising twice as high as the orphan house. Their twisted trunks and uneven branches made for easy handholds to the top, where the flowers bloomed amongst the highest twigs.

Ash tossed her overcoat onto the ground below the first tree. Most villagers wore the sleeveless garment to protect their clothes from the harsh work they did every day, but it would only get in Ash's way as she climbed.

It shouldn't have been hard. The rough bark under her hands was much easier to grip than the stone of the necropolis walls.

But halfway up the final tree, she found a branch broken at the trunk, leaving a jagged end only a couple of inches long. She lunged to bridge the gap and caught a higher branch before planting her thin shoe against the broken end.

It seemed solid enough, and she shifted her weight higher.

Wings fluttered above her, and she jerked her head up. A magpie tilted its head from the branch just above her.

Ash swore. "Shoo," she said, and freed one hand to wave at it.

The bird cawed and flapped its wings, bobbing its head at her.

"Go on!"

The magpie startled and flapped away, and Ash sighed.

Then, her foot slipped against the broken branch.

Ashwyn fell, branches whipping by her face. She grabbed for one, fingers closing desperately on air, and a gray blur struck her cheek. A starburst of pain cascaded across her vision.

One of the lowest branches caught her shoulder, and she grabbed for it. The movement wrenched her arm nearly out of its socket, but it slowed her fall, and at last she collapsed to the ground beneath the tree.

Her shoulder ached, and her left eye stung, but she was more embarrassed than anything and glanced around to be sure no one had seen.

"I guess that's it for today," she said, rotating her arm with a wince. Then she hurried back to the village with her baskets, very deliberately not limping.

By the time she got to the herbwoman's house, her eye itched fiercely, and she could barely keep it open.

The herbwoman took one look at her bruised cheek and reddened eye and snorted.

"Scratched," she pronounced, taking the baskets. "Probably not serious. But you should keep it closed for a few days. Dark and rest will help it heal."

But Bayna snorted when Ashwyn tried to tell her the same thing.

"Rest?" she said, throwing out her hands to indicate the village. "When the babies are sick and everyone is worried and tired and there's work to be done? Get on with you. The clearers will need another pair of hands this week. You might as well fill in while you can. We don't do lazy in Edgefall."

Ashwyn tried to protest, but then she thought of the babies coughing and flushed. At least she could still breathe. And if she could breathe, she could help. In the end, she tied a scarf around her head to keep her eye closed and secretly pretended she was a highwayman while she joined the clearers in the fields.

The next day, her head felt thick and swimmy, though she didn't dare say anything to Bayna, who would just think she was shirking again.

She staggered to the fields with her axe and did her part. Pride kept her upright, clearing the space between the field and the Devastation even as the plants went crooked and wavy and the spring air flowed hot and cold against her skin all at once. It wasn't until later that she collapsed to her hands and knees, breathless and delirious.

Dell Fairhand found her there, but by then she wasn't aware of anything but the thickness in her skull and the blood pounding in her ears. Fragments of reality melted together, a confusing mix of anxiety that drove her to move, to do something, go somewhere, be something. But her limbs remained heavy against clean sheets, and her chest constricted as she coughed, her lungs on fire.

Bits of conversation wafted to her through the blurred thoughts and twisted images. Words she had to pause to understand.

"Infection," came the croaking voice of the herbwoman. Surely the woman had a name. They'd lived together in the same village forever, but Ash had only ever heard her called the herbwoman. "She's caught the cough from the babies. And an infection along with it. See how red that eye is. She shouldn't have been out in the sun with it."

More muffled sounds. Like when she and Cass swam in the pond during the summer, and they tried to yell at each other underwater, and they'd come up to the surface and guess what the other had said.

"—be all right?" Cass's murmured beside her. Ashwyn tried to turn toward it, but she was too weak.

"—hardly matters." That was Bayna, though her words fled in and out of Ash's consciousness, and she didn't care to chase them. "Costing us...Care takes time and money. And she's already got so much to repay just for being who she is."

"It's not her fault she has no family."

"It's not our fault either. Yet we're the ones paying the price."

"I'll sit with her."

Bayna made an affronted noise.

"I've already had the cough," Cass said. "So I'll be fine. And that way it won't cost anyone else's time."

If Bayna replied, Ashwyn didn't hear it, but the argument ceased, and the next time she surfaced from the morass of worried dreams, Cass was there. And Ashwyn clung to her hand and fell back asleep until the dreams faded and unawareness crept in. She barely noticed when Rafe visited, only remembering his voice as she tried to wake up and failed.

When she finally woke for real, the herbwoman leaned over her again, but this time the bed didn't sway beneath her. She no longer sweated under the blankets, and while her limbs trembled, it was with hunger instead of fever.

But a blur still smeared one side of the room, and gray specks floated across her vision, so she had to blink and twist to see.

The herbwoman took Ash's cheeks in both hands and tilted her head, checking the temperature of her skin and looking deep in her eyes.

The stark contrast between her white hair and dark face was much easier to focus on. But it made Ash's head hurt, and she squinted, trying to see through the blurriness along the left side.

"You're awake," the herbwoman said. "And aware."

"Yes." Ashwyn's voice rattled as she spoke, and she realized she was parched.

"Here." Cass's voice came from her left. Ash hadn't seen her over there. The blurred edge of her vision had hidden the other girl.

A cup of clear water came across her chest, and Ashwyn reached for it. Her fingers trembled, and she had to grip it with two hands.

"You're through the worst of it," the herbwoman said. "You haven't coughed in a whole day, which is a good sign, and your fever's broken. Concentrate on rest and food and drink from here on out, and you'll be better in a week."

How long had she been feverish? She still felt weak, but the disorientation had faded. So, that wasn't what worried her.

"What's wrong with my eye?" she said, turning her head so she could see Cass out of the right side.

The herbwoman stilled. "What do you mean?"

"I can't...It's blurry. And there are things..." She raised her hand as if to catch the gray bits that flitted through the mess. "Things floating."

Cass bit her lip, fingers combing through the hair that lay over her shoulder, and the herbwoman sighed.

"What is it?" Ash snapped, panic sending strength along her trembling limbs.

"I was hoping it wouldn't be permanent." She sat on the edge of the bed and touched Ash's cheek just below her eye. "You damaged it, remember? That should have healed just fine except for the infection. I've seen it before. My herbs took the swelling down, but I've no way to tell what damage remains on the inside."

Ashwyn swallowed. "This...this is forever?"

Cass clutched her hand, and Ashwyn held onto her thin fingers tight, as if that would change anything.

"Yes," the herbwoman said. "And likely it will get worse. There's nothing I can do inside the eye. Not without a Mender."

And their little village had never warranted a normal Nexsaint, let alone a Mender. They were too important to the Little Wars. And Ashwyn was too unimportant to call for one. Maybe if it had been the elderman who'd been climbing the tree. Maybe if it had been Cass who had scratched her eye, then Bayna would have insisted on taking her to Vitamorn, where a Mender could see her.

"I'm sorry," the herbwoman said.

"Not your fault," Ashwyn rasped.

"No," she said. "I did what I could. But I still hate to see something I can't fix." She packed up her basket, tucking precious glass vials beside clay jars, all nestled in dried grass to keep them from rattling.

"I lost three babies this round and a mother," the herbwoman said as she stood. "But you'll live. That's the important thing. Life is hard, but we're harder."

Ashwyn turned her head to face the wall as the herbwoman pushed out the door of the orphan house. The other beds were empty, the other war orphans off attending to their chores. The most skilled would be assigned to their apprenticeships soon, and the rest would take the more menial jobs around the village. All of them were hustling to prove they were the right match for a coveted position.

"That's the important thing," Ashwyn muttered. "I'm not useful to Edgefall if I'm dead."

"What?" Cass said with a gasp. "That's not...Ash, that's horrible."

Ashwyn swallowed the lump in her throat. It was true even if Cass didn't want to say it out loud. Everyone had to pull their own weight. And some of them had started with a deficit, so they had to pull double.

The villagers would never let her stay and use up their resources if she remained in this bed. She had to move. She had to regain her strength and finish what she'd started. They'd never make a Bladesaint leave. Then she'd be able to stay and build her house right next to Cass's and—

She had to close her left eye to ignore the blurriness and pretend it wasn't there.

"She said to rest," Cass said as Ashwyn tried to push up on her elbows.

"I will," Ash lied. "But I'm hungry." And eating would help her get her strength back.

Cass hurried to the cupboard where Bayna stored the bread and cheese allotted to the war orphans. And Ashwyn pushed back the tension that crept up her throat. The feeling that she was running out of time.

Chapter 11
Concordim

The herbwoman wanted her to stay in bed a whole week, but Ashwyn saw the way Bayna sniffed every time she saw Ash lying there. So she ate her food, drank her water, and quietly exercised her limbs under her covers until she could stand without getting winded, and four days after she woke with half the world gone blurry, she followed the others out of the house in the morning.

Her sight kept catching her off guard, making her feel like a veil had fallen down over the left side of her face, and she had to turn her head to see what lurked in the blind spot. But Bayna waited outside to pass out chores for the younger children and work assignments for those who were older. Ashwyn straightened and kept her gaze front and center, hiding the way she wanted to twitch.

"Should you be up?" Cass whispered, sidling into place with the others.

Ashwyn raised her chin as Bayna sent the littles off to pull stray weeds from the road and between the houses.

"I'm fine," she said.

Bayna counted off down the line of those who were a little older, just shy of their apprenticeships.

"Three, four, five—" She got to Ashwyn and looked her up and down.

Ashwyn met her eyes, daring her to say anything.

Bayna's lips twisted. "You six go with the clearers today. And make sure they don't neglect the south path. Roderick said the vines were close enough to grab him yesterday."

She shooed them off, and Ashwyn and Cass followed the others as they picked up their saws and axes. Three men and two women waited at the edge of the field, beckoning them toward the space between the Devastation and the field.

Their forest was hungry. It crept closer and closer every day and had to be cut back to leave room for them to eke out their existence in this little corner between the forest that grew on three sides.

The village used to have more fields, but the new Devastations had eaten them. Every time a new Little War cropped up, the Saints would clear the Malady, and after their victory, a new Devastation would grow in its place, stealing more and more land. Like a greedy toddler stealing all the sweets.

Edgefall had had a sister village once. Anton's Grove.

But it had disappeared. A new branch of the Devastation had flowed in to take its place, stretching all the way to the necropolis and merging with the ancient portion of the forest.

A demonstration of the Goddess's power, both sacred and deadly. And forbidden.

Every day they cleared out the new growth that threatened to swamp their fields and creep up the roads. The littles pulled the seedlings found in the road bed, and nothing more sinister than grass was allowed to grow between the buildings.

The clearers spread out in a line at the edge of the field, stepping over vines that had grown overnight.

Ashwyn hefted her axe over her shoulder, turning her head so she could focus on what was in front of her. She'd regained her strength enough that she was hardly winded even after the walk. But she didn't like the blur along her left side. It made her feel like something was creeping up on her.

She angled herself so the Devastation spread from her good side.

Rafe and Ingrim stood watch at the corners of the fields, their black uniforms standing out among the others. They watched the woods, and Rafe kept his hand on his sword hilt even as villagers greeted him.

Ashwyn bent to hack away the vines that nestled into the edge of the field, cutting them off and kicking aside the sliced ends. Roots were harder, but she'd been doing this for years and knew the trick of angling her blade and then twisting it so the woody incursions snapped off. The others were already heating a cauldron of pitch. They'd come along behind and paint the sticky stuff on the cut ends to keep them from growing back.

Ash concentrated on the area around her feet, leaving Cass on one side and Lev, a fellow orphan, on the other. They made slow progress forward, pushing back the overgrowth foot by foot.

Ashwyn paused when the sun was high enough that the edge had started to disappear behind the soul well. She lifted her arm to dry the sweat on her cheeks.

Spring was better than winter, where they had to do this in the bitter cold and clear snow away from the vines to find the roots that hid underneath. But there was always extra to do after the snow melted, clawing back what the Devastation had tried to take in the dark months.

While she stretched her back, she glanced into the dense growth of the forest, checking for anything white traveling through the trunks or between the curving roots and vines. It was habit now. A bit of a thrill on long boring days.

Light caught on something bright, and there was a flash.

Ashwyn held her breath and then let it out on a little gasp.

Three magpies flitted out from between the trees, swooping up high overhead before diving down to alight on the fence posts around the fields.

One of the Fairhand boys cried out and flicked his free hand beside his eyes in the ward against evil.

Ash gritted her teeth as one of the children ran through, chasing the birds away with a switch.

The magpies croaked overhead, returning to the Devastation, and Ashwyn's gaze followed them, still looking for white between the trunks.

"Hey, Ash. You going to do any work or are you just going to dream about it?" Lev called from her right.

Ash jerked and realized Cass and Lev and the rest of the clearers had pulled ahead of her and she was behind.

Cass caught the direction of her gaze and rolled her eyes. "You're never going to see her, you know?" she whispered.

Ashwyn flushed and didn't answer. It was an old argument, and Ash would never admit that she still liked to watch for the mysterious witch of the Devastation.

Lev squinted at her. "You sure you're really blind?"

Ash whipped around. "What?"

"You can't tell. Your eyes look normal."

"That doesn't mean—" Did he think she was faking it?

"I'm partially blind," she snapped. "So now you're only partially ugly to me. That's an improvement."

Lev growled, but Renner stepped between them. "You training for overseer, Lev?" he asked. Renner was only a year younger than Lev and Ashwyn and had come from Anton's Grove after it was destroyed. "Cause you're really interested in everyone else's business."

Lev glowered for a beat before turning back to his work. "Why not?" he said. "Then I'd get to yell at everybody."

Ash sniffed. "People do what you say better when they like you," she said under her breath.

Cass snorted.

"What about you?" Lev asked Renner.

"Josef said I could have an apprenticeship at the forge."

Ash kicked aside a particularly large chunk of root and stretched her back.

"What are *you* going to do now, Ash?" Renner asked.

Most of the other orphans had been refugees, villagers who had been lucky enough to escape the Little Wars before the quarantines had fallen. None of their parents had been Bladesaints.

They'd grieved, they'd recovered, but they'd fit into life in the village in a way Ashwyn had always envied. She'd never quite figured out how to be perfect so Bayna wouldn't look at her with that exasperated eye roll.

Ashwyn frowned as she bent to hack at the rest of the root. It was so deeply entrenched it might have been there all winter. "What do you mean?"

"Where do you want to be assigned?" Lev said.

Ashwyn straightened up, her axe hanging lightly from her hand. "I'm going to be a Bladesaint. I was always going to be a Saint. You know that."

Lev and Renner exchanged a glance, and Ashwyn's gut clenched.

"You *were*," Lev said. "But you can't see out of one eye."

Renner snorted. "Saints are the best of the best. They're not going to take someone who's broken."

Blood rushed in Ashwyn's ears, and her whole body went hot and then cold enough to make her shiver.

She'd lain there for days, watching as the blur got worse and worse, and this was the first time it had occurred to her that this one little thing might ruin everything for her.

"Ash?" Cass said behind her.

She couldn't breathe. There was something stuck in her throat and knotted in her chest.

"I can still hold a blade," she croaked.

Lev tipped his head back to look at her with narrowed eyes. "But can you hit anything with it if you can't see?" He shook his head. "Father Liman said he was going to be a Saint before his accident. Now he's just a priest."

Renner rolled his eyes at Lev, but he didn't stop the terrible words. Or say anything to counter them.

"You were always so good at pretending you were better than us with that climbing and training," Lev said. "Can't pretend anymore."

Rage and grief swept through her, turning her gut into a cold, hard stone. She lunged forward and planted her fist in Lev's face, proving there was nothing wrong with her aim.

"Hey!" Renner called.

"Ash!" Cass tried to drag her back by her arm, but Lev was coming for her, blood streaming from his nose, and Ashwyn couldn't see straight, and it had nothing to do with the blur in her left eye.

"You little Malady rat," Lev gasped. "That hurt."

He yanked her from Cass's grip, and she landed another hit across his cheekbone before he raised his arm to block her. Just like when they were kids.

Lev stooped to grab a loose rock like he was going to hit her with it.

A hand grabbed the back of her overcoat and hauled her away.

"Stop this," Rafe hissed. "Stop this right now. Look! The Devastation feeds on your anger. It takes it and uses it for itself."

Lev froze and stared out at the twisting vines and roots. The gray-green mass shuddered, and vines stretched like tentacles.

Ashwyn's mouth went dry with horror, and Cass's hand tightened on her arm.

"The Devastation reacts to emotion," Rafe said. "Never show it anger when you stand this close. It will swallow you. It will swallow all of us."

Lev dropped the rock and gulped. Renner pushed him back a step, and the two boys glanced at Ashwyn and Cass. Lev sniffed before they stumbled back toward the farmers, who stared at the Devastation, whispering.

Renner jerked his thumb over his shoulder, as if telling them to blame her.

"I hope they never find your body when you go Absent," Ashwyn muttered.

Cass gasped.

"Ashwyn," Rafe snapped. "Control yourself."

Ash glanced at the seething roots of the Devastation—how did plants even move like that?—and yanked her arm from Cass's grip. Refusing to retreat, she stalked along the edge of the field. She wasn't afraid of the woods. She wasn't. Even if she couldn't see it all with her head turned the wrong way.

She breathed in and out and finally turned back to Cass and Rafe when she could finally look at the others without wanting to hit something.

Lev, and Renner, and the farmers huddled in the middle of the field as the Devastation settled and the growth stopped moving. Cass and Rafe watched her instead of the roots, waiting with sad eyes and tight lips.

Because it was true. They knew it just like Lev and Renner. She'd been fooling herself, refusing to think the worst ever since her fever had broken.

She'd never be a Bladesaint.

She sat right there on the stony ground amidst the cut ends of the growth and buried her head in her hands.

Cass crept closer and squatted in front of her. She took Ash's hand and ran her thumb over the knuckles of the first two fingers.

Ashwyn winced at the unexpected pain.

"You're bleeding," Cass said. She took the edge of her overcoat and dabbed at the torn skin of Ashwyn's knuckles.

Ash's throat closed up yet again.

She was so gentle and kind. Cass was always the one trying to take care of her. Trying to keep her out of trouble. She was the one who laughed at Ash's jokes and cared if she was going to die of fever or not.

Ashwyn tried to swallow the lump in her throat.

And now the villagers wouldn't let her stay where she could see Cass every day. Hear her voice and lean on her when everything else seemed to want to crush her.

Hot tears slid down her cheeks.

"Why is it so important to be a Bladesaint?" Cass asked her quietly. "There are lots of things you can do. Things you'll be good at."

Ashwyn had no idea how to answer. How to tell her that the pressure under her breastbone built every day, pushing her to do more and more. So Bayna would look at her with something other than disgust. So the elderman would remember her name for once. So Cass would smile at her.

She raised her chin and looked at Rafe standing behind Cass.

"Are they right? The Bladesaints won't take me now?"

His lips pressed into a thin line under his beard. The hair at his temples had gone white, streaking through the dark strands.

"It's true that they only recruit able-bodied soldiers."

"Then I'll never be a Saint," Ash said, her voice flat. Everything in her had gone numb.

"Now, I didn't say that."

Ashwyn's chin jerked, and Cass looked up at him.

"There are different ways to be a Saint. There are the Bladesaints like Ingrim and me. Like your mom." He tilted his head. "And there are the Nexsaints."

Ashwyn's breath caught. She'd seen a Nexsaint exactly once. One of the Absent had Returned when she and Cass were twelve, and a Nexsaint had come to escort him to Vitamorn.

Ash remembered little about him except for his long robes and the way he and the Divine had disappeared into thin air. Rafe had scoffed and called it showing off.

"Nexsaints are soldiers like us," Rafe said, plucking at his uniform. "Fighters who protect people from the Malady. But their weapon is the Nexum instead of a blade."

Ashwyn's fingers clenched. "But you said there's no way to learn to use the Nexum. It's a gift. It has to be given to you. By the Goddess."

He raised his eyebrows. "How badly do you want to be a Saint?"

She snorted. "You know the answer to that."

"Well, Nexsaints are made. You have to go to the city. Present yourself at the temple with an appropriate offering and meet Deavita herself. She's the only one who can anoint Nexsaints."

"Just walk up to her and ask?" Ashwyn squeaked.

"That's how it's done." He tilted his head. "The *only* way it's done. For those who are brave enough."

Ashwyn stood. "But it can be anyone? Anyone can go and ask her?"

Rafe nodded. "Yes. Anyone can become a Nexsaint. Anyone the Goddess chooses. It doesn't always happen."

Ashwyn bit her lip. Cass stood with her and wrapped her hands around Ashwyn's wrist. The grip steadied her.

"But if you don't ask," Rafe said. "Then the answer is always going to be no."

Ashwyn's breath came faster. Nexsaints were important. Even more important than Bladesaints. Bayna would never be able to complain that she was useless or taking up village resources if she were a Nexsaint.

Cass squeezed Ashwyn's arm, and she looked over at her best friend.

"You'd have to go to Vitamorn," Cass whispered. "You'd have to leave."

For a while at least. Was it worth it?

Cass stared back at her, brown eyes wide. She was worth anything.

"You could come with me," Ash said, keeping the hope from her voice. It was a stupid idea. Another game of pretend.

But then Cass laughed and said, "What?"

"We can both go." Ash's heart thumped. "We can both be Nexsaints. Do you want to go with me?"

Cass looked away, and Ash thought she might throw up if she heard the wrong answer.

"Please," she said before Cass could say no.

The other girl's full mouth tilted in a smile. "I've been going with you my whole life."

Ashwyn sucked in a breath. "Is that a yes?" She'd been the one working so hard all this time to stay with Cass. Maybe Cass had been working to stay with her too, and she'd just never noticed.

"If I'm a Saint," Cass said, thinking it all through. "Ma won't be able to make me the next elderman."

Rafe gave them both a sly smile. "It's a pretty important calling. More important even than elderman. Even Bayna would be impressed."

"Don't tell my mom," she said. "Not yet."

"It'll be our secret."

As a Nexsaint, Ash would be too important for the village to ignore. She'd be needed. She'd get to stay with Cass.

And no one would care how much she could or couldn't see.

Chapter 12
Concordim

While the others all prepared for apprenticeships and taking on more adult roles in the village, Ashwyn and Cass prepared to meet the Goddess. No one under twenty was allowed to become a Saint. Rafe explained that the Order wouldn't risk recruiting anyone younger to fight in the Little Wars, considering the Malady's strange attraction to children and Absent.

So Ashwyn had years to pester Rafe for everything he knew about the Goddess.

"It's not much, Ash," he told her. "I only saw Her once when I was anointed. The process for Bladesaints is different. My whole squad went together."

"Well, then what was *that* like?"

"It was a lot of men and women all crowded into the Greater Temple. I barely even saw Her. I was way in the back. And kneeling."

"But She's actually there? In the room."

"She is. That's the point. The Greater Temple is the seat of Her power."

"What does She look like?"

Rafe gave her an indulgent smile. "I guess you'll just have to find out when you get there."

She gave it up as a lost cause and switched to asking him about the Nexum. But that was even more fruitless.

"It's all connections," he said with the blustering authority of someone who knew exactly one fact about a subject. "The Nexum is a network connecting all life and matter. And the Goddess's gift allows you to see it and manipulate it. For more than that you'll have to ask a Nexsaint. They train for a lot longer than the Bladesaints."

But he couldn't tell her *how* they trained. And whenever she pressed him, he'd say, "You'll have to ask your Rector when you get there."

Cass seemed content with that. But then, Cass never showed the world anything other than peace. Ash wished she could borrow some.

She had to content herself with imagining her new life in between battling incursions of the Devastation and chopping firewood. On good days, she could nearly see the glowing strands that connected all life.

On bad ones, she thought if she just wished hard enough, she'd feel them wrap around her body to carry her off to Vitamorn.

At seventeen, the council called each war orphan to the little chamber beside the Temple to assign apprenticeships. Lev and the others smirked as they left the orphan house to take their places among the adults. Ashwyn watched them go one by one with a strange sort of pang. It wasn't like this was goodbye—they'd still see each other around the village—and she'd never been good friends with any of them, preferring to push their faces into the dirt whenever they insulted her or Cass. But there had always been the chance that they could get along. They were the only other ones in the village who understood what it was like to not belong to anyone.

Ash was only the oldest one in the orphan house for a month before the elderman summoned her on her birthday.

Ashwyn smoothed her hands down her overcoat and made sure it covered the worst stains along her shirt and pants. Then she stepped into the council chamber. It was just a square building off to the side of the Lower Temple with windows along one wall and a line of tables along the other. Nothing fancy. But it made Ashwyn's gut clench when she realized the elderman sat there with the entire village council beside him.

Redd Fairhand sat to his left, representing the farmers. Father Liman was there to ensure every decision had spiritual oversight. The herbwoman made sure the craftworkers and tradespeople of the village had a voice. And Bayna sat to the elderman's right, representing everyone else.

"This one's Ashwyn?" the elderman said.

"Yes, Elderman," Ash said, biting back what she actually wanted to say. It never paid to be rude to the one who held your fate in his hands.

"Seventeen already?" He tapped the big leather-bound ledger in front of him. The ancient man's hair hung limp and unwashed against his frail shoulders. He'd led the council for as long as Ash could remember. Far longer than anyone had thought he would. Especially Bayna, who'd been grooming Cass to take his place since they were little.

"Well, where are we going to put you, now that you're grown?"

Ash's breath caught. "I'm going to be a Saint, elderman. I—I was always going to be a Saint." Everyone knew it. Had he forgotten that along with her name?

He waved a spotted hand as if to bat away her pesky words. "Yes, so you've said. But it's three years before you can go."

"You can't laze about for that long," Bayna said, eyes pinched at the corners.

Ashwyn's teeth clenched. She'd never lazed around in her life. She knew what was at stake here on the edge of the Devastation.

"Besides," the elderman said, resting his hands on the ledger. "Travel to the city won't be cheap. And there's no one to pay your way."

She hadn't even thought about that. She flushed when she realized her entire plan had been to set off down the road and walk until she reached the Greater Temple.

Bayna smirked, but the herbwoman took in Ash's panic and tilted her head.

"She might not have family to help her out," she said. "But it wouldn't be a terrible thing to have a Nexsaint who owes us all a favor."

She winked at Ash.

Ashwyn held her breath.

The elderman raised his eyebrows. "This is true. We will make you a deal, Ashwyn. If you work hard for the next three years, we will pay your way to the city."

Was there a downside to this? This was exactly what she'd planned to do, anyway.

"Yes," she blurted out. "Yes. I mean, I agree."

The elderman held up a finger. "And you will have to wait till we can spare you. Obviously not during an incursion when we need the extra help."

"Of course not," Father Liman spoke up. "Ashwyn knows the dangers here. She will not leave us when she's needed." He nodded to her, and Ashwyn let out the breath she'd been holding and smiled at him.

"So, where to put you in the meantime?" the elderman said.

Bayna examined her fingernails. "The clearers always need more hands."

Ashwyn closed her eyes. *I can endure anything to become a Nexsaint. Even three more years of clearing. Strong and clever. I'll bet Nexsaints have to be as strong and clever as Bladesaints.*

"Hmm," the elderman said.

"I can use her help," the herbwoman said. "She's smart enough to know which plants to pick and which ones to leave alone."

Father Liman lifted his chin. "Actually, I could, too. There are many things in the temple I could use some help with, and they always get a lower priority."

Bayna's mouth twisted. She must not love the idea that they were suddenly fighting over her.

The elderman opened the ledger and made a note. "Very well. She'll divide her time between the temple and gathering herbs."

Bayna opened her mouth, but the elderman spoke before her. "And yes, she'll fill in with the clearers when they need her." He pierced Ashwyn with a look. "Without grumbling."

"Yes, sir," Ashwyn said.

She didn't mind the work. The herbwoman taught her all the right plants to look for, including the ones that grew in the Devastation.

"I don't have to tell you to be extra careful with those," she said. "We only harvest the ones that grow on the edges, the ones we can reach without setting foot in the forest. Even that is too dangerous for most people. But they're valuable to us. Some of those blooms are the only defense we have against certain illnesses."

Ash didn't mention it to Cass, but it gave her a lot more time up close to the Devastation, where she could stare off between the branches, searching for flashes of white.

"Watch your step now," the herbwoman would say, pointing past the first tangle of roots and vines. "The ground drops there. You go any farther, and the forest will swallow you."

"What's down there?" Ash asked, leaning just far enough to see the edge of the cliff and the trees plunging into the depths beyond. It looked like the edge of a crater. Had the Devastation grown in the middle of it?

"Ask the priest," the herbwoman said with a snort. "He claims to know all the answers."

Ash understood why the old woman would want her help. She could reach the greenery much easier than most, and her blurred vision didn't hinder her climbing at all.

But she still wasn't sure why Father Liman had claimed her. So she asked him the first time she showed up at the Lower Temple.

He gave her a sly look and said, "Oh, I just can't fetch and carry with this leg. I need a young, strong back to lift."

Ashwyn looked around at the heavy pews lined up along the floor. He'd already moved them to sweep and mop and shifted them back even before she'd shown up.

"Right," she said. "I'm pretty sure lying is a sin, Father."

He laughed. "Alright, yes. I'm sure you've heard the Goddess chooses Nexsaints. I figured it can't hurt your chances to be closer to Her."

Ashwyn glanced up at the statue over the altar and grinned. "I guess not," she said.

"And you'll need time to find and meditate over your offering. That's always easier in the quiet."

"But what am I supposed to offer?"

"Something special to you. Something that would be a sacrifice to give up. It's supposed to indicate your willingness to leave your old life behind to serve Her."

"I don't have anything like that."

Father Liman turned to head toward the cloister, saying over his shoulder, "Then you'd better start thinking of something to give Her."

Cass still worked mostly with her mother and the council and had less and less time to spend with Ashwyn. Which just gave Ashwyn more time to walk the edge of the Devastation.

"Father Liman, what's in the crater?" she asked him after her morning with the herbwoman.

He looked up with a frown from sorting altar cloths. His dark hands stilled against the creamy fabric. "Hmm?"

"The crater in the Devastation. What's down there?"

"The forest, of course. It's sacred to the Goddess. Sacred and deadly, just like Her."

"Rafe once said it's guarding something."

Father Liman straightened. "Well, yes. She protects us from the original source of the Malady."

Ash sucked in a breath. "Source? You mean it's still down there?"

His eyes widened, and he lifted his hands. "No! No, it's gone. Defeated. Only small outbreaks occur now and are always easily scoured. But the original site could still be dangerous. It's forbidden."

She gulped. "Some good things can come from the forest. Greta sent me after Devastation lilies today. That's the herbwoman's name. Greta. No one else calls her that, but I think it's important that someone remembers. The lilies only grow along the roots of the trees in the forest, so you have to get real close to find them. But they're pretty, and they treat infection."

Without thinking, she raised one hand to touch her eye. Then she shook her head. No use crying about the past. Greta had done her best.

Father Liman straightened. "I don't like that she sends you so close to the Devastation."

"I'm careful," Ashwyn said.

"It's not always enough to be careful. The Goddess's power lives there, and it is dangerous."

Ash carefully dusted the edge of the altar without looking at him. "Do you think any people live in there?"

"Absolutely not!" He stared at her with enough horror that she dropped the subject.

"Father Liman thinks the forest belongs to the Goddess," Ash told the herbwoman the next day. "But the forest snatches people. Wouldn't that mean that the Goddess is responsible for Mikel and all the others it's taken?"

Greta snorted. She knelt close to the roots that crept from the edge of the forest, sifting through the dry grass that grew up from between the bark.

"Oh, I would pay to see you ask him that."

"I didn't want to make him cry."

The old woman barked a laugh. "So you pester me instead."

Ash grinned. "Of course. Do you think he's right? No one can live there?"

"The danger is real," Greta said. "But I don't care if it's a person with a white face or if it's just a bunch of branches and leaves growing too fast for their own good." She saw Ash's look. "I know the rumors, girl. I'll protect against the danger I can see and understand, not the stories that people tell."

Greta held out a handful of dry grasses, all different colors. Some stalks were green and yellow, and others were a dull purple. "Tuck these in your basket," she said.

"Are they medicinal?" Ash asked.

Greta snorted again. "They're useful. They're strong when woven, and I like the colors. They're pretty." She gave Ashwyn a sharp look. "We survive in Edgefall. We pride ourselves on it. But don't forget to try to live, too, while you're surviving."

That was easy for Greta to say. The herbwoman had a place. She was useful and respected. It was hard to live and thrive when you were still worrying about what the food that went into your mouth was costing someone else.

Three more years, she told herself. *I can last that long.*

Chapter 13
Concordim

Ashwyn turned twenty on the snowiest day of the year, two months before Cass's birthday. Enormous drifts gathered under the eaves of the orphan house and tore branches off of the feverdusk trees Ashwyn had enjoyed climbing as a child. The heavy wet layer built up along their wide brown leaves until the weight was too much and the branches came down, leaving long jagged scars in the trunks.

Even the Devastation seemed quiescent, buried under a weight so great that the roots and vines lay still and frozen for once.

It should have left time for the clearers to finally be idle. But instead, they were out with the rest of the village shoveling paths and tunnels between the houses and the Lower Temple, walls of white rising around them as they sweated and swore under their woolen layers.

The sun had disappeared behind the dark tangle of the Devastation by the time they'd plowed their way to every last porch and made sure the villagers could get out. The elderman and the council laid a huge fire in the central brazier of the temple and bid everyone get warm before they returned to their homes. Several of the village wives laid out what little they had on the tables— bread and roasted potatoes and a lumpy pudding that no one wanted to admit to bringing.

It wasn't much. This deep in the winter, they couldn't afford to feast. But it was nice to not have to huddle lonely in their houses and wait for the snow to melt enough to see who had made it through the winter.

And after a day like that, Ashwyn felt completely justified in taking her portion along with the rest. Until Bayna entered the room with Cass in tow and Ash surreptitiously returned a roll to the basket. Just in case.

Cass found her after she'd sat in the corner and taken her boots off so her wool socks could dry a little. The other girl sat beside her, pushing her long scarf back from her face.

"I made you something," Cass said and pulled a plate from behind her back. A tiny pie sat in the middle, small enough to fit in the palm of Ash's hand.

Ashwyn made a delighted noise.

"It's just the dried berries left over from fall. So it won't taste like much. But I wanted you to have something just for you today."

Ash bit into it and made sure to make all the right noises so Cass would know what it meant to her.

"I'm sorry you couldn't leave today," Cass said quietly.

Ash's lips twisted in a rueful smile. Cass was the first to mention it. The first to acknowledge that today was different in any way whatsoever. And the knot wrapped tight in her chest loosened just a little bit.

"Yeah, I know." Ashwyn glanced at Cass. "But I was waiting for you, anyway. You can't go till you're twenty. Which means I can't go till you're twenty."

Cass's gaze flicked away, the corners of her mouth pulling down.

Ash's stomach flopped, and she tipped her head back, pretending she hadn't seen the tiniest bit of hesitance in Cass's response.

"Besides," she said, overly cheerful. "Travel will be way easier in the spring."

Cass turned back, a small smile erasing whatever thought had made her wince, and Ash felt it as sunshine against her skin, even in the dead of winter.

As the other girl talked, Ash slipped her hand into her pocket, running the strands of grass through her fingers. She'd been working on the offering just like Father Liman had suggested, sitting at the base of the Goddess statue in the spare moments he gave her.

Praying wasn't really something Ashwyn did. She gathered in the temple with the others every time the bell rang for the services, but actually speaking the words was Father Liman's job.

But the priest had said to meditate, so she bent her head over the strands and thought harder than she'd ever thought about anything before. Thought about kneeling before the Goddess. Thought about strands of light connecting everything. Thought about why she wanted to leave Edgefall just to come back.

And Father Liman didn't have to know the way those thoughts turned more and more toward Cass than toward the Goddess who stared down at her.

The snow had melted by Cass's birthday, leaving the space between houses muddy, but at least the road to Vitamorn sat above the mire.

Every spring, the village sent a wagon to the city carrying their annual tithe, and Cass had spent months arranging to accompany it. And of course, Ashwyn would go too, to present herself at the Greater Temple.

It was all planned. Ashwyn had dreamed it, but Cass had made it a reality. They really were going.

And then, the night before they were scheduled to leave, the alarm bells rang throughout the village.

Ashwyn woke to the clanging and the shouts of the clearers as they banged on the door of the orphan house.

"Incursion!" they cried.

"It's coming!"

Ash yanked on her pants in the dark, her heart thudding, and she stumbled out to find torches lighting up the night.

At the edge of the fields, roots crept along the ground and vines twisted down from the branches, spreading in a visible onslaught of vegetation.

Ashwyn tried to swallow but found her throat was too dry. She leaped forward, swinging her axe against the overgrowth, severing a vine in two. It fell to the ground, writhing as if in pain. Ash shook her head.

It's just reacting to our fear. It's not sentient.

She worked side by side with the other clearers, passing torches and saws, calling out to keep track of whoever was beside her in that moment. The forest grew too fast to heat the pitch. They could only cut and slash and keep hacking the growth back to regain ground against the incursion.

Beside Ash, Nial Fairhand screamed and went down, a vine wrapped around his foot. It yanked him toward the forest.

"It's taking him!" someone yelled.

The flashes of torchlight made the blur on Ash's left side even worse, but she leaped toward the sound of Nial's screams. She grabbed his hand to keep him from getting pulled any farther. The others followed and hacked at the vines dragging at him.

"There's too many!"

"Keep cutting," Ash called. "Now pull!"

Two of the others dropped their tools and wrapped their arms around Nial alongside Ashwyn. Together they pulled, and the half-cut vines snapped.

They yanked him back toward safety and torchlight, leaving the tools behind to be eaten by the forest.

By the time the sky turned gray and they could finally see, they were each covered in grime and sweat and smoke. The ends of Ash's dark hair straggled into her eyes, and she dragged the stray pieces back to tuck into the haphazard knot on the back of her head.

She ran her sleeve over her face to wipe away some of the trailing dirt but was careful not to rub her left eye. It had long since healed, but she hated to touch it more than necessary. A leftover fear that she might make it worse somehow.

In the dawning light, the fields looked terrible, the ground broken and jagged where the roots had dug it up, and their boots had tromped through the mud. The farmers had already gathered along the edges, discussing how they could salvage what had been ruined.

Murmurs swept through the clearers, and Ash heard more than one relieved, "Life is hard, but we're harder," spoken like a call and response in the temple.

They hadn't lost anyone, but that was the best that could be said. They still had days' worth of work to cut back the overgrowth to where it had been the night before the incursion. And then they'd have to come through with pitch to seal off the cuts so it wouldn't come back.

At least not right away. One thing they knew in Edgefall was that the forest always came back, eventually.

But for one moment here at dawn, they had a chance to breathe.

And that's why Ashwyn heard the creak of wheels on flagstones and Cass's voice raised in anger.

With a sudden drop of her stomach, she remembered what day it was and what she was supposed to be doing. She tossed her axe and sprinted for the village square. There wasn't even time to stop at the orphan house to grab her pack or her overcoat.

Ashwyn raced past the houses and burst into the square. Before the Lower Temple stood the wagon, canvas covering the crates loaded in the bed. Rafe sat on the bench as Cass stood beside the wheel. Bayna and the rest of the council faced them from the steps.

"We're not leaving without her," Cass was saying. Her normal soft-spoken tone had risen, and it made Ash's heart rate pick up.

"I'm here," Ash said, rushing up to them. It wasn't the run that made her voice come out so wispy. It was the thought of Cass on that wagon without her.

The elderman looked her up and down, taking in her torn and dirty shirt and the streaks of soot and mud across her face. Father Liman bit his lip and glanced toward the fields.

Bayna crossed her arms and sighed. "It would have been better if you'd stayed with the clearers," she said, her voice weary and not unkind.

"What?" Ashwyn said. "Why?"

"You're not going." Bayna jerked her chin at Cass. "Climb up, Cassarah."

Something burned in Ash's chest, lodging in her throat so she could barely breathe. "What do you mean I'm not going?"

Bayna extended a hand toward the forest. "There's an incursion. The Devastation is advancing. We can't spare any of the clearers today, or tomorrow, or likely for the rest of the month. Everyone is going to be pitching in for this."

"Then I'll wait," Cass said, stepping close to Ash. "I won't leave for the city yet."

"The tithe still needs to go," Bayna said. "And you're the one person we *can* spare to go with Rafe."

Ash couldn't speak past the dryness of her throat. But she didn't have to.

"You can't do this to her," Cass said. "This is her dream."

"She's been working her whole life to get to this point," Rafe said.

It was the elderman who answered them. "I'm sorry, child." He met Ashwyn's eyes. "Our deal was that you could go unless you were needed. I think we can all say that that qualification has been met."

She nearly laughed in his face, but she choked it down, too worried it would turn into a sob.

She'd wanted this. She'd wanted them to need her like this. And now it felt like a tether tied so tight she couldn't breathe.

Cass would fight for her. So would Rafe. They both waited, watching her face. If she insisted, they would help her. She could just climb up onto the wagon, and Rafe would drive away. She'd never have to see Edgefall again if she and Cass didn't want to.

But...

They weren't wrong about the incursion. She'd left her fellow clearers gasping for a short break before they dove right back into the fight against the Devastation. Greta was already there tending Nial's leg where the vines had torn his skin. And the magpies had gathered on the branches at the edges, watching everything with their beady eyes.

The others were just as exhausted as she was. If she left now, they'd be shorthanded. She'd be the reason someone got hurt next, or the Devastation sucked them in.

What kind of Saint would leave people who needed their help?

Ashwyn shook her head, not only for Rafe and Cass but also for herself. She needed to make the decision that would break her heart. And she needed to do it out loud.

"You go," she whispered to Cass. "I'll wait."

"No!" Cass cried.

"Do I have time to say goodbye?" she asked Bayna and the elderman.

The elderman nodded while Bayna huffed, and Ash pulled Cass aside, behind the wagon where they could speak as Rafe raised his eyes to the sky and pretended he couldn't hear.

Tears already welled in Cass's eyes and Ash was glad for the sweat trails down her own face so no one would be able to tell she'd been crying, too.

"It's not fair," Cass said.

Ashwyn just shook her head. It wasn't, but that was Edgefall. She'd known it a long time now, and there wasn't even a little bit of surprise buried in the ache in her heart.

She took Cass's hands in hers. She'd always loved the contrast between Cass's light fingers and hers darkened by too much time in the sun. "I'll leave as soon as I can. As soon as the incursion is taken care of. Maybe I can catch up."

"But I don't want to go alone," Cass said. "And I don't want you to go alone either."

"You're going to be a Nexsaint, Cass. That's the important part. If you're there, then your mother doesn't have you and, and..." The words ran out. It was so hard to believe them.

"Here." Ashwyn dug in her pocket and pulled out two bracelets woven from the colored grasses Greta liked so much. Ash had spent those days sitting under the Goddess statue, tightening the strands, imagining the day she'd hand one to Cass on the steps of the Greater Temple.

"Take this." The bracelet wove strands of deep blue with lighter purple, Cass's favorite. "Father Liman said that when you ask for a favor from the Goddess, it's customary to leave a sacrifice for Her. I thought these would be ours." They were supposed to lie side by side.

Ash wrapped the bracelet around Cass's wrist as Cass sniffed. "I thought of you the whole time I wove it. And I'll think of you while I wait."

Cass nodded as if she didn't trust her voice. She squeezed Ash's hands before she climbed to the wagon seat beside Rafe.

"We'll come back for you," Rafe said with a nod to Ashwyn.

Ash stepped back as Bayna and the others said their goodbyes, but she didn't climb the steps to join them.

She waited on the street as the wagon pulled away, as if they could change their minds and come back for her now. As if she could change her mind and run after them.

Chapter 14
Animatim

Banners hung from the towers of the Greater Temple, purple and gold glinting in the sun as the breeze fluttered the edges of the fabric. Bits of bright paper cascaded from the upper stories of the surrounding building as onlookers threw handfuls onto the parade below.

Vitania grinned and raised a hand to wave at those crowded along the street.

Technically, she wasn't supposed to be any different from the other novices on their way to the Greater Temple. They were all the same age and some of them had even trained together. But there was no hiding the gold circlet that flashed on her brow or the long honey-colored hair that was a match for her mother's or her deep blue eyes they remembered from her brother.

And the last difference... Despite the celebration, the rest of the novices all shifted nervously, glancing up at the towers. The one on V's left bit her lips until they were white and bloodless. The one on her right couldn't stop adjusting his collar as if it choked him.

No matter how disciplined, how skilled they'd grown with a blade, most of these novices would be leaving today without becoming Nexsaints. The Goddess rarely gifted more than two or three new Nexsaints a year. Most of the novices and supplicants would leave disappointed.

That was not an option for Vitania.

The crowd surged as they reached the steps of the temple, a wave of sound washing over the parade.

Gifting Day was always an affair. People lined the streets starting at dawn in order to get a good spot, and, later, vendors would hawk berry pies and grilled vegetables from every corner.

But V wasn't imagining the fact that the crowd cheered a little louder when she came into view.

It made sense that they looked for her. She was the heir to the Abdicancy. They revered her because of her title, not because of anything she'd done. Just another facet of her existence, like the color of her hair or her height. She tried not to let it distract her.

Her mother stood beside the open archway of the temple, her black robes stark against the white marble. Behind the soaring towers loomed the dark walls of the volcano, mirroring the flare of the Abdicant's sleeves perfectly.

Ahead of the novices, a nervous group of supplicants walked dressed in a hodgepodge of styles. V guessed they'd drawn hopefuls from farmers to merchants and everything in between. They were the ones who'd traveled from their families to be here. To kneel before the Goddess and ask for Her gift, despite the fact they had no formal training.

V admired their bravery, but their disappointment in the end had to be less than the others'. They had homes to return to and lives they could pick up again if they weren't gifted. The novices, on the other hand, had been tithed to the temple. They'd spent years waiting for this day. If the Goddess's answer to them was no, they had only one option: to become a Bladesaint. She supposed they could choose to leave the Saints' Hold and blend back into society with a normal life and a normal profession. But how devastating would that be, to spend your entire life training to be a Saint, and then have to resign yourself to clearing fields for the rest of your life?

Yes, the supplicants definitely had it better than the novices.

Sahvia nodded to each and every one of them as they passed her, her expression revealing nothing but a serene welcome. Even as V passed, she betrayed no worry.

As she had for years.

Just that morning, V had sat across from her at the breakfast table, her hands steady on her fork as her heart beat a thunderous cadence in her chest. And Sahvia had made conversation, laying out her plans for the day, the week, the month.

"I'll have to set aside time for the annual review," she'd said, staring over the paperwork lying next to her. "Perhaps you could take up my tasks along the front line next month. They require a Judge, but I will be double-booked."

As if today were a foregone conclusion.

V squared her shoulders. Because it was. There was no other option. If the

Goddess denied her Her gift today, V would be the first princess since the Descent to not be a Judge.

No pressure.

Sahvia's eyes passed over Vitania, and V straightened herself out and quirked her lips in a confident grin. Judges did not show fear. They did not waver or whine. They let others lean on them and took the weight without staggering.

Her mother's gaze flickered, a trace of warmth crossing her expression for a moment before she turned to head inside.

The crowd gave one last cry, and V waved to them before she held her breath and stepped into the darkened space of the temple.

The supplicants gathered at the crossing of the nave, where the altar stood. Beyond them, the Goddess sat on Her throne, a shaft of sunlight from the stained glass window lighting Her in blues and greens and reds.

Priests and priestesses waited in the crossing on either side of the altar, directing the supplicants into an orderly line. One priestess glanced back toward the novices and caught V's eye. She blushed and bit her lip.

V's lips quirked, and she gave the priestess an appraising look. She'd just broken things off with Melara, but that had gone amicably, and V hated spending too much time alone. Perhaps she wouldn't have to this time.

And the view was certainly a nice distraction from what she'd come here to do.

From back here, V couldn't see much of what was happening with the supplicants. They should be moving forward to kneel one by one at the Goddess's feet, leaving their sacrifices for Her. And shuffling to one side or another after it was done.

V waited, pretending the knot in her throat was an oncoming cold or a result of the trees blooming outside. Every disappointed face made her stomach twist, so she stopped watching as the supplicants moved forward.

As she fought down the discomfort, her fingers twitched, forming the first sign of the Saint's Petition.

"Deavita, keep us in goodness, gentleness, and joy. For your freedom we pray."

It came to her hands during any rise in emotion. A flaw she'd worked hard to stamp out. How many times had her mother's sharp eyes latched onto the movement? How many times had V stuffed her hands under her arms and sat through the burn of shame? Even now she couldn't help hearing another voice, deep and reverent, intoning the words with her.

She suppressed it ruthlessly and turned her attention back to the supplicants.

A girl with long blonde hair and a beautifully round face approached the throne. She wore a gray overcoat to protect her clothes, like they did in the outer villages, where the work was dirty and often dangerous.

The girl glanced over her shoulder as if she was waiting for someone, and she dragged her feet as she moved forward. Finally, she stroked her wrist in what looked like a habitual movement and took a deep breath before she stepped forward to take her place at the foot of the Goddess.

The girl knelt, lips moving as she stared up at the face of divinity. She pulled the thing from her wrist and hesitated, fingers clenched around it. Then she held it to her cheek for a moment and laid it at the Goddess's feet.

It nearly disappeared into the pile of other sacrifices, but V could just make out a grass bracelet dyed blue and purple.

A couple of the nearby novices snorted and hid laughter behind their hands. But V's breath caught, seeing the humble offering settle among the coins and jewelry already glinting at the Goddess's feet.

Tavian had once told her that, long ago, the offering had represented a real sacrifice. Something that was painful to give up or cut away from one's life. Over the decades, the offerings had grown shallow and cold, a mere scatter of coins or a discarded possession, instead of something given from the heart.

This girl dragged her fingers away from the bracelet, as if reluctant. Maybe she wondered if the sacrifice was worth it. What did those simple grass strands mean to her? And how painful was it to leave behind?

At the far end of the hall from V, the Goddess stirred.

A collective gasp echoed from the high walls as the priests and novices noticed the subtle shift and movement on the throne. They waited to see if She'd open Her eyes and bestow Her gift.

But the Goddess's eyes remained firmly closed.

After a long moment, one of the priests gestured, and the girl finally stood, her head bowed. She passed V and the other novices on the way out, and V forced herself to memorize the pain etched across her face.

Perhaps she'd been wrong. Perhaps a supplicant's pain was just as great as a novice's.

V swallowed and turned, staring straight ahead.

She brought up the rear of the line. The pretty priestess gestured her forward after the last novice, and she went, her legs clumsy like she trudged through deep mud. Her chest seemed heavier, and her breath came in great gasps. She clenched her fingers at her sides so they wouldn't betray her by praying.

A flicker of movement to her left made her glance past the pillars that lined the nave. A Bladesaint stood in the shadows, eyes fixed on her, and with a jolt V recognized his dark hair and trimmed beard.

Her father. She'd seen him exactly once in the last twelve years, when she'd been out with her mother. The Abdicant's mouth had gone narrow and tight when she'd seen him, and the next V had heard, he'd been assigned to the outskirts of the city.

But he'd come to see her Gifting Day.

Unexpected thickness rose in her throat, and she choked it down.

He was ruining you.

The politics of Vitamorn made more sense now that she was older. A network of threads stretched across the streets from the Palace of Divines to the Abdicant's Court to the Saints' Hold, like the Nexum. V was the last Judge, the last strand in a cradle that kept the continent safe. If she broke, the Abdicant and the Primarch Divine, then the entire continent would come crashing down with her.

And her father had done his best to ensure she broke. Whatever hate he bore the Abdicant, he'd taken it out on V. And had threatened the entire world because of it.

V raised her chin and scowled. She would walk out of here a Nexsaint and a Judge, and none of that had anything to do with him.

She kept her gaze straight ahead and walked forward.

Beside the Goddess, the air shimmered, and the Primarch Divine stepped out, stopping beside the throne. The priests and priestesses murmured as his white robes settled around him, and he placed a tender hand on the Goddess's shoulder.

The shock of his appearance hit her much less than the sight of her father.

Of course the Primarch Divine would come to see her. She was the heir. The next Judge. Everything around her always escalated. If the other novices faced a test, she faced the same test, but she had to take it blindfolded with the entire Hold watching.

V's eyes went to the Goddess, searching Her face, but it remained serene and Her eyes closed as if asleep.

The Primarch Divine gave her a wide smile and then gestured her forward.

V knelt and reached into her gambeson. She pulled out the silver circlet she'd worn when she'd first come to Vitamorn. It sat across her palms, so small now compared to the one on her brow. Tavian's was hers rightfully, and she wore it with pride in memory of him.

But there was something about this one...

She'd worn it while she ached for a father who had betrayed her. She'd worn it while she struggled through muffled voices and ill-adjusted hearing. She'd worn it while her mother raged at her faults.

With a twinge, V laid it atop the pile at the Goddess's feet. And let go. She let go of the circlet. She let go of the child she'd been. She let go of the pain. The silence...the abandonment.

A blue and purple grass bracelet was just visible within the hoop of her own circlet.

It hurt to draw back, but she did not feel the same devastation she'd seen on that girl's face.

It hurt to leave the circlet, but the one she wore hurt more, with the weight of duty and grief digging into her brow.

She was the Abdicant's heir. Things would never be simple for her.

She raised her eyes to the Goddess and found white eyes filled with all the sparks of color of the world staring back at her.

V drew in a sharp breath as something in her chest broke. She sucked in a breath, clamping her jaw tight on a scream as a shattering spread through her torso, as if hands tore her open so something cool and soothing could leak in.

A space inside her nudged at her awareness, and V knew with the certainty of lessons drilled over and over that it was her connection to the Goddess's power opening inside her. But she was too consumed by the threads of black lined with gold that sprang across her vision, stretching from floor to ceiling, limning the limbs of the Primarch Divine and the Goddess before her.

The entire world wrapped in power, connecting V with it all.

Chapter 15
Concordim

Ashwyn did her best to finish her work in the village after Cass and Rafe left, but the incursion bled into the next emergency and the next one after that. A spring fever to treat. A flooded field to be dammed. A Devastation monster to be hunted down. One thing after another, and it was always Bayna who delivered the news with a sympathetic smile.

Ashwyn traipsed down a lane between houses, her boots squelching in the mud, when she realized this was forever. There was no such thing as "finished."

There would always be something more important than what she wanted and needed. The village would always put itself before her, and she was stuck. Mired in the space between the houses, sunk into the mud so that she could never free herself. She'd always be covered in it.

She had worked and hoped and dreamed of the day that the village would find her so useful that they'd let her stay. And she'd done it so well that now they would never let her leave.

Ash fell to her knees there, the muck seeping into her overcoat and up her trousers. She buried her head in her hands as her shoulders shook and her lungs burned with everything she'd trapped inside.

Bayna had done this on purpose. The elderman had gone along with it. Father Liman and Greta were as trapped as she was in the never-ending cycle of crisis.

Life is hard, but we're harder.

How hard did you have to be before life broke you and you shattered and your pieces disappeared into the muck at everyone else's feet?

But...the alternative was to leave. To walk to the city alone. Arrive alone. She could miss Cass on the road entirely. If the other girl became a Nexsaint, then Ash could run away and join her. But if she didn't, then she'd be on her way home, and Ash would be alone in the city.

No, she couldn't just leave now.

And staying here was even worse. She missed Cass every day with a longing that made her breathless. Their lives had grown around each other like the trees at the edge of the Devastation, one type of bark melding with another until there was no telling where one ended and the other began. Cutting them apart would kill them both.

But here Ash was, with bleeding pieces sliced out of her. And all she could do was wait.

Her fingers dug into the sides of her face, anchoring her as she breathed the tension away. Then she swallowed and climbed to her feet. And walked back to the orphan house.

A month after Cass left, Ashwyn carried bushels of rushes toward the Lower Temple. A heat haze had settled over the flagstones now that it was summer, but the sun had disappeared behind the soul well, leaving a large swathe of shadow for a few blessed hours in the middle of the day.

Ashwyn shifted the burden in her arms so the rushes wouldn't poke her, and as the rustle of the dried fronds faded, a new sound replaced it. Hooves on flagstones and the creak of wooden wheels.

Ash looked up, and her heart froze.

The sun peeked out from the edge of the soul well, sending a shaft of light to fall across golden hair.

Cass.

Cass had returned.

Ashwyn couldn't move; she could barely breathe. A piece of her heart slotted back into place, and her entire body hummed to Cass's presence. She stepped forward before she'd even realized she was moving.

Oh. Sudden clarity swept through her, leaving calm in its wake. *Oh, that's what this is.*

Rafe pulled the empty wagon up in front of the Lower Temple's steps. Bayna waited as if she'd known Cass would return today. Perhaps she had. If Cass had been able to send letters, there was no way Bayna would have told her.

Ashwyn stumbled forward in time to catch the older woman's words.

"Finally." Bayna took her daughter in her arms and gave her a kiss on the forehead. "I didn't realize the trip would take you so long."

Cass pulled away, and her eyes found Ashwyn with one foot on the first step. Her lips pulled sideways in an unhappy smile. "I didn't just drop off the tithe, Ma."

Bayna stepped back and looked at Cass. "Oh? Did you do some sightseeing?"

Cass raised her chin and met her mother's eyes. "No. I knelt before the Goddess. To ask to become a Nexsaint."

Bayna gaped. "What?"

"You don't have to worry, though." Cass pulled her hair over her shoulder and stroked her fingers through it. "She didn't take me."

Ash swallowed, her heart returning to a normal beat.

Bayna's mouth worked before she finally found words. "I'm...I'm sorry, Cassarah. I didn't even know you were going to try. Becoming a Nexsaint is a hard thing. But I'm glad you're home now."

She enveloped Cass in another hug, and Ashwyn stepped back behind the wagon where she couldn't be seen. She dropped the rushes on the cobbles and pressed her calloused hands against her cheeks, struggling to keep her breath smooth and even.

"Hey, kid," Rafe said, coming around the edge of the wagon and speaking quietly, like he didn't want to startle her.

Ashwyn lifted her head with a sniff, pushing aside whatever she was feeling. The tangle in her gut could be sorted out later.

"Do you want to go to the city now?" Rafe said. "It's past time it was your turn."

Her breath hitched. Leave now? Without Cass? Escape the thankless work and the pitying looks of the other villagers?

"Ashwyn?" Bayna called and stuck her head around the end of the wagon. "Father Liman needs those rushes. Now. And after you're finished with that, the Fairhands have asked for your help with their fencing. The Devastation tried to break through in the last incursion, and no one's fixed it yet."

Rafe glared at Bayna, but Ash squared her shoulders and stuffed down the burning sensation that tried to creep up her throat.

Bayna would never let her go. There would always be some work to do, some emergency that would make Ashwyn more useful as manual labor than as a Nexsaint. And they would always use that as a way to control her. The threat of exile always hanging over her head, making her compliant.

But Cass was back. This was what she wanted. She wanted to stay with Cass. So why did she feel so trapped?

"Yes, Bayna," Ash said, giving Rafe a sharp shake of her head. She'd talk to him later. She gathered her rushes and trudged up the temple steps.

Much later, when she dragged herself to the orphan house, she found a stack of stones on the windowsill over her bed.

Her weariness fell away like an unwanted overcoat as she headed for the necropolis. Cass sat on the wall, staring out at the Devastation. Ash climbed up easily and took a spot next to her without a word.

Cass remained still, eyes ahead.

Everything was different now, but Ash didn't know if it was different for Cass the same way it was different for her. And she was too afraid to ask.

Nothing felt anchored in the moment, as if everything could float away depending on what she said next.

"What was Vitamorn like?" she asked quietly. The Absent had already been tucked away in their sanctums, and Uniah had finished her sweeping, so they sat entirely alone here above the sleeping Devastation.

Cass tipped her head back and closed her eyes. She smiled. A real smile. It had been so long since Ashwyn had seen her joy that she caught her breath at the sight of it.

"It's beautiful. The walls of the mountain wrap around the whole city, like the volcano is embracing it. And the streets are all laid out like a temple with the Greater Temple in the middle. There were banners and streamers, and the bells rang until they echoed through the streets."

She held out her hand as if reaching for something, then curled her fingers and brought it toward her chest. "I can't even describe it right."

"And the Goddess?" The words came out no louder than a breath, and Cass turned to look at her finally.

"She was the most incredible thing of all." Cass sighed, and her cheeks went pink in the fading light. "You walk into the temple, and She's at the very end, sitting on a black throne with Her hair all around. It's a brilliant red, like fire, and it grows and grows, just like that picture in the Lower Temple."

Ash glanced down at Cass's wrist, but it was empty. She had left the bracelet with the Goddess. Just as Ash had intended.

"She never opened Her eyes for me, Ash," Cass said, her face falling. "I got to stare into the face of everything good and divine, and...and I wasn't enough."

That couldn't be true. Cass was perfect. If perfect wasn't acceptable, then there was no hope for the rest of them.

"Why didn't you leave?" Cass asked, turning away. "I thought you were going to come meet me."

Ash bit her lip. "They wouldn't let me."

Cass sucked in a breath and spun back to her. "They kept you here? Against your will?"

"No." Ash held out her hands. "Nothing like that. It's just that we're always barely surviving with incursions and Devastation beasts and chores. It was just like when I tried to leave with you. There was always some crisis to solve, and I felt terrible if I tried to leave. And..."

She didn't even know how to describe it with Cass sitting there waiting with her gaze open and welcoming.

"They needed my help," she said. "I couldn't leave when they needed me. I don't know why. I guess I still want to do something important. To *be* something important. Something more than a war orphan. I should have left, but I didn't. And then you came home and suddenly I can breathe again."

Cass shifted forward to take her hands, and Ash's mouth went dry.

"I'll help sneak you out of Edgefall," Cass said. "At night. No one will notice, so no one will be able to stop you or ask for something, and then you won't have to feel guilty for leaving."

Ash let out a shaky laugh. No one had ever seen her as Cass did. No one had known her this way. And she knew Cass back. Knew her laugh, knew her kindness. Knew the fierceness she hid under the surface.

"Cass."

"I mean it—"

Ash surged forward and planted her lips against Cass's.

It was fast and awkward, and she caught Cass by surprise with her mouth open, so there were teeth, but somehow it was the sweetest moment of Ash's twenty years.

Cass pulled back and touched her lips with her fingertips, her eyes wide. The silence drew out, and Ash thought her heart would never start beating again.

"What was that for?" Cass said.

Ice swept through Ash's chest, encasing her heart. "Because I love you."

Cass laughed, and the ice shattered. Then Cass leaned forward to meet her halfway, and this time everything was warm and soft, and the tingle spread down her arms into her hands as she held Cass's neck to keep her close. Ashwyn sank into the moment, knowing that every piece of her life had been leading to this.

When Cass finally pulled back, Ash only let her go so far, keeping a hand on the back of her neck where her thumb could stretch to stroke down the brilliant fall of her hair.

"I don't want to go if it means leaving you," she whispered.

The whole point of becoming a Saint had been to earn her place in the village so she could remain with Cass. It meant nothing if they lost each other in the process.

"Then don't," Cass said, voice fiercer than it had been even a moment ago when she'd offered to break Ash out of Edgefall.

Ash tried to match her bright smile, but the dream dying inside her filled her with bitter pain.

"You could still come with me," Ash said. Her free hand trembled at the idea. "You could show me the city and—and we could finally get away."

Cass chewed her lip and glanced away. "I...I can't leave my mother like that. I just got back and...I can't do that to her."

Ash suppressed a groan. Cass would do much better away from Bayna's oppressive influence.

But Ash couldn't force her to leave. As horrible as the woman was, Bayna was Cass's mother. She was family.

If Ash wanted her own family with Cass, she couldn't start by ripping Cass away from hers.

Cass met her eyes, as if she knew all of the thoughts cascading between Ash's ears. "Please stay," she whispered.

Ash closed her eyes and let out a long breath. The dream of being a Saint slid away with it. Cass was what she wanted. Cass was the important part. It had been a long shot anyway, and now she had something even better. It was only hard to let it go because...well, life was hard. But they were harder.

She turned Cass's hand over and kissed her palm, delighting in Cass's shiver.

"All right," she said. "The council seems to like having me around, so I don't have to be a Saint."

"I'm sorry," Cass breathed. "Being a Saint was your dream."

Ash smiled at her. "You were my dream the whole time."

Chapter 16
Concordim

It should have been enough. She tried so hard to make it be enough. But days went by and then weeks where she worked toward nothing, and she felt like nothing because of it.

I'm making them safe, she told herself. *I'm making the entire village safe, including Cass.*

And that was true. But she woke early, before Cass, and would leave the house as quietly as she could only to go work in the fields with the clearers. Late at night when they were finished, the fields would be clear, but the next morning the growth would have crept closer, and they had to do it all over again. An unending cycle where she changed nothing.

And she couldn't shake the feeling that no one would notice if she weren't there. As long as another willing and able worker replaced her, then there was no difference if she was there or not.

Maybe it would have been easier as Greta's apprentice. The herbwoman had offered years ago, back when it had made sense, but Ash had declined. She'd assumed she would be leaving in just a few short years and hadn't wanted to leave her or the rest of the villagers in the lurch. But now Greta had a young apprentice from the orphan house who was willing to work long hours to earn her place in the village. So she needed Ashwyn's help less and less.

And Father Liman wasn't training any little priests, even if Ash had wanted to spend all day within walls, praying. Which she didn't.

That meant that Ash was a clearer now in all but name.

Meanwhile, Cass acted as a liaison with the other villages around the

Devastation. She often traveled, carrying letters to and from the eldermen of Laststand and Endhaven. Bayna had talked the council into giving her the position, saying she was the most well-traveled of them now that she'd visited Vitamorn.

Cass hadn't argued.

"What else am I going to do?" she'd asked Ash late at night. "There aren't any other apprenticeships right now. And the position comes with a house and a small income. I can support us."

Ash had kept quiet. The words had made it sound like a last resort, but Cass seemed so happy to have something of her own. And she let Ash sleep over at the house instead of with the other war orphans, where Ash didn't fit anymore either.

Maybe it would have been easier if Ash could have married her. But Cass insisted on secrecy.

"For now," she told Ashwyn. "Just for now."

Ashwyn swallowed through the pain. "Is it because your mother's never liked me?"

Cass had glanced away. "Of course it is. You know I love you. I just don't want you to bear her ill will. I'll figure out a way to tell her, I promise."

It would have been easier if we'd left. But Ash kept her lips tight on the words.

Cass saw her expression and laughed. She skipped close to Ash and brushed a kiss across her cheek. "You feel everything so big and so loud. I love that about you. I love that you want everyone to know how you feel. But sometimes I want to keep something small and just between us. At least for a little while."

The words had made her smile and haul Cass back for another kiss.

But they hadn't stopped the undercurrent that surged beneath Ash's skin, making her antsy and discontent.

She had to move, had to walk, had to run. It was just because she was so used to climbing. Or at least that was what she told herself.

Maybe it would have been easier if there had been anyone else to talk to. But Greta had patients to tend to. And Father Liman's response to every problem was prayer. And more often than not, interactions with Lev or the other boys in the village turned into fistfights behind the temple. Someone always ended up limping home with a bloody nose.

In the rare moments when the clearers weren't working, Ash strode along the edge of the Devastation. She walked too close, stepping over the roots that grew over the lip of the crater, axe in her hand. The vegetation trembled, reacting to the emotions roiling inside her.

Every few steps she stopped, peering between the trees. Magpies nested in the branches, their white wings flipping in the gloom underneath the leaves.

Ash found herself holding her hand out to them, as if omens of ill luck were better than whatever this life was she was living. Her stomach clenched, and she snatched her hand back.

Did they work for the witch? Did she control them? Could she see through their eyes, watch her standing here on the edge of everything, staring into the darkness?

"What are you doing?"

Cass's voice came from behind her and made Ashwyn jump.

"Nothing," she said, shoving her hands under her arms.

Cass glanced between her and the trees, her mouth pulling down in a frown when she saw the magpies.

"I'm walking, Cass," Ash said. She took a dancing step that carried her closer to the edge of the crater. "I can't help it if bad luck likes to keep me company."

"You're looking for *her*."

Ashwyn raised her chin, heart pounding. "Looking for who?"

"The Devastation witch. The witch with the white face." Cass let out a huff of frustration. "You always do."

"I do not."

"Don't lie to me, Ash. I've known you for as long as I can remember. Mother of Life, it was just a story we told as kids. It has nothing to do with real life."

Ash turned and followed the edge of the forest.

"You're walking too close," Cass cried. "Why do you do that?"

"I don't know," Ash said. "I like it."

Cass hurried to catch up to her, fingers reaching for the bruise along Ash's jawbone. "You've been fighting again."

Ash pulled away. "It's nothing."

Cass's shoulders jerked, and she turned away like she had to take a deep breath before she could keep talking.

"Come back with me," she said after she was calm. She held out a hand to Ashwyn. "Please, before someone sees you out here."

Ashwyn shook her head.

"I'll make something to eat. I know you've been in the fields all day."

Ashwyn whirled on her, throwing down her ax so she could fling a hand out toward the village. "Do you like this, Cass?"

"What?"

"The work and the house and the endless circle of our tiny lives."

"Why?" Cass planted her hands on her hips. "Am I not allowed to like it?"

"We had so many plans, and now this is it."

Cass's face crumpled, and Ash's heart constricted.

"I don't understand why you're unhappy," Cass said. "This is our life now. This is what we wanted. I'm making the most of it. Why can't you?"

Why couldn't she? Even she didn't know. Her breath came faster, and she tipped her head back to stare up at the gray sky. Autumn always brought afternoon thunderstorms, but it had been such a short summer that Ash hadn't even noticed the air cooling.

"I worked for so long toward something else," Ash said quietly, trying to put it into words even though none of them fit. "Something that was bigger than me. How am I just supposed to settle back into this life?"

"This is the life you would have had after becoming a Saint," Cass said. "Like Rafe and Ingrim and your mother. You were always going to come back here."

But she would have come back different. She would have been someone the other villagers actually wanted. Someone they would have begged to keep. Now she was just Ashwyn. The orphan no one knew what to do with. The one who cost them resources. The one who couldn't just slip quietly into her place and be content with it.

Cass's eyes were wide and deep, and they still saw her as no one else did. "You've always wanted more danger than Edgefall could give you."

Ash laughed. "Right. It was danger I've been looking for."

Cass gestured to the Devastation that loomed too close at Ash's back. "You climb necropolis walls, you walk too close to the forest, you wanted to be a Saint and battle monsters. Even as a child."

"So did you," Ash whispered.

"To be close to you," Cass said. "But...I've grown up. And I thought you would grow up with me."

The worst part was that the words didn't sound accusing or angry. She sounded sad. And that just made Ash feel guilty and angry about it.

She grabbed her axe from the ground beside her.

"Where are you going?" Cass asked.

"The necropolis. Uniah said some of the Devastation is getting too close to the walls."

"So you're taking care of it now? Alone?"

"It's called growing up." Ash shouldered her axe and turned her back on Cass. "Remember?"

Chapter 17
Concordim

The sky rumbled as Ashwyn trudged down the flagstone paths and through the gray feverdusk forest. Brown leaves fluttered overhead, as full and as lush as they'd been all spring and summer, but you could still see the jagged scars left from where the snowstorms had pulled branches down. Still, the trees survived, proving you could always keep going. No matter how much of you was cut away.

Ashwyn scrubbed at her face, willing her eyes to stop burning. Cass had been right. Ash had no reason to be angry. So why was she so restless? She'd be so much happier if she could just accept things the way they were. Like Cass did.

A shout and a bellow made her stop and look up. What...what was that? It had come from the direction she faced, but the only thing over there was the necropolis.

Another cry made its way through the trees, and she broke into a run. Her hand curled around her axe.

She didn't bother with the gate that stood locked tight, just like usual. She sprinted around the corner, along the wall, and stopped with a gasp.

The broken section that Ash and Cass had climbed as children had never been fixed. There'd been enough intact wall that the council had never made it a priority.

Now, blocks of black stone tumbled across the clearing, leaving a jagged tear where something large had punched right through.

Ash's heart pounded, and she rushed to the broken wall to peer inside. She scrambled over tumbled stone, the edges catching at her overcoat, and her breath caught when she finally reached the opening.

Uniah crouched in the courtyard, her black uniform torn at the shoulder and blood seeping from her arm. But she held her sword in her other hand, its metal gleaming even in the gray light.

In front of her snorted a Devastation beast. It had to be. No bull had ever grown that large or had a crest of bone along its spine. Mortis, Ash had never seen anything so big. Or so terrible. An amalgam of bull and boar with a nightmare or two thrown in.

It stood twice as tall as Uniah, and with the massive horns curling from its brow, it could have easily torn through the wall. The beast lowered its head, blood glistening from the tusks that jutted from its jaw.

The spikes of bone along its spine rippled as it snorted. The Fairhands had lost a bull a few years ago. It had broken free of its pen and disappeared into the Devastation. Had the forest turned it into this...this monstrosity?

Uniah lunged, slicing with her blade, and the beast leaped back. She ran, free hand reaching for the bell that hung just inside the gate. The bell that would call the Bladesaints and the rest of the village.

The beast turned its head as Uniah darted past and caught her leg with its tusk. It flipped her in the air, and she landed flat on her back with a thud Ash could hear from her place by the wall.

Ash winced and half-turned. She should run to get help. She could reach the bell at the edge of the village in less than five minutes if she dropped the axe and ran unhindered.

But...the bull would tear Uniah apart in that time. And if her body was too badly damaged, she might never Return. Or worse, she would Return to scattered pieces.

Ash swallowed down bile.

The beast lowered its tusks and snorted. Uniah lay still, dazed from the blow that had knocked the breath out of her, and Ash realized the darkening stain underneath her wasn't shadow. It was blood.

"Hey!" Ashwyn cried from the broken wall then jumped down to the courtyard.

She grabbed a shattered piece of obsidian and threw it with all her strength at the beast. It thudded against the beast's thick skull.

It turned its head, slow enough that Ash had enough time for terror to creep up her throat. She had to clear it away before she could yell.

"Yeah, over here! Come and get me, you lumbering mass of muscle!"

The beast charged. Just like she'd planned.

Ashwyn dove out of the way, counting on it being too big to turn quickly.

She raced for Uniah. The open courtyard provided little cover, just clear flag-stones and a few benches. But Ash hauled on Uniah's shoulders and dragged her out of the open. She propped the Keeper against the wall where she would have at least a little protection from the beast.

"Uniah?" Ash said, patting her face. "Uniah, hang on."

The Keeper's head lolled, and she didn't answer. She must have struck her skull when she'd landed.

Ash didn't have time to bind up the gashes in the other woman's leg or shoulder. She didn't even have time to check Uniah's pupils the way Greta had taught her.

Oh, Dea, I could really use a Mender right about now.

But it was just her. Against a creature made from malice and chaos.

The beast had realized her trick, and it finally hauled itself around to rush her again.

Ashwyn ran for the nearest bench and bent to put her shoulder against it. She heaved, and it fell over, blocking the beast's path to Uniah. It had to swerve or trip over the stone.

Ashwyn took the opportunity and raced for the bell as the beast sprinted past.

She should have had plenty of time. Something that big couldn't turn very quickly.

But the thunder of its passing shook the ground and made it roll beneath her feet. She missed her next step and landed face first against the flagstones. The breath shot from her lungs, and she struggled to get to her feet.

The beast rushed forward, and she had no time to get to the bell. Instead, she flung her axe. It whooshed through the air end over end and hit the bright metal with a cheery clang that she knew they would hear in the village.

The beast caught her, lowering its head to snag her with its tusks. Luckily, she was still wearing her overcoat, and the sharpened points tore through the cloth, yanking her off her feet but leaving her unhurt.

She laughed, a desperate huff that recognized just how ridiculous her escape had been.

But it was too early to celebrate. The beast swung its head back, catching her in the middle, and the force of it flung her across the courtyard. She hit the ground with a thud and rolled into the wall.

Mother of Life, help me, she pleaded in her head. *I'm going to go Absent, and I'll never be able to apologize to Cass.*

That was the worst part of it all. She'd tried to do the right thing—the only thing—in that moment, but Cass would just see her running after more danger. Another mistake that made Ash into someone she just couldn't understand.

Ashwyn climbed to her feet, wheezing, but the beast was already charging again, its horns lowered, and Ash knew she'd never be able to dive away again. She could barely breathe.

Thunder rumbled, and a gust of wind rushed past her, making her stagger. A stream of green sparks went with it, completely incongruent with the gray sky and black walls.

The sparks swirled on the flagstones in front of her, spiraling up into an opaque column, and a woman appeared directly in the bull's path.

Ash opened her mouth to cry out a warning, but she froze, the words dying on her tongue.

Behind the woman, the Devastation beast hung in midair, its head lowered for the charge, its legs bent as if to churn the ground with its hooves. But it seemed completely frozen.

The air around Ash had stilled as well, and the trees beyond the wall bent over, their leaves folded as if in a non-existent wind.

The world around her waited, poised as if holding its breath.

Ash's gaze caught on the woman. She stood with her eyes closed, glowing as if in full sun despite the weather. Her deep red hair cascaded down around Her shoulders, long enough to drag across the ground, and leaves and vines bloomed between the strands, flowers catching the light. It grew even as Ash watched, spreading and pooling across the flagstones.

She wore a green dress that hung across Her shoulders and hugged curves that made Ash's mouth water. A simple gold chain hung between Her breasts, the pendant—a circle with silver and gold highlights—resting just above Her belt.

Between Her fingers, She held a bracelet of woven grass, the purples and blues matching the one that Ash still wore on her wrist.

But Ash didn't need that to recognize Her. She didn't need to remember Cass's description or the mural in the Lower Temple. She knew this was the Goddess, Deavita, the Mother of Life, without being told. Something in her recognized Her, as if she'd always known Her but only just now remembered.

Ash felt like she should fall to her knees. That was what you did before a deity. But she was rooted to the spot. The idea of taking her eyes off the presence in front of her for even a moment made her want to weep.

The Goddess stepped forward and took Ash's hands in Hers, the grass bracelet pressed into Ashwyn's palm. And She opened Her eyes.

They glinted, a strange silvery white, but She focused on Ash as if She could see just fine. Little bits of color floated through them like butterflies.

Ash held her breath as the Goddess leaned forward and pressed Her lips to Ash's forehead. The shock of it went through her, leaving a raging heat in its place. Fire swept down her limbs, reminding Ash of the first time she'd kissed Cass. But this didn't fade. It grew stronger, until every vein burned, and a space opened in her chest. Beside her heart.

The scorching heat burned through her, leaving something deep and gaping inside. Then a coolness washed through her, easing the pain and making her stagger.

The Goddess pulled back, and Her lips curved in a sweet smile that made Ash's heart pound to life again.

And then over Her bare shoulders, a gold light tore through the air with a sound like a dying calf. The screech made Ash jump.

The Goddess's eyes went wide and panicked before the streak of gold sucked Her in. Her hands gripped Ash's at the last second, but She was torn away fast enough that Her nails left gouges against Ash's palms.

And Ashwyn was left standing in the frozen courtyard, holding two strands of dried grass. One purple and one blue.

Across from her, the beast twitched, its legs slowly unfolding into its next step, like time had been stopped and now it ground forward again.

She should be worried about the beast. It was coming for her.

But the gray courtyard was so full of light; black threads highlighted in gold wove through everything in surprising sprays of glory. And Ash couldn't look away. Like she was seeing the world for the first time.

The lines pulsed with life and ran across the ground, connecting everything from the flagstones and the broken rocks to Uniah's limp form and the outline of the Devastation beast that was gaining speed. She reached out and twined her fingers around one strand, feeling the warmth of it as it called to the fire in her veins and the space in her chest.

These were connections. Just like Rafe had said. The Nexum connected everything in the world, and she could see those threads.

She could touch it.

The Devastation beast bellowed, and its hooves pounded the ground, leaving divots in the flagstones the size of her head.

Black threads pulsed through the beast and the ground and even in her hands, and she had no idea how they all connected.

But she didn't need to understand them to be able to disrupt them.

She reached for a strand pulsing in the flagstones, and she yanked.

The thread burned against her hands, making her eyes water, but she didn't let go. She screamed and hauled back.

And the ground heaved, breaking the stone around her and tripping the Devastation beast. It crashed to the ground with a surprised snort.

Ash didn't let it get back up again. She reached for the strands traveling through the broken flagstones and pulled up and over.

The stones flew through the air, and dirt cascaded around her.

The beast bellowed as it disappeared under a heap of rock and dirt, and Ashwyn didn't stop burying it until she could no longer hear its voice, and the ground lay still.

Chapter 18
Animatim

Vitania stepped down the streets of Vitamorn, the wet cobblestones reflecting sparks from the lanterns on every corner. It was only late afternoon, but the sun had disappeared behind the edge of the mountain, and the clouds had stolen what little light remained in the sky.

Few people passed, but the ones who did glanced curiously at her, noting her hair and eyes.

V pulled her hood forward to shield her face. She didn't wear the circlet right now, but her breastplate and the obsidian-lined sword at her hip gave her away just as readily.

She walked quickly, boots thumping the cobblestones, as if she could outrun the chaos on the front lines. But the sodden tent filled with endless rows of infected still hung in the back of her head. The feel of their bodies crumbling to dust as she delivered the Last Death...it lingered in her hands long after she'd left the tent behind.

Was this why there'd always been a hint of sadness behind Tavian's smile? Had his mirth and goodwill covered a well of pain placed there by endless duty?

V shook her head and pushed through the doors of the Greater Temple. It had been awful and necessary, but now she was home, and she didn't need to think of it anymore. She'd grab a drink with the few friends she'd made at the Saints' Hold and climb through Yaria's window to find comfort in the priestess's arms for a few hours. By morning, the feel of the front lines would have faded, and she'd be able to go on.

She just had to check in first.

All Nexsaints returning from the fight with the Malady were required to present themselves at the temple for cleansing and inspection.

As if anyone would be careless enough to get infected and not seek a Judge immediately.

Normally, someone would have been here to greet her, to escort her to the Throne for her obeisance and then back to the ablution pools. But the nave stood empty, the altar dark. She must have done a better job maintaining her anonymity on her way home than she'd thought.

V pushed back the soggy fabric of her hood and freed her arms from the ends of her cloak. A piece of hair straggled from the knot at the base of her neck, sticking to the wet surface of her pauldrons, and she grimaced as she fought with the locks.

The Goddess waited, serene and still in the single shaft of sunlight that penetrated the murky day. Vines crept over Her arms, curling around Her and the black throne.

The sight of them made her stomach lurch, and her parents' words warred in her memory.

"I love our Goddess. But it is our need that holds Her here. That's what makes me sad."

"I've always hated that he made you feel guilty for something that wasn't your fault. Her tethering was a gift to us. You don't say no to a gift, no matter how it makes you feel."

She pushed aside the mess and focused on the one bright memory she had in this place. The day she'd received her gift. Only a few weeks ago now, and fresh enough to keep the argument at bay.

V knelt, kissing her knuckles and then touched her heart, already looking forward to sinking into one of the heated ablution pools.

But as she rose, a flash of purple caught her gaze.

V had visited the Greater Temple many times in the last twelve years. The initial awe of the Goddess had given way to familiar affection. She knew the way the vines lay; she knew the folds of Her dress that rarely changed. The only thing that ever changed about Deavita's appearance were the flowers in Her ever-growing hair.

But today, a bracelet sat on the Goddess's lap.

A simple weaving of blue and purple grass that V recognized.

She sucked in a breath. It seemed like such a small thing, but the incongruity of it hit her like a Malady-crazed beast at full sprint.

This should have been incinerated weeks ago, along with the rest of the sacrifices of the failed supplicants and novices. Why was it here?

In the glow around the throne, Deavita...flickered.

Later, V would swear her heart stopped before it thundered back to life with realization. The Goddess was coming untethered.

How? She'd held herself here for hundreds of years. How could she be fading now?

V spun to cry out for help. But shadows crept through the empty nave.

She was utterly alone, watching the world break.

Deavita was the source of all life and the reason the Absent could Return. Without Her, they'd face true death; everyone in the necropoli all across the continent would crumble to dust.

And V was just standing here letting it happen.

She lunged forward, grabbing the Goddess's arms, but the skin under her fingers faded. Around the throne, the vines holding Her collapsed, empty.

"No!"

Every Nexsaint carried a connection to the Goddess within the space beside their heart. The one Deavita gave them during their gifting. But she couldn't follow it. Traveling down the connection to a deity would mean death for a mortal.

Where were the guards who should have been lining the walls? The Saints who were supposed to protect her?

V had no one. Except one connection she kept anchored within her chest.

"Mother!" she screamed down the black thread that kept her tied to the Abdicant.

In a whirl of colors, Sahvia stepped out of the air, her brows drawn down. She took one look at the empty throne, and V sprawled across it with vines in her hands.

Then Sahvia swept forward.

Another swirl, and the Primarch Divine appeared beside them. Sahvia must have called him.

V's heart leaped. If anyone could bring the Goddess back, it was the one who'd helped Her descend in the first place.

The Primarch Divine stared at the empty throne, his face hard and implacable. Then he met V's panicked gaze.

"Sahvia," he said to her mother. "Guard the crossing. Make sure no one comes near."

The Abdicant nodded and swept down the stairs to the crossing where the nave met the other wings of the temple.

"What happened?" the Primarch Divine asked V.

Her words came muddy and garbled; she had no time to make sure they were clear. "I don't know. She—she just flickered out. Like a—a lamp. I didn't even touch her, I swear."

The Primarch Divine's gaze dropped to her hands and a heavy frown dragged at the corners of his mouth and eyes. V realized her fingers were moving. In her distress, she'd signed the words as well. She dropped her hands and gripped the edges of the throne, keeping them still.

"I know," the Primarch Divine said. "It's not your fault. But quickly now. You must help me bring her back."

"Me?" V said. He was ancient. The original Divine. The one who'd helped Deavita descend centuries ago.

V had been a Nexsaint for barely a month.

"Now," the Primarch Divine said, and the calm in his voice soothed her. He knew what to do.

He gathered threads of the Nexum, and her heart lurched. They were connected to the throne. They stretched away, through the walls. To the Goddess? To wherever she'd gone?

Of course, the Goddess would keep connections to Her throne. Connections formed between people and objects all the time, between the things that they used or loved every day.

V reached for the threads, wrapping them around her fingers for a better grip.

And she pulled.

The strands pulled taut, digging into her arms for a second, as if she hauled on some immovable wall with a tiny thread.

Then the threads all went limp, and Deavita flickered back into her place.

V staggered back, giving her room, and the vines along the throne twined up Deavita's legs and arms, securing Her against the world that tried to thrust her out.

The Goddess slumped, eyes perpetually closed, but Her face had gone milk-pale, and She seemed somehow thinner and frail, Her skin sunken across her cheeks.

The Primarch Divine lowered his head, breathing heavily, and he placed his hand on Hers. Then he tenderly lifted his other hand and dabbed at the sweat glistening on Deavita's brow, keeping it from running into Her eyes.

V's chest heaved with great gasps.

It's over, she tried to tell herself, but her heart wasn't having it. *It's done. She's back, and the world isn't breaking.*

The Primarch took a deep breath and stepped back from the throne, eyes traveling over the vines to check them for security.

"Well done, Your Serene Highness," he said quietly into the silence of the temple.

V swallowed and looked at him. Her first instinct was to sign, "what?" completely forgetting her words for a minute.

But the look on her face was obvious enough for him to guess her question.

He came to stand beside her, staring back at Deavita. "She came back for you, Vitania."

She stared at him, then glanced at the Goddess, her throat dry enough to choke her. "Me?" she grated out.

A murmur behind them made V turn, and she jumped when she realized her mother was single-handedly holding back a crowd of priests and priestesses and Saints and several people who had wandered in from the street wondering what the commotion was.

They had to have seen. They had to have seen the Goddess flickering back into existence.

Her chest seized as the murmurs grew louder and echoed off the walls. Surreptitiously, she reached up to adjust the connection wrapped around her ears, tuning it till the thunder died to a dull echo.

She still heard the Primarch's words clearly as he turned to address the crowd. "The Goddess is safe. She returned. She returned for Vitania!"

Chapter 19
Concordim

"Ash!" Cass's voice made her jump. "Ashwyn!"

Ash spun to see Cass peering through the hole where the Devastation beast had come through, her face stark against the black of the wall.

"Cass?" Ash's voice came out as a croak, and her chest shuddered as she tried to draw in a clear breath.

Cass slithered down the tumbled wall and landed in the courtyard before darting forward.

"I followed you. I didn't want you to be alone after we argued. But then I heard the fighting and came running." Cass surveyed the courtyard, and her eyes went wide when she noticed the pool of Uniah's blood and the disrupted flagstones where the Devastation beast lay buried.

Ash blinked. The edges of everything seemed sharp and clear, lined with light, but her thoughts struggled through the thick fog of disbelief.

"Did...did you see her?"

"See who?" Cass said, reaching for her hand. "Are you all right?"

When they touched, Cass gasped and stared down at Ash's palms. "You're hurt," she said.

Ash lowered her gaze to her palms. Burns striped her skin, criss-crossing the scratches left by the Goddess's nails.

"What happened?" Cass said.

"There was a Devastation beast." Ash shook her head slowly. "It hurt Uniah. I had to fight it. I...I had to, Cass."

Cass scanned the courtyard again, a line forming between her eyebrows. "Where is it?"

"I buried it." She jerked her chin at the broken ground. "With the Nexum."

Cass's mouth fell open. "What?"

"The Nexum." The fog fell away as Ash stared at the evidence on her hands. She hadn't imagined it; she hadn't dreamed it. "I'm a Nexsaint." She grabbed Cass's hands again, and this time a sharp bite of pain came with it. "I'm a Nexsaint!"

She pulled Cass in close to kiss her. Cass let her, but then she pulled back with a frown.

"How?" She shook her head.

"She came," Ash said. "The Goddess. She was here. She kissed me, and then I could see the connections."

Cass drew her hands back, the crease between her brows deepening. "The Goddess doesn't leave the temple."

"But She did." Ash rubbed her forehead where the Goddess's lips had touched her. She was surprised Cass couldn't see the difference in her. There had to be some mark, some difference, that showed the change.

Ash surged forward, barely noticing the way Cass stepped back. "Cass, She made an exception. And if She made an exception for me, maybe She'll make an exception for you, too. We can still be Nexsaints together. Like we always wanted."

Her heart felt so close to bursting. After all these weeks of misery—and she could finally admit that she'd been miserable—things were finally right. Things were finally the way they were supposed to be.

But Cass pulled away, her arms going around herself. "No," she said. "You don't understand. It's not just that the Goddess *doesn't* leave the temple. She *can't* leave the temple, Ash."

Why was talking to her so hard all of a sudden? Cass had always been the easiest part of Ash's life.

"Then how do you explain this?" Ash gestured to the broken ground where the Devastation beast lay buried.

Cass's eyes flicked to the rubble, and her mouth went thin and tight. "I don't know."

"Why are you unhappy?" Ash said, realizing she was echoing their argument from earlier and unable to help herself. "I don't understand."

"You'll have to go to Vitamorn," Cass said. "To get training and...and who knows what else."

Ash's brow furrowed. "So? I'll be back. That was always the plan. And we'll be together this time."

Cass stepped away, not meeting her eyes.

A knot rose in Ash's throat, threatening to choke her, and the tightness drove her to apologize, but she didn't know what she'd done wrong.

A hollow thud rolled through the courtyard. At first, Ash thought it was thunder, but it hadn't come from above.

"What was that?" Cass asked, glancing up.

"I don't—"

The door to the nearest sanctum shivered, as if a hundred bodies had hit it at once, and the sound came again.

"The Absent?" Cass said. "Are they...is there a Returned trying to get out?"

The door shook and, with a crash, it fell open, spilling Absent into the courtyard.

These were not newly-awakened Divines. The Absent still had those vacant expressions. They still moved as though their bodies didn't quite remember how muscles worked.

But they surged forward with more purpose than Ash had ever seen. They stumbled over each other, trampling anyone in the way.

The horde came their way, and for a moment, the sight of the Nexum traveling through them struck Ash like a blow. It didn't pulse like it did through the rest of the world. The threads lay still, waiting. As blank as the Absent.

Cass glanced at Ash, horror dawning across her face. "What do they want?"

Ash fought down the sudden idea that they wanted her. The Absent had been quiescent until she'd become a Nexsaint. "I don't know."

Cass stepped toward the Absent, speaking in the soothing tones they'd always heard Uniah use. "Now, now. Don't you want to go back to your rest? You have some nice beds inside, I hear."

The Absent kept coming, fast enough that Cass stumbled and fell.

"Cass!" Ash cried. She darted forward and grabbed Cass's arm to pull her upright.

A blank-faced man with dark hair and hollow eyes reached for Ash, and she pulled away with a shout.

The Absent weren't physically fit or bright enough to fight. But there were hundreds of them. Thousands. And they could easily overwhelm the two young women.

And Ash had no idea what to expect when that happened.

Why did they want her? And would they hurt anyone else to get to her?

She pushed Cass toward the opening in the wall. "Go!" she said. "Get out. I'll follow."

"What?" Cass scrambled up the stones. "Where are you going?"

Ash sprinted for the prone form of Uniah as the herd of Absent turned to follow her.

It wasn't easy to fling the other woman's dead weight over her shoulder, but it didn't stagger her either. She could thank all those exercises Rafe had given her.

She skirted the lumbering Absent, avoiding their reaching hands. Ash tossed Uniah as high up the broken wall as she could and started clambering up the tumbled blocks.

Cass waited at the top, and she grabbed Uniah's jerkin to help haul the other woman to safety.

They slid down the other side, into the clearing between the necropolis and the Devastation. Cass collapsed beside Uniah, heaving a sigh.

But Ashwyn couldn't celebrate. The hole behind them still gaped, and the Absent were already climbing the rubble on the other side.

"Get back," Ash said as she scrambled to her feet.

Cass gave her a look, but at least she stumbled back, hauling Uniah with her.

Thunder crackled, much closer than it had been, and the clouds roiled above them. But Ashwyn concentrated on the lines that pulsed in the stones before her. Each jagged block had its own matrix of threads winding through it, and as her hand passed over them, feelings came to her. Like a warm breeze on a cool day. Or the weight of a solid body on top of hers.

She tried pulling on the weighted one, but suddenly her limbs went hard and heavy, and she quickly let it go. She had the feeling that if she pulled on that one too hard, it would make her throw up.

Another thread spread smooth under her fingertips, and her muscles tensed, like lifting something just a little too heavy. That was familiar enough.

She strained, and the surrounding blocks wobbled.

The Absent clambered forward, eerily silent. Another moment more and they would escape and be upon them. Or they'd be lost in the Devastation. She couldn't let either of those things happen.

She gritted her teeth and pulled. It felt like the spring planting, when the clearers removed stumps by tying ropes around them and lining up to pull.

Except she had no one to help her.

The first of the Absent appeared in the hole above them, and she screamed through her teeth. Her arms strained and finally, the stones around her rose, and she pushed them into the opening.

They tumbled into the hole, filling it until the only gap left was barely wide enough to admit a rat.

Each stone balanced on the next, and Ash could feel the points where they would tip through their connections. But she had no way to make them stick there. All she could do was wedge them as tight as they would go.

An enormous puzzle that would crush someone if she fit the wrong piece in the wrong hole.

She pulled back, carefully letting go of the lines of power running through each block until she was certain they would hold.

Then she dropped to her hands and knees, her arms shaking as the sky above them opened, and rain poured down.

Chapter 20
Concordim

Shadows crowded Ash's vision, or at least what was left of it, and she fell to one knee, breathing hard. Her muscles quivered as if she'd lifted each block individually and personally placed them in the gap, one by one.

I guess I did. I just didn't use my hands.

A soft gasp beside her made her tense and realize she had no time to recover.

She lifted her head and turned it, every movement setting fire to a new ache. At the edge of the Devastation, Cass clutched the unconscious Uniah, but she stared at Ash, her eyes wide and her face pale as the rain darkened her hair.

"Cass?" Ash whispered, the look in her eyes making Ash tremble. She reached for Cass, but the other girl leaned away.

The sound of many feet on stone made Ash look up.

Rafe stood at the corner of the necropolis, his eyes going from Ash to the wall and back again. Bayna and the elderman stood behind him, and the rest of the village lurked in a blurry crowd beyond.

Ash's breath came faster, and she struggled to her feet.

"What...?" the elderman started. "What happened here?" He also stared at the wall and then at Ashwyn.

They had seen. They'd seen everything. Or at least everything after she and Cass had tumbled out of the necropolis.

"There was a Devastation beast," Ash said, her voice coming stronger as she got her breath back. "It knocked a hole in the necropolis and attacked Uniah."

Greta slipped past Rafe and came to kneel beside the Keeper. A little of the tension went out of Ash's shoulders when the herbwoman bent to check Uniah's skull and peeled back her eyelids to peer in her eyes.

"But what did you *do* here?" the elderman asked. Rafe's eyes narrowed.

Ash swallowed. "The Absent were going to get out. So I fixed it."

"How?" Bayna snapped.

"With the Nexum. I—I'm a Nexsaint."

Bayna scoffed, and the elderman shook his head.

"That's not possible," Bayna said. "You didn't go to the temple Seat. Even if you'd snuck away, there wouldn't have been time."

"No. I didn't go. The Goddess came to me."

"Stop lying," Bayna snapped. "No one sees the Goddess outside the temple."

"I'm not lying! She had long red hair that was growing with flowers and leaves, and She wore a green dress."

Bayna rolled her eyes. "Cassarah described her that way to all of us. I could make up stories using her words, too."

Ash couldn't stand the way Rafe was looking at her. Just like Bayna. Like Ash didn't understand how serious this all was.

She reached for one of the lines crawling through a loose stone at her feet and yanked. This one was much smaller and hadn't fit with the others in the wall. The weight of the thread didn't burn her hands, and it floated free of the ground as she balanced it in front of her.

Bayna sucked in a breath and stepped back. The entire crowd recoiled, and Ash let the block drop to the ground with a thump.

Bayna's mouth tightened, and she flicked her fingers beside her eyes in the sign against evil. "If you can see the Nexum and you didn't ask the Mother of Life for the power, then there is only one possibility."

She jerked her chin at the elderman. "She stole it."

"What?" Ashwyn couldn't help the breathless laugh that escaped her lips. The words were so ridiculous. But no one else laughed.

Ash spun toward Rafe. "You don't believe that, do you?"

Rafe flicked a glance at Cass, who sat, eyes on her hands.

"The Goddess doesn't leave the temple, Ash," he said, and the gentleness in his words broke her. He didn't believe her either.

"She can't." Cass climbed to her feet. "She's grown into the throne. She couldn't move even if She wanted to."

"She didn't tell you that part, did she?" Bayna said it with a smile. Like she'd finally backed Ash into a corner she'd been preparing for Ash's whole life.

Ash looked at Cass, her eyes stinging. It felt like a betrayal. Like she'd failed some test. But it wasn't a test. Not for her. She knew what she'd seen. She had the proof on her hands. It was everyone else who was failing.

She still held the pieces of a grass bracelet clutched in one hand, but she wouldn't hold them out as proof. Cass might recognize them, but everyone else would just assume she was lying about it.

Because that's how they preferred to see her. As a liar.

"How would I steal power from a Goddess?" she whispered. "That doesn't even make sense."

Rafe glanced back at Father Liman, but the priest stood with tears in his eyes as he looked at Ash. "I don't know. But I don't know that it's not possible, either."

"If anyone could find a way, it would be you, Ash," Rafe said. "We all knew how much you wanted it."

Ash stumbled back as if struck. That hurt worse than any of the rest. She'd given up her dream for them. For the good of the village. A dream she'd only had because she'd wanted them to accept her. To love her.

"Stealing from the Goddess is heresy," Bayna said. "Punishable by the Last Death."

"I didn't—"

"Ashwyn of Nowhere, I charge you with heresy," the elderman said. "And according to the laws of the Vitian Order, we will call a Judge to deliver the Last Death."

"Wait."

Ash's heart seized, and she spun to Cass. Yes, Cass always did the right thing. She would speak sense. The rest of them trusted her.

"It should be exile."

Pain staggered Ash, and she braced her hands on her knees. "What?"

"Her crime is against the Goddess. So the Goddess should decide her fate. Exile her to the Devastation."

Ash gaped.

Cass met Father Liman's eyes. "It's sacred to Deavita. If Ash survives, then we have our answer. If she doesn't...no one will find her body anyway, and you'll get what you want."

"This could be a way to satisfy all parties," Father Liman said slowly. "And the Goddess."

"It doesn't satisfy me!" Ash cried.

The elderman waved a hand as if he couldn't be bothered to think any more on the matter. "Fine. Ashwyn, you are sentenced to exile within the Devastation. To live as long as you are able and to be lost forever once you become Absent."

"Now, wait," Rafe said, stepping forward.

"Bladesaints are not members of this village," Bayna said with a sneer. "You have no say. And we all know how you feel about the girl. Granting her a reprieve will only teach her that she can do this again."

"I didn't do it a first time," Ashwyn cried as two of the Fairhand boys stepped forward to grab her arms. "Stop!"

Dell and Nial dragged her, her cheap boots leaving furrows in the mud.

She tried to plant her feet and haul her arms away, but they were too weak from moving the wall. And even though she could see all sorts of lines coursing through their bodies, they held her tight so she couldn't reach.

Ashwyn threw back her head to scream. "Deavita! Tell them!"

But the Goddess didn't leave Her temple. Not for anything. The only thing that answered her was the rain growing heavy against her face.

The Fairhand boys dragged her through the feverdusk trees toward the edge of the original Devastation, to the very edge of the crater. To the place where the Order had first fought the Malady and won. The place where the heat of their fight and the force of their victory had melted away the ground to leave a cliff and a bowl of devastation.

Ashwyn had been here at the edge so many times. To collect herbs for Greta. To search for the witch of the Devastation. To wonder what was beyond and shudder in fear.

Ash twisted in their arms. "Cass! Cass!"

But Cass stood at the back of the crowd, her hands knotted in front of her. Kind and gentle Cass, who had never spoken harshly before. Who always did the right thing. She'd have no idea how to fight back even if she wanted to.

And when she lifted wet eyes to meet Ash's gaze, she knew Cass didn't want to.

Cass hugged herself, her hands trembling, but her eyes held heartbreak. As if Ashwyn was the one who had betrayed her.

The roots and vines at the edge of the Devastation surged in response to her pain.

"It was for you," Ash cried. "Everything I've ever done was for you!"

Cass's throat moved as she swallowed. "You shouldn't have loved me so much, then."

They threw her over the edge.

Part Two

Chapter 21
Concordim

Ash plummeted through the trees. Leaves and branches whipped her face and hands, and she opened her mouth to scream, but the wind stole her breath. So she fell in startled silence, the white faces of the Fairhand boys disappearing between the writhing boughs of the forest.

Something wet and sharp struck her cheek, and she shut her eyes, remembering the last time she'd fallen and something had scratched her. But even behind her eyelids, she could see lines of light stretching in every direction, twining and twisting in a parody of the foliage around her.

Maybe she could grab one. She reached for the confusing blur of lines, but they burned her already battered hands, like trying to hold a rope attached to a runaway bull. She cried out and snatched her hands back.

A huge band of the Nexum rose below her and struck her in the chest. The breath left her lungs in a whoosh, and something in her chest cracked with a sharp pain that sent stars shooting across the darkness behind her eyelids.

But it slowed her descent.

She opened her eyes and scrabbled for purchase against the branch, but the rain made the mossy bark slick, and she slid down again.

The next branch didn't hurt quite as much, and she caught it long enough to hang from one arm before dropping. Thick vines snapped under her weight, and finally her feet struck something soft and springy, and she dropped to the ground with a gasp.

Her fingers flexed against the bed of leaves and broken vines where she'd landed, and she rolled until she could curl around the pain in her chest and her heart.

Ashwyn lay there for an eternity, mind blank as she concentrated on forcing air in and out of her lungs without succumbing to the sharp stab of something broken every time she drew a breath.

Full coherent thoughts were too much right now. The last few moments had fragmented in her memory, the faces and actions making no sense together. Cass's last words replayed in her head over and over as she tried to come up with a response, even though it was far too late for it to count.

They'd thrown her out. Just like she'd always been afraid of. But this...this was far worse than she'd ever thought it could be.

They hadn't just exiled her. They'd sentenced her to the Last Death. The people she'd grown up with and worked beside and tried to protect—they'd called her a liar and left her to go Absent. And without someone to keep her body, she'd lost the chance to become a Divine. When she went, it would be forever. No second chances.

Even the people she'd loved the most hadn't believed her. No. Not just that. They'd lied to her. Over and over again.

Rafe had told her she could be a Nexsaint. The elderman had said they'd send her to the city. Cass had said she loved her.

Just thinking her name hurt.

Ash had built her whole life around Cass. She'd given everything up for her. And until an hour ago, she would have been willing to swear on the Greater Temple steps that Cass had felt the same. How could she have been so wrong about someone who had been so important to her?

Slowly, Ash uncurled her fingers, and the bits of Cass's bracelet fell out of the creases of her palm, the faded blue and purple still vivid against the green foliage where she'd fallen.

Ash pushed herself up, gasping at the pain, and ripped the bracelet from her wrist. She drew back her arm to fling it away and froze, hand raised. Her head bowed under an invisible weight. Tears slipped down her cheeks and dripped from her chin. She used the sleeve of her overcoat to wipe them away with a vicious swipe.

None of them were worth her tears.

But they still came, as much as she hated them.

She grabbed the strands of Cass's bracelet and hers and stuffed them into the pocket of her overcoat. The fabric had been torn, and wet seeped into the cloth, but she pulled the edges closer around herself as she pushed Cass's name and face and her last words—everything—to the back of her mind where they didn't slice her with every other thought.

She'd lost everything, even the happier memories, and now she was just going to go Absent. To slip away until no one remembered her or everything she'd done for them.

She sucked in a breath and winced at the pain before finally looking up to take in her surroundings.

Her eyes widened, and she barely kept from gasping again, only stopping herself because she knew how much it would hurt whatever had broken in her chest.

She'd lived beside the Devastation her whole life, but this was the first time she'd ever seen it from the inside.

It wasn't just a forest. This was an overgrowth. She'd seen it trying to eat fields and take over the village, but the truth of it was impossible to ignore, here in the thick of it.

Layers of vines and roots twined together in thick layers where she sat, so much so that she couldn't tell where the foliage ended and the ground began. Even following the strands of the Nexum, she couldn't sense the bottom underneath all the plant life. Everything grew on top of each other in varying shades of green and brown and gray. Thick trunks rose toward the sky, with ferns and flowers snaking around the mossy bark and reaching out their own branches and vines to confuse the matter.

She could see why the villagers had tossed her in at the edge of the crater and hadn't worried about her climbing back out again. She couldn't even see the cliff from here. And with the leaves and vines crisscrossing above her and blocking out the sky, she had no idea which way was north.

A snarl wended its way through the trees and sent a shiver down her spine. She pulled herself to her feet, holding her breath till the pain passed. With no ground, she had to balance on the mat of roots and vines as she peered through the dense foliage, trying to figure out which way the sound had come from. Which direction would reveal the Devastation beast.

But it was impossible to tell. And night was coming soon. Faster than it would on the surface. It was already hard to see in the gloom under the trees, and she hadn't seen well in the dark since the accident that had damaged her eye.

She was going to go Absent. She knew that.

But that didn't mean she wanted it to happen *yet*.

Ashwyn chose a direction and went. Everything hurt, not just her chest. The cuts and bruises from her fight with the Devastation beast and then her fall all combined into one solid blanket of pain. She held her breath as she moved, then stopped and braced herself against a tree as she gasped.

And when she moved again, she held her hand across her ribs, as if she could hold together whatever had broken inside her. But she couldn't just sit while whatever it was that was making that snarling noise got closer.

Moving was worse than she'd thought it would be, though. She climbed over roots and across odd gullies where the vines had sunk and felt too soft to stand on. She skirted the edges of the soft valleys and just kept moving forward.

A cacophony of caws and the sound of wings made her flinch, and she glanced up to see a flock of shadows wing overhead. Their wings and underbellies flashed with white, and with a jolt she realized they were magpies. She grimaced and ducked out of their path, hiding under a mess of tangled vines.

But as she crowded close to the trunk of the nearest tree, the sole of her boot slipped against the slick bark of a root and she slid down. She turned so her shoulder hit the tree instead of her chest, but it meant she didn't have a hand free to catch herself, and she rolled into one of the thick tangles of vines where it felt too soft to walk.

A hiss and a slither lit along her nerves, and she caught her breath as a narrow head raised and wet scales glinted in the gloom. Bodies heaved under her, and she scrambled backward.

She'd fallen into a whole nest of snakes. Except these snakes had little legs all lined along their long thin bodies, and two black horns rose from the ridges just over their eyes.

They'd obviously started as snakes, but now they were something else entirely. Something more.

And she didn't wait around to see if they were even more deadly this way.

Ashwyn scrabbled at the roots behind her, trying to climb free, but the snakes wrapped around her legs, their little feet scraping at her pants, claws prickling her skin.

She let out a horrified squawk and pushed at their bodies with her hands, then snatched them back as one of them lunged for her, fangs out.

She yanked her hands up above her head, an instinct so new and unfamiliar that it took her a minute to remember why she wanted to keep her hands free.

And then it struck her, as the snakes twined, and the lines flowing through their bodies twined with them.

The Nexum.

She grabbed for a pulsing black line in one snake's body, but nausea surged in her gut as her fingers brushed it, and she yanked back.

What was that? That feeling? Ash could only describe it as a wrongness deep inside her.

But the snakes still climbed up her body, tongues darting out to taste her clothes and the skin of her face.

Could she tie them down somehow?

Ash swallowed hard and braced herself, then gathered a handful of strands from the snakes, ignoring the jolt in her stomach. She hauled a bunch of threads from the vines underneath them with her other hand and tried tying them together.

The strands slipped and stung her fingers like heated wire. And they didn't want to tie nicely. But she knotted them together in a tangle, and suddenly the snakes fell still.

She pulled back in surprise. Had she done it?

The snake that had wrapped around her legs fell away, limp, and she breathed in relief. But underneath it, the vine writhed.

"What the—"

The surrounding vines twisted and twined while the snake lay there, its skin going dull and mossy like the vines.

And the nausea rose in her gut, sending streaks of pain into her head. Under her skin, she saw the threads in her arms wither and curl up, like they were sick.

"Oh, Dea," she whispered, horror racing along her veins.

She fought free of the writhing vines, panic lending her strength.

Ashwyn scrambled up onto a solid root and swallowed down bile, turning her face away from what she'd wrought.

She'd...changed them somehow. By combining their strands, she'd changed the nature of the snake and the vines. And damaged herself in the process.

She held out her arm, staring at the deadened strands under her surface. The rest of the Nexum flowing through her seemed fine, but a raging headache pulsed in her temples, and it seemed to stem from the strands she'd damaged.

She gulped and wiped the cold sweat that had gathered on her brow, then stumbled away, as far as she could get from the snakes.

Which wasn't very far.

She had to stop to lean against a trunk, and when she looked up to take stock of her surroundings, a magpie sat on a nearby vine, tilting its head to look at her.

"Shoo," she whispered, heart in her throat. She did not need its meddling right now. Enough evil had followed her here.

The magpie croaked and clacked its beak.

"Go on. Go away."

But it seemed fearless, fluffing its feathers up against the damp. It wasn't really raining down here. But a steady trickle fell down the nearest trunks, and a haze of mist hung between the foliage.

The magpie wasn't remotely concerned about her. It was just sitting there, bringing its bad luck, as if it couldn't care less that it was ruining an already broken life.

Heat burned in her chest as she looked at it, noting just how much it didn't care. She lifted her hands and flicked her fingers in the sign against evil.

That movement finally startled the bird enough that it flapped away. But only to another branch a little farther above. There it clacked its beak again as if mocking her.

The cheekiness of it made the back of her throat burn.

She couldn't fight the villagers who'd thrown her in here. She couldn't fight the Devastation monsters who lurked in the shadows under the trees. But she could fight this one insolent little creature.

She climbed up higher, reaching for the bird, but it flitted away. Again, it landed close enough for her to chase. The vines and branches formed enough of a ladder that she could climb up the side of the tree.

The magpie led her higher and higher. Maybe it led her to something terrible, and she was just falling into its trap. But the need to fight something drew her along until finally she looked up and found the magpie had winged away somewhere she couldn't reach.

The breath went out of her all at once, and something washed through her that she didn't want to recognize. Because it felt strangely like loneliness.

She turned to brace herself against the trunk and found a network of branches wide enough to walk on stretching away from her feet. Vines draped between them in a pattern thick enough to hold Ashwyn's weight.

It was a canopy. Another layer of the forest above the first. No snakes here that she could see. The vines that crawled up the trees could be parted and woven into a kind of curtain. Her own little nest where she'd be out of sight of anything prowling below or above.

She let out a breath far too close to a sob and collapsed into the cradle of vines, arranging them around herself before she fell into a deep sleep. The last thing she saw before she nodded off was the flash of a white breast, but she didn't have the energy to shoo the magpie away one last time.

Ash woke with the odd feeling that she'd somehow overslept but that it was also still night. She fought her way to wakefulness, and the moment she saw the vines surrounding her, she remembered the previous day.

She groaned and pushed the living curtain out of the way only to be confronted by the sight of the Devastation in the dim light that counted as full sun down here.

The rain had stopped sometime during the night, and golden-green shafts filtered through the upper layers of the forest, bathing everything in a softness the place didn't deserve.

Despite the villagers' best efforts, and despite the Devastation's obvious dangers, Ashwyn was still alive.

A laugh burst from her, and a flurry of wings rose above her nest, startling her. She winced as the magpie flock winged away, and she wrapped her arm around her chest. The sharp pain in her ribs hadn't subsided or dulled overnight.

But the fear had.

She was alive, and now she was angry.

It wasn't just the people she'd trusted who had betrayed her. The Goddess Herself had betrayed her.

Why had She bestowed Her gift and then not defended Ash's right to use it?

None of the answers she could think of made her feel good, and she buried the question under a wave of outrage.

Ash stared out at the network of connections. The Nexum that linked all life to the world that it lived in. One of the magpies swooped overhead, black and gold outlining its wingtips.

The broken strands in her arm were growing back, extending under her skin as if they wanted to reach out to the tree she'd climbed. One stretched from her chest, spearing off into the distance, and Ash could feel something vague and familiar at the other end. Like the feeling she got when she'd sat in the sun on top of the necropolis wall.

She could even see glowing bits of the Nexum lighting up the ruined side of her vision, as if her mind followed the connections where her eyes could not. She'd lived for so long with the darkened blur on her left side that being able to see anything there threw off her balance. But it also felt like a separate sense. One that she could use if she practiced.

And the Nexum had helped her yesterday. At least against the Devastation beast in the necropolis. It would surely help her here once she learned to use it.

Well, the Goddess had abandoned her, and the villagers wanted to kill her, finally and completely. But there was no way she was going to let them.

She would deny them their victory. She would survive. And thrive.

She knew it was possible because she'd lived through the night when everything she'd been taught growing up said the forest should have killed her already. No one had searched for Mikel because it had already been too late.

But she'd survived because she was strong and clever, just like Rafe had made her. And she had the power of a Nexsaint.

It seemed fitting to use that power to survive, since it was what had gotten her into trouble in the first place. And she would learn to use it herself, since the Goddess couldn't be bothered to speak to someone She'd chosen.

She took hold of the strand that stretched from her chest—the one that felt like home—and she yanked and pulled at it until the thread parted under her fingers. The snap echoed in her chest, a short, sharp pain, and then it was gone, and her last connection to Edgefall fell away.

Chapter 22
Concordim

Ashwyn stepped out onto the wide branches that formed pathways through the canopy and breathed deep, determined to see not a deadly wasteland, but to see the Devastation as her new home. It was still dangerous, and it would be foolish to let her guard down, but something had changed.

She reached out and let the dappled green light shift over the back of her hand, highlighting the lines of the Nexum she could see through her own skin. The stubborn light reminded her of a patch of moss growing irreverently between the flagstones of the necropolis.

For the first time in her life, there was no one to tell her to step back. She could finally allow herself to be fascinated by the forest, and it wouldn't mean a slap or a lecture later.

She drew her overcoat off and draped it over a knobby piece of the trunk that stuck out between the moss and vines. The day before, it had caught on every thorn and branch, slowing her down, and Bayna wasn't here to complain when she destroyed the clothes underneath.

Ashwyn took her time climbing down from the canopy, mostly because her rib still stabbed her with pain any time she bent or twisted. But it let her actually see the Devastation for what it was. Diffused light and plants that never went Absent. With no one to cut them back, they grew forever, incorporating new growth as they renewed themselves over and over.

She reached the mat of vines where she'd first found her tree and stepped onto what felt like solid ground. But she still hadn't seen any true dirt with everything so overgrown.

The magpies that circled overhead finally dispersed, as if they'd been waiting for her to reach safe footing. Only one remained, a big fellow with a curled-up foot, like he'd hurt it long ago and it had never healed right. He landed just above her head with a curious caw, and she rolled her eyes at him.

Her stomach rumbled after her exertion, and she rubbed her chapped lips.

She might not trust the magpies, but she *could* use them.

She spent most of that day following the flash of black and white wings through the trees until she spotted the flock feasting in a thicket of bright red berries. They avoided the black ones nearby.

That made it easy. She gathered the red berries in her shirt, leaving the others as toxic.

It wasn't much, but the meal did help. And as she walked, she found other things as well. The bright yellow flowers called Dayshine, sprigs of greenery known as Mother's Blessing, and the bark of a spreading tree she barely recognized under all the vines that grew up it. Greta had prized them all for her brews. Ashwyn might not need their healing properties at the moment, but they were all perfectly edible, and she gathered as many as she could carry.

Food there was in plenty, but no water. She'd have to find some tomorrow.

There was a bad moment after she filled her arms when a sudden thunder carried through the trees. Ash ducked out of sight as a herd of deer, all bearing a ridge of scales down their backs, bounded through the forest.

They didn't look dangerous, but Ash didn't take any chances, staying hidden until the rumble of their passing had faded.

It was only as she thought about returning to her tree to stash her finds that she realized how far she'd come. She spun, trying to pinpoint her tree among the rest.

Which direction had she come? She couldn't see the sun at all under the canopy, and without its help, she couldn't navigate.

She took a few panicked steps before stopping and taking a deep breath. Rushing wouldn't do her any good. It would only get her more lost.

Something croaked above her, and she glared up at the big magpie. He clutched the side of one of the tall, straight sentinel trees so he hung sideways, and he tilted his head to look at her.

"Oh, go away," she snapped. "It's hard enough doing this without an audience."

Her voice didn't bother him in the least. He blinked bright eyes at her, then rubbed his beak against the vines on the tree.

"You're no help."

She sighed and leaned against the tree. This wasn't going that well if she was already talking to birds.

Her brow furrowed, and she shifted her weight so that her shoulder parted the vines. They were significantly thicker on this side of the tree than on the other. But on the next tree over, the side facing her had a significant amount of bark visible.

She shifted her armload of greenery and moved closer to examine the next tree. The vines were thicker on the other side. Again. In fact, all the trees around her had a thicker layer of foliage on the same side. If she unfocused her good eye, it almost looked like stripes marched across the forest.

If the vines always grew thicker on one side, say the north side or the south side, she could use that to navigate.

She closed her eyes and struggled to remember the tree where she'd slept. She could clearly picture the big tree with the mass of vines. And when she'd climbed down, she'd rested her hand against the trunk, and bark met her fingertips.

Good, at least she knew which direction to head.

She set out, keeping the bark side of the trees in front of her. What made the vines grow thicker on one side like that? It couldn't be sunlight. The sunlight that made it this far had filtered and diffused through so many layers of canopy that it felt like walking through dusk.

But something had made them grow in such a distinct pattern.

She shook her head as her tree finally came into sight, and she breathed a sigh of relief. She'd made it.

Climbing with one hand was more difficult than she'd thought it might be, but she found footholds among the vines, and they were thick enough to form a set of nearly vertical stairs. As long as she kept one hand on the tree, she could balance.

She did have to stop halfway up to catch her breath. The stabbing pain in her side wasn't getting better. Greta's voice echoed in her head. "Splinting and rest for broken bones." But how was she supposed to rest when the safest place to do it was in a tree?

She pushed it to the back of her mind and set about cleaning up her nest, making it more secure and stashing her dinner in a nook of the trunk under her overcoat.

As long as she breathed shallowly, she could stand to be upright for a while. And it was strange, despite the fact that she had to keep one hand wrapped around her middle to remind herself not to bend a certain way, she still found herself smiling.

What was this feeling building under her breastbone until she had to huff a breathless laugh? It wasn't simple happiness. She'd felt that before, lying with Cass's arms around her as the morning sun crept over their windowsill.

She shied away from the memory with a wince, but the question remained. This felt...open. Like she could spread her arms and embrace the world.

And that openness gave her the word she was looking for.

Freedom.

Even lying with Cass she'd felt tethered somehow. If she'd said the wrong thing, done the wrong thing, the entire illusion of their happiness would have shattered. As it had eventually. She'd spoken the truth and had lost everything.

Here, there was nothing left to lose. Who would exile her from the Devastation? The magpies?

She tilted her head back and laughed, ignoring the way it hurt because that pain was physical. It was nothing compared to the greater pain of her childhood, and that was behind her.

She was alive. And she'd keep living.

The next morning, Ash chewed her lip while staring at her tree. She needed an easy way to find her way back here. She couldn't be sure she would always remember to check which way she traveled with the bark side and the vine side.

But she had more resources at her disposal that she needed to learn to use.

Threads crawled through the heart of the tree and traveled along the branches, and she reached out cautiously to sift between them with her fingers.

The lights lay under the surface of the tree, and she couldn't actually push her fingers past the bark, but it was like when she reached, she could see the threads respond and snake toward her grip until she could feel them against her skin.

I wonder how far I can reach for these? Could she manipulate strands across a clearing? Across the world?

Different feelings shifted against her skin as she twined her fingers through the threads. This one felt rough and sturdy under her fingertips. This other one pulsed with what seemed like a heartbeat. And another felt like sunlight against her skin.

She gently detached one pulsing thread and held it in her hand. If she brought it with her, she would always have a connection to her tree and a way back to it.

An image flashed in her mind of the snakes flopping lifelessly to the ground as she'd connected their strands with the vines.

She almost dropped the tree thread as bile rose up her throat.

"Dea."

Ash grimaced as the Goddess's name came easily to her lips. No, she refused to swear by Her anymore. Deavita was the reason she was here in the first place, and she wouldn't honor Her with even a thought.

Ash raised her chin and wound the thread around her wrist. She just wouldn't connect herself with it. Not like she had with the snakes. She'd keep it with her but not a part of her.

The thread stretched as she moved away from the tree, but as long as she walked slowly, it didn't snap the line or bend the tree.

All that day she searched for a stream or a pond, some water source she could mark and use for herself, but there was nothing. The vines and the roots were too thick to even see the ground, and there didn't seem to be any fresh-water sources strong enough to penetrate the foliage. Were there pockets of water underground that she couldn't reach? How else had the forest grown so deep and so thick?

Maybe she could do the same thing she'd done with the magpies and follow a Devastation beast to its watering hole. She would just have to find one. And stay out of sight while she stalked it.

As she climbed her tree in the twilight, a chill swept through the forest, and Ash glanced up, looking for the cloud that had covered the sun. But no sun made it this far into the depths. Something else must have caused the cold.

An inhuman shriek rose from below, and Ash threw herself at the trunk of the tree, pressing herself against the bark.

She dared one glance over the wide branch where she stood and caught sight of movement below the trees. A long, thin shape slid between the trunks, impossibly tall with too many angled joints along its limbs. A full rack of antlers rose from its head, each point sharpened to a deadly tip.

Frost crept up the bark under her fingers, and her breath came in foggy clouds. But even as the air grew frigid, heat rose in Ash's cheeks, and she recognized the feeling only because she'd experienced it herself so recently.

Rage. It slid along her limbs, stealing her breath and urging her to fling herself at the nearest threat.

Except this didn't feel like *her* rage. It lingered, separate. Almost like it belonged to someone or something else. Something that stalked the forest below, with ridged gray skin like bark and burning eyes the color of coals.

Ash hid her face and held her breath, praying that the monstrosity would keep walking.

She had no idea how long she stood, fingers pressed into the tree as if to hold herself there. But eventually she realized the chill had gone and her limbs shivered from tension, not rage.

She slid to her knees and hugged her torso.

What...what was that?

That was no mere Devastation beast. That had been something entirely different. A walking glimpse of fury and hate, and Ash realized that her freedom came with a cost. She might live here now, but she had to share the woods with that thing.

Chapter 23
Concordim

Ash clung to the side of one of the sentinel trees with one hand, the other wrapped around her middle as she squinted past the screening foliage. A stream trickled past on the other side of the mass of leaves, but she could finally see why water had been so hard to find.

This creek wasn't on the ground. To be fair, she hadn't even found the ground in the Devastation yet. Just masses of vines and roots.

Here, a thick mat of moss had created a low point in the canopy, and water had collected in the depression. The pool hung between the trees, and it must have gathered its water from the afternoon storms and the morning's dew. The magpies swooped low to splash through the surface.

But they weren't alone.

A crowd of creatures lined the vines and branches surrounding the pool, so many that Ash couldn't even count them.

Enormous bull mutations like the one she'd fought in the necropolis pushed aside smaller beasts that might have once been pigs. A couple of deer with lizard feet clustered nervously on the bark end of the pond, watching a sleek cat with scales crouch low to take a drink.

Each one of them seemed like an amalgam of two or more animals. Bulls mixed with boars, deer and lizards, cats and reptiles.

All except the magpies.

Even the tree trunk under her fingertips was striped with smoother bark between the rougher pieces.

Father Liman had always spoken of the Devastation as sacred to the

Goddess. Life thrived here in a way it didn't in the outside world. Thrived and evolved. The Devastation allowed for a blending of life outside the normal rules.

But Ash wondered what Father Liman would say if he knew she'd caught them eating each other. Was it sacred if predators hunted prey for food? The thought made her gorge rise. No human dared eat meat. What would happen if the butchered animal Returned while it was being digested...

Mortis. If one of them caught her, would she become its meal? Ash quickly turned back to the watering hole, shoving the horrific thought down. She'd never thought she'd long for the Last Death.

A fight broke out between a thick, tusked bear and one of the bull-boars.

She ducked away and pressed her back against the trunk, blocking her ears against the roars and the sounds of blows against fur and flesh. She steadied her breathing and tried to be as still as possible.

Something big hit her tree and made it shudder. She flinched, her arm wrapped around her middle to protect it.

A furry paw reached around the tree before it was dragged back, its claws leaving gouges in the vines at her feet. The tusked bear roared again and slammed into the bull-boar, carrying it into a dense thicket.

Ash gritted her teeth. This might be her only chance to reach the water, while the fight distracted the rest of the creatures.

She ducked around the other side of the tree, keeping it between herself and the combatants, then she held her breath against the pain and sprinted for the edge of the pool.

Her feet splashed through a trickle that traveled down the vines, just like a stream would on the surface, and the strange deer crosses snorted and bounded away from the noise. Their claws dug into the vines of the canopy as they loped out of sight.

Good. Maybe she was one of the scarier things here.

She skidded to a stop beside the pool and leaned forward, fingers cupped for the water.

There was no sound that warned her. She was still learning to sort out the mass of connections she could see, so she didn't notice anything strange about the threads surrounding her.

It was the gentle shift of the vines under her knees that told her something had put its weight on the same branch where she sat.

She turned her head, and a giant scaled cat came out of the blur on her left, where her ruined vision had hidden it. Deep blue scales glinted in the filtered light, but Ash could imagine it would blend into the night, and her only warning would be those slitted golden eyes blinking at her from the dark.

Ash sucked in a breath. It slunk toward her, angling around the pool like a house cat stalking a bug, only this house cat was at least as long as she was tall and weighed twice as much.

She didn't let it get closer; she stood to her full height, ignoring the twinge in her ribs when she straightened, and she spread her arms to make herself as large as possible.

I'm one of the scariest things here, she told herself. Then she yelled and lunged at the cat.

It stepped neatly out of the way, its ears forward.

Mortis, it's not frightened at all.

It turned, its body bending back on itself almost like a snake, and it swiped at her.

She dove out of the way.

The midnight blue cat surged forward, and Ash knew she wasn't quick enough to stay out of its way. Not with her ribs aching.

She ran instead.

The vines shifted under her feet like a springy platform, and she fought to stay balanced. The cat bounded behind, using the vines as a springboard to leap over her head and land in front of her.

She skidded to a stop, lunging back out of reach of the claws. She stumbled and fell on her butt, the big paw swiping through the air where her chest had been.

The cat pounced, and her heart pounded as she rolled aside.

She couldn't outrun it. She sure as the Malady would never be able to outclimb it. What was left?

They fought on one of the wider platforms of the canopy, where the vines stretched between branches. Just past her grasping fingers, a gap opened between the vines as the cat's weight came down opposite her. She could see the next layer down winking at her in the opening.

The cat lunged, and instead of rolling out of the way again, Ash leaped forward, diving for the hole. As the cat sailed over her, Ash's arms slithered through the opening, and when the vines bound around her hips, she ripped free.

And dropped.

The next layer caught her, and she rolled awkwardly into a tree. The world tilted at an angle, but she still caught the flash of blue scales through the opening she'd just tumbled through.

In her desperation, the vines around her shuddered and writhed. But it wouldn't be enough to keep the cat from following her. An angry yowl tore through the trees.

Ash reached up and grabbed the threads in the vines, then she yanked them together and wound them around each other, closing the gap, praying it wouldn't make her sick the way the snakes had. The threads in her arm had finally returned to normal after days of healing.

A scaled paw reached through the opening, swiping at her, but it was too far away. The vines closed around its limb as she wove them together. It hissed, short and sharp, before it withdrew its arm and the gap closed completely.

Ash lay back with a gasp, and the vines around her ceased their writhing, responding to her surge of relief. Her hands stung where the threads of connection had bitten into the burns that were already there.

But she didn't feel that rush of sick, and the strands of her own Nexum remained a healthy, pulsing black.

Mortis, that was close.

She closed her eyes as her lungs burned with exertion. All she'd wanted was a drink of water. But there was no way she was going to be able to slip in between all the creatures like the magpies did.

She was going to have to come up with something else.

She rubbed her eyes, then opened them again, noting the intricate pattern of vines twisting above her. They wove together tightly enough that the water had pooled there in the canopy.

But even a tightly woven basket would leak. At least a little bit. Was that the answer? Could there be somewhere on this level where water collected that would be a little less obvious and therefore less contentious?

Ash climbed to her feet, keeping her arm wrapped around her middle. The pain had faded to a dull ache over the last two days, but it hadn't disappeared entirely.

She kept her gaze half on her feet and half on the canopy above, trying to retrace her steps back to where the pool would have been.

There wasn't anything so obvious as a stream or a trickle on this level, but here, finally, she found a spreading damp where the vines grew thicker, soaking up the residual water that leaked from above.

Ash frowned. She'd hoped for more flow that she could take advantage of. But clearly, that's why no one congregated down here. As dangerous as the pool was, it would be a lot easier to steal a mouthful of moisture there.

She had two options. She could sit underneath the pool with her mouth open, hoping to catch the errant drip.

Even alone in the woods, she couldn't help barking a laugh at the image.

Or she could dig down and see where the moisture finally ended up.

That was hardly a choice. She set to work.

Ash had yet to see the ground here in the Devastation; it was so densely covered with vines and roots. But it had to be down there somewhere. And maybe if she found it, she'd also find stones to line her own little pool where she could catch enough water to actually drink.

A soft spot stood just beside the dense tangle of damp vines, and Ash deliberately stepped into it, hoping to weaken it so she could push through and dig down. The mat held her weight, but as she shifted, the vines parted a little.

She knelt and used the Nexum to clear a path through, hauling the threads aside and anchoring them to each other to open a hole through the vines. She angled herself toward the damp, hoping to find its terminus. And a water source.

Once the opening was big enough, she peered in, wondering if she'd have to make a shovel to dig through the dirt underneath.

Except there was no dirt.

The vines opened onto another space, a little darker than this level. She climbed down cautiously and found another whole layer of the forest. Deeper portions of the trees she'd become familiar with stretched down through more vines, more roots.

She'd assumed the layer where she'd been living and surviving was the surface. The ground level. But underneath that, it was all just more layers.

How far down did it go? Where was the floor of the crater?

A delicious shiver went down her spine, just like when they were kids and the older orphans had told them ghost stories. Or when she'd first heard of the witch. That sense of something not quite right but so fascinating she couldn't help but inch closer, needing more details. Needing answers.

But answers would have to wait. She needed water if she was to last much longer. The berries and other plants she'd found to eat were sustaining her for now, but she had no idea how long she could live like this.

She pushed through the vine curtain, hoping to find the base of the pool. Then she fell back, staring.

Her movement had revealed stone.

A wall hung suspended in a tangle of roots and leaves, and her breath caught under her breastbone.

"What?" she said aloud. Her fingers ghosted over the surface of the stone, almost expecting it to be a hallucination or a delusion. But they splayed against the rough surface, tips picking out imperfections in the stone where lichen and moss had eaten away at it until it crumbled.

She pushed forward, finding the edges of the block, and discovered the next one sitting below it.

This wasn't natural. This was manmade. A piece of civilization sitting in the middle of wilderness so thick it choked itself.

Frantic now, she pushed aside the vines, tearing them down where she could and thrusting them over her shoulders where she couldn't.

The wall stretched as tall as she was, but it cut off abruptly above that, and she shoved her way along it until she found a break, a jagged edge traveling diagonally across the wall as if it had broken free from a bigger building.

She pushed past the break, her heart in her throat as she climbed over the wall into the remains of a room.

Two walls met at an angle with smooth flagstones stretched between them. As if the corner of a building had been cut from a village and transported here, where it hung in the middle of the forest. Forgotten.

Ash's fingers traveled over the square blocks, cut and fit so precisely that even the mortar still held.

Someone had carved little angular bears along the strip of stone at the top of the wall, the style primitive and strangely beautiful at the same time.

She'd never heard of a village in the Devastation. It had always just been the forest for as long as anyone could remember. For the entire history of the Saints and the Order.

As her fingers traveled along the wall, a short buzz against the back of her mind made her stop.

Her gaze returned to the center of the room, where the floor had been broken away. A strange smear of white marred the flagstones, glowing gently against the darkness.

Ash wanted to step closer, to see what it was, but something about the sight of it made her swallow.

Once, when she was ten, she'd slipped while climbing and banged her head so hard on the ground the headache had made her sick to her stomach. This made the back of her head ache and her stomach roil the same way.

The stone looked ashy, the color of a burnt-out tree. She bet that if she stooped to touch it, her fingertips would come away white.

In a sudden flash, it reminded her of the mural in the Lower Temple. The one with the Primarch Divine and the silver flash of lightning lining the gate to Obitullas.

How many deadly little secrets did the Devastation hide?

She had no idea what the white could be, but somehow, deep down, she knew it would be very, very bad to touch it.

Ash backed away, panic rising in the back of her throat. It was inert; it wasn't going to reach out and grab her, but she couldn't shake the feeling that she was suddenly in more danger than she'd been when the scaled cat had leapt for her.

The vines around her shifted, reacting to her fear. Pushing her toward the white.

With a strangled yell, Ash lurched back over the broken wall, shoving through the vines where she'd come in.

They shoved back, and her heart pounded in her ears. The vines wrapped around her arms, and she tore through them, her side stabbing with pain.

A root reached up her legs, and she sobbed.

"The Devastation feeds on your emotions," Rafe said in her memory. "Never show it anger. It will swallow you. It will swallow all of us."

Clearly, it did the same with fear. It had come alive as the Fairhand brothers threw her into the Devastation. The vines had writhed when she'd escaped from the scaled cat.

It was feeding off of *her*. She was the one doing this.

Ash forced herself to stillness in the roots' embrace. She breathed in through her nose, out through her mouth, until her heart rate slowed.

The roots around her arms loosened, just enough.

She slid free and gasped out a sob. Then she swallowed down the last of her panic and reached for the threads connecting each of the vines.

She pulled one into place here and wove it with the next one there. Over and over, she guided them into place and threaded them together to create a staircase that led out.

And when she put her foot to it, it gave just a bit under her boot and then held.

She laughed as she climbed out of the hole she'd made and stepped up onto the layer just below the canopy.

The sun was setting somewhere far above, past the growth of the Devastation, and the light had gone dim gold with just a hint of red.

She held her hands out to it, feeling the little flickers of warmth against her fingers. Tiny flowers climbed the trees around her, opening as dusk fell, catching the very last rays of dim light on their petals, just like she was.

She should be terrified. She'd found yet another way the Devastation was trying to kill her.

But she couldn't help but catch her breath at the beauty. Her new home was unique and full of mysteries. And Ash had never been able to resist a mystery.

No one else in the world got to see what was under the leaves of the Devastation. They never got to see floating ruins, or night-blooming flowers, or the sleek shape of a cat with deep blue scales. The danger was just a challenge, something that called her to be better, stronger, cleverer.

She was going to belong here one day. That was a promise.

As she climbed back toward her sleeping tree, using the thread tied around her wrist as a guide, the back of her neck prickled, warning her that something watched her through the trees.

She stepped up onto the wide branch she called home and turned, peering into the gloom.

Down below, through the curtain of vines and hanging roots, she caught the barest outline of lighter fur against the darker trunk of a sentinel. The lines reminded her of a wolf, but black horns rose from its head. Blue eyes pierced the dark to stare at her for a moment longer.

And then the shape was gone.

Chapter 24
Animatim

V made her way through the streets of Vitamorn with her teeth clenched and her smile fixed.

The short walk from the Abdicant's Court to the Palace of the Divines had turned into a circus, complete with jugglers—the vendors selling cookies in the shape of her face—and performing animals—the herd of sheep a single shepherd had brought all this way to receive her blessing.

The crowds blocked the street that would normally take her down past the temple and back up to the palace.

Sahvia glanced at her out of the corner of her eye, a sardonic tilt to her lips.

Mortis, it would take forever to navigate everyone if she had to stop every three seconds.

Her mother jerked her chin at an alley and whispered. "Go. I'll catch up."

V cast her a grateful look and ducked a mother holding out her child for a kiss. Sahvia blocked the mother as V slipped into the alley and ran.

Sahvia stayed behind to administer the blessings instead, and V just caught the shepherd's disappointed pout before she made it around the corner.

No one in the city knew the details of what had happened in the temple the day before. All they knew was that Her Serene Highness, Judge Vitania Abdicantus, was now Deavita's chosen. Favored of the Goddess. And bringer of miracles.

And everyone and their dog had a miracle to ask for.

V drew her hood up, despite the sun shining down on her bright head, and hoped her black gambeson would provide a little anonymity. It looked just like any other Bladesaint's uniform as long as she covered the trim and the hilt of her sword.

By the time she popped out of the alley just south of the Palace of the Divines, her neck prickled with warning. Another crowd waited on the steps, and she had to sprint up the stairs before they realized who she was.

As she reached the top step, Sahvia appeared along a thread of connection, the air smearing with color as she arrived. V should have done the same except she'd only been a Nexsaint for a month. She hadn't bothered to collect connections to anywhere yet. A mistake she'd rectify today.

"Lovely day," the Abdicant said, flashing one of her rare smiles. "Isn't it, chosen of Deavita?"

"Don't start with that," V said, pushing through into the palace.

"Or soon you'll start believing it?" Her mother quirked an eyebrow.

V sighed. "It's not that I don't believe it…" She couldn't deny that one moment she'd been grasping empty air and the next Deavita had returned to Her throne. "I just don't think getting me to kiss your baby is going to do anything for it."

Sahvia shook her head as she led V up the stairs. The Bladesaints on guard bowed as they passed. "It helps *them* to believe," she said. "That's the important thing."

Sahvia led her daughter into the Primarch Divine's office. The Primarch himself stood at the window and turned as they entered.

"Thank you for coming," he said and gestured to the chairs beside the fireplace. "We need to discuss what happened in the temple."

V winced. "I'm sorry."

"I don't mean your sudden rise to fame," the Primarch said with a raised eyebrow.

V flushed. "Of course not," she said, though that's exactly where her mind had gone. "You mean the untethering."

His face grew grim. "I do. It is more dire than you know."

V laughed. "You mean the Goddess leaving, the Absent disappearing, and death coming back into the world isn't dire enough?"

"Vitania," her mother snapped, and V clenched her teeth.

"That alone would be a disaster to end the world we know and She loves, yes," the Primarch said. "But the subtle evil that makes it worse is that it was not an accident."

V stilled. "What? How do you know?" V had been standing right there, and even she didn't know what had happened.

The Primarch paced in front of the fire. "The wickedness of the world pushes Deavita out of it constantly. Making Her presence here a battle that so far, She has always won. The world is wrong, and Deavita is good, and the two together is only conflict. I was the one who helped Her overcome that, and I helped Her tie Herself here."

V nodded. This was common knowledge.

"Her will has always been enough to maintain that balance. Therefore, Her untethering had to have been a deliberate and malicious attempt to subvert Her will."

"Heresy," V whispered.

The Primarch nodded. "Of the worst kind. The kind that could destroy the world."

He sat heavily in one of the chairs beside the fire, head in his hands.

"I was thinking that. When She faded," V said quietly. "That without Her the Absent would all fall to dust."

He raised his head, his brows pulled together as if considering her, and Sahvia glanced at him, lips tight.

V flushed, feeling like she had missed something. "What is it?"

The Primarch hesitated, then jerked his chin at the door. Sahvia stepped across and made sure it was locked.

V's brows went up as her pulse thumped.

"This is not a thing that is known outside these walls, Vitania," the Primarch said, drawing her attention back to him. "I am trusting you with this knowledge because of your place in our ranks and because of the trust Deavita has already shown in you."

V held her breath.

"She chose to tie herself here for many reasons. To free us from death. To grant Her Saints power over the Malady. But also..." He lowered his head to catch her gaze. "To protect us from Her power."

V swallowed. "What does that mean?"

"Unbridled life is dangerous," her mother said, stepping back toward them. "We know this from the Devastations."

The Primarch nodded. "Deavita's power has always been as deadly as it is sacred. She chose to protect us from it by descending. But if She were to be untethered by design or accident..." He shook his head. "I don't know if the world would survive."

V rubbed her chest. She'd thought she'd panicked when the Goddess had flickered out. But bile rose in her throat as she realized how close they'd all come to destruction.

The Primarch reached out to lay a hand on hers, his eyes soft and intense. "But we don't have to worry about that happening now. We will be prepared.

And we will hunt down the one who did this and make sure it can never happen again."

V knew what he would say next. She was a Judge. This was her entire purpose. To deliver the Last Death to those who committed heresy or were infected by the Malady. Or both.

She sat up as he caught her gaze and held it.

"Find them, V. For Her sake. Find them and make sure we are all safe."

Chapter 25
Concordim

Ashwyn blinked awake the next morning with her tongue firmly stuck to the roof of her mouth. She tried to swallow but could barely get enough moisture to make it work. Her hands shook as she pushed herself up to sit.

She was going to have to find water soon or this place wouldn't be her home. It would be her tomb. Her very own necropolis.

A series of hoarse chirps and beak clacks greeted her, and she craned her neck to see the flock of magpies roosting in the branches around her. The light flashed from an army of black and white bodies as they flipped their wings and warbled to each other.

Their big leader with the curled foot spread his wings and dropped gracefully to alight on the vines over her head. He tipped his head to caw at her.

She waited for the familiar instinct to shoo him away, but it didn't come. The stories all said that they caused the bad moments. But the villagers had said plenty of things about Ashwyn, too. And she knew how true those were. Every terrible moment of her life, they'd been there. But that just meant they were starting to feel like good company.

She let the magpies stay and pulled out the food she'd been storing. The berries lay in her palm, looking shriveled and unappetizing. Ash grimaced. They were just going to make her thirstier. And there were plenty of fresh options she could find later.

She tossed the berries out onto the wide branch that served as her front porch. The big leader of the magpies immediately floated down and snatched up a piece.

The air filled with the thunder of wings as the rest flocked to join him.

Ash's stomach clenched, but she held still and waited, sitting back to admire the iridescence of their feathers as they landed. Bits of blue and the occasional green flashed along their backs, even in this low light. How many colors did their wings actually contain? Maybe the black wasn't actually black. Maybe it was an amalgam of all the colors in the world.

Ashwyn shook her head at herself. Thirst was making her maudlin. She shook out her overcoat, which she'd been using as a pillow, and hung it back up on the knobby portion of the trunk.

As she moved, she caught the glimmer of a thread stretching from her chest toward the bark side of the forest, thin and ephemeral, as if it had only just formed.

Ash could feel Edgefall sitting at the other end. Again.

She growled and yanked the thread under her foot, then snapped the thin thread easily.

Mortis. The threads inside her had grown back after she destroyed them by accident and now the ones she'd destroyed on purpose. Did that mean she'd be connected to Edgefall forever? Would she have to wake up every morning and snap the thread just like she had to relieve herself and clean her teeth every day?

A whirring noise made her jump, jarring her ribs, and she sucked in a breath of surprise. The lead magpie had fluttered in beside her, crowding the little space in her nest.

He dropped something that clanked against the bark of her tree, then he bobbed his head at her as if proud of himself.

A knife lay on the floor, glinting in the light coming through the layers. It wasn't large or terribly wicked looking, just a table knife. It lay there dirty and tarnished, as if he'd stolen it from the village trash heap.

He bobbed his head again and fluttered back out of the opening. She watched him go, her mouth open.

"Wait, is this a gift?"

He landed on a branch at eye level and cawed.

She picked up the knife. It wouldn't do much to defend her against Devastation beasts, but it was better than nothing. And she'd take all the help she could get in this place.

"Thank you," she called, and the magpies lifted off in a wave of clacking beaks and flashing wings.

She just laughed as she tucked the knife into her belt.

Later, it gave her the courage to sneak up to the pool where the Devastation beasts crowded. She was going to have to make this work. If this was going to be her home, then she would have to learn how to carve a place for herself. She pressed against the trunk of a tree, keeping well behind it, but she'd already glimpsed some more of the tusked bears and at least one deep blue cat. And today, there were a bunch of goats jostling for position on the opposite side. Compared to the others, they didn't seem that formidable, but each possessed a set of fangs that Ashwyn would have sworn belonged on a snake.

She gritted her teeth and used the knife to saw pieces off a nearby branch. She'd have to be strategic about throwing them, but they should make enough noise to startle some of the beasts into leaving.

Ashwyn braced her shoulders and stepped out from behind the tree.

Before she could surge forward, a whir broke the peace of the clearing, and the vines and leaves around her shuddered as an army of magpies flew overhead. They swooped and cawed, diving for the Devastation beasts already gathered.

The cat yowled and batted at the birds, but they were too fast, ducking its claws and pecking at the exposed scales under its arms. The magpie leader dove for its eyes, and the cat finally gave up and retreated, snarling as it disappeared into the underbrush.

A pair of tusked bears snorted and snuffled and skipped back as the storm of magpies came at them. But the big predators didn't even last as long as the cat, bellowing and backing away, until they'd left a cleared space at the edge of the pool.

Ashwyn blinked at the opening as the magpies settled on the vines in a jagged perimeter. The leader gave a hoarse chirp and bobbed his head, waiting.

They'd cleared a space for her.

The magpies could grab what they needed between the great animals that gathered there. So the only reason they had done this was for her.

Individually, they were no match for any of the creatures they'd driven away. But together they could easily harry a beast a hundred times their size and scare it into leaving her alone. All because she'd shared a little of her life with them.

Perhaps she did belong here after all.

She stepped forward, into the circle of their protection. And for the first time since she'd entered the Devastation, she knelt and took a long drink as the magpies acted as her shield.

She drank her fill and raised her hand to wipe her mouth, wondering how to carry some water home with her.

And then suddenly the air was full of wings as the magpies took flight. They flapped away, leaving her alone at the edge of the pool.

Ashwyn's heart skipped. Had they tricked her?

No, the other Devastation beasts moved too, dashing away from the pool.

Ash surged to her feet, ears straining as she scanned the clearing. What could have scared them all at once?

The answer had to be bad enough to scare her, too.

She followed the Devastation beasts into the forest, but she wasn't nearly as fast as the other creatures here. It was smarter for her to hide. Ash raced for the nearest sentinel and hit it at a run. She planted her foot against the trunk, just like the necropolis wall, and leaped for a thick branch with screening leaves. Her side twinged, but she didn't have time to coddle it.

Alarm rang along her nerves, urging her higher, to safety. But the mystery itched at her. What scared Devastation beasts?

Ashwyn waited, half-buried in the lowest layer of the canopy, twisting her neck to see.

A huge gray wolf stalked into the clearing, its footpads silent against the vines. Black horns rose from its brow, and when it turned its head, blue eyes flashed.

Ashwyn held her breath. She'd spied this creature the night before, prowling across from her nest.

The creature padded around the pool, its nose lowered as if it checked to be sure everything in the area had actually left.

Ashwyn was so intent on the wolf she didn't notice the sounds of something approaching until it shook the branches under her tree. Rustling foliage and the harsh sound of panting carried up to her as a man burst through the screening vegetation and fell into the clearing.

Ash froze, her breath caught between one inhale and the next. She'd never thought to see another human being again, and she almost dropped from her tree to throw her arms around him.

But a buzz along her nerves stopped her.

Beneath his filthy hair and the dirt marring his face, streaks of white traveled through his skin. They stretched from his cheeks and down his neck and then crossed his chest, where she could see it through his torn shirt. The stark white lines reached for his heart and swirled above it in an ashy circle.

The man staggered upright as if his limbs didn't want to work, and his movements went short and jerky.

He used a hand to help steady himself against a tree, and beneath his fingertips, the bark turned a chalky white.

Just like the spot in the ruins Ashwyn had found.

Ash turned her head and saw the path he'd made through the forest stretching along as far as she could see. Broken and jagged foliage stained white from his touch.

She swallowed and found her throat dry again.

This was somehow worse than the broken building. This was a person.

Bile rose in the back of her mouth, and she wished she could spit it out.

The man glanced behind him as if he was running from something. He got his limbs all working in one direction and staggered for the other side of the clearing. But the wolf snapped at his outstretched fingers and kept him back with a growl.

And sure enough, the bushes below Ashwyn's hiding spot parted again. And another figure stepped into the clearing.

This one had long ash-blonde hair tied in a severe bun at the nape of her neck. Her black robe had been tailored close to her body, but the slits around her legs allowed her to move. The hem hung frayed and ragged from years of wear and tear, but even so, it was still obviously the robe of a Nexsaint.

The woman carried a double-headed scythe, its wickedly sharp edges catching the filtered sunlight.

She stepped forward, graceful and powerful, as if she was used to moving through the overgrowth of the Devastation.

All that would have made Ashwyn think this was just a lone Nexsaint, far from home, if it weren't for two details.

When she turned, the light glinted from a porcelain mask, smooth and unfeatured, covering her entire face with only two dark holes for her eyes.

And white streaks traveled through the veins in her hands. Just like the man's.

Except she moved nothing like him. Her gait remained smooth and unhurried, and she wasn't turning the vegetation white as she moved.

In fact, she kept herself between him and the forest, stepping carefully across the uneven terrain. Like she owned the Devastation. Like she was protecting it.

Ashwyn found herself holding her breath.

This was the witch. The witch with a white face who roamed the forest and killed anyone who set foot inside.

Her grip shuddered on the branch where she clung, but she did not let go. She couldn't afford to be seen now.

The man fell to his knees and turned to face the witch. He shuffled back and raised a hand as his marked face went slack with terror.

"Please," he whispered, but the words carried clearly to Ashwyn. "Please don't. Please let me live."

"I'm sorry," the witch said, her voice muffled behind the mask, but somehow it managed to be as implacable as the walls of the necropolis and so full of regret that it made Ashwyn ache. "You cannot be saved."

"Please, please!" His voice rose as he pleaded, and the hair stood up along Ash's neck.

The witch bowed her head. "This will be quick."

As the witch raised her scythe, Ashwyn fought to hide her face, but she couldn't help staring straight at the horror below.

The witch swung one end of her scythe behind the man's head in a smooth motion and then yanked it forward, the blade cutting cleanly through his neck and spine.

Ashwyn's blood pounded in her ears until that was all she could hear, but she could see just fine from her good eye. The edge of the scythe had cut through the pulsing thread that connected his head and his heart, and all the black and gold strands throughout the rest of his body went dark.

As the ends curled up like twigs in a fire, the man's body cracked and flaked and crumbled to dust, leaving nothing but a splash of ash across the vines.

The Last Death.

The witch hadn't just separated his soul from his body. He wasn't Absent like the people in the necropolis. He was gone in a way Ashwyn had never seen before. He would never come back, never have a chance of Returning or becoming a Divine.

A little moan escaped from Ash's tight and aching throat.

The witch looked up, spinning her scythe to line up beside her.

Instinct made Ash reach out and haul on the threads pulsing in the leaves around her, pulling them to form a protective screen.

Between the cracks, Ash could just make out the witch's profile. She and the wolf exchanged a glance almost as if they spoke to each other, though Ash could hear nothing.

The wolf continued his patrol around the pool as the witch bent beside the pile of ash. Her voice came quiet and reverent, and if she strained her ears, Ash could make out the words.

"From Her arms you came; into Her arms I send you. Deavita keep you, amen."

It sounded a lot like the Keeper's rites when an Absent arrived at the necropolis. Except more final.

In a whirl of black and gold that Ash barely followed, the witch formed a net of strands then released it with a twist. A burst of wind scattered the dust before her until it disappeared into the vines and roots of the Devastation.

Ashwyn's chest hurt and her throat ached from holding back her ragged breath. Terror still rode high in her veins, but...

There was something in the way the witch spoke and in the care she took with the man's ashes that was gentle at the same time. Kindness and ruthlessness kneeling there in the dappled sunlight where Ashwyn had taken a drink just moments ago.

The witch rose to her feet, taking up her scythe in one hand. Then she passed under Ashwyn's tree and retreated along the path the man had made. As she went, she used her scythe to sever the connections in the plants that had gone white and chalky, and one by one, they fell in her wake, turning to dust. The wolf followed.

The witch was gone, but in her place, she'd left a trail of death.

It was a long time before Ash could climb down from her hiding place. Her arms burned, and she slipped and dropped the last few feet to the carpet of vines, jolting her damaged ribs.

And she didn't even care. She lay there struggling to breathe for who knew how long before she finally climbed to her feet.

Ashwyn stepped close to the trail the witch had made and bent to examine the damaged foliage. The connections had been severed, just like in the man.

Ash hadn't even known that plants could be given the Last Death.

Ash held up her hand. The threads in her arm that had withered after her brush with the snakes had regrown and pulsed with a healthy glow. But the thread the witch had severed in the man's neck had taken all the others with it.

So it was true. The witch of the Devastation killed anyone who ventured into her forest. From his clothes and demeanor, that man had been a villager. Ash hadn't recognized him, so he wasn't from Edgefall, but maybe he'd been from Laststand or one of the others around the rim of the Devastation.

And she'd killed him just for wandering in here.

But what were the white marks that had marred both of their faces? Why would the witch pray over someone she had hunted down? And why would a Nexsaint be prowling the Devastation in the first place?

Ashwyn should run. She should put as much distance between herself and the witch as possible. She had no desire to die a true death at the witch's hands any more than at the Devastation's whim.

But...something pulled at her, drawing her toward the path of destruction. And it felt just like standing on the edge of the Devastation trying to glimpse white between the tree trunks.

Only, the draw was stronger now that she'd seen the witch. She wanted to know more. She needed to see her again. And it had nothing to do with the austere beauty of the smooth white mask.

Ashwyn's hands clenched. She could justify it to herself easily. This woman clearly knew what she was doing in the Devastation. She belonged here in a way Ashwyn was only pretending to. Ash could learn from her. And she didn't have to introduce herself for that. She could just follow and observe.

She'd be careful. She'd stay out of sight. And she'd solve another of the Devastation's mysteries.

Ashwyn made sure the knife was still tucked securely in her belt, and she plunged into the forest, following the trail of death as a lone magpie winged its way over her head.

Chapter 26
Obitusim

Someone follows, the wolf said.

The executioner checked behind her, lips pursed tight enough to ache. "Are you sure?"

I can smell them.

The executioner saw nothing, but she trusted Felleron more than anyone or anything.

She swung up into the trees, using the scythe to fling herself higher to catch the strands of the branches above. The wolf bounded up behind her, finding his own route through.

And now she saw it. Telltale signs of someone else in her forest. Vines and roots that had been cut away then regrown around someone's trail. The flash of something light coming at her through the trees.

She huffed under her breath, half annoyed and half impressed. How had she missed that there was someone else in her woods? Not just a trespasser, looking for a faster way to the city. This was an interloper. An invader who'd made themselves right at home in the deadly forest she'd called home for ten years.

Clearly, she'd grown complacent in that time.

She could turn and solve the problem right now. But if she really had grown complacent, it was just as likely that she had grown sloppy.

She had to do this right the first time or she wouldn't get a second.

She used the edge of her scythe to pull herself to the next layer and sprinted for a wide branch, the wolf keeping pace with her.

What now? Do we leave them alone?

The executioner shook her head. "I can't. If they ever left the Devastation, they would have proof that someone is here. Rumors are one thing, but the Order can't know that I exist."

Then we hunt, the wolf said. *And our kill will be swift.*

Her grip tightened on the shaft of her scythe. "Yes. We hunt."

Concordim

This was going to be a lot more complicated than Ash had realized. She'd imagined following the clear trail of death through the forest and finding the witch's lair.

She hadn't counted on the vastness of the Devastation, the rate at which it regrew, or how fast the witch herself was.

"It's going to take a while," she told the magpies as she returned to her nest in defeat. "And I'm going to have to leave."

She stood in the opening of her nest, oddly reluctant to leave. She'd carved out this space out for herself, made it into a home. It was a terrible one, but it was still a home. The first one she'd ever had for herself. The orphan house had always been noisy and crowded, and the house she'd shared with Cass hadn't ever been hers at all. It had belonged to Cass, no matter how much Cass tried to tell her it was theirs together.

The magpies took flight over her head with their usual squawking, and she glanced up to see them winging away, unworried about finding their way back. Because they didn't have to worry. Their home was the forest itself.

Ash laughed. She was acting like she was tied to this place, but she was as free as they were. She owned nothing. If she wanted to move, she could. She could just leave and rebuild what she needed elsewhere.

She detached the thread that connected her with her tree, a sigh escaping her as it fell back into place. Then she grabbed her overcoat and made sure to tuck her knife into her belt before returning to the trail that started at the watering hole.

Already the Devastation was trying to reclaim what was lost, new roots creeping over the dead spots, so she had to follow the trail carefully and pull aside young vegetation to get a look at the old.

Here the witch had burned away all traces of white where the man had passed, but what was it before it was dead?

A niggling memory caught her off guard. This was where the Malady had first appeared centuries ago.

But that couldn't be it. The Saints had won the great battle. They'd eradicated the Malady from the Devastation long before it was even the Devastation. And they'd done it ever since. Every time the Malady cropped up, they were there. Fighting and winning the Little Wars.

And the witch might have been a Nexsaint once, if her robe was anything to go by, but she couldn't be anymore. Saints didn't live in the Devastation. Saints didn't kill innocent villagers.

The trail of death led her farther into the Devastation than she'd ever been. But it ended abruptly in an area below the canopy layer where she'd been traveling.

Several paths tore through the forest, leaving jagged scars of destruction, ending in a small clearing, where everything had been killed and cleared away.

It was a strange little pocket of calm in the otherwise overwhelming tangle of the Devastation. Above and below, more vines and branches stretched, cutting her off from the rest of the world, but here there was only death.

Ashwyn stood in the middle of the silence with her hands on her hips. She had the strangest feeling that she should find the place eerie. But instead, she was annoyed.

She would have to search each trail separately, and the Devastation was already reclaiming its territory, making it much harder to find the paths.

But...maybe she could use that. Ash pulled aside the vegetation, searching for the ones that looked newer.

Unfortunately, most of them were either so overgrown that they had clearly been here a long time or they led to dead ends, and she couldn't figure out what connected them all. Why did these paths end here? What had they led to?

The fifth trail she checked led to another piece of stone held captive in the depths of the Devastation. This one wasn't cut or manmade in any way Ash could tell. It was just an enormous boulder tangled between roots and vines. But it held a broad scorch mark across its center—a white mark that had died? And another path stretched out behind, lined with dead and ashy plants.

This trail cut through the underbrush as if it had been sliced, its edges still fresh and jagged.

The witch had been this way recently.

Ashwyn plunged into the forest. Her chest still twinged when she moved too fast, but she couldn't afford to let this lead get too old. If she could find the witch's home, then it would be a lot easier to keep track of her as she moved through the Devastation.

But thirty steps later, she pushed aside a screening curtain of vines and found that the path disappeared. Everything on the other side of her stretched green and brown and normal.

Ash bit back a scream of frustration. How could it just disappear? What was it that she was following?

She kicked a dried-out seed pod and growled as it bounced away.

Then it disappeared, too.

She gasped and scrambled toward the end of the trail. Sure enough, it didn't just disappear. It plunged downward through a gap in the vines.

She'd forgotten to check the lower layers of the Devastation. How many other trails had she assumed were dead ends when they'd just moved to a different layer?

She berated herself as she parted the vines and climbed down.

Here, the light grew even dimmer. Roots grew thicker and wove together with the vines to create walls. They seemed to close in on Ash, forming a chamber or a tunnel. The root below her feet narrowed to a solid path wide enough for her and nothing else.

The path of death stretched ahead of her, and she could only just avoid stepping in the worst of it. A fine layer of ash covered her boots. But the dead parts didn't give her the same sick feeling as the white had.

Every now and then, another path crossed hers, a place where the vines and roots formed a tunnel leading in a different direction. But she stuck to the trail of destruction, following it deeper.

Soon it would be too dark to see, but Ash squinted and used the pulsing black and gold threads of the Nexum to navigate. They spread through the walls and ceiling, and she raised her head to study the interwoven branches arching over her head, but while she wasn't paying attention to her feet, she stepped into a soft spot.

The soft spot hissed.

Ash lunged forward, falling to her knees, and she spun around to face a nest of horned vipers.

Mortis, she'd been careless.

The vipers surged forward in a mass of scales and fangs, and she scrambled backward. Ash drew her knife and waved it in front of her, hoping the movement would scare them away because the edge certainly wouldn't.

But they kept coming.

She nearly reached for their strands and jerked her fingers back at the last second, an image of her own deadened threads flashing through her head.

But she'd never gotten sick from manipulating the Devastation itself.

She yanked the threads at her feet, pulling up so that the floor of the tunnel heaved. The force of it threw the snakes back.

Ash dropped the strands and scrambled to her feet. The impromptu wall wouldn't hold them for long.

She turned and ran down the dim pathway, putting as much distance between herself and the snakes as possible.

Her breath came fast, hissing between her teeth. It masked the roar for long enough that it was almost on top of her before she noticed.

A thick shape barreled out of one of the cross paths, slamming into Ashwyn without warning.

She lost her footing and spun through the air before she struck the vines of one of the walls and slid down.

She groaned, her ribs on fire, and she rolled to catch a glimpse of her attacker.

An enormous badger stood on the path where she'd been, the white stripe of its face easy to see even in the dark. A tail rose through the shadows behind it, and Ash could just make out the shape of a scorpion's stinger.

"Mortis," she muttered.

The badger huffed, and that was her only warning. She lunged, just avoiding the stinger as it plunged into the vines where she'd been lying.

Her free hand hugged her middle, and she avoided thinking about whatever was grating in her ribs as she sprinted down the path.

The creature roared and came after her, proving that bulky didn't necessarily mean slow.

Ash swore and tried to think. Jerking the floor vines like she had with the vipers would only slow this thing down. She needed to stop it entirely.

She put enough distance between herself and the badger that she could spin around. A dangling vine gave her an idea, and she hauled it across the tunnel. She reached for another, but her fingers grasped on nothing, and she glanced down in surprise.

The trail of death that she'd been following cut through the tunnel, leaving nothing behind. No glowing bits of the Nexum, no threads or connections. They'd been severed, and the burnt, curled ends wouldn't do Ashwyn any good.

She had to reach around the dead zone and find living branches to use. She pulled them into place, locking them around each other.

The badger hit the other side of her barrier, making it creak.

Ashwyn winced and kept adding layers.

Finally, a thick wall of vines stood between her and the creature, and she stepped back, her shoulders drooping.

She wouldn't place any bets on the wall holding for long against the badger though, not with the huge digger claws it had on each paw.

She used the space she'd created to turn and continue her flight down the path of death.

The lower layers of the Devastation were clearly more dangerous than the upper. She'd never had this much trouble above, except for around the watering hole where the Devastation beasts congregated.

She held her side against the pain as she gasped for breath, but she dared not slow down.

Just ahead she could see light, a narrow shaft filtering through the many layers until it penetrated some looser weave of vines.

The trail led up toward a break in the ceiling, as if something had crashed through here.

Ashwyn didn't wait to catch her breath. She pushed through the vines and used one as a step to climb up out of the tunnel.

Clear, fresh air hit her lungs, and she took a deep breath, ignoring the pain. She raised her head and gasped.

No wonder light had filtered into the tunnel.

She'd come out into an enormous clearing, as if the entire Devastation had been peeled away. For the first time in days, Ashwyn felt the sun on her face. She could see the edge of the soul well to her left and realized the village must be in that direction.

Ashwyn tipped her head back with a laugh and held out her arms.

Then she spotted what had made the clearing.

A huge hole tore through the middle of the Devastation, plunging down farther than she could see from here. Vines and roots wrapped around to form the walls of the chasm. But every one of them shone sickly white in the afternoon light. The same white that she'd seen in the ruins and in the witch.

Ash stepped closer, inching along until she could peer into the hole. The white crept across the vines where she stood, just beyond her boots, as if it reached for freedom.

But everything in this area had been cut back and leveled, like a firebreak. The vines and roots where she stood had been killed and burned, leaving a swath of death all around the hole.

Ashwyn swallowed back the taste of bile. The sun didn't feel so warm anymore.

All throughout the white, she could see strands of the Nexum. But this was the first time she'd actually had a chance to observe the difference between this and the rest of the Devastation.

The strands here pulsed with a sick light, and the strands themselves writhed, reaching as if they wanted to cross the firebreak to the healthy forest and the Nexum beyond.

"Mortis," Ashwyn whispered.

That's what had happened when the man had touched the plants around the watering hole. The strands within him had...corrupted everything he touched. The Nexum had sickened. And that sickness had come from here?

Everything around her had been cut back in order to starve the corruption that had eaten its way through all life here at the heart of the Devastation.

She only knew one thing that could corrupt the threads of life itself.

This *was* the Malady. This was the sickness that had tried to doom the world hundreds of years ago. The invasion that the Saints kept pushing back.

This was the enemy that should have been defeated long, long ago.

Ashwyn stood at the heart of the Devastation. Where the war against the Malady had started. And where the Saints had won their first victory.

Except they hadn't, had they? The Malady was still here, still reaching and grasping, trying to spread and end all life.

Her stomach roiled, but she couldn't look away.

She made sure her boots stayed firmly on the deadened vines, but she leaned forward, craning her neck to try to see the bottom of the hole. How far down did it go? And what was down there that had started all of this?

A hand grabbed the back of her overcoat and yanked her away from the edge, flinging her backward. She sprawled on the vines, the wind leaving her lungs in a whoosh.

From her blind side came a swirl of dark cloth, and she had just enough time to glimpse the flare of a black robe and the glint of sunlight against the edge of a scythe blade.

She'd found the witch.

Chapter 27
Obitusim

The executioner's blade spun, whistling through the air as it arched toward the interloper's throat.

The younger woman—hardly more than a girl really—gasped, and her eyes went wide.

How many times had she seen that fear directed at her through the holes in her mask? The Goddess's voice had been right all those years ago. The horror of it had not faded, but she had grown harder. And so the terrible task had grown easier.

But in that moment of panic, the girl reached out with her hand and grabbed at the threads traveling through the executioner's scythe.

The executioner staggered, and the blade skittered away from its intended path. She lunged to catch her balance and her breath.

A Nexsaint. The girl was a Nexsaint.

Mother of Life, the executioner hadn't come face to face with one in years.

She spun her blade to balance and brought it back to a ready position.

Her breath steadied her. The presence of a Nexsaint changed nothing about her goal. It only made her more careful and more determined.

She pressed forward, her blade whirling, and the girl scrambled backward, lunging out of the way. But the executioner stepped quickly, feet sure on the uneven vines.

The girl reached again for strands of the Nexum, but she reached for the dead threads under their feet and found nothing but curled, blackened ends.

She twisted and instead pulled threads from the forest behind her, and the vines raced to obey, twining around the executioner's feet.

The move was so amateur it nearly tripped her.

She gestured, the edge of her hand slicing through the strands, and the vines fell away and disintegrated into dust.

So she might be a Nexsaint, but she wasn't a very good one. Anything she did, the executioner could do better and faster.

The girl surged to her feet and used one hand to sweep the scythe out of the way before grabbing the executioner's robe in the other.

She was strong; the executioner would give her that. But the move merely brought back endless days of training with the Bladesaints, and the executioner brought her hand up between them and twisted it out and down, breaking the girl's hold.

She huffed as if surprised.

And the executioner used her unbalance to throw the girl off her feet. She landed in a tumble against the vines, her face going white with pain. She choked on a gasp.

The executioner thrust aside the surge of sympathy and swept forward, swinging the blade of her scythe behind the interloper's neck.

All she had to do was pull, and the girl would lose her head. She'd fall to dust the way so many had before her.

It would be easy. The sharp edge of her blade had never failed. And her nerve had been honed to its own kind of weapon.

But the girl stared at her, dark hair tangled around her sun-darkened face. She hadn't spent so long in the forest to lose that weathered look.

The executioner clenched her teeth and braced herself, grip shifting on her scythe for the final blow.

A thunder of wings and a cacophony of cries burst from the forest behind the girl. White and black feathers flashed and formed a wall as magpies swarmed between them. Their beaks tore at the executioner's robes, and she flung up a hand to protect her face.

The fury of their attack forced her to step back, and the girl scrambled out from under the scythe, gaining her balance amongst the vines.

Through the magpies' fury, the executioner saw the girl's eyes. She saw the moment she realized she could run. And the moment she decided not to.

A bark made her smile.

The wolf, Felleron, leaped from the forest, snapping at the flock that surrounded her.

A group of birds broke off and swarmed the wolf, and he yelped, swinging his head to catch them with his dark horns or his teeth.

But the magpies swooped and dove in and out, harrying them without leaving any openings.

The girl lurched upright, sucking in deep breaths, her arm wrapped protectively around her middle as she swayed on her feet.

A weakened target.

The executioner brought both hands close to her chest, twisting her fingers through her own threads before flinging them out in a net.

The magpies burst away from her in a flare of feathers and claws, the Nexum pushing them back.

She set the shield so they couldn't dive on her or Felleron again, and the birds whirled around above them, then winged away from the dead zone, disappearing into the trees with a strident storm of affronted squawking.

One lone magpie remained, circling above them. He held his foot curled, and as he flashed by, she caught the way it bent unnaturally.

The executioner curled her left hand around the space where her last two fingers should have been.

Magpies.

Her heart twisted in her chest, leaving her breathless. A different set of wings flashed in her mind, more angular and made of stone, but with the same pattern of black and white feathers.

"My lady," the executioner whispered, still following the bird's path against the bright sky. "Did you send these?"

The voice didn't answer. But then She almost never did. It was the times in between the silences that kept her on her knees, praying.

The executioner dropped her gaze to the girl who still stood, lips pulled thin in pain. The silence left a mystery, then.

"You've been following me," she said, and she couldn't keep her voice from going low. The feeling of trespass, of someone walking through her space, didn't fade easily.

The girl shivered, her dark eyes closing for a moment before she met her gaze again. Not without fear but as if the fear wasn't nearly as important as whatever this moment was.

The executioner swallowed. How was she supposed to meet someone's eyes without memorizing them for remembrance after they were dead? After she killed them?

She shook aside the feeling and focused on the outrage and the feeling of violation.

"If the Order sent you to kill me, they shouldn't have bothered with a half-trained novice," the executioner said. "It's as insulting as it is ineffective. Are there no more Judges?"

The girl flushed, and the executioner noted the color and the way it disappeared all the way under the neck of her dirty overcoat.

"I'm not here to kill you," the girl said, voice breathless and strident. "You were trying to kill me first."

The executioner's eyes narrowed, and she jerked her chin at the girl's hands. "You're a Nexsaint. What else would a Nexsaint be doing in here?"

The girl snorted, and for the first time the executioner had the feeling she was missing something.

"You're pretty full of yourself, aren't you?" the girl said. "It's a big Devastation. Not all of it has to be about you."

The executioner's mouth opened and then closed again under her mask, and her gaze raked the girl up and down, taking in her torn and stained overcoat and the loose shirt and pants underneath. Both were filthy, but under the grime, neither of them was in Nexsaint black.

But she had seen the girl reach for the Nexum. She'd seen her pull threads.

The executioner used her scythe to reach out and turn the girl's hand over, revealing the still-healing stripes where threads of the Nexum had burned her.

Not a full Nexsaint then, but a novice.

Rage rose in her chest, stifling her, and she couldn't tell who she was angrier with. The Order for letting this girl out of their sight during her training, or the girl for getting herself lost in the most dangerous place on the planet for one who'd been anointed by the Goddess.

She should kill her now. Deliver the Last Death and be done with this before the Malady could infect her. Or she took stories of the executioner back to the city.

But the magpie circled above them, its wingbeats echoing a voice the executioner could barely hear but trusted more than her own life.

If her lady wanted her to point this girl in the right direction...so be it.

The executioner huffed, blowing out her anger and frustration and leaving her chest empty.

"You're too young to be out without your Rector. Dea save you from such foolishness, for I will not."

She stepped forward, raising her scythe to her shoulder. The girl's eyes went wide, and she raised her arm as if to ward off the next attack.

But the executioner shook her head.

"Go home," she said, the words grating out against her better judgement. "Go home and forget what you've seen here." She spun away, and the wolf turned with her.

"I can't," the girl cried behind her, a burst of grief and anger that made the executioner stop, feet planted against the vines.

She tilted her head. Not turning, but listening.

"I have no home. They exiled me. They threw me into the Devastation."

The executioner's throat went dry between one breath and the next. The Order would not exile someone to the Devastation. Not for anything. This place was forbidden to Nexsaints for a reason. Only the ignorant would choose this place as a punishment.

"You're from one of the villages," she said over her shoulder. "Not the city."

The girl nodded, then shook her head.

The executioner turned to eye her. "Exiled for what?"

The girl's eyes twitched in confusion, and the executioner wondered if it had been so long since she'd spoken to another human that the ease of conversation had left her. She snorted. She'd never been particularly gifted at human interaction to begin with, so there hadn't been much to lose.

"What crime did you commit?" the executioner asked, trying to gentle her voice and utterly failing. Her throat wasn't used to speaking out loud so much anymore.

The girl swallowed and met her eyes. "Heresy."

The word echoed through the executioner's chest, tightening in her heart and stomach. She wouldn't have thought it would have so much power over her anymore.

The girl took her reaction as a question and raised her chin. "They said I stole the Nexum's power from the Goddess to become a Nexsaint."

More ignorance. The executioner choked on a laugh. "That's not possible. No one can steal from the Goddess. She is absolute. It is *Her* power we use, yes. Because it is *Her* power that She gives to us. You cannot just take a piece of a goddess."

The girl rolled her eyes. "That's what I said."

The knot in the executioner's chest loosened, and she drew a breath that was nearly another laugh. Duty urged her to take her scythe and lay it along the girl's slender neck, but with every word, the feeling retreated.

She turned to face her fully. "How *did* you come into your power, then?"

"She gave it to me," the girl said. "In a necropolis, while a Devastation beast attacked."

An image flashed in the executioner's memory, joy and pain tangled in each other so as to be indistinguishable. The Goddess sat before her, vines growing along Her arms, tying Her to the stone beneath Her.

The executioner shook her head. "Deavita does not travel. She has grown into Her throne. No one is gifted without visiting Her in the Greater Temple."

The girl threw out her arms. "Either She can't travel or no one can steal Her power. Both can't be true because I'm standing right here."

Behind her, the vines and roots of the Devastation rose, reacting to her anger.

The executioner's eyes narrowed, but before she could admonish a novice who'd lost control of herself, the girl closed her eyes and breathed through her nose, settling the Devastation around them.

Finally, she opened them again. "Which do *you* believe? That I'm a thief or that I'm a first?"

Her gaze remained steady, though her voice shook and her breath came in shallow gasps, revealing just how much the question cost her.

The executioner could kill her in an instant. End this mystery and keep the girl from wandering into the Malady or revealing her location. She could believe the heresy and execute her for it far more simply and painlessly than the villagers had.

But the voice of the Goddess threaded through her mind, too distant and muffled to make out actual words. Filling her with the sense of a friend just out of reach but still close.

The Goddess did not travel. She did not gift Nexsaints outside of Her temple.

But She also did not speak to Her Saints. She did not order them to corrupt themselves for Her work.

The executioner knew the feeling that sat in the girl's eyes. The fear and resignation that came from being an anomaly.

She glanced at the magpie above them, her mouth twitching in a rueful smile.

Very well, my lady. I will not kill her. Yet.

Then she sighed and squared her shoulders.

"You shouldn't be here," she said. "Nexsaints are especially vulnerable. You need training and a Rector. Go to the city and tell them what happened. If you stay here, then I will be forced to deliver the Last Death." She readied her scythe, its wicked blade dripping sunlight. "I cannot risk a Nexsaint spreading the Malady."

The girl staggered back a step. Fear would have been the obvious cause, but her eyes were on the executioner's face, not her blade.

"You believe me?" she whispered.

The executioner cocked her head, scythe still ready. "Yes. Why?"

"No one's believed me yet."

Oh. The force of it hit her like a blow, knocking the wind out of her. Trust could be a sudden thing and so fleeting.

The girl's eyes caught on the white streaks in her hands, and the executioner fought the urge to tuck them under her arms.

"Who are you really?" she said.

The executioner raised her chin. "It's best you don't know my name. When you go to the city, I do not want you to be able to speak it."

"I'm not going to the city," the girl said, though she'd had exactly no time to make that decision for herself.

Had she no sense of self-preservation? The executioner's eyebrows twitched. "Then I will be forced to kill you."

"Then there's no reason not to tell me your name."

A wheeze escaped her lungs as she teetered on the edge between outrage and a sense of the ridiculous. She was glad for the mask covering whatever her face was doing, but still, the girl's mouth stretched into an uncertain smile.

"Have you always been this stubborn?" the executioner asked.

The girl shrugged. "Pretty much. I'm tired of people lying to me. Or just omitting the truth to manipulate me. I'm not letting it happen anymore."

The executioner shook her head. Such cynicism from someone who looked like they'd left the cradle less than a month ago. "Who has lied to you so that you're this jaded?"

The girl opened her mouth, an answer ready on her tongue. But then she glanced behind the executioner, and she set her jaw.

She pointed to the Malady tearing a hole in the middle of the Devastation.

"That is not supposed to be there," the girl said.

The executioner stepped back, her face going still and serene, all trace of amusement fleeing. This was a thing she could understand. A thing she'd never thought to share.

The girl swallowed before continuing. "The Order says they wiped it out. That every time it comes back, they get rid of it again. They said they were victorious. That lie is bigger than anything in my broken life. Are you going to add to it?"

The executioner hung her head, and her shoulders dropped with her next breath. Then she spun her scythe and hooked it behind her, using the threads in her body to connect it there.

The truth had cost her so much. But the pain had never stopped her from speaking it. She'd left her name behind so long ago and now she only thought of herself as the executioner, but it had belonged to her once. An identity she'd chosen when she was young and learning who she was. It had hurt to give it up.

It was still there, as if waiting for her to pick it back up again. She settled it around herself and the truth of it seeped into her. This was who she had been when the Goddess had called her to leave everything and follow.

"You are right," she said, her deep voice going quiet. "I am no liar." She raised her head and drew the mask from her face. "My name is Morlinna."

Chapter 28
Concordim

The name shot through Ashwyn, striking her with a jolt.

She'd seen it carved into the Saints' record. The bronze plaque outside the temple. The name had been one of five that had been struck through.

This woman was an apostate. A Saint who'd embraced the Malady. According to the Order, she was damned for eternity. And had been executed for it.

Ash gazed at the face revealed under the mask. High cheekbones, long jawline, stark blue eyes surrounded by white streaks traveling through her veins. They were the same color as the Malady.

Maybe the Order was right.

Morlinna waited, eyes intent on Ash's face as if waiting for her reaction.

Ashwyn cleared her throat. "You...you seem pretty healthy for someone who's supposed to be dead."

Morlinna's eyes went wide for a moment before she laughed, short and sharp. And Ashwyn was pretty sure she wasn't going to die today.

Her voice, even as she laughed, was deeper than Ash had expected, and it sent a shiver all through her.

Morlinna stepped away from Ash, toward the hole in the center of the Devastation. She skirted the edge, gaze sweeping the vines and the roots as if she was checking for something. Ash had never seen eyes so strikingly icy, a shade even lighter than the sky above them.

Ash tripped forward. "Are you making sure it hasn't spread?"

Morlinna glanced at her sharply. "How do you know about that?"

Ash had thought it was obvious. "That's what you've been doing. You've been severing the connections to keep it from spreading. Like a firebreak." She indicated the dead vines at her feet. "We do something similar in Edgefall. We clear the weeds from between the houses and along the roads. But I don't think anyone expects that we'll actually need it."

"No," Morlinna said. "They don't. But as you've seen, the danger is much closer to the surface than they realize. And it can take even the most diligent along with the unwary."

Ash bit her lip, remembering her own brush with the Malady. "That man that you...killed. Was he one of the diligent or the unwary?"

Morlinna's face remained serene, but something flickered in her eyes, too fast for Ashwyn to catch. Something that made her gut clench.

"You saw him," Morlinna said.

"I was in the tree."

Morlinna raised her chin. "He strayed into a pool of the Malady. They happen sometimes out in the forest, and if I don't get to them in time, they pose a risk to anyone who gets too close."

"And you killed him just for that."

There'd been a moment with Morlinna's blade against her neck where Ash had known Morlinna was going to kill her, too. The witch's scythe was perfectly shaped to slice through the thread connecting her head and her heart, and she would have fallen to dust.

But even then, Ash's fear came with a strange sort of admiration. It had made her limbs tingle as she stared up at the witch's implacable face and thought, *I guess I'm glad it's her.*

Morlinna drew herself up, and Ashwyn realized the witch was nearly a head taller than her. "Understand this now. There is no cure. If left alone, he would have died the Last Death anyway, but not before he spread the Malady throughout the entire Devastation. And the world beyond. That's what it does. It doesn't just kill. It seeks to spread."

Ashwyn swallowed. But the words didn't make her want to run. That time had passed when she'd realized she'd never outrun the other woman.

She stepped up beside Morlinna, staring at the writhing connections within the Malady. The ones that had been corrupted. She didn't have to ask Morlinna if letting it spread would be bad. But was it bad enough to kill someone who had done nothing wrong?

"Where did it come from?" she asked.

Morlinna's gesture took in the great chasm and its seemingly endless depths.

"The war against the Malady started here, centuries ago. No one knows why, but this is where the first incursion happened."

"I meant...why is it here now?" Ash said. "The Order tells us it's gone from here. That the Devastation grew in its place. Are they lying? Or just incompetent?" It was hard to imagine Rafe as either. His convictions had been as steadfast as the sunrise. And he'd trained every day she'd known him. "Do they even know it's here?"

"They don't know." Morlinna stared down, thoughts clearly far away. "They believe they are winning the Little Wars. And they believe they are doing the right thing keeping people out of the Devastation, regardless. The Malady affects Saints in worse ways than anyone else. There are many in the Order who are superstitious about the danger even after victory. They've never set foot inside the Devastation for fear of being declared an apostate. And as long as the Malady does not spread, they don't know that they have a reason to."

Ashwyn stole a glance at her face while Morlinna was distracted, taking in the white streaks outlining her veins.

She was the reason it hadn't spread outside the Devastation. She was keeping it back.

And killing anyone who might spread it. Or take the secret back to the Order. But why wouldn't she want their help? Just because she'd been cast out?

Even as her breath came fast and painful, something under that swelled and pulled her forward, toward the other woman. It was the same feeling that had urged her to walk too close to the forest and search for that white face between the trees. Now that they were finally face to face, Ashwyn was starting to understand it.

She'd spent her life trying to get the villagers to respect her and accept her as one of them. And they never had.

But here was someone who had no one and nothing and was thriving and powerful despite it. Or perhaps because of it.

Ashwyn wanted that. She didn't want to care what any of them thought anymore. She didn't want any of them to have any power over her again.

"But...*you're* corrupted," Ashwyn said quietly, wondering if pointing it out was the last thing she'd do.

Morlinna's focus returned, and she met Ashwyn's gaze. "What's your name?" she said.

"Ashwyn."

"I have been corrupted, Ashwyn. But I did this to myself."

And she'd been declared an apostate for it. Did she know? Had she ever seen her name stricken from the plaque in the temple?

"You aren't corrupting everything you touch."

"No."

"Why?"

"That is not for you to know."

Ashwyn made a face. "I thought we did this already. Why won't you tell me?"

Morlinna turned to face her fully. "If the Order finds out that I live like this —" she gestured to her face and the white there. "They will hunt me down and ensure that the truth of my existence is never known. I'm making it so there is less for you to reveal about me when you begin your training in Vitamorn."

"I already said I'm not going to Vitamorn, and even if I did, I wouldn't tell them about you."

Morlinna twitched back, eyes going narrow. "Why not?"

Ashwyn had no idea. She couldn't explain why she already felt more loyalty to a stranger who'd threatened to kill her over and over than to the Order she'd spent her whole life trying to join. All she knew was that she wasn't going to the city.

The Goddess had given her this gift and then She'd gone silent, leaving Ashwyn to deal with the consequences alone. The Order was full of people dedicated to the Mother of Life, and Ashwyn had exactly no reason to trust any of them.

But this woman had survived when the Order believed she'd died. She'd left them for something, and it had to have been big.

She lived apart from the system that had created her. And she could teach Ashwyn to do the same.

Morlinna's face tightened as Ashwyn took too long to answer.

The other woman spun away. "You must go to the city. There is no other choice."

Ashwyn scrambled after her. "I can't. I've been exiled. You think they'd just let me walk into Vitamorn?"

"If you go to the temple, then the Goddess will vouch for you and all will be well."

Like She'd vouched for Ash the first time? Ash burst out laughing, desperation creeping in past the sense of ridiculousness.

The sudden onslaught of mirth sent a stabbing pain through her side, and she gasped, dropping to one knee.

Morlinna sucked in a breath, standing there with her empty hands flexing, like she didn't know what to do. "I didn't think I'd hurt you so badly."

Ashwyn clenched her eyes shut, trying to catch her breath between surges of pain. "It was finally healing." She cracked one eye open to spy Morlinna's face and couldn't help adding, "You probably made it worse."

Morlinna knelt to get a closer look, then hesitated, palms raised, and Ashwyn noticed she was missing two fingers on her right hand.

"I don't see any blood," she said.

Ashwyn grimaced. "I think it's my ribs. I hit a tree on the way down."

Morlinna went still, face blank. "The way down. They dropped you from the crater's edge. You meant it literally when you said they threw you in here."

"Yeah."

Her lips thinned, the only change in her otherwise serene expression.

"I am not a Mender, but I believe I can fix this." Her fingers spasmed. "It will require me touching you."

Ashwyn wasn't sure if that was for her benefit or if Morlinna was preparing herself. How long had she been living alone in the wilderness, anyway?

"All right," Ash said, still breathless, but now it was for an entirely different reason.

Morlinna might not be used to people, but her hands were gentle when she raised the edge of Ashwyn's shirt and checked the ribs there.

Ash fell back on her elbows and tried to ignore the grating feeling as Morlinna explored the extent of the damage. Morlinna's fingertips were cool, but the rest of the experience was unpleasant enough that Ash couldn't even worry about feeling awkward.

"What's the difference between a Mender and any other Nexsaint?" she asked to distract herself.

Morlinna's gaze flicked to hers before returning to her work. "A Nexsaint trains for years in combat and Nexum theory in order to fight the Malady. A Mender does all that and then trains for years more to know the human body well enough to manipulate it."

Morlinna's fingers moved down the threads of the Nexum just under Ash's skin. One day she might have to replicate this. But Morlinna moved quickly, and Ash had a hard time following it while her side throbbed.

Morlinna reached for a thread in her own body and drew it toward Ashwyn.

Ash tensed, an image of the limp snakes flashing in her mind.

But whatever Morlinna did next made the pain vanish, and Ash sagged against the dead vines with a sigh of relief.

Morlinna wove the strands together and somehow snipped one so they weren't connected anymore.

She might not have been a specialist, but Morlinna at least knew how to manipulate the Nexum. Which was more than Ashwyn did.

"How did you do that?" Ashwyn said, sitting up and breathing deep. Nothing twinged.

"I used the properties that I wanted from the healthy body to remind yours of how it is supposed to be."

"Oh," Ash said, though she didn't think that actually answered the question. She gave Morlinna a sidelong glance and a sly grin. "Thanks for fixing it. Nice of you, considering just a few minutes ago you were trying to kill me."

She'd been hoping to get Morlinna to laugh again. But the other woman stood abruptly, and Ash lurched back to avoid the flapping edge of her robe.

"Now you are healthy enough to travel, you must leave the Devastation," she said, adjusting her cuffs though Ashwyn could see nothing wrong with them. "If you do not, I will be forced to kill you."

Ashwyn scrambled to her feet. She'd said it enough in the last hour that the words were losing their urgency, though Ash had no doubt Morlinna actually meant to carry out the threat. She hurried to find something to say that would allow her to stay. Here. With Morlinna.

"Then why haven't you?"

Morlinna's eyes dropped to slits. "What?"

"Why haven't you killed me yet? You keep saying you will, but you don't. In fact, you helped me." She could bend and climb and shout now without the stabbing pain.

Morlinna drew herself up, and her gaze went icy, lips thin. "Do you think I like slaughtering simple people who lose their way in the Devastation and stumble into the Malady? Do you think it pleases me to murder baby Nexsaints who don't know any better? It does not."

She spun away, robe flaring. "But I do what I must because that is what I am for. That is my purpose." She drew in a long breath, and when she spoke again, her voice had gone calm and flat. "You have two days to reach the edge of the Devastation. After that, I will hunt you down to prevent your inevitable corruption."

Cass would have known this was the worst way to convince Ashwyn to do something.

And Ash would have known just what to say to get Cass to agree to something maybe a little bit unwise.

But this wasn't Cass, and Ash had to change tactics.

She wanted what this woman had. This powerful, independent Nexsaint who had made the Devastation her own.

But this Morlinna spoke in flat, implacable tones and became an insurmountable wall the moment Ashwyn challenged her. Between her cold manner and all the threats to Ash's life, she was getting the impression that Morlinna didn't want her there.

But the brief flashes of bafflement in her eyes or the twitch of empathy quickly hidden told Ashwyn that there was an expressive person buried under the weight of duty and murder.

She just had to find the right leverage to unearth her.

"Fine," Ash said and let her shoulders droop a little.

Her gaze caught on the white edge of the Malady just beyond Morlinna's shoulder.

She knew so little about this woman. But she did know that she was dedicated to one thing above all.

Ash limped to the edge of the forest. She hadn't had a limp two seconds ago, but Morlinna didn't have to know that.

Then she paused as if she'd just thought of something.

"You said the Malady crops up other places," she said. "Does it leave a trail every time or can it be random?"

Morlinna jerked as if the question had startled her, and her eyes went out to the Devastation, where she had left trails of death through the foliage. "It can be random. It does not always spread through touch. It's why the Order is still fighting the Little Wars. Sometimes the Malady appears out there without any visible connection to this place." She tilted her head. "Why do you ask?"

Ash turned just enough to gesture to the chasm. "This isn't the first time I've seen the Malady."

Morlinna stepped forward, eyes catching on Ashwyn's face. "Where?"

Ashwyn glanced up to orient herself with the edge of the soul well. She'd spent a long time under the surface, and she couldn't be sure, but Edgefall was probably in that direction.

"Near the crater's edge. I'm not sure how far or how to describe it. But I saw it not long after I was thrown in here. It was buried in a layer, deep down where you couldn't see it from the surface."

Morlinna stared at Ash, then she met the wolf's gaze. When her eyes flicked back to Ash, the creases at the corners had deepened with worry.

Ashwyn swallowed and went for it. "I could help you find it. Before I leave the Devastation."

Morlinna hesitated a moment longer, clearly torn. Ashwyn waited, breath held. She wasn't going to push. She would wait, and it would pay off, and she'd get what she wanted while Morlinna got what she thought she wanted.

Finally, Morlinna nodded once and hooked her mask to her belt as if she'd been thinking about donning it again this whole time and had only just decided not to.

"All right. Show me."

Chapter 29
Concordim

Here in the very center of the Devastation, Ashwyn finally realized why the vines and moss grew thicker on one side of the trees. All of the vegetation faced the chasm in the middle of the crater. Perhaps because the enormous clearing had more light. Or for some other reason related to the Malady. Either way, she had to use the bark side of the trees to navigate because the moment she led Morlinna under the branches, the soul well disappeared.

She stopped for a moment, turned around.

"Are you lost?" Morlinna said.

Ash flushed. "No," she said, too quickly. "I just came most of the way under the surface."

"Do you have a connection to the place we are going?"

Ash turned with a frown, thinking of the strand from her tree that she'd carried around for so long. And dropped before she'd come here.

"No."

"Hmm. That is too bad. You can travel instantaneously along threads. It will be harder without."

"Yeah, too bad. This would be a lot easier if I could talk to magpies," Ash muttered, glancing up at the leader of the flock who winged above them, his white feathers flashing between the trunks. They knew their way around just fine.

Morlinna gave her an odd look. "You've really had no training at all?"

"Of course not," Ash said with a huff. "Edgefall only had Bladesaints. And it wasn't like the Goddess explained anything while She was here. Everything I know I learned myself." She folded her arms. "I can move most things just fine, but some of my early experiments went...badly."

"Did your frog explode?" Morlinna asked.

"What?" Ashwyn cried. "No. Nothing like that."

"Oh, well, you're doing better than most, then," Morlinna said with entirely too much calm.

Ashwyn's eyes narrowed as she imagined all sorts of unpleasant scenarios behind that statement.

Morlinna kept her gaze straight ahead as they continued to walk, but her next words were clearly for Ashwyn. "Moving things is the first and simplest technique a Nexsaint learns. Yank on a Nexum thread hard enough and you can move anything. Though if you're trying to move something larger than you, you can easily hurt yourself if you don't do it the right way."

Ashwyn tucked her hands under her arms, though the burns from the threads when she'd fought the Devastation beast had long since healed.

"But a Nexsaint's true strength lies in forming connections and changing them."

Ashwyn thought for a moment of the thread Morlinna had used to heal her ribs. "Is that what you meant by borrowing a healthy body's properties?"

Morlinna gave her a surprised glance. "Yes, you can use different strands from different objects or creatures and weave them into other things, sometimes yourself, in order to change the original's properties."

Morlinna reached and Ashwyn saw her pull a strand from one of the nearby sentinels. She wove it into herself in a complicated pattern Ash could barely follow, and when she held out her arm and pushed up her sleeve, her skin had changed, becoming ridged and rough.

Just like the surface of the tree.

The snakes. That's what she must have done. She'd given the vines' properties to the snakes and the snakes' properties to the vines.

Morlinna shook her arm, and the strands fell away from each other, leaving her skin as smooth and pale as it had been. "But that's the third and most complicated use of the Nexum. What we need here is a simple connection. We don't need to borrow anything except knowledge."

She paused amidst the vines of the Devastation and called, "Felleron."

The wolf that had been pacing them came ambling through the trees, and now that Ashwyn was looking, she could see the thin thread that glinted between him and Morlinna.

"Oh," she breathed.

"You see?" Morlinna said. Felleron stopped beside her, and Morlinna smoothed her hand over his horns and the gray fur of his head. "Through this, we can communicate and form a deeper connection. What he knows, I know."

Ash looked up at the lead magpie flying above them. "You're saying I can just ask him?"

Morlinna raised her eyebrows.

Ash rolled her eyes. "All right, I'll just ask him," she muttered.

As the magpie alighted on a vine just ahead of them, Ash reached for one of the black and gold strands running through him and pulled.

The big bird squawked and flapped off of his perch, giving her a beady glare before he winged away through the trees.

"Well," Morlinna said as Ashwyn flushed. "Would you want to be grabbed out of the blue?"

"I guess not."

"To manipulate another creature's strands, they must agree to the process. Without consent, you will make yourself sick and destroy your own strands one by one. Destroy too many or sever the heart thread that connects you here—" Morlinna pointed to her heart and then her head. "—And here, and you could kill yourself without realizing."

Ashwyn gulped, the writhing wrongness of the snakes spinning through her head.

"I understand," she said, voice hoarse.

This time she teased out a strand from her own network of connections, which she'd never tried before. Separating the thread felt a lot like warm water trickling over her skin, except it was somehow in her veins.

Morlinna watched patiently while Ashwyn tried approaching the magpie again and again until she finally succeeded by bribing him with the berries she'd been planning to eat for her dinner.

That got him close enough that she could finally reach him while he gulped the little red morsels.

"Connect the strands," Morlinna said as Ashwyn hesitated. "Don't weave them. Weaving will allow you to share properties, but I doubt you want to learn to grow feathers today."

Ashwyn laughed, then realized abruptly that Morlinna looked as serious as she had when talking about consent. Ash gulped and used the next moment to reach out for the lead magpie.

The bright strand in her hand snapped into place along his smaller network of threads. He tilted his head, peering at his own back as if he could see what she was doing.

A flurry of thoughts flapped through her mind, borne on black and white wings. An image formed of a group of nests built high in the canopy, little fuzzy black heads peering over the edges. Another magpie gave a hoarse chirp overhead, and Ash recognized his mate by the sound of her voice.

And finally she saw the swirling landscape of the Devastation below her, and she recognized the watering hole.

"Yes!" Ashwyn cried. "Yes, there. Can you take us there?"

The magpie bobbed his head and clacked his beak.

Ashwyn laughed, the sound bursting from her as the magpie took off and flew in a straight line through the trees.

"The connection can be heady," Morlinna said, watching him. "But you must be careful with it as well. It changes them. And it changes us. A day won't hurt either of you, but the deeper the bond, the more it hurts to separate."

Ash scrambled after the magpie as Morlinna followed more gracefully. "How long have you two been connected?" she asked, jerking her chin at the wolf who ranged ahead.

Morlinna was quiet for a moment. "A lifetime," she finally said.

The magpie swung back overhead to check on their progress, and Morlinna tipped her head back to smile at him. "It's funny. I've never been able to get them to sit still for me."

Ash shrugged. "I just fed them. Nothing special."

"Yes, I tried that," Morlinna said, but she didn't press the issue.

The older woman used her scythe to climb up into the canopy and stepped along the branches as if they were a roadway. Ash raced to keep up, fighting down the feeling that Morlinna had slowed down for her.

"Where is this place?" Morlinna asked as they got closer. "Can you describe the terrain where you found the Malady?"

"It was under a layer of vines in a pocket just underneath a pool of water. Near where I saw you the first time." Where she'd killed the man.

Morlinna frowned. "Any defining characteristics?"

"It was gathered on a bit of stone. Like the corner of a building buried in the Devastation." Ash looked at Morlinna, hoping the other woman would have an explanation for that.

"That does happen in areas. As things grow, the ruins move, carried along like a raft on a wave."

Even having seen it, Ash could barely believe it. "I'll admit, I never thought I would see buildings again," Ash said, remembering the strangeness of it.

Morlinna's mouth went tight. "You will see many in the city."

Ash rolled her eyes behind Morlinna's back. She should have expected the conversation would end up there again.

Their path twined with other branches and tangles of vines, and Morlinna stepped across, leaving Ashwyn to hop awkwardly across the spaces.

Finally, the long branch they'd been following sloped downward, and the magpie dove to follow it.

Ashwyn glanced around as they slid down the steep incline.

"It's here," she told Morlinna. "I recognize this place."

Just below them, Devastation beasts gathered around the watering hole, snorting and stamping if any of the creatures got too close to each other.

Ash didn't have to fight for space today. They hopped off the branch into familiar territory, and Ash led them down another layer, past the hole where she'd escaped the blue-scaled cat.

"I was looking for water," Ash explained.

The section where she'd yanked back the vines to create a stairway for herself had already grown over with tendrils of thin roots and a fresh layer of leaves. She had to haul back the new growth to find the faintest trace of the path she'd made.

Morlinna shared a silent exchange with the wolf beside them.

"Felleron will stay here," she told Ash as the wolf ranged to the other side of the hole, sniffing. "I don't think there will be enough room for him below."

Ash nodded and used her feet to hold back the vines, giving Morlinna enough room to drop into the cramped space. Then Ashwyn climbed in beside her as Morlinna surveyed the ruined wall peeking between the foliage.

But as Ash moved forward to show her the way around the broken ends, Morlinna held out her hand. She didn't touch Ash, but the gesture was clear, and Ashwyn froze.

"Carefully," Morlinna said. "It has spread already."

It was much harder to tell in the dark. The dim light hid the streaks of white stabbing through the stones and the nearby vines, but when Ashwyn focused on the strands of the Nexum, their corruption pulsed in time to an unknown heartbeat.

"Is that normal?" Ashwyn said. "For it to spread so quickly? Even without any animals or people to help it along?"

Morlinna's lips thinned. "Yes."

Ashwyn drew in a breath. "All right then." She yanked at the vines blocking them from the end of the wall, avoiding the ones that were already corrupted. "It's around the other side. This is one wall of a corner, and the Malady I saw was back there."

"Stay back," Morlinna said. "I will handle the infection. If it touches you—"

"You'll have to kill me, I know. We've covered that. But I can at least help you get in there."

"As long as you understand the danger and are cognizant—"

"Trust me, I'm cognizant. Just get moving—"

As she held back the vines to let Morlinna pass, the other woman sucked in a sharp breath, and Ashwyn glanced up to survey the space they'd finally entered.

It was just as she'd remembered it, a ruined room complete with walls and a flagstone floor that had been pushed up into this part of the Devastation. The vines and roots twisting above closed them in from the layer above.

But the pool of ashy white in the center of the floor had grown, stretching deadly fingers in all directions until it formed an enormous sunburst that took up all the space in this little hollow of the Devastation.

And lying directly in the center was the blue cat that had threatened Ashwyn's life just days ago. It lounged across the white-stained stones, great paws stretched like a house cat in front of the fire.

But when it raised its head to stare at them with slitted golden eyes, white streaks marred the blue scales of its muzzle, stretching up and lining its eyes with corruption.

"Oh, mortis," Ashwyn whispered.

Morlinna said nothing, but she set her feet and suddenly her double-ended scythe was in her hand.

She leaped at the cat even as it growled and surged to its feet.

She caught it mid-lunge and brought her scythe down, but the cat slid to the side and her blade drew sparks against the stones.

"Whatever you do, don't touch the corrupted strands," Morlinna called as she spun to face the cat.

Ashwyn huffed. She hadn't been planning on it, because she wasn't an idiot, but the space in here had already been tight, and now there was a cat the size of a horse twisting around, trying to slash at her. With every step, white strands cascaded from its paws, the Malady spreading in its footsteps.

Felleron howled from somewhere over their heads, but there was no way the large wolf was getting in here.

Morlinna's scythe spun as she ducked and wove closer to the cat.

Ashwyn dove for the opening, deciding it was better to give Morlinna her space rather than trying to be a hero, but the scaled cat swiped and caught the end of Ash's overcoat in its claws. It yanked her backward, and she had to twist to avoid a spot of corruption.

Morlinna's robe swirled as she slashed, but the cat didn't seem to care. It scrambled out of the way as Morlinna tried to corner it and snarled before lunging at Ashwyn again.

She swore and fell to the ground in a ball, letting it sail over her head.

From across the ruined room, Morlinna reached and grabbed several strands of the Nexum, then pulled.

And suddenly she appeared in front of the cat as it landed, catching it across the face with her scythe.

Ash gaped.

The cat yowled, falling back to paw at its face, but even that didn't turn it toward Morlinna. It shook the blood from its eyes and swiped her out of the way, reaching for Ashwyn again.

Mortis, it's coming for me.

And she had no defense. All she could do was avoid its touch. And avoid the pools of Malady it left behind. And none of that was easy.

Ash was running out of clear space, and every time she reached for a strand to try to help—to do anything—it was corrupted the moment the cat got close, and she had to drop it or risk falling to the Malady herself.

The cat lunged, backing Ash up against the only clear space along the wall. It passed so close she could see the white creeping through its gold pupils, wide and feral.

Then Morlinna appeared in front of her again, the strands of the Nexum swirling around her and falling away.

The cat screamed in frustration and swiped, dragging Morlinna under its paws.

Its eyes stayed locked on Ashwyn as it walked over top of her, pinning the other woman.

"No!" Ashwyn cried.

The cat came for her.

And in the process, stepped into one of the last clear areas among the vines.

Before its corruption could spread to the threads around it, Ashwyn reached and yanked up, pulling free an entire wall of roots.

She hauled them up and over the cat and slammed them down on the other side, feeling the threads connect with a click.

She yanked them taut and then let go, lunging away as the threads touched the corrupted cat and the Malady surged through them, leaving them pulsing with sickly white light.

Morlinna rolled out from under the spasming claws and leaped to her feet, scythe in hand.

She didn't hesitate. The cat thrashed under its net of roots. They creaked and strained, but Morlinna stepped forward, slid the blade of her scythe along the cat's neck and pulled.

Ashwyn turned away. Her breath came heavy and fast, and her stomach tried to climb out of her throat.

But when she turned back, Morlinna stood in the single shaft of sunlight that penetrated this deep in the Devastation. The light struck white sparks along one end of her scythe while the other glowed black. Her dark robe showed no stains, but blood spattered her neck and face, and tendrils of her light hair had fallen down to brush her cheeks.

Ashwyn had never seen anything so luminous.

Morlinna's wide eyes caught on Ash crouched against the wall.

"Are you hurt?" she said, voice rough from her exertions. "Corrupted?"

Ash's throat went thick and gummy, and she didn't trust herself to speak, so she just shook her head, never taking her eyes off Morlinna.

There was something there in the other woman's eyes. Something more complicated and tangled than fear.

Morlinna took a deep, steadying breath, and when she blinked, it was gone, replaced with the serene expression she'd worn even as she'd threatened Ashwyn's life.

Ash was starting to find it comforting.

"You did well," Morlinna said. She glanced around the ruined room and at the cat lying in a gathering pool of blood. "Even in this space. Even surprised."

Ash's pulse fluttered, but Morlinna had already moved on, sweeping along the edge of the sunburst pattern on the floor.

She swung the scythe around and brought one of the blades across the writhing strands, severing them until they curled up, twisted and burnt. She followed the trail of them, tracking each to the end and cutting it off until the corrupted vines and roots lay dead and fell to ashy dust.

Ashwyn dragged herself up off the broken flagstones, following her smooth movements around the room and out into the cramped space outside the ruins.

She glanced over her shoulder at the cat, taking in its white-streaked scales before it too crumbled into dust, erasing all traces of its existence.

She finally cleared her throat of the fear and awe and tangle of other things underneath, deep and unspeakable.

"It was trying to get to me," she said, and it wasn't a question like she'd thought it would be when she started.

"Yes," Morlinna said. She cut through the last of the Malady, and now Ashwyn could see she wasn't imagining the difference between the two blades of her scythe. The one she used on the corrupted strands was lined with white threads of Nexum. Just like the ones across her face.

She came to stand beside Ashwyn, where she looked back into the ruined room, searching for any bits of Malady she might have missed.

"The Malady corrupts everything inside you until you are completely consumed by one thing, destroying all life. Spreading your infection to all things."

Ash didn't think it was an accident that Morlinna used the word 'you.'

"It saw the Malady in me," Morlinna said. "And it knew I was dead already. But you are life. And it wanted to take that."

Ash struggled to control her breathing. "The man you killed. He would have become that, too. Before he died."

"Yes. He would have lost his senses and tried to spread his corruption as far and as wide as possible before he died."

"You said it affects Saints differently." Ashwyn swallowed. "What would I have become? If it had corrupted me?"

The corners of Morlinna's mouth went flat and stretched thin. "Our deaths damage the heart of the world."

She turned to climb out of the hollow, and Ash followed.

Above, the wolf had raised his snout to the lead magpie, as if comparing notes on their humans.

When they reappeared, Felleron bounded toward them, nearly bowling Morlinna over as he got close.

A fine mist soaked everything around them, and Ashwyn realized that somewhere far above them, it was raining. The water hole overflowed, drips cascading down the vines to plunge under the layer where they stood.

Now that she didn't need it, there was plenty for everyone, of course.

Ash waited for Morlinna to notice she was still there. To threaten her again or run her off to the edge of the Devastation herself.

But the other woman was silent as she ran her hands down Felleron's horns.

"That's what you're fighting, isn't it?" Ashwyn said into the silence.

No one had forced her to. In fact, they thought she was dead, and she did it anyway. She fought because somehow she could. She'd said she'd been the one to infect herself. And it had made her a deadly weapon against the Malady.

"Yes," Morlinna said, then she met Ashwyn's eyes. "Does the Malady frighten you?"

Ash drew herself up. "Of course it does."

"Good. At least you are not a fool. Now you—"

"But being frightened doesn't make me want to run."

Morlinna jerked. "What?"

"This is my home. More than Edgefall ever was. I'm not leaving it to become whatever that was." She waved a hand at the hole they'd climbed out of. "There are questions here, things I haven't found answers to and...and I need answers more than I need to breathe."

Ashwyn struggled to find the words she needed, the words that would portray the mix of terror and determination that made her want to move, to fight an invisible enemy. And she only found one.

"Please. Please let me stay."

Chapter 30
Obitusim

The executioner stared at the young woman she should have killed hours—days—ago. She should have done it before she had the chance to feel this creeping hesitancy. This strange respect for someone who would face the Malady and what it did to the living and still stand there, voice steady.

But if Morlinna had killed Ashwyn the first chance she'd gotten, she wouldn't have found this pocket of the Malady before it spread and made her work that much harder.

It didn't matter. She was not a Rector. Rectors had to guide their students as they learned from their mistakes.

The Devastation did not allow for mistakes. And neither could she.

"Morlinna," Ashwyn started, as if sensing the direction of her thoughts.

After years of trying to forget, the sound of her name made her shiver. She'd suppressed who she'd been. And who she'd *chosen* to be. Something deep in her chest loosened, and she had to tighten everything else in response, to make sure she wasn't caught unaware or unguarded.

She clenched her teeth and glared at Ashwyn. But the other woman just stared back, breath unsteady but her gaze unwavering.

Morlinna studied the planes of her face. Smooth skin stretched over muscles toned by hard work. Deep brown eyes flecked with bits of green glinted in the dim light, matching the determined set of her jaw.

"Why don't you want to go to the city?" Morlinna said before she realized she was going to.

A little of the tension went out of Ashwyn's shoulders. She'd probably assumed Morlinna was going to escort her to the edge of the Devastation and dump her.

"The Goddess gave me this gift," Ashwyn said. "And then She abandoned me. The villagers kicked me out of the place I spent my whole life trying to fit in. And the Order is lying to everyone. I don't trust any of them."

Morlinna blinked. "But you trust me?"

"They abandoned you, too."

It felt like a blow, and the breath whooshed from her lungs. Faces flitted past, ancient memories from a life so far gone it might as well have belonged to someone else. Faces of people she'd loved and left dying. People who had left her for dead.

"I chose my exile," Morlinna said through her teeth, knowing it was true. Her choice had driven them to try to kill her.

"Why?"

"Deavita asked it of me, and I obeyed. I trust Her even if you don't." The Goddess's voice whispered through the back of her head, bolstering her.

But Ashwyn's posture sank, and the power of her own words struck Morlinna hard enough to make her flinch. It had been so long since she'd had the power to convince anyone of anything. Even before she'd disappeared into the Devastation and lost her voice in society, no one had listened.

But this girl had. And they'd changed the Malady's hold on the Devastation because of it.

Morlinna had known for ten years what her fate would be. She'd faced it, waiting, knowing she would die alone and in agony without anyone to stop it.

what if it didn't have to be alone…

Her voice wove in the back of Morlinna's head, familiar and comforting. But there'd been a moment in the layer under their feet, with a corrupted cat bearing down on her, when her mind had rung with the silence. An absence that sent alarm surging through her.

But this untrained Nexsaint had filled the gap, trapping the creature and giving Morlinna the opportunity she'd needed.

What if she didn't have to die alone?

"We'll see, my lady," Morlinna whispered.

Ashwyn jerked and her eyes narrowed. "What?"

"I trust Her. I trust She gifted you differently for a reason."

The girl's mouth screwed up like she didn't quite believe what she was hearing. "I like where this is going, but why did you change your mind?"

"My Goddess is limited by nothing, least of all by rules. Everyone knows

She doesn't travel outside of Her temple. But everyone also knows that She does not speak." Morlinna spread her hands. "She speaks to me."

Morlinna waited for the shock and the disbelief.

Ashwyn's mouth dropped open in the expected surprise. But her next question wasn't the usual one.

"Did She tell you to trust me?"

"No," Morlinna tilted her head, a smile playing with her lips. "In fact, She was silent."

Ashwyn wrinkled her nose. It must not sound like a good thing to her.

Morlinna chuckled. "She is the one who watches my back. She tells me what's behind me and where to strike. This time She remained quiet. Because you were there."

Ashwyn waited. She was patient, then. A good quality.

Morlinna took a deep breath and decided.

"I will teach you," she said. "On one condition."

"Anything," Ashwyn said, far too quickly for one who knew next to nothing.

Morlinna shook her head. "I will teach you on the condition that you know what I am preparing you for. This is our fight." She gestured down the hole, where the vines were already slowly creeping back to cover the opening. "If you are to become a Nexsaint the way I am a Nexsaint, then this will be your fight, too."

Ashwyn opened her mouth, but Morlinna held up her hand. "Do not answer now. We'll have plenty of time later."

Felleron jerked his head up with a snort just as the lead magpie took off with a flurry of black and white wings. The wolf disappeared into the branches, and Morlinna straightened, alert to every sound coming from the surrounding layers. Every feeling.

"Something comes." She beckoned and used her scythe to grab the nearest branch. "Follow me. Quietly."

Ashwyn climbed into the branches behind her.

Morlinna took a spot on a wide branch in a lower layer of the canopy and crouched low. She waited, still as one of the stone angels that guarded the Greater Temple.

Ashwyn crept up beside her as the wolf stopped on the tree behind, his paws making no noise against the bark.

Morlinna glanced at her and then placed a finger to her lips, though she assumed Ashwyn didn't need the warning. Already, a feeling rose from below, a deep miasma thick enough to breathe in.

Morlinna extended one end of her scythe and held aside a spray of leaves, giving Ashwyn a clear view of the layer just below them. The one where they'd just been standing.

A figure stepped through the gloom, the shape coalescing from the darkness between the trees. Long, thin arms and legs with too many joints to be called human and a bulbous head protruded from the torso. A set of antlers rose over its brow, steeply slanted and sharp enough to cut.

Morlinna's breath fogged as frost crept across the leaves.

An inhuman shriek rang out, making the hair on the back of Morlinna's neck stand up. The feeling rising from below solidified into a rage so deep it sucked everything else away. Even the memory of joy fled in the face of such hate.

It didn't matter how many times she'd heard it, the noise still tore through her.

Around the creature, vines and roots writhed and shivered. The Devastation reacting to the creature's anger.

Ashwyn reacted, too. Her fingers clenched against the branch where they knelt, bits of moss flaking away under her nails, and her lips pulled back from her teeth.

Morlinna knew the thought that was taking root in her mind. This thing had to be erased from the world. It had to be killed. It was the only way to get rid of this feeling.

"Are we going to fight it?" Ashwyn grated out between her teeth, so quiet it was only a breath.

But Morlinna's hand slashed through the air.

"No," she said, the word only the faintest of sounds. "This is the first rule of the Devastation. If you see a dread, run. They cannot be corrupted; they cannot be killed. They are creatures of pure hate that will destroy you in a heartbeat. And they hunt Nexsaints above every other life on this planet."

Ash's breath stopped.

"Come," Morlinna whispered, and she led Ashwyn away as the creature's shrieks rose to a crescendo behind them.

Chapter 31
Animatim

Vitania waited in the corner of the Greater Temple as the Primarch Divine finished morning prayers and raised his hands in blessing.

The city folk who crowded the nave all bowed their heads to receive it, and Vitania scanned the space, looking for the telltale black uniforms of the Bladesaints. Four stood at the four corners of the Goddess's throne and one stood on either side.

The Primarch Divine lowered his hands and turned, disappearing in a swirl of color as he returned to the Palace of the Divines. The people in the crowd straightened and murmured to each other as they left the space, streaming through the doors and out into the sun.

V pushed through the crowd, moving against the current. Several people glanced at her, then glanced back as they noticed the circlet, but she ignored the looks. Past the altar, the crowd thinned, and as the chaos melted away behind her, the guard changed.

An unobtrusive side door opened, and a black-clad figure appeared to salute the lieutenant, who stood at the Goddess's right. The lieutenant saluted back and stepped aside, allowing the newcomer to take his place.

V stalked after the off-duty Bladesaint. He slipped through the door, and the new guard shifted, ready to stop V from following.

She tilted her head so her circlet caught the light and threw back her cloak so her breastplate gleamed. The uniform she wore underneath was the same cut as theirs, but only Judges on a hunt wore the plate.

The Bladesaint swallowed and jerked his chin back up.

"Sorry, Your Serenity," he whispered in the spreading quiet of the temple. "You're permitted to enter."

"I know," she said, but her lips quirked in a grin to soften her words.

The door led to a narrow hall built against the sides of the central throne hall. Bunks lined one side, and tables and chairs stood pressed against the other wall with a narrow walkway between. Three bunks were currently occupied, their blankets rumpled around sleeping bodies.

The Bladesaint V had followed stood beside one of the beds, hands on the straps of his leather cuirass.

"Lieutenant Julianus," V said.

He looked up, startled. His eyes flicked to her armor, and his face paled.

He straightened with a sharp salute. "Judge Vitania," he said.

"At ease," she said, returning his salute with a languid touch to her forehead.

Her mother would have made him stand there at attention with his jacket flapping open. But the Abdicant wasn't in charge of this investigation. Vitania was.

V stepped down into the hall. It sat lower than the temple so its walls wouldn't block the tall stained glass windows that lined the Temple seat.

She ran her finger along one of the tables and inspected the tip of her glove, then rubbed it and shook her head as if disappointed.

Lieutenant Julianus gulped.

"You may sit," she said, indicating the chair that sat uncomfortably close to her. "I'm just here to ask a few questions."

Julianus licked his lips and glanced at the chair, then at her. He didn't sit. "About what, Your Serenity?"

"You were the commanding officer on duty the day of the Goddess's untethering," she said. It wasn't a question.

He gulped. "Yes, Your Serenity."

She smiled. "Sit, Lieutenant, please. This is all routine. I'm just making sure everything was as it should have been on that day."

She didn't even have a specific line of questioning yet. No idea or speculation on how the untethering had even been possible.

But she did have the evidence of her own eyes.

Julianus glanced at the chair again, then he must have decided resistance would get him nowhere, because he sat.

V kept her gaze on the furnishings, the worn tapestries on the walls, the notches cut into the posts of the bunks. Tavian had told her once that soldiers kept track of their "conquests" that way. She'd been too young then to know what he meant.

But now, she smirked at the sight and made sure Julianus saw the way she dismissed them. They were amateur numbers anyway.

She stepped behind him, keeping her body close enough to his that she could see the sweat bead against his temple.

"I was there that day," she said conversationally. "Did you know that?"

"Yes, Your Serenity," he whispered. "The Goddess came back for you. She chose you."

"Hmm," was all she said, watching the bead of sweat grow.

"I noticed...the temple was empty that day. Not a Bladesaint in sight." She tilted her head, but the look was wasted on him as he stared straight ahead. "But that can't be right. Because I know six Bladesaints serve as the Goddess's honor guard at all times. Or did I get that wrong?"

He shook his head violently, and the bead of sweat finally slid down the side of his face.

"No. No, Your Serenity. Of course you're not wrong. We were there—"

"Were you?" she said, sounding surprised.

"We were called from the hall. There was a disturbance in one of the ablution pools. A pregnant woman came for a blessing and a cleansing and—and she gave birth early. Right there in the pool."

She came around the front to stare down at him.

"The priests called, so we ran to help. It was a mess."

"And you left the Goddess unguarded."

"No!" the lieutenant cried. "Your Serenity, please believe me. We left Saint Tayrin in position. Just as the regulations state."

V sat in the chair opposite him. "Tayrin?"

"He's served the Goddess for ten years. He's loyal and a skilled Bladesaint, and I trusted him more than the others, who are a bit newer."

"So he was in the hall?"

His eyes slid away from hers. "He...he was supposed to be."

"But?"

"But he wasn't at his post by the time we returned."

She raised an eyebrow, daring him to elaborate.

"I reported him missing, Your Serenity. Immediately. He hasn't been seen since."

V clenched her teeth to avoid swearing. The report would have gone through the normal channels, and V was decidedly not a normal channel. Her investigation, while officially sanctioned, was a very special circumstance and worked outside of the Saints' structure. The report of the missing Bladesaint had likely gone up while she'd been coming down and missed her entirely.

She gave herself a single moment to tap the table with her fingertips, her mind working. The missing Saint Tayrin was obviously the next step as a witness or a possible suspect, but there was already a system in place to find missing Bladesaints, whether he was shirking his duty or something more sinister had happened. And that system would be working from Lieutenant Julianus's report. She didn't have to waste her time tracking him down herself.

But she needed to corroborate the lieutenant's story first.

"Thank you, Lieutenant," V said, and Julianus's shoulders slumped in relief. She glanced at him sharply. "However, five Bladesaints to help a woman in labor is ridiculous and a clear dereliction of your first duty, which is to protect the Goddess. I am writing this up. Report to the Saints' Hold for imprisonment. At least there I will know where to find you should more questions about your role in this arise."

His face went white, but he stood and saluted, open jacket flapping.

She unhooked the connection with the Saints' Hold that she'd carried with her and held the end of the black and gold strand in her hand.

Lieutenant Julianus bowed his head as she stood and accepted the bond when she attached it to him. That was a good sign. Or it could just mean that he was smart. If he ran now, she would be the one hunting him down. Not one of his fellow Bladesaints, who might have been more sympathetic to his plight.

And Judges were not taught the word mercy. Once they were anointed for a hunt, they did not rest until they'd delivered the Last Death.

The strand of the Nexum she'd used pulled him inexorably from the room, and she didn't have to follow him to know it would tug the entire way until he presented himself at the door of the Saints' Hold.

The figures in the beds lay still, not even breathing as she left. She could have called their bluffs and interrogated them to verify Lieutenant Julianus's story, but it would be easier to believe coming from someone who wasn't under his direct command.

She didn't have to go far to find her corroborating evidence, though.

Several priests and priestesses moved throughout the temple, attending to their duties, but V sought the one helping the Saints and the occasional city dweller in the ablution pools.

V stopped at the corner of the hall and waited in the shadows, watching. Yaria held out her hand to a Nexsaint who, from the mud caked on the robes lying beside the pool, had just returned from the front. The Nexsaint took Yaria's hand with a weary nod and stepped down into the pool, letting the water close over her head.

Yaria murmured a blessing over the water, then stepped away to fetch a basket of soaps. The wet hem of her un-dyed robe dragged against the ground, its weight pulling the cloth flat against her figure, and V gave herself a moment to appreciate it.

Then she cleared her throat and stepped forward.

"Priestess Yaria," she said with a grin. "May I speak with you a moment?"

Yaria glanced up, eyes going wide in her dark face. Her throat bobbed. Then she gestured to one of her fellows to take her place.

"Yes, Serenity," she said, her voice soft. V loved the way it sounded like velvet, though it didn't usually wobble so much.

She extended her hand to steady the priestess across the wet floor. V's boots would have better traction than Yaria's bare feet.

V led her to a quiet corner where they could speak. She could have taken her to the priests' quarters. Technically, V was allowed there, too. But she planned this interrogation very differently than the last. She didn't have any reason to believe Yaria was at fault for anything. She was just looking for information.

"You were on duty the day of the untethering, weren't you?" she asked.

Yaria sucked in a breath, and she drew her hand away from V, smoothing it down her robes. "I was," she said. She did not look up, and V missed the dark softness of her eyes.

"You're not in trouble, Dayshine," she said, trying to keep her voice as warm as possible. The nickname came as an easy reassurance. She'd used it often enough with the priestess, telling her how much she reminded V of sunlight and the way it fell on the bright yellow flowers. "I'm just putting together what happened. Where were the priests and priestesses during the time between the fourth and fifth bells?"

"Here in the ablution pools. I believe all of us came to help. There was a pregnant woman who gave birth early."

V lifted her eyebrows, as if she hadn't already heard the story. "I imagine that was a bit of a surprise."

Yaria nodded, and she almost lifted her head to meet V's eyes before she ducked her gaze again. "It took ages to drain the pool and replace the water afterward."

"Did anyone else come to help?"

Yaria bit her lip. "Yes, the Bladesaints came running. Six of them."

V frowned. "All six?"

Yaria's gaze flicked to hers, startled. "I think so...wait, no. Lieutenant Julianus said something to Saint Tayrin. The Saint returned to the Throne Hall after that, I think. I don't...I don't remember. I was busy."

"Catching a baby," V said with a grin. But Yaria had ducked again and didn't see it. "I bet they're slippery when they come out."

"Yes," Yaria said, but she didn't rise to the bait.

What was wrong? Just two nights ago, Yaria had laughed under the covers, telling V the only way to stop her mouth was with a kiss.

This felt different. Full of fear. Like Lieutenant Julianus.

V shifted her body, leaning against the nearby pillar. Trying to look less aggressive. She couldn't do anything about the armor. The law was the law.

She slipped one hand down the woman's arm and laced their fingers together.

"Well, you do have steady hands. I would certainly trust them to catch a baby."

Yaria's fingers lay limp in hers. "Thank you, Serenity."

The wrongness jarred her so hard she had to steady herself against the pillar. And she had no idea how to make it all go back to normal. To the soft laugh and welcoming glance and the warmth of Yaria's arms around her.

"Maybe I can come by later, Dayshine. Test their steadiness myself."

A muscle in Yaria's jaw twitched. "You may come whenever you like, Judge Vitania."

V jerked back, dropping Yaria's hand. The priestess had never called her by her title. As if she hadn't wanted to remember what V actually was. And V had been happy to forget herself for those hours.

She shifted her feet, and the breastplate flashed in the light, and the hilt of her sword dug into her elbow. And the wrongness slipped into context finally.

Neither of them could pretend she was anything else here. Not with her hunt declared for all to see and her questions hanging between them.

Yaria hadn't told her not to come. She'd said yes because she thought she had to.

Oh, Dea. Had V done something to make her think she didn't have a choice?

Or...was it simply the fact that she was a Judge on a hunt? And everyone in the temple that day was under orders to aid in her search.

V held all the power here.

And Yaria would never be comfortable with her again. Not completely. The Judge's authority had shattered whatever trust they'd shared before.

Even after all this was over, there would always be this lingering feeling. V outranked her, and she couldn't trust that anything Yaria gave her was freely given. Not anymore.

V took a deliberate step back and swallowed the bitterness rising in her throat.

"Thank you, Priestess Yaria," she said, and signed the name she'd given to Yaria in the secrecy of her own mind. A little sweep under her eyes. Yaria didn't speak in signs at all. She would just think it was because V liked the color of her eyes. Not a little piece of her soul slipping through the cracks of her careful veneer.

Finally, Yaria gave her a careful smile, and V decided that was as good as she would get. She ignored the ache in her chest. Judges did not show weakness. They did not show heartbreak.

She would come by later to end things cleanly. It would be better for both of them. V wouldn't be distracted. And Yaria wouldn't feel pressured to say yes.

Actually, maybe it would be better to send a note. So there was less chance of Yaria misinterpreting her visit.

"I should speak with the rest of the priests." She had her corroboration, but Judges were nothing if not thorough. And she still had questions.

The rest of the priests' stories lined up with Lieutenant Julianus and Yaria's tale of the woman giving birth.

She saved the Archpriest for last as he oversaw all the rest and answered only to the Primarch Divine.

"He trusts us to care for the Goddess," he told V. "We are the ones who wash Her, tend to Her. We trim Her hair when it overwhelms the space, and we carry the flowers away to the hospitals as blessings for the patients."

"And none of those things disrupt Her?"

He stared down his nose at her.

She held her ground, raising her eyebrows until he answered the question.

"Of course not. We have very strict protocols to keep from untethering Her. Not one of my people was careless that day or ever."

V blew out her breath. She believed it. All the priests had said the same thing. Whatever had happened had not been intentional, and any accident had been slight enough to be forgotten.

"Thank you for your time," V said. "I'm sure we'll get to the bottom of this soon."

"I hope so," the priest said as she turned away. "I hate questioning every move we make, wondering if something new is causing Her distress or discomfort."

Except nothing they'd done was new, according to their testimonies. And V had been there that day. The only thing she hadn't recognized from her many visits had been the grass bracelet sitting on her lap.

She paused. "Do you place old sacrifices with her often?"

The priest's brow furrowed. "Old sacrifices?"

"The sacrifices left by the supplicants and the novices on Gifting Day."

The priest snorted. "Never. They're disposed of as soon as the ceremony is over. Sacrifices are full of emotions. The connections in one might be strong enough to pull the Goddess away."

V froze. She had definitely seen the grass bracelet sitting there. She remembered it vividly, along with the feeling of something out of place.

"You didn't see a sacrifice on Her lap after the untethering? While you were tending Her?"

He snorted. "I would have reported such a thing immediately if I had."

It had disappeared. The one thing out of place. Someone must have taken it after the disturbance had died down.

And V's money was all on the missing Bladesaint.

Chapter 32
Concordim

Morlinna led Ashwyn along the wide branches of the Devastation, finding her way easily, even in the dark. She used them almost like roads through the trees, and Ashwyn wondered if there were some sort of landmarks she used as signposts.

"Where are we going?" Ash called up to her.

Morlinna didn't pause; she just spoke over her shoulder. "To my home."

Ash's heart rate sped up.

They'd been traveling through the dark for hours by the time they reached a spot where the curtain of vines had been cut back recently. A soothing yellow glow beckoned them farther until Ashwyn finally saw two lamps hung from the wall of a ruined tower. The tower itself sat suspended among the roots and vines of the Devastation.

Broken walls extended on either side, forming the unique fork-like shape of a temple. Morlinna led her through the door and into the building itself, where tall, narrow windows still held some colored glass. Roots and branches grew through the gaps in the roof, crisscrossing above and obscuring the vaulted ceiling. And around the tops of the walls were carvings of interlocking triangles, black and white paint flaking with age.

"What are those supposed to be?" Ashwyn said, strangely drawn to the shapes. They seemed reminiscent of something, though she couldn't quite put her finger on what.

Morlinna followed her gaze, and her lips tipped in a soft smile. "I've always thought they looked like magpies. When I first found myself lost in the Devastation, the Goddess led me here. I took them as a sign of good luck instead of bad."

Ash snorted. "So that's why you didn't kill me."

The lead magpie dove in through an empty window and settled on one of the branches above.

Morlinna's eyes followed him. The wolf, Felleron, tipped his head back and huffed before stalking to one corner of the building and plopping down in a nest of blankets. In the corner of the long nave, Morlinna had created a hearth out of loose stones, where a pot steamed over a banked fire.

"I've learned to trust their judgement," Morlinna said. "At least when they're being serious. They're terrible tricksters the rest of the time."

Her expression had softened the moment they'd entered the temple, the lines around her mouth disappearing when she smiled.

Ashwyn eyed the wrecked remains of furniture and the stone altar at the end of the long room. If she just closed her eyes, she imagined she'd hear Father Liman beginning morning prayers.

"Some people might think it strange to make their home in a temple," she said, keeping her voice carefully neutral.

Morlinna raised an eyebrow as if she knew exactly who might be uncomfortable here. "Maybe," she said. "But I grew up in the cloisters of the Greater Temple. Right next to the Temple Seat. I was a novice. So I suppose I'm less comfortable outside the temple than I am in it."

"What's a novice?" Ash asked, hyper-aware of the fact that she'd grown up in a tiny village on the edge of a vast wilderness and had never even set foot in another town, let alone the one city on the continent.

"Sometimes victims and orphans of the Little Wars are bequeathed to the temple to be raised there. It means I was raised to become a Saint. If the Goddess had not given me Her gift, I would have been a Bladesaint."

"How did you end up here?"

Morlinna went to the hearth and stirred the coals into a flame.

"I served on the front lines of the Little Wars," she said, her gaze going distant. "That's where I first heard the Goddess's voice."

Hearing the Goddess was supposed to be as unlikely as meeting Her outside the temple. But Morlinna had believed Ashwyn's story. The least Ash could do was believe Morlinna's.

"What did She tell you?"

Morlinna shook her head and took a ladle from the hook beside the hearth. She took a bowl from a stack of two and spooned something thick and savory into it.

"She told me there was another way to fight the Malady. Something the Order wasn't willing to use."

Ash glanced around at the evidence of Morlinna's exile. "I take it that didn't go over well."

Morlinna gave her a sly look over the bowl. "How did you guess?"

Ash shrugged. "I've had my own brush with heresy."

Morlinna handed her the bowl and a bent metal spoon. "The Order didn't want to hear about it, and their reaction was...violent, to say the least. They declared me a heretic, then an apostate. I had to run or be hunted down."

So she did know her name had been stricken from the Saints' record.

Ash cleared her throat. "Well, it's probably not that bad if you like peace and quiet."

Morlinna dropped her gaze as she stood, brushing out the folds in her robe. "Sleep now," she said. "There is enough to learn to fill a lifetime, and you have nowhere else to be, I hear."

The other wing of the temple was missing, sheared off along the corridor, but the cloisters remained, and Morlinna showed Ashwyn to a room full of sacks and crates that she'd clearly used for storage.

Where do the supplies come from? Ash wondered. *The villages? Or deeper in the Devastation?*

The setup should have been terribly uncomfortable, but Ash had been sleeping on tree branches and roots for days now.

She sucked down her dinner and fell asleep among the sacks.

The next morning, Morlinna led Ashwyn through the Devastation. Ash was starting to feel crusty, and her scalp itched fiercely, but she didn't dare interrupt Morlinna to ask if she had a way to bathe when the other woman finally seemed willing to answer questions.

She hadn't told Ash where they were going, but judging by the bark side of the trees, they were heading toward the Heart of the Devastation, where they'd met the day before.

Over and over they passed places where a trail of death snaked through the forest. Or there had once been a pool of Malady, and now there was only a dusty smear with reaching arms.

Ash paused to examine the dead and curling ends of the threads.

"Everything comes down to the Malady," Morlinna said.

Ashwyn hurried to catch up to hear her words.

"A Saint's entire purpose is to protect from the Malady. Our home grew out of its destruction." She gestured to the Devastation around them. "And it has hidden its rebirth. Our entire existence is a call to action.

"But I'm not going to tell you the history of the Malady the way the Order tells it. I am going to tell you the history of the Malady that I have learned here, which is very different.

"This is where the corruption was first encountered, a hundred years after the Primarch Divine invited the Goddess to descend. That part is true. He rallied Deavita's chosen and named them Saints, and so the Vitian Order was born."

Ash wondered if this was how Morlinna had been taught, because she sounded just like Father Liman.

"They fought the First War of the Malady here. You already know it was lost."

They reached the edge of the vast clearing, and Morlinna led her up into the canopy, high enough Ash could look out across the chasm, but even from here she couldn't see the bottom. She could only see endless walls of corrupted Nexum and the white roots and vines that stretched under them.

They'd been here just yesterday, but already bits of Malady crept across the open space, slowed by the absence of life, but not frozen by it.

"But we keep fighting it," Ash said. "That's what Nexsaints are for. We can use our power to stop the spread. Right?"

"No," Morlinna said, making Ashwyn jump. "That is the first lie the Order told. A Nexsaint cannot manipulate corrupted threads of the Nexum. One touch is enough to infect them. And a Nexsaint who deliberately infects themselves is an apostate."

The words made Ash's breath catch. More lies that completely changed the way she saw the world. And under that cruel revelation was another. Morlinna said "them," not "us."

"But everyone knows Saints fight in the Little Wars. If they can't actually do anything, then how..."

"They have one technique. One weapon. The only way the Order knows how to fight it is to kill everything around it. They starve the Malady until it withers and dies."

Ash looked out at the Heart, trying to peer into its depths.

"But there was a town down there," she said, voice rising with horror. "Or a village or something."

There were ruins floating through the Devastation. Places where people had once lived and loved and worshipped.

Had the Order killed everything there in the First War? And what about all the places lost in the Little Wars? Anton's Grove and all the others?

Morlinna sighed, eyes on the chasm. "They do what they can to evacuate, and then they destroy it. A concentrated use of the Nexum requiring hundreds of Nexsaints to maintain until the Malady is starved out."

Ashwyn gulped.

"The cost is enormous. Entire towns and villages have to be relocated. And the Goddess's creation is destroyed."

"That's what happened here before the Devastation came in and took over?" Ash said.

"We know this because this is what always happens. We destroy everything to scour away the Malady, and the Devastation grows over what's left. I thought the cost was too great. I argued with them to find another way. But they wouldn't listen. That is when the Goddess whispered in my ear. A corrupted Saint would be able to manipulate the Malady."

The hair on the back of Ash's neck stood up. It was heresy. Wasn't it? Did it still count as heresy if your god told you to do it?

"So you corrupted yourself."

"The next time they called for an evacuation, I went in while everyone else fled."

"They thought you died. No, wait." If they'd been ready to scour the area... "They think they *killed* you."

Morlinna was silent a beat. "Yes. From their perspective, I died corrupted."

"I've seen your name on the list of Saints. It's crossed out."

Morlinna's smile was full of pain. "Yes. But it was all worth it. Because I was right."

She reached out to the corrupted strands of the Nexum and wove two together, forcing white-streaked roots to rise and twine together.

And it didn't corrupt her because she was already corrupted.

"Why doesn't it kill you?"

"It is trying. My life is a constant conflict. A push and pull where I allow it a certain amount of myself, and I spend every moment of my life keeping it from taking any more than that. When I sleep, or if I slip, the Malady creeps closer to my heart."

Morlinna held her hands out and pushed up her sleeves so Ashwyn could see the white streaks traveling up the veins in her arms.

"These were much shorter once," she said pensively.

"How did you know you could push it back?"

Morlinna's expression went rueful. "I didn't. I assumed I would die. But before the Malady took me completely, I hoped to prove my point. I hoped to leave behind enough knowledge for others to build on."

She'd sacrificed herself, knowing her only reward would be death and damnation.

Ash stared at her profile, heart thudding in her ears. "Will you teach me?" she whispered.

"No," Morlinna said, startling her.

"But then why—"

"Not yet. Maybe not ever," Morlinna said. "It requires great strength in addition to skill. Skill you don't have yet. And one day, sooner or later, it won't be enough, and I *will* die."

Ashwyn gaped as Morlinna stepped away from the chasm and beckoned over her shoulder. She huffed and followed.

"Why did you tell me if you weren't going to let me help?"

"There are more ways of fighting than the path I have chosen."

Not far from the chasm, another dead spot spread through the Devastation. But this one was different. In the middle, corrupted strands still writhed, lining a...a gash. That was the only word Ashwyn could use to describe the hole that lay before them. The tear slashed across the Devastation, but unlike the chasm behind them, corrupted roots and vines didn't line this one. This was a pool of Malady lining an endless black void. Beyond the edges, flashes of silver lightning flickered across the space.

Like the gate to Obitullas depicted on the temple wall.

Morlinna cut a twig free from a nearby bush and tossed it over the tear.

The twig caught in midair and stretched almost like wet paint running across an unfinished painting. Then, a white flash made Ash's eyes water, and when her vision cleared, the twig was gone. Sucked into the tear.

Ash's mouth went dry. "Where does it go?" she asked.

"A realm of death. Wherever we went before the Goddess's descent. Whatever goes in is gone from this world."

She turned to Ash, lowering her chin to meet the shorter woman's gaze. "In my first year here, a Judge came hunting for me and found the Malady instead. I foolishly thought I could save him. I did not. I failed to kill him, and now this is what remains."

"What?"

"This is what is left when the Malady takes a Saint. After days of suffering, they become a gap in the world."

Ash couldn't look away even as her chest heaved trying to catch her breath.

"Why?" Ash whispered. "Why are we different?"

"I can only guess. But the Malady is a corruption of the Goddess's gift. And we carry Her mark of blessing. Even Bladesaints are anointed by Her personally. The Malady hates that, and so even our death is a corruption of Her world."

She drew herself up. "This is what you are agreeing to fight if you stay here.

This is what I have done to myself. It is not pretty nor heroic. It is monstrous. But it serves its purpose. And one day I will turn into a gap. It will be your job to kill me before that happens. Before I tear a hole in the world."

Chapter 33
Concordim

"It will be your job to kill me...before I tear a hole in our world."

Morlinna's words lurked in the back of Ash's mind thereafter, overshadowing everything the other woman said.

They echoed there while Morlinna taught her how to find her way along the upper reaches of the canopy—"It's safer in the branches. Fewer Devastation beasts make their home in the trees."

They echoed while Morlinna showed her which tunnels came out where in the lower levels—"It's not just creatures you must worry about down here. The vines and roots constrict and move. They can trap you easily."

In the mornings, Ashwyn would come out of her little cell to start breakfast, wondering if today would be the day when she would find Morlinna overcome by the Malady. It never was.

Most days she found Morlinna kneeling before the altar at the end of the temple, prayer beads clicking between her fingers.

The other woman never mentioned the conversation again, and Ash worried desperately that she'd made Morlinna a promise with her silence. But there had to be some other way, some other end they could find that didn't involve Ash murdering Morlinna. She just had to keep quiet until she found it.

Morlinna took her out into the forest every day to track the subtle trails of the Malady as it tried to spread through the Devastation. The spikes of white rot hid everywhere, and Morlinna knew exactly which leaves to turn over to reveal the ashy surface underneath and which tunnels allowed the Malady to hide in dangerous gloom.

In the darkness under the layers of growth, Ash watched her use the scythe and finally realized that it wasn't just a tool to behead corrupted villagers or creatures. Both ends served a unique purpose.

One blade cut the clean, uncorrupted threads of the Nexum, allowing her to deliver the Last Death to anyone and anything. This was how she created the firebreaks around the Heart of the Devastation.

The other blade had been lined with obsidian and imbued with a piece of Morlinna's corruption. It wasn't just a trick of the light when it reflected white from its threads. This side allowed Morlinna to cut strands that were infected with the Malady.

Morlinna touched the band of stone set into the haft. "The obsidian keeps the Malady from spreading. And the blade allows me to manipulate corrupted threads without...without succumbing too quickly."

While Morlinna hunted down the Malady and burned it out of the forest, she showed Ashwyn how to weave strands together, borrowing the properties from one thing and giving them to another.

"Each strand in an object or a plant or a person represents a specific piece of their essence. Properties that make them who and what they are. You'll learn to recognize them by feel. Pull one to manipulate it." She pulled a thread to make a loose branch snap into her hand. "Or weave them with yourself to borrow strength and resilience and anything else you can separate out."

She twisted her hands and neatly severed a piece of the Nexum from the branch.

Ash glanced at the branch, which still pulsed with life. "You can cut pieces out of things."

"As long as it is not the heart thread, yes."

That made sense. She'd forcefully snapped the connection to Edgefall again that morning, and she was still alive.

"But remember..." Morlinna held up her arm, measuring the edge of her scythe against the strands under her skin. "Removing threads takes its own toll. It is painful, and be aware that you are removing your own properties until they grow back. But smaller pieces can be useful."

She wove the Nexum strand into the threads of her arm.

"The more strands you weave, the more variety. But the harder it is to control. We will start with two."

Ash looked around for something to use, but Morlinna pointed at the knife she kept in her belt.

"In order to cut strands of the Nexum, you will need something sharp. You can practice imbuing yourself with the properties of steel."

"Can't I just use a blade like yours?" Ash asked, glancing at the wicked edge of the scythe.

Morlinna cocked an eyebrow. "You can. But it is like taking a shortcut down a road you've never seen before. You might end up at the wrong destination. I am attempting to teach you how to reach the end before you start changing the route to get there."

Technically, Morlinna was acting as her Rector. Her teacher. But Ash avoided using the title. She already worried about how Morlinna saw her inexperience. It wasn't something she wanted to remind her of.

Ash didn't expect the lesson to be hard. But as she gripped strands of the Nexum, feeling the strength of the steel beneath her fingertips, the threads slipped, like cool metal slicked with rainwater.

"Threads themselves have different weights and different properties," Morlinna said, watching her. "Fire, for example, is notoriously hard to work with. Steel is inflexible but much stronger and will hold its weaving. If you're patient."

Patient, sure. Ash could be patient. She twisted the thread, trying to get a better grip, and spun it around one of her threads, locking them together.

But the moment she let go, the two ends unraveled and fell away from each other.

Ashwyn huffed, and her eyes flicked to Morlinna, who stood nearby, her head turned so she could keep an eye on their surroundings as Ash practiced. The white streaks under her skin lit it from within, making her seem to glow in the Devastation's gloom.

Ash swallowed, tearing her gaze away from Morlinna's austere profile. She gathered the threads again, forcing herself to breathe deeply and at least look like she was calm and attentive.

It took three more tries to get the threads to knot in a way that held them. She twisted her hand, examining her work with a frown.

"Good," Morlinna said.

Ash laughed. "Really?"

Morlinna cocked her head. "Yes, really. Weaving threads is the hardest technique. It takes Nexsaints years to learn. Most don't leave the city to join the fight with the Malady until they've been proficient for more than a year."

Ash tipped her head back to squint at the much taller woman. She had to turn her face to focus with her good eye.

"How long did it take you?" she asked.

Morlinna shook her head. "I am not a good example."

Ash's brows came down. "Why?"

"I was twenty-one when I joined the Little Wars. But I was a special case."

Ash gaped. Supplicants weren't even allowed to become Nexsaints until they were twenty.

"Why? I mean, how?"

Morlinna stared at her for a moment more before she held out her right hand. The last two fingers were missing, the skin puckered where they'd been removed cleanly. Ash had been too afraid to ask her about them.

"This," Morlinna said. And for a second Ash thought that was all the answer she was going to get. But then Morlinna turned her hand to stare down at her palm as she continued.

"When I was a child, the Malady overran my village. One of the very first things I can remember is the evacuation. The panic, the crowd, the pig that had gone white and enraged. It ran at me, and my mother didn't grab me in time."

Ashwyn held her breath.

"I was luckier than most. A Mender was stationed at the evacuation camp. The moment she saw me, she acted. She cut off the area of infection before it could spread to the rest of me. It was incredibly fast, no time for pain management or preparation. But it saved my life."

She folded her fingers over into a fist so her hand looked nearly normal.

"My parents gifted me to the temple after that, convinced Deavita had spared me for a reason. I spent my whole life in the cloisters, studying. I knew how to fight the corruption, how to manipulate the strands of connection before I ever knelt before the Goddess to beg for Her gift. After that, it was just a matter of practice."

Ashwyn blew out her breath and turned her head to hide Morlinna in the dark side of her vision. She could imagine a black-clad girl no older than Ashwyn on her knees begging for the thing that had set her apart.

Ash hadn't even had the chance to ask. She'd been given this and all the consequences regardless of what she'd wanted.

It didn't help to think about how much she'd longed for it before. She looked back at that younger Ashwyn and cringed. How naive she'd been. How desperate.

Ash sucked in a breath and held up the hand she'd imbued with the strength of steel. Her skin looked normal, but underneath, the joints felt stiff. Like a dagger.

She carefully chose a thread in a nearby bush and slashed through the connections with the edge of her hand. They parted and shriveled, succumbing to the Last Death with ease.

It had taken her a while, but she'd done it.

She detangled the knot in the connections so she could try again, ignoring the sweat that prickled the back of her neck even in the cooling air.

"How fast does the corruption travel?" she asked. "Can you slice through something and not be infected? If you're fast enough?"

Morlinna held up her damaged hand and gave her a mirthless little smile. "I would not try it."

Ashwyn winced. "Sorry," she mumbled.

"It is a good question with a terrible answer. The Nexum is a part of the body. So any infection will affect it instantaneously. And then I suppose the question is how many parts are you willing to lose?"

Ash's hand crept to her eye. "No more," she whispered.

"No more," Morlinna echoed. "But if it saves a life?" She shrugged. "The cost might be worth it. But only if the infection has not spread to the heart. And that is a hard thing to hold off."

"You did it," Ash said. "Right? It's why you're not a gap." She nearly winced again. She hadn't meant to remind either of them of Morlinna's fate and the terrible promise that went unsaid between them.

But Morlinna merely tilted her head. "This is true. But I have had much practice fighting to be who I am."

Ash's brows drew down. What did that mean?

But Morlinna was turning away, to take them back to the temple where she lived.

"What does it feel like?" Ash asked, scrambling after her. "Fighting off the Malady?"

Morlinna paused, her hand pressed against her chest. "It is a battle inside. When the Goddess gifts us, it opens a space within ourselves where we can fight. Nexsaints know it as a piece of our Goddess's power within us. I think of it as the battleground."

She glanced at Ash. "You have one too, though you may not have been there yet. One day you may learn to set foot there."

A battleground. The word echoed in the space in Ash's chest, and she could almost feel the opening she'd felt when the Goddess had kissed her forehead.

She glanced down surreptitiously at her chest and then flushed. There was nothing there, obviously. Morlinna wasn't talking about a literal space.

Was she?

It took nearly a week, but Ash concentrated only on the one steel strand until she could weave it perfectly every time. The same ease eluded her with other threads, but she was beginning to realize that being a Nexsaint was work. And being a Nexsaint like Morlinna was even more work.

She spent her days clearing the Malady as it spread, and occasionally scaring off merchants who thought it would be a good idea to cut through the Devastation on their way to Vitamorn.

When that didn't work, it turned into hunting them down when they inevitably got themselves infected.

Ash didn't wonder where Morlinna got her supplies anymore. Too many foolish souls thought they were smarter than the locals who tried to warn them away.

Morlinna didn't let her help with the day's work, so Ash spent her evenings beside the hearth, practicing the one weave she'd mastered. Over and over, until the slide of steel against her threads felt like the most natural thing in the world.

Morlinna frowned at her as she settled beside the simmering pot. "Why do you push yourself?"

Ash gave her a quizzical look. "To get better." She'd thought it was obvious.

"Dedication is admirable," Morlinna said. "Determination is the core of a Nexsaint's success." She lowered her chin to examine the cookpot. "But so is self-awareness. Knowing why you are driven is essential. Otherwise, it is only work with no end."

She looked up to meet Ash's eyes. "So why do you push yourself? What do you hope to gain?"

Ash's mind shied away from the question. Too much writhed under the surface, and it felt toxic to touch. Like the Malady. If she brought it out into the light, it would corrupt everything. Make her feel things she'd pushed down and buried.

But Morlinna waited, still staring at her with those light eyes that made Ash shiver.

"If I don't, you'll make me leave."

Morlinna cocked her head. "That...was never part of our agreement."

Ash flushed as she remembered the unspoken promise. "S-sorry. I guess I'm thinking of something else."

"Or someone?"

Ash gulped.

"Who?"

"It doesn't matter."

"The ones who threw you in here?"

Ash scrubbed her face. There was nothing for it. She'd never been able to hide what she felt.

"I lived in Edgefall my whole life," Ash said. "I thought it was my home. At least, it was supposed to be. Now...I don't know. I never fit. But I wanted to fit. If I fit, then she..." Ash shook her head. "I tried every day, every year. And none of them noticed. I was supposed to go to Vitamorn with her, to become a Saint. And I gave that up. To help them. And sh-*they* thought the worst of me. After everything, they couldn't believe that I was telling the truth. They couldn't believe anything good about me. And nothing I said or did mattered."

Morlinna waited until her words trailed off. "So you want revenge," she finally said.

Ash's hand slashed through the air. "No! I don't…I don't want anything to do with them. I just want to be able to control what happens to me. I want to be someone no one can—or wants—to exile again." Ash sucked in a breath. "I don't want them to have any control over me ever again."

"Them?" Morlinna asked, voice soft as she stared into the flames. "Or her?"

Ash wrapped her arms around her knees and leaned against the edge of the hearth. "Both," she whispered.

"Does she have a name?"

The jagged edges of the memory stabbed at Ash. "Cassarah," she said.

Morlinna didn't say anything more, but the damage was already done. The thoughts swirled like bright points of light that speared her eyes when she caught one from the wrong angle.

"If she'd just spoken up for me," Ash whispered. "The rest would have listened. They always listened to her over me. Between Cass and Rafe and Greta, they would have listened."

Morlinna's eyes went to her. "This is the one who was supposed to go with you to the city?"

Ash nodded, clearing her throat. "We had plans. We'd both be Nexsaints. Then no one could make me leave. Turns out I should have been more worried about how they wanted to keep me."

Morlinna stirred her pot and then hung the spoon on a hook above the hearth. "Jealousy can destroy even the strongest friendships."

Ash blinked at her. "You think Cass was jealous?"

It was Morlinna's turn to glance away. "Perhaps. I had few friends before I became a Nexsaint. Even fewer after."

Ash sat with her jaw slack as Morlinna served up dinner.

She hadn't thought Cass *could* be jealous. She'd always been the level-headed one. The practical one. She'd just wanted to get away from her mother. And becoming the council liaison had done that.

But maybe being a Nexsaint had meant more to Cass than Ash had thought. Enough to throw Ash into the fire when trouble had come?

"Perhaps," Ash echoed. It didn't dull the ache in her breast, but it twisted it, veiled it, and turned it into something far more bitter.

In the afternoons, Morlinna patrolled the woods, ranging from Edgefall's side of the crater in the north, all the way around to the southern lip and Last-stand, the village that stood on its edge. The Devastation was always changing, but Morlinna knew it so well, she could track a blundering human's movements days after they had passed.

Ash trotted along behind, trying to learn what she was looking for.

Not long after Ash had mastered her first weave, she followed Morlinna through the forest, studying the dense foliage, looking for signs of passage. Broken branches, scuff marks against the vines, anything that might have been made by a human and not a Devastation beast.

Intent on the dense foliage, Ash lost sight of Morlinna quickly.

She wasn't too worried. She knew which direction the other woman had been heading, but when she rose to her feet to catch up, a familiar hush fell over the woods.

Ash froze, a shiver creeping over her skin. The gloom of the Devastation deepened, and a gut-wrenching sense of rage rose in her throat.

A dread, Morlinna had called them. The long, gangly creatures crowned with knife-sharp antlers that swept a curtain of hate before them.

Morlinna's words rang in her ears. "The first rule of the Devastation: if you see a dread, run."

Ash took the space of a single breath to decide the feeling was coming from down and to her right. So she headed in the other direction, dodging tree trunks and launching herself over roots.

"Morlinna," she whispered as she went. But she could no longer be sure which direction the Nexsaint had gone.

No magpies flitted through the trees above her. In fact, she couldn't sense anything within her reach. Just the knotted growth of the Devastation.

Her breath came in fierce gasps, and her chest hurt. She could no longer be sure if the deepening gloom was from the dread or if the good side of her vision was clouded from exertion.

A great gray wolf with curving horns rose in her path, and she skidded to an abrupt halt.

"Felleron," she gasped.

She glanced behind her but saw nothing except hanging moss and criss-crossing vines. Was the panic beating in her chest her own or a product of the approaching nightmare?

"Felleron, where's Morlinna?"

The wolf stood stock-still, his eyes on her. He lowered his head, eyes narrowing.

"Felleron?"

There was a crack in the woods behind her.

They both flinched, and Ash rocked forward.

"Felleron, it's a dread. Let me pass."

The wolf's lip lifted, and a low rumble echoed from his throat. Morlinna had said once she'd named the wolf for her favorite poet, and Ash had laughed because she couldn't think of anything less fitting for the grumpy old wolf.

"What is wrong with you?" Ash whispered. "Let me by. We have to find Morlinna."

The wolf snapped at her as she tried to move past him.

Ash reacted, reaching out to grab one of his threads. If she could just connect with him, she could make him understand the danger and get him to take her to Morlinna.

The wolf jerked as she took hold of his thread and yanked one of her own forward to connect it with his.

A jolt went through her, and the threads in her hand went dark and shriveled. The pain spread up her arm and radiated to her head and stomach.

Just like it had with the snakes.

Ash dropped the strands and fell to her knees retching. Her fingers clutched at the roots underneath her, and she had the vague notion that she saw a set of gray paws pacing in front of her. But everything had gone blurry around the edges, and she squeezed her eyes shut to concentrate on not heaving her lunch onto the woven vines and roots where she lay.

She had no idea how long she lay there before a cool hand touched her head, bringing a tiny sliver of relief to the pounding in her skull.

"'Linna?" she croaked, trying to raise her head.

"Hmm," Morlinna said, not like a question or even just a soothing noise. More like Father Liman when she'd gotten the answer wrong, and he'd moved on to ask Cass to give him the right one.

It didn't matter. Morlinna was here. She'd take care of everything. There was nothing the woman couldn't defeat.

"You tried to control Felleron, didn't you?"

Did she? She'd just tried to get him to move or talk to her or something helpful. She hadn't meant to hurt him.

"Unfortunately, you'll just have to wait it out. That is the only cure."

"Th-there's a dread—coming," Ash gasped out. She cracked her eyelids open to see Morlinna's profile checking behind her.

"Not anymore. I led it away, but we should move quickly."

Ash raised her hand to her spinning head to steady it, but it didn't help.

Felleron's wet nose pressed against the back of her hand, and he sneezed.

Ash groaned.

"I was just trying to reach you, and he wouldn't listen. It's the same thing I did with the magpie."

Morlinna shook her head and helped Ash sit up. "The magpie agreed and didn't fight the connection. Felleron did."

"I didn't mean to make him angry."

Morlinna sighed somewhere to her right. Ash was still having a hard time seeing. "He was once the pet of a great lord. A very unkind lord. I found him after he freed himself."

"How did he manage that?"

"I don't think you want to know."

Ash gulped and tried to shake away the image of blood-matted jaws and horns glinting red.

"I think he trusted me because he recognized a fellow killer. But he has a hard time with other humans still."

Morlinna looked over her shoulder as the big gray wolf stalked away through the trees. "I think he has a mate and cubs in that direction. He's been secretive about it for weeks. He won't even let me in to see them."

Ash could just keep herself from throwing up, but she had to keep swallowing down bile. "Lesson learned," she said.

"He forgives you. And he will forget the incident far faster than you. Especially once the cubs are grown and can fend for themselves. Just remember next time, if the answer is no, it means no. Not try harder."

It wasn't the wolf Ash was worried about angering. She used a nearby tree to climb to her feet, then pressed the heel of her hand into her temple in a vain attempt to keep her head from spinning.

"There doesn't have to be a next time," Ash mumbled.

Morlinna raised one eyebrow. "What was that?"

Ashwyn raised her chin, blinking her vision clear. "I was trying to reach you. We should be connected. Then we'd never lose track of each other. It would let us communicate over distances and...and maybe it would help me learn easier if I could see the way you do things from your perspective."

"I know it sounds like the easy way out," Morlinna said. "But there is a reason Rectors make their students learn on their own. In the city—"

"But we're not in the city," Ash said. "We're in the Devastation, and the Order has lied about plenty of things. This might be one of them."

"There are other reasons, Ashwyn," Morlinna said and held up her hand. The white veins under her skin caught the light. "At least half of me is corrupted. I can keep it from my surface, but the threads inside of me are not safe. It is too dangerous for you to have access to any part of me. At least for now."

"If I were corrupted by accident, I'd be able to fight it off. Just like you." Her voice rose, gaining conviction. "I survived Edgefall. I survived the Devastation. I could survive the Malady, too."

"Why do you want this so much?" Morlinna asked, head cocked. Ignoring the rest of what she'd said.

Ash faltered. "I-I respect you. You know so much."

Morlinna cocked an eyebrow. "Enough to respect that I know what I'm talking about?"

Ash swallowed, knowing she'd lost the argument and feeling like a child for having argued in the first place.

Morlinna had the grace not to rub it in, but Ash had never known when to stop talking.

"I just want to help you. I need to help you." She whispered the last part, wondering why the words beat so hot in her chest.

Morlinna paused, and her gaze went softer somehow. "You know you don't have to earn your place here."

"What?" Ash started.

"You don't have to earn your food or your bed or your life. With me, you have the right to exist without having to prove you are worth something."

Ash froze. Was that what she was doing? Was that what drove her to work and learn and challenge herself? Had Edgefall left such a deep scar that it had changed her even here in the Devastation?

Morlinna used her scythe to cut a branch from a nearby tree and held it out to Ashwyn.

"Lean on this. We'll get you back home."

Morlinna rarely touched her. Ash had thought it was because of the corruption, but if she could keep it from her surface as she said, then perhaps the reason went deeper. She had been alone in the forest for many, many years. The Little War she'd referenced, where she'd told Ashwyn she'd deliberately corrupted herself, had been ten years ago. She'd been roaming the Devastation ever since. That isolation had taken its toll.

"You are right about one thing," Morlinna said suddenly, and Ash drew in a breath.

One thing didn't sound like much, but she would take whatever she could get.

"What's that?" Ash asked.

"You survived the Devastation when most wouldn't. You are unusually resilient."

"Maybe," Ash said with a laugh. "Or maybe I trained myself to be a Blade-saint from the time I was eight. Rafe said...Rafe said I needed to be strong and clever. So I made myself stronger."

"Why did you want to be a Bladesaint?"

Morlinna had already guessed about earning her place, so she must have been asking about something deeper. Something Ash hadn't ever put into words.

"My mother was a Bladesaint. She went Absent during the Little Wars."

"And that is why you were in Edgefall?"

Ash nodded.

"Who was your father? Why did he not come to care for you?"

"I don't know." Ash leaned on her stick for a rest. "He wasn't around. And Ma was gone before I could ever ask her. And Rafe said he didn't know. It wasn't important. I was where I was, and no one was coming to get me."

"It might be important for other reasons," Morlinna said, voice distant, as if something had just occurred to her.

Ashwyn cast her a sharp glance. "Why?"

"We've both been wondering why the Goddess would have made an exception for you. Why She came to Edgefall when everyone knows She never leaves the Greater Temple."

"You think it's because of my parents?" Ash said, straightening up. It made her head spin, but Morlinna's words had already added to that.

"Your mother was a loyal servant until her end. And your father is a mystery. Perhaps he served Her as well. Your gift could be a reward for their service to Her."

Ash's mouth worked, but she couldn't think of anything to say. The thought rolled around in her head, comforting and disquieting in turn. She hadn't wanted to believe that the circumstances of her gifting were random. But if the thing that had ruined her life had nothing to do with her at all...that was somehow worse.

"Did She tell you anything?" Ash asked. "Did She say it had something to do with my parents?"

"No," Morlinna said.

Ash sighed. "Yeah, that seems about right."

Ash moved on, but Morlinna didn't follow. Ash had to stop and look back at her. Morlinna's brows were furrowed.

"What do you mean?"

Ash sighed. "She might speak to you, but She never seems to say anything useful."

"That would be hard for you to gauge," Morlinna said, voice cold. "Considering you are not the one who hears Her words."

Ash flushed. "Fine. You can trust Her all you want, but that doesn't mean I will."

"You are a Nexsaint—"

"An exiled Nexsaint. And don't pretend She's been a great friend to you, either."

"I don't know what you mean."

"You think it's fair that She would ask one of Her most faithful followers to corrupt herself and then instruct all Her other followers to declare her a heretic?"

Morlinna went still. "It wasn't Her fault. You cannot blame Her when Her followers make mistakes."

"But She didn't defend you," Ash cried, the vines at her feet raising up.

Morlinna's face and voice remained calm. "Are you angry because She didn't speak for you either?"

Ash snapped her mouth shut and forced down feelings that were making the Devastation react.

Of course she was angry. But she'd seen Morlinna praying. She'd seen her unshakeable loyalty and piety. Arguing with her wouldn't go well. But she didn't think much of a Goddess who wouldn't speak for the ones She called.

Morlinna could believe what she wanted. But Ash wouldn't make the mistake of believing in Her again.

Morlinna shook her head, like she knew what Ashwyn was thinking.

"I don't have answers for you. But even the biggest boulder can be moved by the smallest stream, eventually. I learned to see the Goddess's care in the little things."

"Like what?" Ashwyn said, feeling like she had to say something.

"Like this place." Morlinna stepped away from the tree, running her hand along the edge of the stone block held suspended in the foliage. "The life that thrives here. The beauty and the danger wrapped up into one. I cannot believe it is unguided."

Ash pressed her lips together, tight enough to hurt. She'd seen the beauty, too. Felt it in her bones. But that didn't mean there was some all powerful force guiding it.

Morlinna closed her eyes. "There's always been a mystery to this place. Where did the Malady come from? Why did it start here? I always thought the answers were buried under the Devastation. But keeping the Malady in check has demanded all of my time. I've never had a chance to search. I've always been alone."

Morlinna turned, gaze landing on Ash. "Until She sent you."

Ash couldn't breathe, couldn't move, waiting for something more.

But Morlinna moved on with only a content smile on her lips, leaving Ashwyn to follow or not.

She did, silent. Musing.

She'd also seen the mystery of this place. The Malady where there shouldn't have been Malady. The ruins suspended in the growth. The gaps in the world where Saints had died.

It pulled at her, too.

Morlinna had been here for ten years, alone, unable to solve any of them. Alone except for a Goddess who spoke to her but never said anything useful.

But Morlinna wasn't alone anymore. She had Ashwyn now. And once she learned how to help keep back the Malady, they would have time to explore. She'd make sure of it.

Chapter 34
Obitusim

Morlinna watched as Ash wove the strength of bark into her skin. Living things were always much trickier to work with than inanimate objects like steel or rock. Living things were mutable; they could change as much as the Nexsaint if done improperly.

But Ash tied off the end with a clean cut and held out her hands to examine them, as if she would be able to see the difference.

It was well done. Morlinna had known plenty of Nexsaints that couldn't resist a flourish as they finished their work. And anything extra ran the risk of tangling a person in the connections of the Nexum. Embarrassing at the least and deadly at the most.

"Good," Morlinna said. Her throat had grown used to being used again, though her voice was still lower than most people expected when they saw her.

Ash looked up and beamed, the sheer joy in her gaze striking Morlinna through the chest.

How long had it been since Morlinna had felt something like that? Had she ever looked at the world with such wonder?

Something within her wanted to reach back, but she cut it away, ruthlessly. Too many memories, too many past moments that made trust a fleeting thing.

She cleared her throat and stood, pushing away the mess of tangled memories and feelings that had lived inside her for long enough she no longer remembered which were a part of her and which had been adopted along the way.

Ash scrambled to her feet, her gaze returning to her hands. Then the girl clenched her fist and slammed it into the trunk of a nearby sentinel.

She laughed when it connected with a solid thud and stretched her fingers again.

"It didn't hurt."

"That is the point," Morlinna said with a raised eyebrow.

"Can you change yourself any way you want with the Nexum?" She gestured to Felleron, who napped on a branch above. "What about taking the shape of a wolf or a magpie?"

"It is technically possible, but not the way you're imagining."

Ash's brow furrowed.

Morlinna raised her arms, collecting strands from around them to wind down her arms.

"Everything is mutable, but the question is how much time and effort you want to spend on it. We borrow properties from other living entities. Trees, vines, animals. I can change my eyes to see in the dark if Felleron allows me. But the moment I give up the weave, my eyes will change back. The strands are only borrowed.

"However, if I were to keep the weave in place, then over time my body would learn to behave as his does. My eyes would change, and I would eventually be able to drop the weave and see in the dark as myself."

"How long would it take?" Ash asked.

"Years. Decades even."

Ash bit her lip as she realized the implications. "And it would take just as long to change back."

Morlinna nodded. "Yes. Some Nexsaints have done this and disappeared into the wilds, changed beyond recognition. But not many. The result is too much effort for most and too much time for the rest."

"So not a practical tactic for battle."

"No. But not all of life is a battle. There are other reasons a person might want to change themselves over time."

Ash's eyes narrowed. "You're talking about healing."

"Among other things," Morlinna said with a smile, thinking of days spent in the Hold's infirmary. "Menders can use healthy strands of the Nexum as models for a patient. They can change how much of a chemical an organ produces or convince a broken bone to knit." She spread her arms. "They can change the way a body grows. As long as the person does not mind spending half their time lying in the infirmary for several years."

Ash tipped her head in question.

Morlinna's heart thumped, though her hands remained steady, and she took a bracing breath.

"I was not born a woman," Morlinna said, indicating her long form. "But I knew who I was by the time I was six. The Menders of the temple were able to weave my strands with a friend's." Morlinna huffed a little laugh. It would mean nothing to Ash, but the word friend tasted bitter on her tongue. "They convinced my body to produce the right chemicals during my formative years. Until one day my body could do it on its own and the ties were cut."

Ash blinked, and Morlinna waited for the next question. There were always questions. Anyone who didn't grow up with Menders had a hard time believing the wonders they could produce.

"Why didn't they fix your hand?" Ash said.

Morlinna let out the breath she'd been holding. That...that wasn't at all what she'd been expecting. Ash's gaze remained inquisitive but with none of the judgement or disgust Morlinna had faced in Vitamorn.

Morlinna extended her hand, stretching the three fingers out to emphasize the empty space where her pinky and ring finger should have been.

"Changes to a limb or an organ that is already present are far easier than convincing the body to replace what was lost. But beyond that, it is forbidden to replace a limb that was lost to the Malady. In case it ever comes back to infect them again."

"That can happen?" Ash asked, eyes wide.

Morlinna's lips twitched. "I don't know. It may just be superstition. It is very, very rare for someone to survive a Malady infection. It spreads too quickly. And once the rot has reached the chest, it is too late to cut it out. It will reach the heart, and the person will be gone."

"Unless you can fight it. Like you did."

Ash's brows drew down, like she knew that wasn't the complete story. And it wasn't. Her original infection had happened well before she'd become a Nexsaint. But even Morlinna couldn't explain it. Not entirely.

Her memory of those moments had been lost to age and the panic that had dominated her body then. But she remembered the feeling of fighting. Of pushing back something that was trying to make her other than herself.

But that made no sense. The battleground where she fought with the Malady every day as an adult hadn't been a part of her before the Goddess had anointed her.

"You said the Malady reaches for the heart," Ash said, head down as she thought.

"Yes. Its final target."

"That's when a Nexsaint becomes a gap in the world."

Morlinna went still. This was the thing that ruled her life. The thought that always lurked, even on the warmest days. "Yes. This is why an infected Nexsaint must die."

"But what if it could be cut out? Like the Mender did with your hand."

"It cannot. Cutting the heart thread delivers the Last Death."

"Have you tried?"

Morlinna went silent. The girl couldn't see her failures stacked behind her. She didn't know the agony of holding a friend's insides in her hands as the white spread through his chest.

Something in her eyes must have given her away because Ash reached for her.

Morlinna stepped back.

"A corrupted Nexsaint must die before the Malady reaches their heart," she said, voice rough. "That is what you agreed to. There is no other way."

Ash dropped her gaze, and the weaving in her Nexum fell apart.

They stared at each other. Then the girl swore and turned to rework it.

Morlinna waited for Ashwyn to acknowledge the inevitable. This evasion made no sense. The girl had already agreed to be the one to kill Morlinna.

Right?

Morlinna swallowed, thinking back over the weeks. Ashwyn was as swift and as strong as a Bladesaint. She'd trained herself well over her life, and her diligence extended to her studies of the Nexum as well.

Morlinna trusted her ability in battle. But had Ashwyn ever actually said the words Morlinna needed to hear?

Her one condition. Ashwyn had never actually promised, had she?

Morlinna watched Ashwyn concentrate. The girl refused to meet her eyes, and Morlinna settled into the familiar sinking feeling.

The sense of being alone even when surrounded by people.

None of this would work if Morlinna couldn't trust Ash with the most important piece of her life: its end.

Chapter 35
Animatim

Vitania leaned back in her chair and rubbed her face, blotting out the view of her office and the papers strewn across the desk and floor.

Back when she'd started her investigation, they'd been a happy little web of connections and clues pasted to the wall, but the intervening months had not been kind to her organization. Or the investigation as a whole.

The incessant patter of rain on the roof pounded at her, each plop a spike driven into her skull, and the clang of the hammer felt as real as the edge of the desk against her hands.

She groaned, a guttural noise that made her teeth clench. A Judge didn't show weakness. A Judge didn't show frustration.

She sat forward, the legs of her chair slamming into the flagstones, and she reached up to yank the connection in her ear free. Blessed silence flooded her mind.

Before she'd become a Nexsaint, she couldn't manipulate the little loop of Nexum that hung over her ears. She had to trust Mender Misana to make any adjustments. But once she'd been able to see it, she was surprised by its simplicity.

V tried not to disrupt her hearing often. She needed every advantage, and if the Abdicant ever caught her at it, she'd never hear the end of it.

Her lips quirked despite the grim thought. Literally, she'd never *hear* the end of it, because her mother would make sure it was the last time.

But now she finally felt alone inside her own head with silence enough to think.

She pressed the heels of her hands to her temples.

She was out of leads. Saint Tayrin had vanished from the temple like a Nexsaint taking a Nexum jump. The investigators in the Saints' Hold had turned up nothing. None of the morgues reported an unidentified Bladesaint. And the hospitals all had plenty of patients, but all were well documented.

Tayrin was nowhere. Unless someone was hiding him.

She stood, the chair jolting across the cracks in the flagstones, and she stepped to the window. Rain trickled down the panes, but she flipped the latch and threw it open anyway to feel the cool air against her face.

The rain would be snow by tonight.

She stared across the yard of the Saints' Hold. A few novices practiced below, their blades running with water.

If someone *was* hiding Saint Tayrin, how would she find him?

She'd spent far too long waiting for the Saints' Hold to track down their wayward Saint. She'd even retraced her steps back to the temple and searched out the woman who'd caused enough of a disturbance to draw five Bladesaints from their duty. In case Saint Tayrin had managed to orchestrate the whole thing.

But the woman, happily ensconced with her new baby, had only been able to say that some Bladesaint on the street had directed her to the temple, recommending she get a blessing before her baby was born.

But that had been well before Tayrin had disappeared. According to Lieutenant Julianus, the Saint had still been in the Throne Hall at that time.

V spun and swept a hand across the desk, sending papers flying. A few caught the breeze from the open window and fluttered across the room.

She followed the movement, and her gaze caught on the young man standing in the open doorway, his fist raised as if he'd been knocking.

Mortis, how long had he been there?

She reached up to reposition the Nexum loop around her ears, bracing herself for the sounds of rain and settling paper.

"What?" she snapped.

"Sorry to disturb you, Your Serene Highness," the novice said. "There's been a message for you."

She breathed, stilling the frustration simmering beneath her surface. It wasn't this boy's fault that she'd been stalled for months.

"What is it?"

He held out an envelope marked with the Saints' Hold seal. "They said to tell you Saint Tayrin's been found."

Her heart leaped. "He has?" She snatched the envelope from him and tore it open, eyes scanning the contents before she'd even gotten it unfolded the whole way.

The address made no sense—it wasn't a hospital or morgue—but she was on her way in minutes, a heavy cloak pulled over her armor.

The house sat in the skirting district, outside the protective curve of the mountain. As V walked, the buildings grew closer together, and instead of towering over the streets, they leaned, their upper stories crowding out the sun.

V reached her destination, a cottage nearly at the edge of the river. Five washing lines trailed across the back yard, far more than a little house like this would need, and washing buckets stood stacked under the eaves, protected from the rain.

A Bladesaint already waited at the front door, standing at attention.

He saluted as she approached. "Judge Vitania," he said and opened the door.

She stepped through into a tidy, well-kept living space with a stove and a table against the wall on her right and a hallway leading to some small rooms on the left.

In the main space facing her, a temporary bed had been made in the window seat looking onto the backyard.

A man lay under the covers, his hair shaggy and his beard grown out. A woman in Mender's robes sat on a chair beside him, and another woman rose from the table to greet V.

"Thank you for coming, Nexsaint," the woman said. "We called for you as soon as we knew what was going on."

V took a breath and pasted a smile on her face. "Of course. Now maybe I can find out what's going on as well. Is this Saint Tayrin?"

"Yes. At least, that's what we've learned today."

"Saint Tayrin," she said, meeting the man's eyes. "I'm Judge Vitania Abdicantus, running a special investigation. I've been searching for you."

The woman beside her gasped and sputtered out a garbled "Your Serene Highness" as she sank into a deep curtsy.

V wanted to push past her to her quarry, but she forced her hands to relax by her sides. No one here was trying to run or keep her from the man. Saint Tayrin himself seemed more confused than anything, his brow furrowed and his eyes darting between her and the Mender.

The Mender stood and gave her a low bow. "I'm sorry, Your Serenity. Saint Tayrin has suffered a blow to the head. We weren't even sure he would live and now that he's awake, it seems he's lost much of his hearing."

V felt it like a blow. "He...he what?" That was not the most intelligent thing she'd ever said in her life.

"Deaf as a doorpost," Pallia said with a shake of her head. "Can't even hear the littles when they bang pots right by his bed."

The Mender winced. "There's more nuance than that, but...yes. Basically, he can't hear. Pallia here found him on the banks of the river nearly three months ago," the Mender said. "After pulling him out, it was obvious he wasn't well."

"That's nice speak for his head being nearly caved in," Pallia said. "Scared the kids half to death. But my husband let me set him up in the window to see if he'd get better."

"Why didn't you call for a Mender or a Nexsaint immediately?" V said, giving her a sharp look.

Pallia bit her lip. "We can't afford fancy healings. I didn't think anything of it. He'd either live or he wouldn't. That's all the rest of us do down here."

V flushed. Not only had she insulted the woman, it had been a stupid question here, so far from the heart of the city where so many could afford Menders. If a Judge couldn't know everything, she at least had to be aware of the gaps in her knowledge and work to fix them.

"He didn't have no uniform," Pallia said. "Probably had it stolen off of him before we got to him. So we had no idea he was a Saint."

Or whoever had hit him over the head had stripped him before dumping him in the river. Saint Tayrin could still have been wrapped up in the Goddess's untethering, but it was looking more and more like he was a victim as well.

"Pallia cared for him for weeks before he woke, and when he did, he was very confused with no way to communicate," the Mender said quietly. "I learned of his plight through my work in the area and came to see if I could help. We've been writing questions and answers back and forth."

She indicated the thin board covered in charcoal markings that Tayrin held.

Pallia shrugged. "More than I could do. Never learned to write. Don't need it to wash clothes."

"We sent word to the Saints' Hold as soon as we learned who he was," the Mender said.

V glanced at Tayrin, whose eyes had narrowed as he scratched something across the board. "Does this happen often?" she said. "A blow to the head causing hearing loss?"

The Mender gave her a crooked smile. "Sometimes. Heads are tricky things. Trauma can cause memory loss, permanent paralysis, death. It could be the blow, or it could be infection after being in the water for so long. We might never know."

Tayrin held up his board and V caught the fresh charcoal scrawl.

What's going on?

His gaze darted between V and the Mender.

A dull ache lodged in V's chest at the suppressed panic she saw there. She knew that feeling. Silence was her friend now, but there'd been a time when it had been terrifying. Sitting at the dinner table trying to understand her mother's words and moods and feeling alone even among her family.

V jerked her hand, asking the Mender to move, and she took the chair the Mender vacated.

Hello, Tayrin. I'm V.

It was easier than spelling out her entire designation. Besides, he could probably guess from her uniform.

He leaned over to read as she wrote.

I need to ask you some questions. Can you tell me what happened to you in the temple?

She turned back to the Bladesaint, who pushed himself up in the bed and reached for the board.

From the slant of his scrawl, he wanted to go fast, but he was hindered by the chunky piece of charcoal and the roughness of the board. V swore under her breath. She should carry a notebook for occasions like this.

There was a woman. She gave birth in the pools.

V nodded, encouraging him to go on.

The rest left. I stayed with the Goddess. Lutenant Julanus's orders.

In his haste, he misspelled the Lieutenant's name.

So you were alone in the Throne Hall?

V handed it back to him.

Yes. Until you came.

She knew what happened next from her perspective. But...Her gaze flicked to the two women in the room. She didn't want to say anything about the untethering in front of them. The Primarch had done a decent job smoothing it over so the city didn't go into a panic thinking their goddess could leave at any time.

Instead she moved on to the question that had burned in the back of her mind for months.

The Goddess had a bracelet with her. Made of grass. Do you know what happened to it?

His eyes widened, and he sat up straight, nodding hard enough to make him wince.

The Mender stepped forward. "Gently," she said, though the man couldn't hear it.

V leaned forward as Tayrin scribbled across the board, his breath coming harsh and fast as he tried to tell her what she needed to know.

She couldn't tell who was more impatient: her or Tayrin.

The charcoal broke in his fingertips, smearing his words, and he cried out in frustration. V tamped down on her own reaction. This wasn't easy and getting angry wouldn't help anyone.

Dea, if only she could sign with him.

Her fingers clenched in her lap, holding tight to the guilt that swept through her at the thought. But it was her guilt. Not Tayrin's. He didn't have to worry about looking weak in front of the other Saints. He didn't have to follow rules laid out by her mother.

She looked down at her hands and deliberately stretched her fingers out. Her language could help him. If his loss was permanent, he'd need a way to communicate. He'd need that connection with another human being. And a connection looped around his ear wouldn't work if he really did hear nothing.

Hadn't she gone to Mender Misana longing for a way to make herself heard and understood? How could she deny him this one just because it filled her with an assortment of comfort, nostalgia, and guilt?

She laid her hand against his, where his fingers clamped down on the broken charcoal.

She took it from him and found a clear space on the board.

I know this is hard, and nothing will make it easier. But I think I can help. I speak a hand language that lets me talk and understand even when I can't hear. It can help you. When you feel better, go to Mender Misana in the Saints' Hold. She can teach it to you.

Tayrin's mouth worked as he read. Then he stared at her before writing,

Tell me more. Please.

It will take work. It's learning a whole new language. But I think you should try it.

V made sure she had his attention. Then she pointed to her chest and signed her name, a V across her chest. It was easier for someone just learning than trying to spell out the whole thing.

Tayrin's eyes lit up, and he gleefully repeated her name sign.

Something in her chest loosened upon seeing it. She also had the strange urge to check over her shoulder, and she shook her head when she realized she was waiting for her mother to catch her.

"You know hand languages," the Mender said in surprise.

"Just the one," V said with a rueful smile. "I was born hard of hearing."

The Mender blinked. "I didn't know that," she said quietly.

V turned her face away to hide her grimace. "I'm not surprised." The Abdicant would not have spread the information around.

"Oh, it's a miracle from the Goddess. You really are Her chosen," Pallia whispered, and clasped her hands together over her chest.

V grinned. "More like divine coincidence," she said.

She pulled Tayrin's board toward her and wrote out the Saint's Petition. The one that came to her hands every time she felt lost or lonely. She figured it would help a fellow Saint.

Then she very carefully signed it out for him, making sure he had each one memorized before moving on to the next. It would take years before he'd be fluent, but this, at least, was a start.

Tayrin didn't smile at her, but the look in his eyes was somehow more than that. He held her hands and voiced, "Thank you."

She understood just fine even if the words came out wobbly.

He took the board back and wrote,

The bracelet. The Goddess had a bracelet on her lap. A man came and took it away. I followed him. He hit me. I woke up there.

Tayrin pointed out the window at the river passing behind the cottages. V sat forward in her chair, heart pounding.

Who hit you? Did you see him?

Tayrin held his fist as if he held a sword then wrote,

Bladesaint.

V held her breath as Tayrin painstakingly wrote out a name.
She froze.
He'd spelled it wrong, probably because he was in a hurry, but there was no mistaking who he meant.
There was only one "ex-commander" of the Bladesaints.

V stood outside the hovel where her father had lived for the last twelve and a half years. Six Bladesaints and two Nexsaints flanked her, waiting for her signal. Because arresting the ex-commander of the Bladesaints was too big for one person, even if that person was a Judge.

Especially if that person was family.

V shook her head, swallowing down a misery she hadn't expected. He'd betrayed her. He'd tried to sabotage her place as a Judge, and who knew what else he'd ruined in her early schooling. It shouldn't have surprised her to find more betrayal the deeper she looked.

If her father had attacked another Bladesaint, that made him a traitor. If he had placed the bracelet with the Goddess and then tried to cover it up, that made him a heretic. Only slightly less horrible than an apostate who'd willingly corrupted themselves with the Malady.

She gave the command to break the door down, and it fell under the first blow.

It was an insult. The former commander of the Bladesaints living in this...

this heap, outside the mountain on the opposite end of the city from the Palace and the Court and the Hold. But that's what happened when you crossed the Abdicant.

V stepped through the door, holding her hand to her nose. Flies buzzed around the fish decaying on the table. That was her first clue. The empty cot in the corner was her second.

The house was so small it only took one Bladesaint to make a thorough search.

"No one's here, Your Serenity," he said with a salute. "And there's no sign of where he went, either."

V gestured for the two Nexsaints, both of whom were skilled in tracking the connections made and left by fugitives.

But V was better, and she could already tell they wouldn't find anything. Her father wasn't a Nexsaint. But he'd been one of the greatest Bladesaints to ever live. He knew what he was doing.

His uniform hung on the stand beside the bed, clean and pressed. But his boots were gone. As was the pallet from his bed. It could have easily been rolled into a bedroll.

He'd left nothing behind with an emotional connection. Nothing they could follow to his person. And that was the most damning thing of all.

V stepped out of the house, breathing deep and shoving away everything except the numbness.

Only the guilty ran. Especially when the Judge coming after them was their daughter. There was no other reason her father wouldn't have been here, waiting to explain everything.

There'd been a part of her dreading it. And a part of her that had hoped for it, desperately.

The Saints still on the street stared at her, waiting, and she realized they were waiting for her to take the next step. Or to cover this up and let her father escape.

V's fists clenched, the nails biting into her palms hard enough to draw blood.

"Send a preliminary report to the Abdicant and the Primarch Divine," she said. "The ex-commander has fled. I will follow with the full report in an hour."

Chapter 36
Concordim

It was much harder to mark the passage of time in the Devastation, but Ashwyn was pretty sure she'd been with Morlinna for nearly two months when the other woman shook her awake one night. The rush light had burned down to a few smoldering brands in its wall sconce, and the magpie leader perched on the branch above her, head under his wing.

Ashwyn blinked in the dark, her heart racing. "What is it?" she slurred. Morlinna would not have woken her for something less than disaster.

"There's a problem we need to attend to. Now."

Ash sat up, shoving back her blankets. Her old overcoat hung in the corner where she'd placed it the first day. It was too bulky for use in the Devastation, and Morlinna had let her dig through their pilfered supplies to piece together a wardrobe.

Ash shoved her feet into a pair of supple leather shoes she'd put together for herself. They let her feel her way through the treacherous footing of the Devastation and find footholds within the knots of roots and leaves. And she snatched up the calf-length overcoat she'd tailored down to protect herself from the thorns and noxious saps of their home.

Morlinna had already passed back out into the open cloister, and Ashwyn hurried to follow.

"What's the problem?" she asked, fully awake now.

"A Devastation beast has been infected," Morlinna said.

Ashwyn sucked in a breath. Morlinna worked tirelessly to track down the trails of Malady and cut them off before anything could wander into them, but it was a never-ending task when the corruption could jump to new, unpredictable places. Morlinna said they'd been lucky so far this winter that all they'd found was a couple of bunnies and a squirrel that had to be given the Last Death.

Ash could tell from Morlinna's face this was much bigger than a bunny.

"Which way?" Ashwyn asked. Morlinna had brought her along on every hunt she could so far, but she'd never let Ashwyn help. Only watch. This felt different.

"Felleron is tracking it to the north. He'll guide us to its path."

Morlinna stepped to the door, then hesitated, her marred hand against the worn frame. Ash's gaze caught on the stark white lines through the puckered skin where her last two fingers had once been.

"What's wrong?" Ash asked.

Morlinna didn't answer. She stepped back across the temple toward the altar. Ash had never seen her panic or hurry her steps. She moved as fleet as a wolf, but always with grace and calm.

She pulled a long object from behind the altar and came back to Ash.

In her hand, she held another double-headed scythe. The shaft gleamed as if it had been polished, and one side reflected with the black strands of the healthy Nexum.

A thin sheath of obsidian covered the other blade. Morlinna pulled it free, revealing steel that glinted white with corruption. A band of obsidian kept the Malady from spreading down the shaft.

"It's just like yours," Ash said.

"Yes. I have several. I did not intend to give you one so early." She fell quiet for a moment, eyes on Ash's face.

What was she looking for? Some sign that Ash was worthy of carrying it?

Her breath caught as Morlinna held it out to her.

"Are you sure?" Ash said. She'd never practiced with a blade that could cut through the Nexum before, let alone one that could cut through corrupted strands.

"You need a way to defend yourself and clear the Malady in a fight. And I know I do not have to tell you to be careful with it. The Malady held in this will corrupt you as easily as it will corrupt any strands you choose to touch with it."

Morlinna slid the sheath back into place before dropping the weapon into Ash's palms.

Ash's fingers curled around the shaft, and her chest went tight. She held the weapon close. "I promise I'll only use it if I absolutely have to."

Morlinna nodded once, then turned to glide out into the dark Devastation.

A Nexsaint did not normally carry a weapon. Only Bladesaints and Judges needed blades.

But neither of them was a normal Nexsaint. The thought made her pulse speed up.

Ashwyn connected the scythe's threads with her own, so the weapon lay against her back and stayed with her as she moved through the trees. She'd have to be careful how she went. It would be too easy to get the curved blades caught on the hanging vegetation.

The Devastation lay before them, pitch black, with none of the filtered and patchy light making its way from above, and Ash wondered what time it actually was. The days were getting colder, and a fine layer of snow occasionally sifted between the big leaves and branches, coating the lower layers in slick ice.

Ash kept up as Morlinna stepped from one branch and ran along the next, always north and a little west as she followed Felleron's instructions in her head.

Eventually, the magpie leader dove through the branches to scold her as she raced to keep up.

"Sorry," Ash huffed. "You were asleep. I didn't think you'd want to come."

He sent her an image of a puffed-up mama magpie feeding a nest full of fluffy fledglings.

Ash snorted. "Does that mean you think of me as a nestling?"

He croaked, and she laughed, picking up on the subtleties in his voice. It was more that he thought she couldn't take care of herself without him.

She'd named him Marauder, because every other day he brought her some trinket he'd stolen from some poor human beyond the Devastation, and Morlinna had laughed and said he had the heart of a pirate. She laughed so rarely, and Ash had hoped that the name would make Morlinna smile when she heard it.

He tipped his wings to dart ahead, and she barely caught the glint of white feathers in the darkness. Down their connection, he sent her a flash of warning. As if he whispered, "Brace yourself."

And as soon as Ash caught up to Morlinna, she realized why.

A swath of Malady, white as chalk, wound through the Devastation. As wide as the road out of Edgefall and meandering like a creek with nowhere to be, it corrupted everything from the vines and roots to entire trees.

Ash recognized the trail of a corrupted creature. The Malady had taken root in its mind and driven it to move as erratically as possible, infecting the widest area as it went.

Ash gulped. "This will take forever to fix," she whispered, the weight of the scythe digging into her shoulder.

Poor Morlinna. The mysteries of the Devastation lurked under their feet, but she'd been trapped here in this endless cycle for over a decade. Always fighting, never getting the chance to search for answers.

Maybe there was another reason she'd given Ash the scythe. With it, Ash could help her clear the Malady.

Morlinna shook her head. "After we deal with the creature," she said. "There is no time now. The Malady spreads fast, but the creature will be faster. We must head it off."

Felleron appeared beside them, stalking along a branch just wide enough for his paws. Morlinna paused to touch his head in gratitude, and then she was off, unhooking her scythe to grab the next branch up and haul herself to a new layer.

Ash scrambled to follow. "Where is it going?" she called. "Can you tell?" Maybe if they could get ahead of it, they wouldn't have to follow its trail through the dark.

"The Malady craves life," Morlinna's voice came out of the darkness. "So its creatures will seek out the greatest concentrations of life to corrupt."

Ash's brow furrowed. They were already in the greatest concentration of life that Ash had ever heard of. The Devastation. But Morlinna had mentioned this before. That life was sacred to the Goddess, and the Malady sought to corrupt that. And humanity was the most sacred of Her creations.

They had to be nearing the northern edge of the Devastation. And there was only one great concentration of life along the crater.

Mortis, it was heading for Edgefall.

Ash stopped, her knees locking as the realization hit her. They were heading to save the village that had betrayed her.

Marauder squawked and circled back toward her, drawing Morlinna's attention. The other woman looked over her shoulder and realized that Ash was no longer moving with her.

Ash had no idea what her expression was doing. She couldn't control it at all. Her breath came in a ragged stream between her teeth, and her fingers clenched as if looking for something to hit or to crush.

"Tell me," Morlinna said.

"It's heading for Edgefall, isn't it?"

"Yes."

A jagged sound escaped her lungs, something between a laugh and a cry.

"You told me you did not seek revenge."

"I don't," Ash cried. "I didn't." She swallowed, trying to get past her dry throat. "I don't want anything to do with them."

The thought of seeing Cass or even Rafe made bile climb up her throat, and now she was swallowing for an entirely different reason.

Helping them was the antithesis of ignoring them.

"You would rather leave them to their fate," Morlinna said quietly.

"They deserve it!"

Morlinna glanced away as if Ash's pain cut her, and it was a long moment before she responded. Too long to wait for what they had to do.

"The Malady seeks to corrupt life. If it reaches Edgefall, the Order will come. They will evacuate the ones they can and destroy the rest. And you already know this will not stop the Malady. It will spread. All the way to Vitamorn and beyond. The Order may try to find the source. They may even track it back here."

Ash winced. She didn't care if the Order destroyed Edgefall. She didn't care if Cass had to find a new home. She didn't care if Bayna was forced to leave the village she'd spent her life building.

But she did care if the Order made it back here to the Devastation.

Images flooded her thoughts. Uniforms tromping through the temple, the Goddess statue smashed, Morlinna's prayer beads scattered across the floor, a shadowy Judge slicing Morlinna's head from her shoulders.

Ash pressed the back of her hand to her mouth. The Order couldn't find Morlinna. It would end everything.

Finally, she could move her feet again.

Morlinna saw and nodded, the crisis pushed back. For now.

Ash followed, ignoring the thought that the images in her head would horrify Morlinna.

Morlinna thought of herself as some executioner. A murderer with a sense of duty. But she cared about people. She killed a few in order to save many.

She was the hero here. Ash cared about one person exactly, and somehow, she knew Morlinna would not be impressed to find out it was her.

The trail carved its way through the Devastation, as if the creature had blundered blindly from path to path, leading them from the layer Ashwyn thought of as the surface up to the canopy, where Ash could see stars peering through the gaps between frost-covered leaves.

Here, the path of white, writhing strands plunged through the layers, as if the creature's weight had made it plummet. They followed it down again.

Until the trail dove into one of the wide tunnels where Devastation beasts lurked.

Ash sent Marauder up to fly along above them. He wouldn't be of any help in the tunnels, where thick vines and roots kept everything closed in. Morlinna did the same with Felleron.

They traveled the length of the roots, and Ashwyn concentrated on Morlinna's back, keeping her thoughts to the here and now, not the past where memories—and the feelings that came with them—kept trying to distract her.

So she nearly ran into Morlinna when the other woman stopped abruptly.

Thick vines and roots blocked the tunnel ahead where the overgrowth had shifted and cut off the prior pathway.

Their trail disappeared under the heavy growth straight ahead.

Ash glanced at Morlinna, expecting her to know what to do. But the other woman's nostrils flared and her breath came quicker.

"Felleron," she said aloud. "Can you pick up the trail above?"

Ashwyn obviously couldn't hear the answer, but Morlinna's silence and stillness was all she needed.

Ash reached out to Marauder and the magpies, asking them to search along the nearby layers. She got flashes of branches and vines and leaves as they passed under black and white wings, but nothing gleamed with the sickly white sheen of the Malady.

Morlinna met her eyes, and Ash had to shake her head. "They aren't finding anything either."

Morlinna blew out her breath and spun to the obstruction. She swung her scythe around and slashed through the curtain of vines. But another layer followed the first. And another. The tunnel had collapsed, taking their route with it. Who knew where the creature would have surfaced?

The next step was to section off the forest and search systematically to pick up the trail. The way they did when they were looking for new spots of corruption. But that would take days.

Morlinna fell back, her arms trembling with exertion.

"How long do we have?" Ash asked quietly.

"Given the rate it was moving?" Morlinna said, face grim. "An hour. Maybe less."

Ash's gut clenched.

Morlinna paced to the wall of roots, then two steps back. Then she folded her legs and sat right in the middle of the tunnel.

Ash watched her close her eyes and breathe deep. Her own gaze flicked down the tunnel, looking for anything creeping up on them.

"What are you doing?" she asked.

Morlinna cracked an eyelid to glance at her. Then winced.

Ash realized with a jolt that there were still plenty of secrets that Morlinna kept from her. Trust fluttered fragile between them.

"I'm going to find our quarry," the other woman said quietly. "Please keep watch. I can't do this if I have to defend my physical body as well."

Ash went cold. "Can't do what?" Her voice squeaked on the last word.

Morlinna sighed. "I am going to connect with the Malady."

Ash recoiled. "You can do that?"

Morlinna's face contorted, and Ash immediately regretted the question.

"The corruption is something I have to push back every day of my life," Morlinna said, voice echoing strangely against the root walls around them. "It wants to take me. It takes effort to hold it off. But if I open myself to it..."

"You can find it. I mean you can find where it is nearby."

"Yes."

Then why did she spend so much time roaming the forest looking for spots of corruption? If she had this sense that would lead her right to it? But Ashwyn knew better than to ask that out loud. If Morlinna thought something was too dangerous to use, she had a good reason.

"Once this takes hold," Morlinna said through her teeth. "Do not touch me. The Malady will be close enough to the surface to corrupt you."

Ash swallowed. "Yes, Rector," she whispered.

Morlinna's eyes flicked open in surprise, and her brows twitched down. Then she went still, and Ash felt as if she'd left entirely, even though the woman sat right there.

Ash pulled the scythe from her back. Just in case.

For a long moment, nothing happened, and Ash wondered if she was supposed to see anything.

And then Morlinna seized. Her spine went ramrod straight, and she threw her head back so hard Ash leaped forward to catch her, only remembering at the last moment that she wasn't supposed to touch her.

Morlinna kept herself upright, almost as if a force had reached out to prevent her toppling over. Then she ducked her head and breathed hard, like she ran from disaster.

Ash couldn't see the battle going on in Morlinna's body, but she did not doubt that it was actually a battle. The cords in Morlinna's neck stood out and her shoulders hitched up to her ears, as if she held the gate against an invisible onslaught.

And then she relaxed, her shoulders falling and her head drooping, and Ash wondered who had won.

Except there wasn't anyone else here. Right? Just Morlinna...and the Malady.

Morlinna raised her head finally and opened her eyes.

"Dea protect me," Ashwyn whispered, completely forgetting her resolve not to invoke the Goddess who'd betrayed her.

Morlinna's eyes had gone white all the way through, and the lines in her face writhed.

She slowly rose to her feet, and Ashwyn skipped back a step.

She'd said not to touch her. That was why she retreated. Not for any other white-eyed reasons.

Ash could feel her heart beating in her throat as Morlinna turned in a slow circle. Then the other woman started moving. Back down the tunnel and out into the more open air of the upper layers.

Ashwyn followed her, keeping her lips clamped shut and the scythe held tightly in her hands.

Felleron joined them as soon as they surfaced, twining around Morlinna without actually touching her.

Marauder dove under a branch then squawked when he saw Morlinna. He flashed away through the trees, and Ash didn't blame him in the slightest.

Morlinna moved unerringly through the night, silent as a shadow, and it was all Ashwyn could do to keep up without crashing through the branches and vines she could barely make out. Dark had always been harder to navigate with half her vision gone. She could barely tell where the real world began and the blur ended.

They'd walked for nearly a half an hour when Morlinna stopped abruptly.

"There," she said. "It will surface just below."

At the sound of her voice, Ash's breath whooshed from her lungs, somewhere between a sigh and a sob.

Morlinna glanced at her, eyebrow raised. The expression looked so normal Ash almost forgot about the stark white eyes. Almost.

"What is it?" Morlinna said.

"I thought—" It seemed silly now, but she'd thought Morlinna was gone. Possessed or erased by something or someone who'd taken control of her body.

But that was stupid. And clearly wrong. Morlinna looked back at her with the same sense of steady amusement tinged with regret. Ash was pretty sure by now that she wasn't the source of the regret. But she had yet to erase it from the other woman's countenance entirely.

"Sorry," Ash muttered. "I'm ready now." She settled her new scythe in her palms to prove it to herself as well as Morlinna.

Morlinna gave her a nod. Then her chin jerked, and her shoulders twitched. Like she'd heard something alarming. But she turned away, and Ash realized they stood at the edge of the crater where she'd fallen on her first day in the Devastation.

Vines and roots covered the bare rock, disguising the threshold where the cliff towered over them before plunging below the layer where they stood.

"How far down does it go?" Ash asked.

"I do not know," Morlinna said, staring at the layer under their feet. "I have never reached the bottom."

A snuffling sound broke through the silence of the Devastation, and Ash jumped.

"Ready yourself," Morlinna whispered.

Just ahead, only feet away from the crater's edge, a low spot in the vines indicated a passage to one of the tunnels below. They twitched and heaved as something pushed from underneath.

And a huge bear burst through the vines, sending bits of broken roots and leaves flying in all directions. Spikes bristled along its back as it shook, and tusks thrust from its jaw.

White eyes glistened in the dark as it swung its head, searching. It took one moment to stare up the cliff, toward the distant village. Then it lowered its gaze to Ash.

"Now," Morlinna whispered.

At the same time, the bear roared and charged.

They'd never actually done this together, but Ash knew her place in this plan without having to be told.

Morlinna dove left while Ash dove right.

The bear veered and came after her. But Ash was expecting it. With Morlinna corrupted—and therefore unpalatable to the Malady—Ash's role would always be as bait.

Ash reached for a strand in the branches above and wrapped it around her wrist. With a tweak, she sent herself soaring out of the creature's grasp and landed lightly on the branch. If she stayed above it, she would be less likely to blunder into strands that the beast had already corrupted.

In that moment of peace, she slid the sheath from the corrupted blade of her scythe and attached it behind her. She might not get a chance later.

The bear roared loud enough they could probably hear it in the village, and Ash thought of all those nights she'd lain in bed in the orphan house and listened to the noises of the Devastation beyond.

How many of them had been Morlinna battling a corrupted creature?

Ash shook herself and leaped to the next tree as the bear rammed its corrupted head into the trunk.

She frowned. She hadn't thought of that. She would run out of room fast if it deliberately started corrupting her platforms.

But one thing was going right. The creature was so focused on Ash that it wasn't even looking for Morlinna.

Ash reached out for a strand and swung herself across the open space, feet gliding over the bear's head.

The bear stood up on its hind legs and slashed at her. But she angled herself so that as she passed, it overbalanced backward and crashed to the ground.

Morlinna leaped out of the darkness and brought her scythe around to cut through the creature's corrupted threads.

A great claw met her in the air and batted her aside.

Ash cried out from her perch in the trees.

Another bear stood in the tunnel's opening, and with a menacing growl, it stalked forward to stand over its mate.

The first bear stood and shook itself.

Then they both raised their gazes to Ash.

Ash gulped.

The bears rushed the tree, and Ash threw herself down to wrap her arms around a branch as they slammed into the trunk. The whole tree shook, and Ash gasped and shifted her grip so she wouldn't slip. One of the bears snorted and began climbing.

But that wasn't all she had to worry about. The strands under its paws went white and twisted, and the corruption climbed up the trunk faster even than the bear. It would reach Ashwyn before the creature did.

She glanced toward the vines where Morlinna had landed, but the other woman wasn't there anymore.

Mortis.

The Malady surged through the tree's branches toward her grasping fingers.

Ash let go of the branch.

As she fell, she reached for an uncorrupted thread of a nearby tree and wove it with one of her own. It was sloppy work, but she'd been practicing the different weaves, and this was the second she'd mastered.

Her skin went hard and bark-like just before she hit the ground. It still knocked the wind out of her, but she hadn't broken anything.

The bear swung its head toward her, and it lifted its great weight as if to stomp her.

As it reared back, Morlinna arced overhead, scythe flashing. The skin along the bear's back parted, and the threads beneath withered.

The bear screamed, a wretched sound that brought its mate crashing to the ground from the tree.

Ashwyn lost no time rolling out of the way, avoiding the vines where the Malady spread.

Finally, both creatures turned their attention to the real threat. The one who could end their miserable existence.

Morlinna wasn't nearly so limited in which strands she could weave into herself. She moved with the fleetness of her wolf and the fluidity of a brisk stream, and from the way she darted around the bears, using the shadows to trick them, she had given herself better sight in the dark.

Ash clambered to her feet and skipped back, finding a clear enough space to stand amidst the creeping disaster of the Malady.

On the other side of the clearing, Morlinna ducked and rolled, coming up on the other side of the bear to slash with the white-slicked side of her scythe. She fought like a brawler, getting close and hitting hard.

But she wasn't in a good position. Her strikes angered the creatures but didn't kill them. With two bears to fight instead of one, she had to work twice as hard. And thick muscle and fur covered their heart threads.

Ash stood there uselessly. She swung her own scythe around, but the new weapon felt heavy and clumsy in her hands.

Morlinna leaped over the creatures again as Felleron darted in to snap at their paws, making them duck back. But he couldn't get close, either, unless he wanted to risk corruption.

Morlinna's scythe sliced across a bear's flank, and the creature roared as its blood spilled across the vines. Its back leg collapsed, and Morlinna darted forward.

She brought her scythe across its throat, severing its jugular and the corrupted heart thread at the same time.

But its mate roared and lunged.

And caught Morlinna's arm in its jaws just as she raised her head to see. It swung its head and flung Morlinna aside.

"No!" Ash cried.

Morlinna landed and rolled to her feet, panting, but her arm hung at her side, limp, bloody, and bent at an angle that made Ash sick.

Felleron fell back to guard her, teeth bared as she caught her breath.

And Ash could no longer stand the feeling of being the useless bait.

She leaped forward, swinging her scythe.

The one bear still on its feet met her, and she ducked under its claws, stepping only on uncorrupted spots along the vines.

It reared up, ready to swipe at her or crush her. She didn't care which. It was an opening either way.

She brought her scythe under, using the blade to gut it along the thick fur of its belly.

The scythe did its work against the bear's skin, and the weave along its blade cut through the corrupted threads in its body.

But the white of infection leaped to the blade and raced through the metal.

Ash stumbled forward, gasping.

She'd used the wrong end. This was the uncorrupted blade. Which she'd just infected.

Oh mortis.

The bear's blood poured out, and something darker fell down to trail against the vines, but the beast didn't stop. Just like an Absent person, it would keep going until someone delivered the Last Death.

But if Ash took the time to do that, the corrupted scythe in her hands would corrupt *her*.

Ash staggered back and braced the ruined blade against the ground and stomped on the shaft, right in the middle. The wood snapped, and she sliced through its threads, severing them before the corruption had crept too far.

Now she held half a weapon and faced the relentless beast.

It stood up on its back paws, the rent in its belly sagging and grotesque. In the dark, Ash could only guess at the lumps she saw.

It lifted one massive paw and swung at her.

Ash raised the broken scythe between herself and the bear, but the blade was angled all wrong. It would do nothing jutting off to the side like that.

She spun, turning, so the blade caught the blow.

This time with the edge Morlinna had corrupted for her.

The force of it shivered through her entire body.

But the edge of her blade sliced through skin and muscle and bone like a clearer's axe, and the bear's paw fell away behind her, cut clean from its body.

The bear fell back, howling. Ragged ends of the bear's corrupted strands waved from its severed limb.

Morlinna's figure darted between Ash and the bear, wielding her scythe one-handed.

She surged forward, her feet sure on the corrupted vines, and she swung her scythe around the back of the bear's neck and yanked, severing its head from its body.

The bear fell back and toppled to the ground. Its threads curled up and went dark in a wave, and the bear's body fell to dust beside the disintegrated remains of its mate.

Ash fell to her knees and held out her hands, searching for any hint of infection.

Nothing. Her strands remained healthy black lined with gold.

But where was Morlinna? She'd been hurt.

Ash shook out her arm and rose, spinning around in the dark.

The other woman still knelt beside the piled remains of the bears, hands buried in the dust of their ruins. The fingers of her good hand clenched and unclenched, leaving tracks in the pile. The lines across her face writhed, and she squeezed her eyes closed, but Ash worried what she'd see if they were open.

Had the white spread? Little tendrils of it crept from the corners of the older woman's eyes.

Ash stepped forward and yelped when Marauder darted in front of her.

Bad, came his call along the bond between them. *Bad ground.*

Ash glanced down at writhing white strands. The Malady. Of course. It had covered nearly every inch of the clearing. She couldn't get close to Morlinna. And Ash wouldn't be able to touch her if she did.

She had to fight this battle alone.

And Ash had no doubt she was fighting.

Sweat streaked Morlinna's forehead, and the cords in her neck stood out as the white lines throughout her skin writhed higher and higher, creeping toward her heart.

Morlinna cried out, and a mighty shudder went through her body. She collapsed, her head falling against her arms as she heaved in great gulps of air. But between her arms, Ash saw her blink, and the white had gone from her eyes, leaving them a light, ghostly blue.

The barest hint of light came in the cracks between the leaves and the cliff. Dawn. Somewhere above them, the people of Edgefall would be waking. If Ash strained her ears, she could imagine the temple bell ringing, calling everyone to morning prayers.

Ash glanced at the half-weapon in her hand and then at the corrupted strands separating her from Morlinna. At least she was holding the correct half. She raised her scythe and struck through the corrupted strands at her feet. The white threads shriveled and curled away, leaving nothing but clean husks and a path Ashwyn could follow to Morlinna.

The other woman sat up as she approached, her throat bobbing as she tried to swallow. Ash took her waterskin from her belt and handed it to Morlinna.

Morlinna reached for it with her good hand, and her tattered sleeve fell back, revealing her skin up to her elbow.

Ash stared, forgetting the water.

The white lines in Morlinna's arms no longer writhed like they had moments ago, but they lined her veins all the way to the bend in her arm.

Yesterday they'd only reached halfway between her wrist and her elbow.

Morlinna followed her gaze. She went stiff, and the blood drained from her face. Then she tugged the water from Ash's limp hand and turned away to take a sip.

This was the toll Morlinna had talked about. She'd said she had to hold it back every moment. That it was always trying to take more of her, but Ash hadn't thought about what that actually meant.

The Malady was taking her a piece at a time. When she opened herself up to it, it surged forward, stealing more and more.

Ash's mouth went dry as she recalled her own rash words. "I can fight it."

How stupid she'd been. She'd had no idea.

They'd won. They'd kept the creatures from corrupting the village, but at what cost? Morlinna had lost another piece of herself. And for what? To protect a bunch of people who had already hurt them? A bunch of people who would kill them if they knew they'd taken refuge here.

Morlinna wasn't looking at her, and Ash couldn't shake the feeling that she was the reason why.

Morlinna's other arm lay in her lap, her forearm torn and bloodied, and with a jolt, Ash was sure she could see bone against the mess. She tore strips from her shirt and knelt beside Morlinna. Very, very gently she reached out and took the ruined arm in her palms.

"I can't fix this for you," she said. The words hurt. She had so much left to learn.

Morlinna shook her head, but she still didn't look at Ash. "I will. Later. I... can't yet."

"I'm going to wrap it to keep it still and to stop the bleeding."

Morlinna's breath came faster as Ash carefully tended the wound, keeping her touch as gentle as she could.

"Are you hurt?" Morlinna asked her, voice grating. "Corrupted?"

"No." Ash glanced at her hands again. "I don't think so."

"You fought well. Well done."

Ash ducked her head to hide the way her breath hitched and her cheeks burned.

She finished tying off Morlinna's makeshift bandage. It wouldn't do much for long. They'd need to tend to it soon, and Ash had every intention of making Morlinna walk her through the process so next time she wouldn't be so useless. But Morlinna went stiff, and Ash glanced up.

Morlinna's gaze had gone distant and fierce, then she flinched.

"What is it?" Ash whispered.

Morlinna shook her head. "Nothing," she said as if coming back from a distant thought.

Ashwyn frowned. "It's not nothing. Something hurt you."

When Morlinna hesitated again, Ash huffed. "Please talk to me. *I'm* not the thing that's hurting you."

Morlinna met her eyes, startled. Then her gaze softened.

"No, you're not," she said softly. Her voice was so dark and husky, and it reached a place in Ashwyn's chest that made her feel hot and shivery at once.

"It speaks to me," she said, and Ash had to pull her thoughts back to what she'd asked in the first place.

"What does?" she said.

"The Malady."

Ash sucked in a breath, and Morlinna tipped her head back as if to drink in the sunlight that never reached this level of the Devastation.

"It calls to me. I hear it sometimes, urging me to give myself up to it. To let it take over. It is always worse after I connect with it. Sometimes, then, I'm tired and...I want to let it have me."

Morlinna so rarely touched her, and Ash had wondered if she hated touch. Or if she just didn't know how anymore. Or if she ever did.

Ashwyn slid her fingers under Morlinna's. Not forcing her to hold her hand. Just offering it silently. In case she wanted to.

Morlinna started, and Ash's heart clenched, worried she'd just ruined it all.

But then Morlinna's fingers curled around hers, just enough.

Morlinna met her eyes, and Ash's stomach fluttered.

That seemed to give Morlinna the strength to stand. She held her wounded arm close to her body and used the other to straighten her robe.

Felleron came toward her, her scythe held in his jaws.

Morlinna took a deep breath and then took the scythe. She stepped around the clearing, cutting corrupted strands as she went.

Ash watched her go, noting the circles under Morlinna's eyes. They were dark, not white, but she could see the exhaustion in Morlinna's movements, the way her hands trembled on the scythe.

Ash's muscles twitched and bruises were forming along her back and shoulders where she'd fallen.

"Do we have to clear the trail right now?" she said quietly. "Can't it wait till we've rested?"

Morlinna glanced up the cliff where the morning light was just turning the furthest edge pink. "We must keep it from reaching the village. There is no time to rest."

Ash's lips thinned. "You know they won't thank you for it."

Morlinna gave her a look, one light eyebrow arched, and Ashwyn flushed. All the warmth from their earlier touch fled.

"I don't do it for the thanks," Morlinna said and turned to continue her sweep.

Ash swallowed. She could have said "we," but she hadn't. Because Ashwyn wasn't selfless the way Morlinna was. She wasn't good the way Morlinna was good. It was the corrupted apostate who was protecting people and losing pieces of herself while she did it.

While Ashwyn fought with herself not to leave them all to death and corruption.

Morlinna was the bravest, strongest, most selfless person Ash had ever known. And Ash knew she didn't have any of that in her.

But she could follow the one who did.

She stood and took up her scythe, treading in Morlinna's footsteps to be sure they cleansed away every piece of the Malady from the forest.

Chapter 37
Concordim

By the time they returned to Morlinna's cloister, it had to be late afternoon. The inner clock Ashwyn had developed in the Devastation's gloom told her it was long past dinnertime.

Morlinna had done most of the work, ranging up and down the creatures' path, clearing the Malady from the forest one leaf and branch at a time. Ashwyn had done her best, clearing up the sides and checking their progress so Morlinna could concentrate on the worst sections.

Ash hurried ahead the last few feet and got the fire going while Morlinna staggered inside. Felleron supported her on one side as she held her torn arm against her chest.

Morlinna kept a cistern on the roof where water from snow and rain could gather and melt and be used below for cooking and washing. Ash turned the knob on the pipe and filled a pot and set it over the flames to boil while Morlinna settled herself against an ancient stone pew.

Morlinna had never moved them to give herself more living space. Ash had never been able to make this place feel like home because it was too much of a temple.

But with Morlinna sitting there, watching her, Ash could imagine a time when it might be...if Morlinna was there, too.

The thought struck her like a gust of wind on a calm day, and her feet halted on the worn flagstones.

She tried it again, just to see how it made her feel.

I could live here forever as long as Morlinna was with me.

The words went down her spine and settled in her gut, comfortable and sure.

"Ashwyn?" Morlinna said, snapping her back to real life. "Are you all right?"

She never called her Ash. Always Ashwyn. Ash liked it. She liked the formal lilt of her deep voice. She liked the deliberateness in Morlinna's every movement. The other woman did nothing without thinking it through and knowing herself inside and out. Morlinna would never trust the wrong person or do the wrong thing in the wrong moment.

"I'm fine," Ash said, a little out of breath, and hurried to help Morlinna tie back her sleeve so they could tend to her arm properly.

When they were done, the bone was set, and the skin had started to heal over, taking its cue from a healthy strand in Ash's own arm. It wasn't exactly the connection she'd been hoping for with the other woman, but Ash would take anything she could get.

She helped Morlinna to bed after they'd both washed the blood from their hands and gulped some dried fruit.

Morlinna slept in a room across the cloisters from Ash, and she'd made it into a tidy home, with a straw mattress on a bed strung with dried vines and a crate upended nearby to hold her candle and a book.

Ash helped her lie down and resisted the urge to tuck her in. Felleron curled up beside the bed. The last thing Ash saw before she pushed through the curtain across the opening was Morlinna's long face go soft in sleep.

Ash rubbed her chest, trying to ease the ache as she stepped across the cloisters to her own room. Morlinna didn't have the same round features Cass had. No one would call her a beauty with her strange light eyes and sharp chin. But her nose and brows reflected her strength, and that was what kept Ash awake that night.

Morlinna's quiet countenance hid power and resolve and a fierce need to protect people, even from themselves.

Ash curled up on her side, holding the feelings close to her chest.

It was too early for them. She'd known Morlinna for a handful of weeks. She should not have this wave of comfort every time she thought of her. Compared to Cass...

But that was the problem, wasn't it? She'd known Cass her entire life, and it hadn't changed anything when Ash had ultimately asked her to trust her.

The warmth in her belly should have warned her away. Should have told her to slow down. To stop this before it was too late, and she was betrayed by her own feelings again.

But she'd never thought she'd feel this way again. She'd thought Cass had broken something inside of her.

She finally fell asleep curled tight around it, as if protecting it a little longer would make the feeling strong enough to withstand anything.

In the morning, she found Morlinna praying as she usually did. The woman would have made a wonderful priest if she hadn't ended up a Nexsaint.

Ash was enjoying a bowl of oat porridge when Morlinna finally put away her prayer beads and joined her.

"How is your arm?" Ash asked.

In response, Morlinna held out the arm in question. Her sleeve remained pushed high to reveal a puckered scar where the bear had tried to tear a chunk out of her the day before.

"It will continue to heal over time," Morlinna said. "And you?"

Ash shrugged. The bruises had spread and turned a nasty black overnight, but she could still hold her bowl, so she wasn't complaining. "Same," she said.

Morlinna reached gingerly for another bowl and spooned some soupy porridge into it for herself.

"I have been thinking about how to improve for next time."

Ash paused, spoon halfway to her mouth. "Oh." Her voice went flat.

Morlinna raised her eyebrows and caught Ash's gaze. "You did very well. Better than I would have hoped. This is not a complaint, but rather an acceleration of the timeline because now I believe you can handle it."

"Oh," Ash said again, this time with an entirely different inflection, and she sat up straighter.

"Your weaves are improving, and you already fight like a Bladesaint."

Ash pressed her lips together and glanced down. "I didn't realize...I feel like I could learn faster."

"It is harder to mark improvement when you have no one to judge yourself against."

Ash almost expected her to say, "This is why you should train in Vitamorn," but for once she didn't.

"It would be a good idea to be able to communicate more effectively," Morlinna said. "Across distances but also during battle."

Ash sucked in a breath as she realized what Morlinna meant. "You're not worried I'll get corrupted?"

"I was," Morlinna said. "But I believe you have enough control now to keep from grabbing the wrong threads."

And Morlinna was more complicated than one of the corrupted creatures they fought to kill. Even sitting here eating breakfast in the dim light of the fire, Ash could see she was made up of a tangle of healthy black threads weaving through corrupted strands that pulsed sickly white.

And Ash had a new appreciation for the effort Morlinna went through every day to keep those two separate and not let the corruption have more than its fair share of her.

Ash thought she had done a good job containing her excitement until Morlinna had finished her breakfast and stood, but she couldn't keep her hands from trembling.

Morlinna arranged Ashwyn opposite her as Marauder led a flock of magpies into the temple. They settled themselves on the branches and vines that climbed through the holes in the roof as Morlinna glanced up at them.

"They must think something is going to happen," she said, and Ash flushed.

She could hide her excitement from Morlinna, but not from Marauder. The lead magpie always lived in the back of her head nowadays. She could have disconnected him, but he seemed to prefer to be near her, and she liked having his eyes and ears available.

Morlinna carefully detached one end of a strand and held it out for Ash.

This made it much easier. Ash didn't have to reach through the mess of corrupted threads to find a healthy one. Ash gave her a grateful look and attached one of her strands to Morlinna's.

The weave snapped into place as if they belonged together, and the ends wrapped around each other.

A flood of warmth surged through Ash the moment the connection was in place, filling the empty spaces of her mind and body with a strange sense of someone else overlaid on top of her.

Ash gasped, trying to remember how to breathe on her own when she had a ghostly pair of lungs somewhere beyond herself.

Steady, Morlinna said into her mind. *It can be a lot at first. Take it one breath at a time.*

The brush of thought against her mind sent a shiver through Ash. Morlinna's touch felt like dark honey on bread and sunlight on her skin. Like lying in tall grass facing each other, as if no one else in the world existed.

Did she feel this, too? Was she the one sending this image? Was this what Morlinna imagined when she thought of Ash?

Ash tried to send a thought down the thread of connection, but the moment she pushed it, it raced away from her, spearing straight toward Morlinna. The connection made everything easier.

The thought that had started as a simple greeting dragged a feeling of contentment with it, then a stray appreciation of Morlinna's hair and the way it framed her face, and with that went a whole host of other things until suddenly Ashwyn's entire mind opened, and every thought and feeling she had for Morlinna went racing toward the other woman.

Some were tame enough, but others were things she would have rather kept hidden in the dark of her room at night.

Morlinna's eyes widened as the rush of Ashwyn's thoughts and emotions struck her like a flash flood traveling downstream.

And for one split second, Ashwyn saw her reaction. The one inside her head that she would never have chosen to say out loud if Ashwyn's blunder hadn't forced her.

Nothing came as words, just a rush of shock and beneath it, a tangle that felt like fear and shame and something desperate quickly hidden underneath it.

Morlinna reached out and snapped the connection before anything else could be sent down the line by either of them.

Ashwyn dropped to her knees, feeling the weight of someone else's thoughts and emotions pressing down on top of her. Even though she knew they couldn't be there anymore.

Morlinna kept her feet, but she swayed and pressed a hand to her heart as if it was also beating too fast.

"I'm sorry," Ash mumbled, fighting through the memory of Morlinna's feelings to find her own. She should be mortified; she knew that. But it was buried somewhere too deep to feel yet.

"No," Morlinna said with a breath. Then her shoulders steadied, and she tried again. "No. It's not your fault. The connection can be overwhelming at first. And I did not think to warn you. It can...spin thoughts and emotions until they are far larger and more out of control than they actually are."

It was an excuse. An explanation she could grasp and run with to save herself some embarrassment. To save Morlinna, too.

But...it wasn't true. All the feelings Morlinna had seen, those were true. Out of control, yes, but not any larger than Ash had made them. And now they were out there, hanging between them where they both could see. For good or for ill. And Ash had never been able to deny the things she felt or the degree to which she felt them. She was not going to stuff them back down.

She pushed herself to her feet. "That might be part of it, but that's not all of it," she said.

Morlinna cocked her head as if she was inviting Ash to elaborate, but something hesitant lurked in her eyes.

"What do you mean?"

"You know what I mean."

Morlinna swallowed, and Ash watched the movement travel all the way down her long throat. "No."

"I think I love you."

Morlinna froze, her eyes going wide and panicked before she closed them.

Oh mortis.

"No, you don't," Morlinna said.

Ash huffed a laugh, too surprised to monitor her next words. "You can't tell me how I feel or don't feel. Especially not when you just saw it."

Morlinna opened her eyes again, and her face had settled into that calm, clear expression that told Ash exactly nothing.

"I don't even know what I just saw. Connecting with someone is not an exact science. And without control—"

"You saw everything I've ever thought about you."

"Then you are confused about who I am."

"You are the bravest, most selfless person I know. Why wouldn't I love you?"

Morlinna sighed, and her expression softened a little. "It isn't real, Ashwyn. You respect me as a—as a teacher. Of course, you do. And that is natural. But it is the teacher's duty to protect the student. Even from themselves. There's too much power held by one half over the other. I would never, ever take advantage of that."

Ash's fists bunched. "I'm asking you to," she cried.

Morlinna stepped back and dropped her gaze like she'd realized she'd lost control of the conversation or because she'd decided to drop it entirely.

And something in Ashwyn knew she'd broken everything. Again.

"I do not think you should stay if this is going to be an issue."

The words fell between them, and Ash sucked in a breath, her chest seizing.

Morlinna turned and picked up the breakfast bowls. As if that was it. She was moving on with her life.

"If I am a distraction, then your life is in danger. But more than that. If you cannot fulfill your promise to me, then there is no need for you."

Ash's heart caved. "What?"

Morlinna dumped the bowls into the bucket beside the hearth. "I made it very clear that I wanted one thing from you."

And Ash had never promised it. "I'm not going to kill you—"

Morlinna whirled. "Then I cannot trust you."

Ash had thought they would move past Morlinna's need for death. That they would find a different way forward together. But she could finally see that Morlinna had been holding herself apart this whole time. It was Ash who had pushed her and convinced her and fought for their time together.

And now Ash was angry and embarrassed enough to stop fighting.

Morlinna returned her gaze to the bucket, as if Ash's answer didn't matter to her at all.

"Fine," Ash said, voice hoarse.

Oh mortis, it was Cass all over again. At least she hadn't slept with this one first. But throwing herself at someone so wildly repulsed by her might be worse.

Her broken scythe stood propped by the door where she'd left it the day before, and she snatched it up without really thinking about it. It was her only possession besides her clothes, and it felt good to wrap her hands around the haft.

Marauder dove from his branch, and the rest of the flock took wing around them. Morlinna didn't look up from the bucket.

Ash stormed out of the temple amidst a flurry of magpies.

Chapter 38
Obitusim

There was no door in the ancient building, but the curtain Morlinna had hung long ago swished behind Ash as she left.

She kept her back to the opening, counting silently until she couldn't hear the girl anymore. Then she stepped to the altar, movements smooth and unhurried...

And she collapsed against the stone with a gasp. Her heart still pounded from that overwhelming moment of connection. The flood had nearly taken her with it, overwhelming and drowning her in feeling, and she couldn't even be sure what had belonged to her and what had belonged to Ash.

She shuddered, dragging in breath after breath.

But even as her hands shook, her mind remained clear.

"Go after her," she whispered to Felleron. "Make sure she gets to the crater's edge all right."

But silence greeted her. She'd forgotten the wolf had left early that morning to check on his mate and cubs after the disaster the day before. And she'd suppressed the connection with him to give him some privacy. Morlinna sat in the temple alone.

No, never alone. The Goddess stared down at her as she hunched her head against the altar.

She was never supposed to feel like this again. She'd been so careful. So removed. But it turned out she wasn't the one she'd needed to worry about.

She should have been clearer from the beginning. If Ash had just understood, she would have known Morlinna was...unavailable. Spoken for. She could have spared them both this pain if she'd just faced every blush, every look laden with feeling. She could have stopped it all if she'd just spoken up.

Even now, with the result of her reluctance still ringing along her veins, she shuddered. She'd never been good at speaking when hearts were on the line. Her tongue stuck to the roof of her mouth. Her palms grew clammy.

Maybe if she were better at explaining herself, then people wouldn't leave her when she couldn't give them what they wanted.

And yet, somehow worse, was the ringing silence of the nave where she sat. There'd never been much joy here. Only duty and the quiet peace of acceptance. But she hadn't realized how Ash had brought light and lightness to this place. At least she hadn't until it was gone.

Now she would return from her work and no one would greet her. She would cook for one again, not two. She'd go for weeks without speaking out loud.

Without anyone to use it, she would forget her name.

Morlinna's hand stole to her chest. It was better this way. If Ash loved her the way she'd shown her, then the girl would never have been able to kill her when the time came. And there were so many reasons Morlinna would never have been able to return her affections. This was better for both of them.

But an unfamiliar longing keened underneath the words. What would it be like to look at someone and see a future instead of death?

What would it be like to look at someone and feel safe?

Years ago, she'd offered friendship instead of love and the answer had been no. She never wanted to go back to those years of guilt and shame, feeling like she was broken just because she loved a Goddess more than another person.

And yet here she was, unable to raise her gaze to the statue above her.

She laid her hands against the cold, stony feet and spoke.

"Forgive me, my lady."

The voice in the back of her head remained silent, and she wept.

This is better, she told herself. Over and over. But why did 'better' always come with so much pain?

Chapter 39
Concordim

Ashwyn struck out along the upper reaches of the Devastation, following a wide path in the canopy where she could see the sun. The magpies swooped and dove around her as she trotted down the vine and then grabbed a thread to pull herself across a gap.

Her vision had long since gone watery, but she didn't bother to wipe her eyes anymore. She could still sense the strands of the Nexum, and it wasn't like she had any idea where she was going, anyway. To Vitamorn? To the Greater Temple, where she could stand before the Goddess who had failed to defend her?

No. She might not know where she was going, but she knew exactly where she *wasn't* going.

Right now, she just had to get away. From Morlinna and Cass and Edgefall and everyone who had never wanted her in the first place.

She didn't even know why she was surprised. Cass was perfect, and Morlinna made no mistakes. It was Ashwyn who kept screwing up.

She replayed it, over and over, remembering the swell of feeling that wasn't hers, the warmth. And then the shame and the fear and the moment when Morlinna had cut it all off.

The knot in her gut grew tighter with each iteration. But she didn't know what she would have done differently. She'd always been loud when it came to feelings, and she wasn't going to hide them.

She knew what she wanted, and she wasn't going to apologize for it.

Something flickered on the path just beyond a curtain of vines, and Ash glanced over her shoulder. She caught the telltale flash of gray fur.

Felleron. Had Morlinna told him to follow her? To make sure she actually left the forest?

She took a moment to get her bearings. She'd been traveling blindly, mostly just heading north without any deeper thought.

No, he wasn't following her. He was making sure she didn't stray too close to his mate and cubs. They were somewhere to her left. She'd bet that if she hopped over to the other path, he'd stop shadowing her and make his displeasure very clear.

Well, she didn't need to have anything to do with the old wolf anymore, either.

She veered away, finding another branch that crossed her path and led her farther east than north.

Ahead of her, magpies burst from cover, their wings flashing in the sunlight and their caws grating against her ears.

"What?" Ash froze, instantly alert. The birds could be noisy and distracting, but they didn't scare easily.

Marauder swooped low, catching her attention. The others all flapped in a confusing display of fear, but Marauder sent her a clear warning.

Bad, he said. *Bad touch. Below.*

And somewhere to her left, a wolf howled.

"Mortis," Ash whispered. She hesitated only a second before she climbed down through the trees, plunging into the darkness below the canopy.

What am I doing? She railed at herself in her head. *I'm not Morlinna. She doesn't want me here, she doesn't need my help, and I don't care about this place anymore. I should be getting away, not moving toward the danger.*

But a shiver ran through her as the magpies continued to panic. A yip startled her, and a broad gray shape coalesced out of the gloom.

"Felleron," Ash gasped, but the wolf didn't bare his teeth or block her way.

He twined around her legs and set his teeth into the broken scythe she'd attached to her back.

Ash sucked in a breath. Things had to be bad if Felleron was actually paying attention to her. But why hadn't he called Morlinna?

Marauder swooped in front of her, and Felleron tugged her forward before darting away again.

Ash knelt at the edge of the branch and pulled back the next layer of vines blocking her view of the layer below.

A wide swath of death meandered through the forest where they'd cut back the corrupted bears' trail the day before. Dead and blackened plants fell away on either side, but at least there was no telltale sign of the Malady. No white streaks peeking through anywhere.

A rustle and a groan made Ash stiffen, and she craned to see around the screening foliage.

A figure stumbled into view. A man by his height and build. Stained and tattered cloth hung from his shoulders, so he'd been in the Devastation for a bit. His dirty hair had once been held back by a tie, but most of it had fallen free and obscured his face and neck.

Her gaze locked on his hands. He raised one to touch his head like it ached, and white flashed along his veins.

As he stumbled past the streak of death into healthy foliage, his steps left bits of white writhing in the Nexum.

"Oh, Dea," Ash breathed.

They'd been so careful to clear it all away. But either they'd missed some tiny holdout, or he'd stumbled through it before they'd scoured it away the day before.

Stupid. What was he even doing here? He was obviously some villager from Laststand or one of the others who'd thought he could make it in the Devastation despite all the stories. And now he was putting everyone at risk and forcing her to deal with this.

Her fingers clenched, and bits of snow fell away from the vine she'd pushed aside. Her breath steamed in the air as she huffed.

Morlinna didn't matter right now. She was back at the cloister, oblivious. And this man was going to spread the Malady despite the work they'd done yesterday.

Felleron whined and slipped down the vines and through the trees, probably toward his mate.

He was right. Morlinna wasn't here. It was just Ash. And the scythe Morlinna had given her. At least with that, she could give him the Last Death and stop the spread right now.

Her pulse raged in her ears as she dropped behind him and pulled the broken scythe from her back, unhooking the connections so it swung freely in her hand.

She should have delivered the blow before he turned. But she'd never actually killed a corrupted creature herself, let alone a human. Her mind filled with the imaginary feel of the scythe biting into his neck, and she balked.

"You shouldn't be here," she said over the sounds of his blundering. It gave him a chance to turn, to face what she was about to do.

And it gave her a chance to steel herself.

She thought she was prepared.

He spun at the sound of her voice, wild eyes nearly overrun with white, streaks of Malady crawling through his skin like a carnival mask.

But she still recognized him.

"Rafe," she breathed.

"Ashwyn," he groaned, and his hand stretched out as if to touch her face. But he snatched it back even as she recoiled.

The sudden movement made him sway, and he lost his balance, falling to one knee. His hand touched the vines where they stood, and white streaks spread from his palm.

A lump rose to choke her. Now that she was looking, she could see the tatters of his clothes were his old uniform, but he didn't have his sword. She'd never seen him without his sword. It wasn't right.

"Rafe, what are you doing here?" she cried. He was supposed to be safe in Edgefall, where he couldn't be corrupted. If he'd just stayed there...

Rage swept along her limbs. Didn't he know how dangerous the Devastation was? Hadn't he told her a thousand times not to walk too close?

Her hands clenched on the haft of her weapon.

The Malady climbed through his veins, moving farther and faster even as she watched. His torn shirt revealed a large swath of skin, and the white streaks reached across his chest, tangling over his heart.

It was taking him over.

How long did he have left? His limbs twitched as if he needed to move but was holding himself still by an act of will.

He lifted his head toward her, squinting like the white across his eyes clouded his vision.

"You..." he grated out. "I've been...looking for you."

Her jaw clenched. "Why?"

He shook his head. "No one...should be thrown in here. Whatever their crime. You didn't deserve...this."

She tried to swallow, but it hurt too much. For a moment, she'd thought maybe he'd realized they were wrong about her.

But he still thought she was a thief and a liar. He just thought her punishment was wrong.

"And...Cass?" she forced out through her teeth. Her heart thudded as she waited for him to draw enough breath to answer.

He shook his head. "Still...in...Edgefall," he wheezed.

She hadn't come. Back when she'd first been thrown in here, a tiny piece of Ash had wondered if Cass had plans to follow. She hadn't realized that there was any part of that piece left over yet to die.

It withered and crumbled away like a leaf after the Last Death.

"Ingrim..." Rafe whispered. "Came with me. He...fell first."

The Bladesaint held out his hand, just getting his fingers to cooperate so they could point.

Ash followed his gesture. Behind him, the mark of his path zigzagged through the forest, a white line of destruction crossing the blackened portion they'd already cleared the day before.

A wolf moaned beyond a screening layer of branches.

Ash pushed them back.

Ingrim lay in a pool of the Malady, limbs splayed in an unnatural pile as his wide white eyes stared up at the branches and vines above, unseeing. A gaping hole opened in his chest, stabbing down into the vines below him. A colorless void, specked with pinpricks of lightning. Tendrils of corruption waved around the gap, ripping at the strands of reality and trying to suck them in.

Morlinna had called it a gap in the world. A gate that led to Obitullas.

Beyond Ingrim, a wolf had made her home in the arching roots of one of the great sentinels. A cozy den made of vines and leaves.

But the she-wolf lay against the edge of the Malady, eyes already glazing to white, her great white wings spread against the vines. Her back half trailed away into the gap, being sucked into that void between worlds.

Ash tasted bile.

Felleron whined and scrabbled at the wide walls of the roots. He couldn't get past the Malady and into the den.

Ash stepped forward, swallowing down the sick taste in her mouth.

A form struggled in the leaves—a cub, no bigger than a human babe, with his father's horns and his mother's wings.

Ash swung her scythe around and slashed the threads of the Malady, cutting a path through the reaching pool. She had only seconds. The gate widened behind her, reaching for more life to pull into its void.

She stepped across the space she had made and scooped up the cub as the Malady tried to close the gap behind her.

She reached for a strand above and hauled herself back to safety along with the cub.

"Ash!" Rafe screamed from somewhere behind her.

Ash's breath came faster, but she forced her thoughts to a calm she didn't feel.

"Felleron, get Morlinna," she said. "Now."

The wolf snuffled and took one step before swinging back to her and his offspring.

"I'll keep him safe. Go show her where we are. You'll need speed."

Felleron gave one last howl and sped away up the vines to a higher layer where he could travel faster without the Malady to block him.

Ash swung the wolf cub onto her back and used the Nexum to attach him there like a baby in a sling. He either recognized she was trying to help or was too young to fight her, because he settled there easily without the nauseating aftereffects of trying to force a creature to her will.

Rafe screamed again, his voice rising along with the hair on her neck.

She raced back to him and gasped.

He'd fallen and lay on his back, his spine arching against the vines. The lines of Malady across his chest had spun together in a tangled knot, and a pinprick of void peeked between them.

The gate tore through him even though he still lived.

Anger fell out of Ash like water from a bottomless bucket, leaving her empty and cold inside.

A part of her had wanted this. Yesterday when she'd learned the bears were headed for Edgefall, she'd wanted to see all of them corrupted and gone.

But no one deserved this. Least of all Rafe.

She slashed the corrupted threads and fell to her knees beside him. Her arms ached with the need to grab his shoulders, to hold him while he writhed and cried out in pain. But she couldn't touch him.

"Hold on," she cried. "Rafe, just...fight it. There's a way to fight it. You just have to hold on a little longer. Push it back."

Morlinna had pushed it back. She'd pushed it back when she'd infected herself deliberately. And before that, when the Mender had saved her life. Had it been like this with the pain and the fear pouring off of her in waves?

But Rafe was a Bladesaint. Not a Nexsaint. The Goddess had anointed him, but he couldn't even see the threads of the Nexum, let alone control them.

"Please," Ash whispered. "Just a little longer."

Then Morlinna would get here, and she could fix everything. She could tell Rafe how to fight it. She could...she could...

She could kill him.

It was the only "cure." Morlinna had been trying to tell her for months now. And Ash had thought she'd known better. She'd thought they could find a different way.

Rafe gasped, and the gap in his chest grew, tearing at his flesh and sucking it inside.

Ash could feel it against her skin, like a strong wind blowing past her, trying to pull her with it.

"Can't..." Rafe rasped. "Too late. I'm sor...Ash."

"Rafe!"

"Strong and clever, Ash," he said, his eyes squeezed tight. "Strong and clever."

His whole body shuddered and went limp, and Ash sobbed, her chest caving.

But instead of the silence of the Absent, Rafe's eyes drifted open again and his body shifted.

Ash sucked in a breath.

She'd thought it would be over. That the gap would take him and he'd be gone. Absent enough that she could deliver the Last Death.

But his white eyes stared sightlessly, and he rolled, the gap moving with him.

The wolf cub on her back whimpered as Rafe's body pushed itself to its feet, movements jerky.

Ash fell back, scrambling to stay out of the strands of Malady pouring off of his body in waves.

"Rafe?" Ash cried, hoping a piece of the Bladesaint was still in there somewhere. "Rafe, stop!"

But the Absent Rafe stepped forward, arms reaching. The gap in his chest yawned wider, and the pull sucked at her clothes.

"No," she moaned. The Malady had taken him, turned him into an agent for its cause. Now, the only thing he wanted or cared about was spreading the Malady as far and as fast as he could.

There was no cure. There was no 'different way.' There was only the Last Death delivered swiftly, and she'd already failed at that.

Rafe's body lunged for her, and she rolled out of the way before scrambling to her feet.

He swung for her, and she stepped back, tripping over a root.

The wolf pup yelped and buried its head against her back.

That sent a jolt through her, and her hand tightened on the scythe. There was a creature depending on her.

Rafe's body strode toward her, movements fluid now that he wasn't fighting for control. Ash brought the scythe blade around in an arc and caught his legs before he could reach her. Thankfully, Morlinna had made these with reach.

But without the other half, the angle was off, and the blade caught against the bones in his legs without severing them. She yanked him off balance, pulling her blade free.

He went down, blood pouring sluggishly from the rents in his flesh, and Ash grabbed a thread from the tree above and yanked herself high into the branches.

Rafe's body lurched to its feet again, stumbling a bit as it found its balance on legs that didn't have all the pieces anymore.

Then it calmly laid both hands on the tree trunk beneath her perch. The Malady spread from its touch and raced up the trunk for her.

Ash skipped along the branch and reached for another, swinging between the two. But the unexpected weight clinging to her back dragged her lower than she wanted. She caught the branch in one hand, her scythe still clutched in the other.

Below, Rafe's body staggered to the pool where Ingrim lay, the white stain spreading with every heartbeat.

It stooped and when it straightened again, it held Ingrim's gleaming blade in its hand.

"Mortis."

It touched the tree where she hung, sending the Malady up toward the branches, and Ash had to make another desperate jump. She missed her grab and fell.

The Malady spread below her, and she brought her scythe around in a sloppy arc to slice through the white threads before landing.

They curled and died just as she slammed into the viney surface.

But she didn't have time to catch her breath from the blow. Rafe's body came for her, blade swinging in a perfect parody of the forms he'd used every day of his life to defend their little village.

Ash's heart caught in her throat. His eyes had gone glazed and white, but his face remained Rafe's familiar face. This was the man who'd taught her to swing a blade. He'd given her the means to become a Saint. He'd believed she could be.

He was the only one alive who still remembered her mother.

She cried out as she parried his blow, pushing him back a ruthless step.

Her chest ached, and she knew that no matter how much it hurt, how much it felt like her heart was tearing in two, Rafe's pain at the end had been worse.

The gap in his chest pulsed as if his heart still beat within it, and it pulled at her.

Ash's breath sobbed in her chest, and her hands trembled on her weapon, the only thing that could save her. The only thing that could stop this rotten copy of Rafe from trying to destroy her, too.

She didn't want to have to kill him. Even more than that, she didn't want to have to do it alone.

But that was what was happening. No one else was here. No one else could do what had to be done. Not even Morlinna.

Ash raised her arm to block his next blow. Rafe's blade struck, sparks raining from her Malady-imbued blade, and she thrust him back, using the strength he'd trained into her.

Rafe's body stumbled back, and she surged into the space he'd made, cutting the corrupted strands so she could stand there. Then she hooked him from behind with the scythe blade and yanked, cutting through bone and sinew and muscle. This time she got the angle right.

Rafe fell, his severed legs going in one direction and his body falling in another.

He lay on the vines gasping, white tendrils trailing away from him.

But it was still Rafe's face staring up at her, white streaks barely masking his blank expression.

He'd given her purpose. He'd given her hope. She could remember his smile in the fields as he'd protected them from monsters. His concern when she'd been sick with the fever. His words when she'd thought she'd never be a Saint.

"It's the *only* way. For those brave enough."

He'd been talking about kneeling before the Goddess. He'd never said she'd have to be brave enough to kill him. Brave enough to kill the ones she loved.

His body twitched, warning her, and he swung his blade around to catch her legs, just like she'd done to him.

Ash cried out and bashed the hilt with the blunt side of her scythe, breaking the bones in his hand so he had to drop the weapon. Then she swung the blade around and looped it behind his neck.

When she pulled, the imbued steel severed Rafe's head. And the corrupted heart thread traveling from the gap in his chest.

Rafe's eyes went wide, as if the Malady knew what had just happened, then his entire physical form fell to dust, leaving only the gate swirling endlessly into a pool of white lightning.

Chapter 40
Obitusim

Morlinna soared through the trees, barely touching down on one branch before grabbing a thread to fling herself to the next. She kept her mind carefully blank, pushing aside the one thought that pressed for attention ever since Felleron had howled.

I won't make it in time.

She didn't have a connection to the part of the forest where Felleron said Ash was. It was his space. The den he'd made for his mate and cub and she'd wanted to protect his privacy. And he'd already traveled close enough to her that using him as an anchor would be useless.

His dark shape loomed beside her, and she turned to follow him as he led her down through the layers to a clearing where the Malady sang a discordant hum in the back of her head.

Morlinna clenched her teeth and landed.

Beside the wide roots of a tree, two gaps swirled close enough together that their edges combined into one large pool of Malady. One still stemmed from a body.

Morlinna's eyes skipped over the disaster, searching for...

There. Ashwyn stood in a spot she'd cleared, her half-weapon hanging limp from her hands like she couldn't even feel the weight. Morlinna raked her with her gaze, looking for any trace of infection.

Ashwyn's skin was clear, but her gaze remained distant. The lead magpie had landed on her shoulder, his one good claw drawing blood through her shirt.

Morlinna approached her carefully.

"Ashwyn," she said, keeping her voice low, waiting for a reaction. The Malady could still have taken her, a tiny spot of infection easily overlooked until it ruined the life it had touched.

Morlinna's throat ached.

Over and over, she had threatened Ashwyn with death. She'd executed hundreds in the last ten years, severing their heart threads and scattering their dust into the Devastation. Each one its own private agony.

But here in this clearing, Morlinna knew that if she had to kill the girl now, something would break inside of her. Nothing would be the same, and she needed it to be the same. She needed that status quo to continue her work.

She stepped in front of the girl, staring at the lines of her face.

No. She'd been doing Ashwyn a disservice thinking of her as 'the girl.' She might be young, but her adulthood had been born of pain and survival.

Like Morlinna's.

And Morlinna was exactly the one who could show her the route out of that pain.

She'd still have to say goodbye, but only when she was sure Ashwyn would not crumble before her.

That would be its own kind of pain, but she'd live through the leaving. She'd done it before.

Concordim

A prick against her shoulder and the sound of her name finally penetrated the fog that kept Ashwyn calm. The mist had kept the ugly thoughts and memories from overwhelming her, and she wanted to cling to the last wisps. But there was a tightness in that voice that made pieces of her ache.

Why did she feel so numb inside? Rafe was gone. Ingrim lay Absent under the awfulness of his gap. She should feel *something*.

She tried to suck in a breath, but her throat was so tight. Marauder touched her cheek with his beak, and she lifted a hand to find her face wet.

Oh.

Ashwyn blinked, and a black figure came into focus.

Morlinna.

Felleron waited beside her, a whine straining his throat.

"How long have I...have I been standing here?"

The cub struggled against Ashwyn's back, reminding her of his presence. With one hand, Ash detached the threads keeping him there and let the creature down to the mat of vines. He raised fluffy wings just like his mother's and stumbled to Felleron.

The old wolf lowered his head and shifted to stand over the cub.

Morlinna stared at the carnage, taking in the writhing strands of the Malady and the blackened ends where Ash had begun purging them before she'd succumbed to the fog. She wore her mask hanging from her belt. She only brought it when she thought there was a good chance someone might see her. It had been a long time since Ash had seen her carry it.

Beyond the half-cleared Malady lay two gaps, their edges sucking at each other, creating a terrible gate to Obitullas.

The gaps would remain. An eternal testament to two men who would just disappear into the Devastation. No bodies to corral back to a necropolis so they could one day Return.

Morlinna turned to Ash, and the sudden softness in her eyes nearly broke her. The other woman knew exactly what had happened here, and Ash was struck with the sudden conviction that she didn't have to defend herself. Morlinna wouldn't accuse her of lying or stealing or any other awful thing. Because she *knew*.

A wall of delayed terror and grief rose up, rushing through her veins, and she choked on the tears that started pouring down her cheeks.

"He came to find me," she said, voice breaking. "I didn't think anyone would, but he did, and he brought Ingrim, and they—I couldn't stop it, and now they're just dust."

Dust and a tear in the world that ate life.

Her gorge rose, and she stumbled to the nearest tree, bracing herself against the trunk as she heaved up her breakfast.

A hand pressed against her spine, steadying her.

Her knees trembled, and the moment she could breathe again, she sagged.

Morlinna caught her, and Ash rested her head against the other woman's bony shoulder.

It was the first time Morlinna had ever reached out to her. A voluntary intimacy, and Ash couldn't even appreciate it for more than the sudden comfort it brought.

She rested there, eyes closed, so she didn't have to see the gate swirling into nothingness. "Does it get better?" she whispered. That's what people always said about grief and disappointment and every bad thing in the world.

Morlinna's voice was a long time coming. "No," she said. "It is never better.

We only ever get stronger and better at handling it. It is always the worst when it is a friend."

"Ingrim used to slip us sweets when we were kids. So Bayna couldn't see. And Rafe...Rafe taught me I could be a Saint."

The wolf pup untangled his wings from his sire's legs and wobbled to Ash. He pressed himself against her legs, and she sat up enough to rest her hand on his head, right between the shiny black horns.

A tingle made Ash put a hand to her heart. Deep inside her, a connection was forming to this place. Whether she wanted one or not. She could cut it away, but connections formed when someone had emotional ties to something. It wouldn't matter how many times she cut it; until the pain faded enough for her to ignore, it would keep regrowing. Just like her thread to Edgefall.

Morlinna stood and took up her scythe. She checked the edges of the spread, slicing it back to the very rim of the gate. She looked straight into Ingrim's lifeless eyes, then severed his heart thread, turning his body to dust.

Ashwyn winced.

She tried to remember Rafe as he'd been. She tried to remember all the good things he'd done, instead of the one mistake that had ruined her life and the final moments that pressed into her thoughts hard enough they'd never fade.

But he'd wanted to protect people, and in the end he had died alone, trying to kill her.

"You did well," Morlinna said, her deep voice quiet.

Ash shook her head. "I panicked," she croaked.

Morlinna turned to face her. "You panicked, and you still did well. Both things can be true." She raised her chin. "This Rafe taught you well. The Order will be stronger for a Saint like you."

Those were the words Ash had been expecting. The ones that threw her away again.

"I'm sorry," Ash said, her voice still rough. "I know I shouldn't have said what I said. I know you don't want me here. Don't want me at all. And I'm sorry."

Morlinna studied the ground between them for a long moment before she spoke. "You told me what you thought was truth. That's not something to apologize for. My reaction is not your fault. I also panicked, and I apologize. I should have explained better. But this is not the first time I could not give someone what they wanted. And the last time..." Morlinna sighed heavily. "I lost a friend. She walked away from me when I told her I could not love her. And eventually she came with the Judge to hunt me down."

Oh Morlinna.

"I'm sorry," Ash said.

Morlinna raised her gaze. "I cannot give you what you want while I am your teacher, but also because...I have been dedicated to the Goddess since I was small. Love is not something that was ever supposed to happen to me."

Ash swallowed and then cleared her throat. "Are all Nexsaints proscribed from feelings then?"

A faint blush tinged Morlinna's cheeks. "No. I only feel that sort of thing when...when I feel safe. And I've only ever felt that in Her presence. She takes up all the room in my life. There's never been any left over for anyone else."

I fell in love with someone who's already married. To a Goddess. Ash laughed softly, desperately, to herself. How could she compete?

But...there was more Morlinna wasn't saying. Ash had been there, at the edge of her mind, feeling all the fear through their connection, and now that she wasn't standing in the middle of the flood, she could see more clearly. Morlinna wasn't just afraid of what Ash was offering. She wasn't just afraid of the intimacy and the truth of feeling. She was afraid of being alone.

Morlinna had never had anyone to rely on. She'd lived her entire adult life in the Devastation, knowing that she would die and her death would rip a hole in the world, making it worse.

And Ash's feelings threatened the tenuous connection she'd made with the one other human being she'd allowed herself to trust.

Morlinna had been fighting alone because her fellow Saints had abandoned her and left her for dead. A part of her had to have been preparing for Ash to prove just as unreliable as they'd been.

And that's exactly what Ash had done, leaving her to face her fate alone. She'd ruined Morlinna's trust in her. The woman had been clear about what she needed: a partner to support her efforts and kill her when the time came. And Ash had ignored her or thought she could get around the unpleasant bits.

As for love...Ash grimaced. It was too late for that. Or maybe it was too early. Either way, Ash had twisted them up in an impossible situation, and it would take time and effort and understanding to untangle them.

"Come," Morlinna said, turning so Ash couldn't see her face. "I will help you to the border."

And Ash finally saw the threat for what it was. Morlinna preparing to go on alone.

"No," Ash said. Hopefully for the last time.

Morlinna's shoulders dropped. "No?" Her voice had lost all of its fight.

"I'm not leaving." Ash stood. The wolf pup whimpered in his throat. "I'm not going to Vitamorn. I'm not going to pretend I haven't seen what I've seen, and I won't become a Saint who does nothing."

Morlinna spun, lips thin as she pointed at the gap made by Rafe's death.

"You've seen what doing something looks like. It is killing. It is death. This is the work that is needed. So I can have the space to learn what made the Malady."

"I know," Ash said. "That's the Saint I want to be."

Morlinna heaved a sigh. "You don't want to be like me, Ashwyn." Her voice dropped. "I made myself into a monster to do what had to be done. So people like you don't have to do the same."

Ash stepped closer. Not close enough to scare her away. Just close enough to catch her gaze and hold it.

"You can keep using the worst ways to describe yourself. But I'm not leaving you. And I'm not leaving them." She gestured to what little remained of Rafe and Ingrim, using them as a stand-in for the entire village of Edgefall.

"Does this mean you've forgiven them? For the things they did to you?"

Ash shuddered. "No." Never. "But I don't want them to die horribly, either. You said two things can be true. These are my two."

An image flashed in her mind, provided by some dark whimsy that took the worst and threw it at her. Cass, with her eyes gone white, staring at Ash with the same intense hatred creasing her familiar face.

Ash flinched. "If Edgefall needs monsters to protect them because they can't do it themselves, then let me be a monster with you."

Morlinna pressed her lips tight between her teeth.

Oh, mortis, she hadn't meant it like that.

"I won't approach you again," Ash said quietly. "You gave me your answer, and that's that. You don't have to worry that I'll try to force you."

Morlinna raised a sardonic eyebrow. "Thank you for that. But that's not the promise I need from you."

Ash's breath caught. "I know."

"If you stay, I need you to promise to end me when it is time. When the corruption threatens to take me. Before I become that."

She pointed to the gate, and Ash made a noise in the back of her throat.

All she could see was Rafe's face as he raised his sword. The way his body hadn't been his. The way he'd died trying to kill her.

"That won't be a problem," Ash said, matching her tone.

Some of the tension went out of Morlinna's face. "Good. The infatuation will fade, and then there will be less of a barrier."

Ash just kept herself from snorting. If Morlinna needed to believe that Ash couldn't love her and still manage to kill her, then she would let her believe it. Ash knew the truth. The only reason she'd been able to kill Rafe was because she'd loved him.

But Ash desperately didn't want Morlinna to die alone thinking the worst of herself. She wanted to be the one Morlinna relied on. The one who did the work that was needed so they could fix the problem.

"I promise," Ash said. Because she hadn't yet and that was the first step to trust between them.

Morlinna cocked her head, almost as if she was listening to something, and Ash wondered if the Goddess was speaking with her.

Finally, Morlinna spoke. "Thank you."

"You'll let me help?"

Morlinna's lip twitched in the barest hint of a smile. "Yes. I will teach you to be a monster."

Animatim

V knelt before the Primarch Divine, head bowed, her deep blue cloak flung back over her shoulders. The light coming through the stained-glass windows glinted against her etched breastplate, and she averted her gaze from the blinding glare.

The Abdicant stood at the Primarch's right shoulder, and the Goddess sat on Her throne behind them, eyes closed.

V's pauldrons rang as the Primarch tapped the metal with the tip of his blade, and his voice echoed against the high walls.

"You have been anointed in justice and anointed *for* justice, Judge Vitania Abdicantus," he intoned. "Now go. And deliver the Last Death to the heretic, Wesley Ranimas. He is declared forfeit of any mercy or succor in this world and the next."

The Primarch lowered the sword, and V raised her gaze to meet his.

"He is your sole responsibility, Judge. His life and death belong to you."

"So Dea wills, and I obey," V whispered.

She stood and raised her eyes to her mother's and added. "It will be done."

Part Three

Chapter 41
Concordim

Ashwyn knelt among the vines and the leaves and used both hands to weave a complicated knot in the strands of the Nexum below her. She turned her head to see the glowing threads with her good eye and made sure they were even.

The entire magpie flock settled around her, their wings tucked neatly against their backs. In the last five years, she'd finally taught them to watch and wait without erupting over every little noise and surprise. Now they sat silent, only the nearest ones watching her while the rest kept a lookout beyond.

Ahead of her, the clearing at the Heart of the Devastation opened, and she could see across it in the moonlight that shone unfiltered into the chasm.

A white wolf paced across the mat of vines just behind her, keeping his gaze on the forest. His wings rose half-furled along his back, ready in case he had to take flight. When he turned his head, nostrils flaring, the moonlight glinted against the black horns that rose from his snowy fur.

Are you almost done? His voice came to her through the connection they shared, almost as familiar as her own now. *This is boring.*

"Patience, Wraith," she said, eyes on her work.

You use this word too much, he grumbled. The physical noise he made was more like a cross between a whine and a groan low in his throat. *I don't like it. It makes my insides sad.*

Ashwyn pressed her lips together, hiding her smile.

Felleron's cub had grown big and healthy and had a boundless energy that even Ash was hard-pressed to match.

She finished her weave and laid the glowing strands back into the vines at her feet, attaching them lightly at the surface where they would catch against the threads in anyone or anything that crossed them.

She'd never worked on something so complex before, but it was just a continuation of making her skin bark-like or borrowing the sight of a magpie.

This strand contained the strength of the vines and their tenacity. This one had the keen senses of a wolf. And this one bore the magpies' ability to sense the difference in a corrupted creature.

The glowing strands lay flat and smooth in a thick arc spearing away through the growth of the Devastation. They curved away from her on either side.

One of the magpies flitted down through the trees and alighted on her shoulder. A big female with a sheen of white over her iridescent feathers.

Magpies didn't live long in the wild. Marauder had lived his full life and had gone Absent in his sleep years ago. His Absence had hurt her, just as Morlinna had warned, but Ashwyn hadn't had the heart to break the connection before he went. His devotion had meant more to her than the promise of a pain-less goodbye.

Raider had taken his place for three short years, leading the magpie flock as they patrolled the Devastation with Ash, learning her human words and ways. And when he had finally gone Absent, the big female had stepped into his role.

Ashwyn tipped her head and dug in her belt for a strip of dried fruit to feed her. The female chirped and gulped it down.

Ash had named her Ebonheart for the ruthless way she led the magpies. No battle was too big. No cause was hopeless for the large bird.

"I need to test this," Ash said out loud as she sent the idea down the connec-tion that glowed between them. "Anything in the area worth trying it out on?"

Nothing bad, Ebonheart said. Corrupted was a long word for a magpie. Ash had given up trying to teach it to them. *All clear.*

"Because we worked hard to clear it," Ash said with a sigh. "Don't worry, I'll handle it. Is there anything at all?"

Ebonheart cocked her head one way, then another. *Two goats. Three deer. Family of rabbits. One bear.*

A smile twisted Ashwyn's lips. "Bear it is," she said and stood. "Thank you."

The last thread of her weave stretched between her and the complicated knots waiting just under the surface of the vines. She gave it a little tug to test the connection and felt the pull of it inside her chest.

Perfect.

Felleron padded into view around a wide sentinel tree, his paws nearly silent on the vines. The gray around his muzzle had deepened in the last few years, and Ashwyn suspected his natural lifespan should have been up long ago. But his connection to Morlinna kept him alive. Either on purpose or as a side effect. Ash had never been mean enough to ask and draw attention to it.

Wraith bounded up to his sire, wings giving his leaps more height, and he landed beside Felleron with a thump. The pup's jaws went wide as he tried to fit his father's face in his mouth.

Felleron let him gnaw for exactly ten seconds before he twisted his head out of the way and brought his big paw down on Wraith, flattening him against the vines.

Enough, pup, Ash heard him say through her connection with Wraith. His voice held no anger, just weariness.

Wraith's tongue lolled in surrender, and Felleron let him up. Wraith shook his head hard enough to make his ears flap. A tiny whine escaped his throat.

We'll play later, Ash sent to him privately. *Work first.*

Wraith raised his wings, and the tips fluttered in the slight breeze. *He never wants to play anymore.*

Ashwyn didn't disagree. The old wolf had never been particularly carefree, but he'd changed after his mate had been sucked into the gate to Obitullas. He'd lost a lot of the energy he'd once had. But Ash avoided bringing up Wraith's mother if she could.

I think his joints pain him, she told him instead. *Look at the way he moves.*

Wraith lowered his head and huffed a sigh. *He says, Morlinna said to tell you she is ready on her side.*

A little flash of sick shot through Ash's stomach. An echo of remembered shame.

Even five years after their first attempt changed everything between them, Morlinna had never asked to connect with her. They relied on Felleron and Wraith to relay messages. Ash couldn't even hear Felleron directly. Only the mirror of his words through her connection with Wraith.

Ash shook herself free of the old feeling. It was fine. She and Morlinna didn't need a connection. They knew each other so well that it would be redundant.

"Tell Morlinna we're going to test the perimeter," she said aloud to Felleron, knowing he'd send her words.

Felleron didn't wait for more. He bobbed his head and stalked off around the chasm while Ash gathered her double-bladed scythe from the ground where she'd left it.

She and Wraith headed in the other direction, Ebonheart and the other magpies taking wing around them.

The bear snorted and snuffed just beyond the stand of sentinels that marked the start of the forest proper after the break around the chasm. It stood at least twice as tall as a normal bear that lived its life outside of the Devastation, and saliva dripped from the fangs that hung over its lips.

Every bit as big and belligerent as the ones she and Morlinna had hunted down years ago. Except this one wasn't corrupted. Yet.

"Sorry for this," she whispered under her breath, then caught a thread in the trees above her and flipped herself over the bear's back, slicing through one of its strands with the corrupted end of her scythe.

The severed ends of the healthy black strand paled and turned white, the color of the Malady spreading through its body.

The bear roared and stood on its hind legs as Ash landed in front of it. It pulled back a paw as if to lash out at her, then its movements halted and a shudder ran through its bulk. It blinked, its pupils going white as bits of the Malady spread through the skin of its face.

Ash waited, poised as the Malady took it completely and it staggered back a pace. It fell to all fours with a thud that shook the vines where she stood.

Then it swung its head up and focused on Ashwyn. A low growl rumbled in its throat.

Ashwyn cocked her head. "Perfect. All right, buddy. Let's go."

She leaped as the bear lunged. As its jaws snapped closed on the empty air where she'd just been, she soared over it, landing on the other side and sprinting along the vines.

"Come on now," she called.

The bear spun and raced after her.

As Ash ran, a shadow joined her, keeping pace on her other side.

Ash didn't even have to look to know it was Morlinna.

The bear snorted and shuffled to a stop, glancing blearily from Ash to the shadow. Corrupted creatures always took a moment or two to get used to the feel of the Malady coursing through them.

Ashwyn doubled back and ran straight at the bear. It shook its head and steadied on its thick legs. Then it lunged at her.

Ashwyn let it. She ducked and slid under the blow aimed for her head.

And Morlinna fell onto the massive paw from above, slamming it into the ground.

Ash rolled out from the other side, springing to her feet.

"Go," Morlinna said, spinning out of the bear's path. "I will herd it from behind kend take care of its trail."

Ash gave her a brief nod and sprinted away again, serving as bait for a very enraged bear. It blundered after her, roaring, and Ash led it right across the woven strands she'd just been working on minutes before.

She felt the moment it crossed, a reverberation down the strand that connected her to the glowing weave. In her chest, it stretched taught like a trip-wire. Then snapped.

The bear pounded across the dead vines surrounding the chasm, oblivious to the tripwire.

Ash let it come. She raced to the edge of the chasm, the bear on her heels and as it reached out its wide head to snap at her, she reached for a thread of the Nexum and swung herself into the air, flying across the empty space of the chasm.

The bear thundered over the edge and fell into the white-rimmed pit, plunging into the blackness below.

Ash pulled another thread and changed directions, arcing over the empty space and landing lightly beside the glowing perimeter.

Morlinna came up beside her. The apostate pushed back her hood, and the moonlight picked out bits of white in her light hair.

Ash swallowed. Morlinna was nearly ten years older than her; it could just be that. She tried to tell herself it was that.

But Ash couldn't help but notice the streaks each ended where the white lines of the Malady marking her face began.

Morlinna knelt, the skirt of her robe pooling around her, and her long fingers probed the edges of the weave. The glowing strands of the Nexum curved the entire way around the chasm, forming a perimeter between the Malady and the rest of the Devastation.

The ragged ends had gone white and corrupted where the bear had burst through.

"It broke the weave when it passed," Morlinna said as Wraith trotted up to sit beside them, wings held half-furled.

"We suspected it might," Ash said. "But it still did exactly what it was supposed to. It warned me as the bear crossed. I felt the corrupted creature through the connection."

"I did as well," Morlinna said, sitting back on her heels.

The perimeter would never serve as a barrier. It wasn't built to keep the corruption in or out. But it would warn them if the Malady spread from the chasm far enough to cross the weave.

They'd worked for years to push the Malady back. To hunt down every pocket, every creature, every trail and cut it all back so that this chasm at the Heart of the Devastation was the only place where the Malady had any kind of presence.

Ash smiled to herself. The funny thing was, this was the job she'd loathed so much in Edgefall. The one that had made her feel itchy and anxious, like she was running in circles, retracing her steps every day. Yet it was the task she engaged in the most. Cutting back the growth of the Malady. Retracing her steps every day to ensure it never got away from them.

But with this perimeter, they would be warned if it spread, even if they weren't here.

Morlinna would finally have the space to explore and study and figure out why this place was so important to the Malady.

Ash ducked her head to hide the relief that poured through her at the thought. This was her entire purpose here with Morlinna. To help her fight the Malady for as long as she could, and to be there to end her life when she could no longer fight.

Morlinna wore long fitted sleeves that covered her from wrist to neck, but on the rare occasion that Ash saw her arms, the white progress of the Malady crept up her skin nearly to her shoulders. And every time, Ash had to turn away, bury the question that rose in her mind. How much time did Morlinna have left?

But today they had made progress. And it would help. It *had* to help.

"The perimeter will have to be fixed every time," Morlinna said, standing. "And the Malady cut out so the entire thing is not corrupted." Even now, the white spread along the threads from the break, turning the healthy black to a sickly ash color.

"The corruption is inevitable if something gets this far," Ash said. "But we can tweak the design, add in resiliencies and see if we can slow the spread. For now, this is exactly what we need."

Morlinna glanced at her, and Ash raised an eyebrow.

"Breathing room," she said.

Something groaned and huffed behind them, and Wraith spun, his hackles raised. Felleron rose stiffly, lips pulled back in a snarl.

Ash merely looked over her shoulder and spotted a dark shape climbing up the corrupted vines at the edge of the chasm.

The bear. This one was tougher than most.

The Malady spread along its face, visible even under its thick fur, and its white eyes narrowed on the two women standing at the edge of the Devastation.

With an impossible heave, it pulled itself from the chasm and charged.

Ash just sighed.

"You fix the perimeter," she said. "I'll take the bear."

Morlinna chuckled and turned away from the behemoth bearing down on them.

If Morlinna was a brawler, using her corruption to get close to her enemy, Ash was a duelist, darting through a fight and using speed to stay out of the creature's way.

Ash sprinted right for the bear. It planted its feet, skidding to a stop among the deadened vines, and opened its jaws to meet her charge.

Ash feinted right, then dashed left and slid, feet out in front of her.

She reached beneath the bear and pulled a thread on its other side in order to slide completely underneath it.

Her scythe blade severed the corrupted threads in its neck as the physical blade caught against muscle and sinew.

Her momentum carried her to the other side of the bear, and she heaved the blade, severing its head from its shoulders.

The bear collapsed in a heap, its eyes going blank and glazed just before its body shuddered and fell to dust.

Morlinna was already rising from her work, dusting her hands off along her robes. She shook her head with a smile. "How anticlimactic. You could have done that at any moment."

"Yes, but we had to test the perimeter."

Morlinna cocked an eyebrow. "With the worst creature you could find?"

"The bigger the better," Ash said. "Might as well do it right the first time."

And this way I get to show off for you, she thought to herself. But not out loud. Never out loud. Morlinna was like a bird, a skittish starling that would flee the moment it sensed another presence nearby.

But that was all right. Patience was one of the many things Ash had learned over the years in the Devastation.

Morlinna actually laughed and put out her hand so Felleron could come underneath it for a scratch. "I suppose sometimes loud and bold can be an advantage," she said.

Ash caught her breath, but Morlinna didn't look at her, as if the words had only meant exactly what she'd said.

"We should return home," Morlinna said. "Tomorrow is a new day."

A thrill went through Ashwyn as Ebonheart alighted on Ash's shoulder. The rest of the flock rose around them and winged off through the trees to find their nests for the night.

But despite the successes of the day and the promise of the morning, Ash wasn't nearly tired enough to sleep yet.

She glanced at Wraith, who sprinted from the edge of the Devastation and back, sniffing everything in his path.

"Race you home," she said, then sped forward as he yipped in delight, and the two of them passed Morlinna and Felleron, who strode at a much more sedate pace.

Chapter 42
Concordim

For the first time in years, Ashwyn rose before Morlinna. They'd moved the crates and barrels from her room long ago and built a bed frame in the corner. Her lamp rested on the chest she'd shoved next to the bed. The dusty religious texts Morlinna had given her lay unused on the shelf over her headboard, while a couple of adventure novels they'd pilfered from a lost merchant's cart lay open on the floor.

Ash pushed through the curtain into the nave while Wraith yawned and covered his eyes with his wing.

By the time Morlinna stepped into the nave, Ashwyn was already dishing warm porridge into bowls. The other woman finished adjusting her sleeves and brushed imaginary lint from the black fabric over her knees.

Ash had never taken on the robes of a Nexsaint in her time with Morlinna. Sure, she was a Nexsaint by ability, but it had felt like trying to usurp something holy from Morlinna. Something she hadn't really connected with, anyway.

Instead, she wore a pair of un-dyed breeches and a dark calf-length overcoat, sleeveless and hooded, like the ones they'd worn in Edgefall. But this one was cut close to her body so it didn't catch against the vines and roots of the Devastation.

Morlinna blinked in the lantern's light and tilted her head. "What's the occasion?" she asked as Ash flourished a spoon and handed her a bowl.

Ash bit back a grin. "It's the anniversary of the day you didn't kill me."

Morlinna huffed a laugh. "What?"

Ash loved getting Morlinna to make that noise. She sat at their makeshift table and jerked her chin at the other stool. "It's been five years since I found the Heart of the Devastation. Five years since you almost killed me and decided not to."

"Ah," Morlinna said. "I did not realize we were keeping track."

It was much harder without a calendar. But Ash couldn't help counting out her life in terms of knowing Morlinna and not knowing Morlinna. She was pretty sure that if she stopped and thought about it, she could count the number of times her heart had beat since she'd looked up to see the other woman standing over her with a blade.

Ash shook her head and took two big bites of her breakfast before setting it aside, too excited to eat.

"You've wanted to do one thing since you came to the Devastation," she said.

Morlinna stilled.

"Solve the mystery of the Malady." She met Morlinna's light eyes, breath coming faster. "Learn where it came from so we can fight it without having to murder."

"This is true. But I haven't been able to."

"Until now." Ash set down her spoon. "We've pushed back the Malady and given ourselves enough space to breathe. Now you can focus on the next thing."

Morlinna laughed again. "I don't even know where to start."

"That's all right," Ash said with a grin. "I do."

Ashwyn let Morlinna finish her breakfast, but she was waiting at the door with a pack on her back by the time Morlinna was actually ready to leave.

Wraith and Felleron joined them, and Ebonheart dove from her nest at the top of the nave as they slipped out of the cloister.

"Where are we going?" Morlinna asked, and Ashwyn couldn't help hearing the echo of her own voice from five years before when she'd followed this woman to her home.

"It's a surprise," she said.

They flitted through the trees, swinging from threads of the Nexum. Travel was much faster through the air between boughs and vines, and they had the rhythm of it now. Poor Felleron was the slowest of the group without wings, but he had a knack for finding ways through the growth where no one else could fit, so he barely lagged.

Technically, Nexsaints could travel along threads of connection if they'd been to a place before and remembered to take a strand. Or if they'd formed an emotional attachment great enough to create a thread out of thin air.

But carrying weaves and connections required a certain amount of concentration, and a Saint could only hold so many. Plus, Ash hadn't wanted Morlinna to see anything connecting her to this place and ask about it. It would have spoiled the surprise.

Ash led them to the far edge of the Devastation, nearly to the cliff where Laststand sat. The bells of the temple rang faintly in the morning air, penetrating the depths of the forest.

She finally came to rest on a mat of vines crisscrossing between the trees. As Morlinna landed beside her, Ash held out the tip of her scythe and pointed to the vines at their feet.

A soft spot sagged, the vines loosely woven so gaps opened between them.

Morlinna stepped forward, the flooring shifting under her weight, and she knelt to pull a large vine aside.

Below, another opening gaped in the lower layer.

"I found the passage during the thaw," Ash said quietly. "When everything shifted and reformed in the spring. I only had a chance to explore a little before I was called back for a corrupted creature. But I think it goes all the way down."

"To the bottom of the crater," Morlinna said, eyes still on the opening. "To the source of the Malady."

"Yes." Ash touched the strap of the pack on her back. "I brought supplies. We can finally find out what's under the Devastation. What the Order is hiding. We can go now."

Morlinna didn't say anything, and Ash had to swallow against a dry throat.

"If you'd like," she added softly. Maybe this had been a mistake.

Morlinna's hand crept to her chest, and she pressed her palm against the ribs over her heart. Then she finally looked up, and Ash's own heart thumped. Her eyes had gone wide and a little lost.

But as she stared back, something fierce and full of curiosity and joy seeped into her face—and Ash felt it as a jolt, almost as if they were connected.

"You arranged this as a gift. For me."

Ash had to clear her throat. "Yes."

Finally, Morlinna smiled. "Thank you."

"You're welcome."

Morlinna didn't even stand back up. She pulled the vine farther aside and fastened it to another to keep the opening wide. Then she gave Ashwyn an entirely un-Morlinna-like grin and cocked her head.

"Well, are you coming?"

As she dropped into the hole, Ash had to put her hand to the nearest tree trunk to hide the way her knees had gone wobbly.

"Of course," she whispered even knowing Morlinna couldn't hear now.

Felleron wriggled in after Morlinna.

Wraith watched as Ash attached her scythe behind her and sat on the edge of the opening.

When are you going to tell her how you feel about her? He said across the thread that connected them.

The feeling in her chest faded, veiled by a healthy caution.

"Never," Ash said.

If that was what it took for Morlinna to feel safe around her, if that was what the other woman needed from her, then that was what Ashwyn would give her. Forever if necessary.

It might be what Morlinna needs, Wraith said. *But what about what you need? Silence is not you.*

Ash ignored him.

You will have to go back to being you, eventually.

Chapter 43
Obitusim

How many years had the mystery of the Devastation eaten at her? Fifteen?

For a decade and a half, the whispers of the Malady had crept through the layers and into Morlinna's dreams, calling her to see what lay in the depths.

And now she was headed into those depths to discover why all this had happened. With the one person who had made it possible.

Morlinna didn't need to glance behind her to see where Ashwyn was. She knew exactly how far back she'd stay to give Morlinna her space.

But she felt her presence there, anyway. Steady and safe.

She didn't remember the first moment when she realized she didn't have to check on Ashwyn. She didn't have to think of the next step or warn the other woman about what was coming. Ashwyn was just there.

She didn't remember the first time, but each moment after had solidified Ash's place at her side.

Before ducking down to the next layer, Morlinna paused as Felleron trotted up next to her and Wraith snuffled the vines along the floor.

"The magpies?" she said.

Ashwyn's voice came exactly where she'd expected it. "I told them to stay up above. I doubt there will be room for the flock down here, and I'd rather they keep watch. The perimeter will tell us if the Heart starts expanding. But it won't let us know if any pockets show up outside the weave."

"That is a good plan," Morlinna said.

"I do occasionally have them." Ash flashed her a grin, and Morlinna's heart constricted.

A flush sent sudden heat through her and her fingers itched, almost like they wanted to reach for something. But there was nothing there. No one except Ashwyn.

And just as suddenly a surge of memory swept the feeling away. A face stared back at her with hurt and disgust, and Morlinna couldn't discern the difference between Ashwyn's features and those from another long ago.

Morlinna glanced away and cleared her throat. "Let's...let's go."

As they descended, the growth grew thicker, more tangled. This was always the trouble with going down. The upper reaches felt more like layers where they could move freely between mats of vines and roots. But the farther they descended, the more the space felt like tunnels carved between the growth.

The pathways shifted over the years, the freeze in the winter closing some off and the thaw opening new ones in the spring. Finding new ways through the forest took time, and there was always the chance that the tunnels would shift while they were inside. Morlinna had seen too many Devastation beasts trapped under the weight of the branches, their legs broken but still kicking as their Absent eyes bulged in their heads.

The fact that these openings had lined up to create a kind of passageway that led deeper and deeper into the crater was a stroke of luck Morlinna hadn't expected to happen naturally.

Or...she glanced at Ashwyn. Maybe it wasn't just luck. After all, the Goddess had sent Ashwyn for many reasons.

They found several places where the tunnel had grown over, and they had to tear through new roots and vines. Once, Ashwyn searched along the strands of the Nexum to find a passage nearby that provided an easier route. She and Morlinna used their scythes to cut through to it.

Then they cut back to the original passage in order to avoid a family of groundhogs with fangs nesting in the tunnel.

Morlinna kept her hand on the wall when she could, reading the flutters in the strands of the Nexum, using them to tell her where the next opening was or if there was something dangerous traveling toward them.

The change in the strands was so subtle she didn't even notice it at first.

Every strand in the Nexum pulsed black and healthy, and a trained Nexsaint could use them to read the surroundings. See where things grew and how healthy they were.

Morlinna had gone two dozen paces before she realized the strands under her fingers no longer pulsed with an unseen heartbeat.

They still glowed black against the darkness, but there was nothing inside them. No life, no illness. Nothing.

Morlinna stopped, and Ash noticed the movement, pausing just behind her.

Morlinna held out her hand to Felleron, and the wolf immediately knew what she wanted. He drew close enough for her to pull a thread from his body and weave it with one of her own. The amount of light in the dim passage didn't change, but her ability to pierce it did. She blinked as the vines and roots came into sharp relief.

"What is it?" Ash asked.

"Look." Morlinna reached out to touch the vines themselves. They hung dense and clustered, woven tighter than a basket, as if they'd grown up in a too-small pot.

The thick, healthy roots and vines from above had given way to thin strands gone gray and brittle.

Morlinna broke a piece off in her hand.

The strands under the surface remained black, uncorrupted, but still empty, and that sent a shiver through Morlinna.

"They're not...alive," Ash said. "Not anymore."

"But they haven't gone through the Last Death, either," Morlinna said. "Then the strands would have disintegrated. These are just empty." She scanned the wall of crammed vines, brow furrowed. "And waiting. Like the Absent in a necropolis."

"Absent plants," Ash said. "I've never seen it." She ran her hand down a root as well. "It makes sense. How can they grow here? There is no light. No nutrients. Even the air is close and stale."

Ash shuddered.

They moved on, walking through a necropolis of Absent growth. They couldn't even call this a forest anymore. Just endless caves of eerily blank roots.

They still traveled down at a steep angle, following the pathways where the growth had shifted and left openings.

But they'd left any Devastation beasts far behind. Nothing lived down here.

"Maybe there is no end," Ash said, voice hushed. "Maybe there's no bottom. It feels like we've been descending forever."

"Twenty-three layers," Morlinna said.

"What?"

"We've gone twenty-three layers. I've been counting."

The number should have been reassuring. It was a finite distance. Measurable. Instead, it weighed on her. The miles of growth pressing down upon them. If something shifted, they'd be buried.

But the sense of something important drew Morlinna ahead, making her pulse quicken. There had to be a bottom. There had to be an answer in whatever lay beneath the Devastation.

Their passage ended in a tangle of Absent roots. Hardly any vines made it this far.

Morlinna's heart sank. She'd been sure they'd make it to the bottom. Or perhaps Ashwyn was right. There was no bottom.

She stepped forward to place her hands against the tangle. But here, without any vines to weave through the roots, the floor beneath her feet went bumpy and uncertain.

Behind her, Ash gasped. And as Morlinna turned, the other woman disappeared between two roots. As if the Devastation itself swallowed her.

Morlinna had time to cry out and lunge to catch her, but Ashwyn's strands slipped between her fingers, and she fell through open space.

Concordim

Empty darkness rushed past Ashwyn, making her stomach drop. There was nothing to grab. No roots, no threads.

Then, a glowing strand whipped past her face, and she reached for it instinctively. The thread tightened against her fingers, then pulled loose, and she fell again.

The strand felt rough and heavy against her fingers. Stone. There was stone down here. But stone wouldn't help her survive a fall from this height. She'd shatter against whatever she hit next.

Pouches lined her belt, full of her collection of useful things. Magpie feathers, bark, vials of water, among many other things.

She pulled a strand from the feathers, borrowing their lightness, and wove it into her Nexum. Immediately, the feel of the air across her body changed, dragging less at her limbs.

She reached for strands from the wood of her scythe and the steel of her knife, supplementing her weave with strength and suppleness.

By the time she struck something solid, she was ready. Her legs hit the ground and her body bent but did not break.

She grunted, the breath rushing from her lungs. She would live, but she'd never taken a hit that hard before, and she needed a moment to just breathe.

But strands rushed past her face, and she leaped back as the block of stone she'd grabbed smashed into the ground in front of her.

She lost her balance and fell to one knee, catching herself against the dirt.

Her heart thudded.

Dirt.

She splayed her fingers against the ground. Actual ground.

She hadn't seen ground since the moment she'd fallen from the cliff in Edgefall.

They'd reached the bottom.

"Ashwyn!" Morlinna's voice came faint from above her.

She tipped her head back and imagined she could see a white blur far above her in the darkness.

"I'm all right," she called. She had to cough to clear the leftover fear from her throat. "I'm here."

"I'm coming down," Morlinna called. "I think I can lower myself and Felleron."

A white shape was already diving for her. Wraith, who wasn't waiting for the other two.

"Be careful," Ash said, eyeing the shattered stone. "I nearly hit something on the way down."

"Yes, I see," Morlinna said, and something bemused in her voice made Ash finally sit up and take stock of her surroundings.

Darkness shrouded everything in shadows. Ash drew a piece of flint from a pouch and struck the stone against the end of her scythe blade, creating a spark.

As it flashed through the air, she pulled a fragile strand from the tiny flame and wrapped it through her hand, borrowing the flame's brightness so that her hand glowed and sent light through the cavern.

For that was what it was.

As Wraith landed beside her and whined a worried greeting, Ash stood and stared up at the Devastation growing in a dome high, high above her.

Morlinna lowered herself from the opening where Ash had fallen, using a strand of the Nexum. Behind her, the roots grew in a solid wall, encasing the empty air.

A tower rose just beside Ash, jagged edges thrusting into the air. The block that lay beside her had come from the upper reaches of the tower before she'd yanked on it to slow her fall.

Morlinna landed beside her.

"Are you all right?" The Nexsaint surged forward and stopped short before touching her.

Ash noticed only with a distracted portion of her thoughts. The rest of her was occupied.

They'd expected buildings. The Devastation had carried some of them up through its growth for decades. They'd known there was some sort of village or town down here.

But this was more than that.

An entire city spread before them. They stood on a hill overlooking an entire underground metropolis.

And every building below bore marks of fighting. Toppled walls, scorch marks along broken roofs, little craters blasted into the cobbled streets.

As far as Ash's light stretched, they saw signs of some great battle.

"Is this...is this what it looks like when the Order scours away the Malady?" Ashwyn asked. Somehow, it wasn't what she'd imagined from Morlinna's sterile description.

"No," Morlinna said shortly, stepping forward and raising her hand as if to see farther into the distance. "The Order scours away every living thing. Plants, livestock, people. But it leaves the buildings intact. Entire villages and towns emptied and left like husks. This...this is different."

Ash looked out over the city and gulped.

"What happened here?" she whispered.

Chapter 44
Concordim

"This makes no sense," Morlinna said as she picked her way down the hill, away from the broken tower. Felleron ranged out from her side, nose to the ground, and Wraith launched himself into the air to scout from above.

Ash followed her, staring up at the buildings that crowded close to the streets, looming over them. After years of walking on vines and roots, the ground beneath her feet felt oddly solid. Her body expected some give when she put her foot down, and there was none. At the base of the hill, the dirt gave way to cobbles, which were even worse.

Ash ran her toe across the edge of a broken cobblestone where something had blasted a hole in the street.

"Which part doesn't make sense?" Ash said with a frown. "I'm making a list."

Morlinna spared her an exasperated glance. "This place should not be here."

"You mean the Devastation should have destroyed it?" That was definitely what she'd assumed they would find. A village overrun with the growth.

"I mean, how can there be a city here we've never heard of? There is only one city on this continent. Vitamorn. The seat of the Goddess's power. If the Malady is the reason we don't have another one...we would have known of it."

Ashwyn ran her hand along the wall of a mostly intact building. It soared high enough that its jagged roof was nearly lost in the darkness beyond her light.

Even the Lower Temple of Edgefall wasn't this tall, and this didn't even look like it had been that important. A house or a business, maybe.

Was this what it was like to walk through Vitamorn? To see everything with this sense of awe and disbelief?

"It wouldn't be the first time the Order has lied about something important," Ash said. She tipped her head back. She didn't like the claustrophobic feeling of everything crowded against the edges of the streets. Looming over her, ready to pounce.

Morlinna glanced back at her and bit her lip. "No. It wouldn't." Her hushed voice carried in the still air, echoing down the empty streets.

"How old is this place?" Ash asked. "The architecture is...different." She reached out to touch the large flat blocks, and mortar crumbled away from her fingertips. Rough tool marks marred the edges.

Morlinna frowned. "If it predates the Devastation, then at least three hundred years. Probably more."

Ashwyn snatched her hand from the wall. "Oh."

Morlinna raised an eyebrow. "If it's lasted this long, you're not going to topple it just like that." She poked her head through an empty doorway and pointed to the darkened frescoes painted along the top of the walls. "The art style matches the other ruins we've seen in the Devastation. Geometric shapes to represent animals and people. So the Devastation did push some of the buildings up and carried them along as it grew."

"But not all of them," Ash said. "I thought the growth would be here, breaking through the buildings like it tries to do above in Edgefall. But it's all clear."

The street they followed poured out onto a square surrounded by big, official-looking structures, marred only by the holes ripped into their sides. Across the empty space, a roof had caved in, leaving debris strewn across the cobbles, and the obelisk dominating the center of the square lay toppled and cracked across its base. But there were no plants. No vines creeping up the walls. No roots cracking the cobbles. Even the ancient planters against the walls were empty of anything but dust.

Morlinna stepped to the middle of the street and gazed up at the dome of growth arching over the city. "It's almost as if the Devastation is protecting this place."

Ash grimaced. "Or it's hiding it," she murmured.

Cold had seeped into her limbs and gut, and she couldn't tell if it was because the air was chill down here or if it was the feel of the ruined city.

Morlinna turned. "What was that?"

Ashwyn shook her head, unable to put the feeling into anything so tangible as words. "What are we looking for?" she said instead.

"Anything that will tell us the story of this place." Morlinna turned and met Felleron as he ranged between buildings. They exchanged a glance before he was off again, nose to the ground. "How did the Malady begin? What is it? How did they fight it?"

"With fire, looks like," Ashwyn said, indicating the streak of soot that stretched across the building opposite them. Beneath it, the cobbles had been broken in a circle, depressed and blackened as if flames had scoured them for hours.

Morlinna's brows drew down, and she stepped across the cobbles to examine the edges of the crater. "Perhaps. If this was the first battle, they would not have known that fire has no effect against corrupted threads."

"They would have learned fast, though," Ash said, picking up a chunk of blackened rock. "Fast enough to not destroy the rest of their city."

"That was my thought. I don't think this was the Malady."

Ash picked another structure, one with an intact roof, and stepped through the open doorway. There were no hinges, but a bar hung above her head. Perhaps they'd used curtains instead of doors hundreds of years ago.

Ancient tables and rough stools sat in the wide room. A collapsed staircase led to a second-story walkway, where black openings indicated more rooms. Bayna had petitioned the council to build an inn to house those who came to drop off their Absent in the necropolis instead of relying on just the guest house. But it had never been built. Ash imagined it would have looked something like this if it had.

Morlinna followed her into the room and wordlessly the two of them spread along the edges, searching. Ancient crockery lay on the tables. Clay plates and bowls and spoons had been abandoned mid-meal.

Ash stepped closer and ran her finger across the bottom of a bowl. There was nothing there but stains. "Whatever happened here, took them by surprise. In the middle of dinner." She frowned. "The Order evacuates a place before scouring it, don't they?"

Morlinna bit her lip. "If they have time," she said, voice carrying remembered pain.

Ash winced. "And if the Order was created to fight the Malady, this place would predate the Order."

"Everyone here might have succumbed to the Malady."

"But there's no infection. There are no Absent," Ash said, indicating the empty room and the streets beyond. "Where is everyone?"

"In their necropolis?" Morlinna said, but her voice held more than a hint of question. The details weren't adding up. If they hadn't had time to evacuate or rebuild, they wouldn't have had time to herd everyone into a necropolis.

Ash made a silent note with Wraith to look for a city of the dead on the outskirts of the real city, and the wolf wheeled around far above to find one.

Morlinna left the inn, the edge of her robe sweeping across the steps as she descended to the street.

Ashwyn hurried after her. She kept her eyes on the glowing threads weaving through the ground and the buildings. They remained a healthy black. No sign of the Malady anywhere.

Morlinna aimed down the main street that continued off the square. Almost as if she knew where she was going.

"What are you looking for?" Ash called, her breath coming faster as she hurried after her.

Morlinna hesitated long enough for her to catch up. "I'm not...not sure yet. It's just a feeling. Like I've been this way before."

Ash gave her a look out of the corner of her eye.

Morlinna frowned as if she was trying to find the words to describe it. "It feels like a street in Vitamorn. Like it's laid out in a similar pattern."

"And what was at the end of that street?"

Morlinna's steps faltered, and she stopped. Then gestured upward, and Ashwyn raised her light so it spilled across the street and up the facade of a bell tower.

"A temple."

Ash's brows drew down, and she glanced at the other woman. "Morlinna..."

Morlinna caught her look and shook her head. "It is not an exact replica. The style is different. As I said, the street was laid out in a similar pattern. Perhaps this was a holy district once."

"Maybe," Ash said, but she couldn't help the shiver that ran down her spine. Wraith echoed it across their connection.

Morlinna climbed the steps of the temple. The style might have been different, but it looked very much like an older version of Edgefall's Lower Temple with its long straight nave and the chapel house and cloisters on either side. Even the big double doors made Ash feel like she stood on the steps listening to Cass tell Bayna that she hadn't been chosen as a Nexsaint.

Morlinna paused on the top step, her hand on the worn door handle.

"What is it?" Ash asked.

"It's...strange. It feels like coming home only to find it destroyed."

"But you've never been here before."

"I know."

Ash kept her teeth locked tight on any more observations. Morlinna lived in a cloister. She had made her home in temples her whole life. It made a certain kind of sense that she would feel a connection to an ancient place of worship. That was all this was.

Morlinna shook herself and pressed down against the door handle. It moved, but the door itself stuck, and Ash stepped up to put her shoulder against it with her. Together they shoved, and the door grated open, carving a path through a pile of ancient debris.

Ash stared as Morlinna stepped through the nave, crisped wood falling to ash and dust as she passed.

Broken and blackened ends might have once been pews, and scorch marks marred the walls and stained the colored glass in the windows. Immense heat had cracked the stone of the altar right down the middle.

The destruction spoke of deliberate care. Someone had made sure that nothing survived the conflagration.

Except for the far wall behind the altar.

The paint flaked away, blistered and peeled after whatever fire had raged here, but the mural remained visible, illuminated by the light in Ash's hand.

Two figures stood, portrayed in broad angles and metallic tints. Some brightness still shone through the grime and patina of age, highlighting the lines of their faces and bodies.

The two faced each other over the altar, one tall and slim with white hair done in silver paint. Strong angular lines portrayed her long face and pointed jaw. Triangles, bisected by faint black lines, scattered across the wall behind her, looking like feathers in a whirlwind.

Ash couldn't tell if her eyes had originally been painted black or if the pigments had gone dark over the centuries, but her sable gaze remained fixed on the other figure in the frame.

The sharp angles didn't do her justice, only hinting at the curves of her waist and breasts, but the red paint still held an otherworldly luster as her hair fell behind her in impossible waves, piling at her feet. Flowers and leaves grew in curling lines through the strands.

"It's Her," Ash said even as Morlinna glided to the foot of the mural and dipped to her knees before it.

"It is," Morlinna said. "Deavita."

Ash picked her way through the debris to Morlinna's side. She raised a tentative hand to the mural, but the moment her fingertips brushed it, bits of gold paint flaked away, and she yanked her fingers back.

This was a temple. Of course there would be a depiction of the Goddess. They should have expected it. But...

"Who is this?" Ash asked, tilting her head back to stare up at the taller, silver-lined figure. The one who stood on the same level as a goddess, holding Her hands and gazing at Her with something soft in her still face.

Morlinna's head rose as if called from prayer, and she searched out the figure. "I don't know. I've never seen Deavita depicted with anyone else. She's always been a singular goddess."

Ash tore her gaze from the face surrounded by silver, feeling a strange jolt in her gut as she did so. Why was it so hard to look away? The Goddess stood there, beautiful and compelling even in Her angled style, but it was the other figure that drew Ashwyn. If only because she presented a mystery.

They held their hands high between them in a familiar pose of devotion, and Ashwyn caught her breath.

"Look at this frame," she said, finally taking in the rest of the imagery. The feathers, the flowers, and the woven strands crisscrossing around the couple, enclosing them in their own personal space. "It reminds me of the ones in those books you made me read."

The dusty religious histories Ash had only pored over because they were so important to Morlinna.

"Which ones?" Morlinna rose from the floor, her movements smooth despite the fact that it had to hurt her knees to kneel on the bare stone.

Ash searched her memory for names. "The frames around Saint Gerheart and Serene Highness Viora. And later around Saint Heliora and Saint Pallia."

"Those frames always depict important marriage alliances," Morlinna said. "They're supposed to represent the strands of the Nexum connecting the couple in question." She tipped her head back, eyes traveling over the interlocking lines. "This is very similar. Much simpler, but so is the style of the painting."

Ash's breath caught. It looked like a wedding portrait. The ones in the village were always done in bold colors on a stretched canvas no bigger than her hand. But the positioning, the way they held hands, the frame. It had to be.

"Morlinna," Ash said softly, voice hushed. "Is...the Goddess married?"

"No," Morlinna said, but she couldn't take her eyes off the couple either. "It's never been recorded. She's always been alone on Her throne."

Ashwyn bit her lip. "What else is this, then?"

"I don't know." Morlinna's lips went thin. "The Order might have hidden this. If She married a mortal, it would be..."

"Blasphemy?" Ashwyn raised her brows. "Is it blasphemy if a Goddess does it?"

Morlinna gave her a sidelong look, acknowledging the irony.

Ashwyn huffed a laugh and stepped to the altar, a huge slab of rough-cut stone that had barely survived the fire. Her hands ran over the surface, fingertips catching in gouges stained dark with soot. It would explain why this place was destroyed if someone had wanted to hide the evidence of a blasphemous union.

"Morlinna," she said, carefully not looking at the other woman, who still stared at the figure of the Goddess's spouse. "She speaks to you."

Morlinna let out a soft sigh. Not exactly a 'yes' but enough.

"Has She ever said anything about a spouse?"

She was silent for a long moment before her quiet answer came into the silence of the temple. "No."

"Why—"

"She is allowed to choose what to tell me," Morlinna said, voice sharp. She turned away from the silver figure.

Ashwyn bit her tongue hard on her next comment. Morlinna already knew how Ashwyn felt about a goddess who kept so much to Herself. Especially when it hurt those who placed their faith in Her.

But after many painful arguments, they'd agreed to disagree on this. And Ashwyn didn't want to be the one upsetting Morlinna right now. The Goddess was already doing a fantastic job of that.

Morlinna stalked down the nave, robe gathering ash along the edge.

"None of this mentions the corruption," she snapped. "If this was the original source, we should find some record of it somewhere. The Order fought the Malady for a century before finally defeating it. If this was the battleground, something should be left over."

"Then we keep looking," Ash said, hurrying to catch up as the other woman swept from the temple. "We find the necropolis and see if there are corrupted Absent there. We find an archive where the histories are kept. We'll find something, Morlinna."

Wraith's voice came into her head, making her jump. *There is no necropolis.*

"What?" She was startled enough to say it out loud.

Morlinna stopped on the steps. "What is it?" She was familiar enough with one-sided conversations to recognize Ash wasn't speaking to her, and she waited for the explanation.

I have been the entire way around the city, and I see no necropolis.

Ash's brows drew down. "That's odd."

Morlinna raised an eyebrow. "What's odd?"

"How big is the necropolis for Vitamorn?" Ash asked her.

Morlinna cocked her head. "Enormous. The cliff behind the city has been hollowed out for centuries in order to house our Absent. I've heard the caves extend for miles. It towers over everything. Why?"

"Wraith says he can't find the necropolis for this city."

Morlinna shook her head. "That's not... It would be impossible to miss."

"Could it be underground?"

Necropoli were traditionally built above ground, where the Absent could see the sun at least some of the time.

"Perhaps," Morlinna said. "Many things are different about the way this city has been built."

"Or maybe it's beyond the dome of the Devastation. Who knows what else is out there that was cut off."

I know what I'm looking for, Wraith grumbled. *But you can check if you want.*

Wraith allowed her to see the memory of his pathway through the air, and Ash paused, examining the layout of the streets below. Three parallel corridors connected with one central line.

"Morlinna, I think the whole city is laid out like a temple."

"What do you mean?"

Ash knelt and drew lines in the soot they'd tracked onto the steps of the temple. "Look, we're traveling along the nave here. And the edges are laid out like the cloisters and the ablution pools."

Morlinna bit her lip. "Just like Vitamorn."

Felleron darted up the steps and pressed against her legs. Morlinna put her hand to his head.

"If the city is set up like the temple, then what's at the altar?" Ash asked.

Morlinna took a deep breath. "In Vitamorn, it is the temple Seat."

"Then we go there." Ash stood and brushed off her hands. "That is the heart of this place. That must be where it all started."

Chapter 45
Concordim

This place is making me nervous, Wraith said.

"You're not the only one," Ash muttered.

Morlinna moved as though something drove her from behind, even though it was Ash who had the map in her head. Still, Morlinna guessed the next turn correctly more often than not, and Ash had to force herself to assume it was because of her familiarity with Vitamorn.

That's all it was.

Down their connection, she felt Wraith take a turn at the edge of the dome just as they passed onto the main street that ran down the entire length of the city. Like the nave of the temple.

Ashwyn held her hand high and let her light shine across the half-destroyed buildings to the central square, where the altar would have been if this was an actual temple.

Her breath caught, and ahead of her, Morlinna's steps faltered.

What is that? Wraith asked in her head.

Ash stepped past Morlinna, holding her hand out and tipping her head back to stare up and up at the column of vines and roots wrapped around the city's center. Each strand of the growth flashed white and ashy in her light, the strands of the Nexum underneath pulsing with the Malady.

As she stepped closer, the vines and roots shifted as if growing around each other, closing the gaps to form an impassable barrier guarding the heart of the city.

Morlinna came up beside her and blew out her breath.

Somewhere far, far above her, Ash felt Ebonheart wheeling over the forest, and she caught the dark slash of the firebreak and the white stain that was the chasm.

"It's the Heart of the Devastation," Ash said. "It reaches all the way down here."

They'd always wondered if the chasm went the whole way down. Now they had their answer. This was the outer layer of the chasm made by the corrupted roots that speared all the way to the city buried miles below on the crater's floor.

Each new detail sent a breath of unease through her. Instead of spreading across the cavern floor, the roots—and the Malady carried within them—dove directly into the ground.

Where did they go?

"This must be where it all began," Morlinna said. "Under the Heart. Whatever happened here, the truth of it is in there."

Ash agreed. Everything seemed to be leading them here. And with an empty city behind them, it was their next step, but she didn't like the desperate look in Morlinna's eyes or the feverish way she pushed forward.

"Can we even get through?" Ash said, a step behind her.

"*You* cannot," Morlinna said, then she slashed through the wall of growth, severing the roots and vines along with the corrupted strands.

But instead of a hole she could push through, she found more foliage on the other side, strands of vines grown even tighter. The foliage around the cuts shivered, growing to cover the gap.

Morlinna's hand crept to her chest, and her gaze darted across the barrier. "I can hear it," she whispered. "It's here. The Malady. And I can hear Her. I need to get through."

She cut through the vines again, and Ashwyn pulled her scythe from her back in order to help, but Morlinna dropped her blade at her feet and pressed into the opening where Ash couldn't follow. She held her hands to the corrupted vines, holding them back. But infected strands of the Nexum grew over her arms, and the vines followed, trapping her in place.

Ashwyn gasped and grabbed for Morlinna's robe, but the corrupted tendrils snaked across the other woman's back, and Ash had to snatch her hand away.

Morlinna screamed and pressed herself against the barrier, trying to push through.

"Morlinna!" Ash cried.

The roots and vines tightened, pulling her deeper, but she twisted around, gaze searching for Ashwyn behind her.

Ash recoiled. Morlinna's eyes had gone white, and the veins in her neck strained as she fought off the Malady's hold in her body and against her limbs.

Ash could do nothing to help the internal battle, but her hands clenched on her scythe. She could at least keep Morlinna from being eaten alive by the Devastation. She lunged forward, sweeping her corrupted blade around in an arc to sever the vines and the strands holding Morlinna prisoner.

Morlinna fought against the pull as Ash cleared the area, and finally, the other woman tore herself free and skidded back a step to land on her hands and knees on the cobblestones.

Ash gasped and fell beside her, holding her scythe in white-knuckled hands to keep herself from reaching for Morlinna.

"Are you all right?" she wheezed.

When Morlinna caught her breath and looked up, her eyes were clear blue once more.

But how much of her life had the Malady taken this time? How close to her heart had it climbed?

"I'm...fine," Morlinna said between pants.

She met Ash's tight-lipped look with one of her own. Then her features softened for just a moment around her eyes and mouth. "Truly, Ashwyn. The day has not come yet."

Ash's heart thumped. She stood back and let Morlinna rise.

"I thought you'd lost yourself to it," Ash said softly.

"No. It's only that I can feel it there. Close enough to touch. But I can't reach it. It's...frustrating."

From the agony on her face, this was a colossal understatement, and Ash couldn't help laughing.

Morlinna glanced at her, and the pain faded to self-deprecating humor. "Yes, well, you have always been good at helping me see the ridiculous."

Ash caught her breath, and the laugh fell away.

Morlinna was the first to return to the barrier, the stiff set of her shoulders their own retreat.

"We can't get through," she said.

"Even if we could cut back the vines? I can at least help with that."

Morlinna considered it for a moment and then shook her head. "No. It is growing too quickly, as if working against us. I could barely hold back the Malady, and if I got trapped inside..."

She would be overcome, and Ash wouldn't be able to reach her.

Ash moved to touch her shoulder, then pulled back at the last moment. It was *her* inclination to reach out with comfort. Not Morlinna's. Her touch would not be welcome, no matter how it was intended.

"We'll come back," she said instead. "Now that we've been here, we'll grab a connection. We can come back anytime to find a way through the barrier. Or maybe there is a way to come down through the chasm."

Morlinna laughed a real laugh this time. "Do you remember how far we've come? You want to travel the whole distance down the chasm?"

"So we'll label that plan B," Ash said, rolling her eyes. At least she'd gotten rid of that lost look Morlinna had had moments ago.

Ash was close enough to Morlinna to notice the way her laugh hitched and her body went stiff and straight.

"What is it?" Ash said. Then saw the tilt of Morlinna's head and the distance of her gaze. As if she listened to something Ash couldn't hear.

Ash bit her lip. It wasn't Felleron. The wolf sat at their feet, and Morlinna always made a point of looking at him when he spoke to her.

"Is it the Goddess?" she said. "Or the Malady?"

Morlinna's shoulders relaxed a fraction, and she glanced back at Ash with a rueful smile. "The Goddess."

Ash sighed. "About time," she muttered.

Morlinna gave her a sharp look. "She works on Her own time. Not ours."

Ash kept silent, but the thought that tried to slip between her teeth was that the human lifespan wasn't long enough to be held to a goddess's timetable.

Morlinna sighed, a chink forming in the relentless armor of her faith. "She speaks in words so rarely, Ashwyn. It's best I pay attention when it does happen."

She started forward, and despite herself, Ash stepped out to keep pace, her curiosity piqued. "What did she say?"

"She said, 'there.'" Morlinna raised her hand to point.

The pillar of the Malady stretched across the central square of the city, obscuring whatever the place had been built around. But there were several buildings still standing around it. Morlinna made for one of these.

Ash moved to follow, but a spike of alarm raced down her connection with Wraith.

"What—"

A burst of cold interrupted her, and somewhere to her left rose an inhuman shriek.

Ash! Wraith cried. *Dreads!*

"Where?" she said, trying to determine if the cold was here or coming through the connection.

She felt him flap, turning sharply to follow the edge of the Devastation high enough the dread couldn't reach.

At least one here. There are more in the city. They're heading for you.

More than one? Mortis. She'd never even been sure there was more than one in the forest.

Morlinna had paused on the steps of the building, her head tilted toward the scream.

"We have to go," Ash said.

Morlinna's gaze found hers, eyes tight. "I can't...Not when she finally spoke. We're so close."

Ash swore. This was a very bad idea, but there was no frost yet. No overwhelming sense of rage. Maybe they still had a moment before certain death.

"Hurry," Ash said. "I'll keep watch."

Morlinna pushed through the stone doors. One hung at an angle as if it had been blasted open, and through the opening, Ash caught a glimpse of ancient furniture, broken and left in piles around the large open room.

The space could have been anything, but given its position on the square and the open floor plan where many could gather, Ash guessed it was an official building of some kind. A city hall, perhaps.

Along one wall were the remains of another mural, but this one was too darkened to be seen and half was burned away.

A tablet hung on the opposite wall, but the bottom two-thirds had broken free and lay shattered against the stone floor.

Morlinna hurried to it. "You should see this," she called to Ash, and something in her voice made Ash realize arguing would be pointless.

She glanced down the streets, looking for tall, thin forms in the shadows. But there was nothing.

She blew out her breath and ran for Morlinna.

The top half of the tablet remained legible, the words carved deep into the stone.

It read:

City of Mournefast.

Beloved of Life's beloved.

Chosen of She Who Had Been He.

"She Who Had Been He?" Ash read aloud, a thrill of recognition going down her spine, and she glanced sharply at Morlinna.

But the other woman didn't return the look.

"Beloved of Life's beloved," Morlinna said instead.

"The Goddess of Life's spouse," Ash answered. "Her wife. This was her city."

"Mournefast. The mirror of Vitamorn."

Morlinna stared at the tablet, her face going through so many changes so fast that Ash couldn't track them.

Ash stepped back and glanced through the gap in the doorway toward the white barrier of the corrupted vines and swallowed.

If this city had belonged to the Goddess's wife, and this was the seat of the corruption...what was the connection between the two? Had the Order wiped out an entire city for heresy and created the Malady? Or had the Malady been the reason for the destruction?

Ash opened her mouth to ask the question out loud, but a shriek rose just outside the building, spearing through the open door and ringing against the walls.

Chapter 46
Concordim

Frost crept across the doors and the flagstones of the city hall, reaching icy fingers into Ash's chest as the dreads converged.

She glanced up, but the roof was one of the intact ones. They'd trapped themselves in here.

"We can't stay here," she hissed at Morlinna. "We've got to get out."

Wraith, get back here. We're going to have to jump back to the surface.

Morlinna stared up at the broken tablet at the name of the city. Mournefast. Her long face went bleak and frustrated.

Then she blew out her breath in something that sounded a lot like a growl. It was so uncharacteristic, it made Ash jump.

"We'll come back," Ash said. She reached out to pull a thread from the tablet, weaving it loosely beside the threads she kept for Morlinna's cloisters and the three other places in the Devastation that she could manage. "We'll come back as many times as we have to in order to find answers."

Morlinna met her gaze.

"I promise," Ash said.

Morlinna closed her eyes and took a bracing breath. Then she nodded and swept toward the door. Maybe they still had time to slip out.

Wraith, meet us beside the Underheart.

Ash, Wraith's voice came to her thin and breathy, even though there was no such thing as air along their connection.

She stopped, and Morlinna glanced back with a frown.

What's wrong?

You...you should see this.

Ash sent herself down the thread of their connection, borrowing his eyes.

Wraith swooped at the edge where the city ended and the Devastation began. He turned his head, and Ash caught a glimpse of something white and pulsing.

A root.

Oh mortis.

They'd thought it was odd that the Underheart just plunged straight into the ground without spreading. But they'd been wrong.

"Ashwyn," Morlinna said calmly in her ear, and Ash pulled her consciousness back.

Her breath clouded in the air as long, wicked fingers curled around the edges of the door.

Ash made a split-second decision.

Wraith, land. Now. I'm using you as an anchor.

"Hold on," she told Morlinna.

Morlinna tucked her arm through Ashwyn's, and her other hand grasped the ruff at Felleron's neck. Then Ash reached out for the thread connecting her with Wraith and wrapped it around her arm so she wouldn't lose her grip.

A crown of antlers appeared around the crooked doors, and a shriek raised the hair along Ash's arms as she yanked on the thread.

She, Morlinna, and Felleron speared through the air, their bodies smearing along the thread as Ash pulled them across the city to Wraith.

The three of them staggered, appearing back in the world next to Wraith. Ash immediately straightened and swung her scythe around, but there was no frost here, no chill in the air.

"We have a moment before they catch up," Morlinna said. "What did he find?"

Ash turned, taking in the space where the roots and vines of the Devastation met the floor of the crater in an impenetrable wall. Between the last buildings and the vines, rows of ancient trees stood dead and petrified in their fields. An orchard?

What had it been like here when the Devastation first appeared? Had there still been people here? Had they stood in this very place and watched as vines and roots and trees cut them off from the rest of the world, sealing them in for centuries?

And if they had, where had they gone?

Here, Wraith said, and Ash's attention snapped back to the present. She raised her hand to light up his find.

An enormous root had pushed through the dirt, heading from the city's center and plunging into the thickness of the Devastation. The ground lay cracked and heaved where it had broken through.

Like a root from one of the great trees of the Devastation, it stood at least half as high as Ashwyn. But this one was stained an ashy white, and the strands beneath its surface pulsed with the Malady.

"Mother of Life," Morlinna said under her breath. She stared along the line of the root where it plunged into the dirt before reaching the city. It had come from the Underheart. That mass of corrupted growth had sent out roots into the ground, and at least one of them had grown all the way to the Devastation.

"It's been down here, spreading," Ash said. "For who knows how long. Everything we've done on the surface...and this has just been sitting down here, sending out roots." She met Morlinna's eyes. "Was it on purpose? Was it just keeping us busy, so we'd never know it was down here creeping closer?"

Morlinna shook her head. "That's ridiculous. The Malady isn't sentient. It doesn't think. All it has is instinct."

"It talks to you," Ash said, horror crawling up her throat, thick enough to choke her.

Morlinna drew in a sharp breath. "Not with words." She glanced away, then back, her voice rising. "It has only ever been a wordless call. A feeling that it wants me to give myself to it. I am the one who gives that meaning. No one else."

Ash bit her lip, but Morlinna's pained gaze ate at her. "All right," she said. "I'm sorry."

A thread of thought reached Ash through her connection with Ebonheart. A query.

Us? she said.

She was asking if there was anything the magpies could do.

Search the forest, Ash told her. *Look for the spread from above.*

This one root might have caused hundreds of islands of Malady throughout the forest.

It would be good to have eyes in the Devastation, but the likelihood that the magpies would be able to find a single spot of Malady in the vast forest was nearly zero.

Ash stepped forward, following the line of the corrupted root, twisting to trace its path. It pushed through into the open air and then plunged into the wall of roots and vines, which had pulled back to form a tunnel around it.

Ash turned to examine the tunnel walls. Nearly three feet of clear air surrounded the corrupted root. The vines and growth that made up the tunnel were still Absent like everything else they'd found this deep in the Devastation.

But they weren't corrupted. The clear space they'd left around the white root had created its own firebreak.

"I have never seen the Devastation do this before," Ash said. "Like it's protecting itself. Have you?"

"No," Morlinna said. "Perhaps it is learning to fight the Malady as well. It is to our advantage. We can follow the root to its end and cut it off there."

She hesitated and glanced back along the root.

"What is it?" Ash asked.

"I don't like it. The concentration of the Malady here in this one root is disturbing. And the way it seems to be heading somewhere specific..." Her lips went thin. "It reminds me of a corrupted creature and the way it seeks out the greatest concentration of life to corrupt."

Ash's heart sank. "We should hurry," she whispered.

Morlinna didn't even respond. She just climbed into the tunnel and started up the dense pathway, staying away from the root itself, as if testing the path for Ashwyn, who couldn't afford to even brush the corrupted root.

The journey in this direction was even more surreal than when they'd descended. The silence and the darkness pressed against Ash until she felt the entire weight of the Devastation looming over them.

And as they slowly sloped up, they should have seen more creatures, Devastation beasts making their home in the vegetation. But the tunnel remained eerily empty except for them and the root. Almost like the creatures had learned to avoid it.

They did go up some, but the root remained on the deepest levels of the Devastation that Ash had ever seen. And again, Ash was struck with the thought that it was trying to hide itself. To get as far as it could before they noticed it.

And she had the sinking sensation that she knew where it was going.

Connections formed to places where people had some sort of emotional attachment, and Ash had cut this one out over and over whenever it had grown back.

She sent a thought to Ebonheart, and the magpie spun, calling her brethren to follow her. Far, far above, Ash felt the connection between them stretch as the flock wheeled and followed Ash's path, predicting its end.

Ash climbed along the tunnel behind Morlinna and let her focus go wide, feeling the magpies as a whole instead of riding along inside Ebonheart's mind.

They swooped and dove in a line, spreading from Ash and Morlinna's location deep under the Devastation, following the line of the root to its logical destination.

And as they flew over wide green swaths and open land, sticks and shouts chased them away.

The jolt of familiarity made Ashwyn jerk, and she stopped climbing, resting her head against the wall of the tunnel where the Absent vines wrapped around and around each other.

"What is it?" Morlinna said, turning in the narrow space to check on her. "Are you all right?"

Ash shook her head. "Edgefall," she said. "The magpies are following the trail from above, and they just reached Edgefall."

Morlinna gave her a look, eyes full of empathy. "Of course it's heading to the village."

Ash tipped her head back, blinking. The blur along her left side seemed especially thick in the dim light.

"I don't think it is," she said. Above, the magpies were still wheeling, still spreading out along the route the Malady was taking. "They're being chased from the fields. Because we always chase off magpies. But just beyond that..."

Morlinna leaned against the wall. "What is beyond the fields, Ashwyn?"

"The necropolis," Ashwyn whispered. "If it stays on this path and doesn't deviate, it will reach the necropolis."

Morlinna's shoulders slumped. "Dea protect us. How many does it house?"

"Thousands," Ash said. "Hundreds of thousands. Ten generations from across the whole area from here to Vitamorn."

She raised her gaze to the woman who'd taught her and sheltered her when everyone else she'd loved had tried to destroy her.

"Morlinna," she said, voice hoarse. "My mother is housed there."

Chapter 47
Animatim

V returned to the little town of Squallhaven on a day as gray and oppressed as she felt. The town was far enough from the front lines of the current Little War that it felt like another world. But the change in scenery wasn't enough to scour the memory of bodies falling to dust or the white, contorted faces of infected victims.

It had been months since she'd left this place—and her hunt along with it—but her pack lay in the corner of the inn's one room and her second best set of leather armor waited on the dresser, untouched.

And now that she was back, she couldn't get her head straight. The Malady lurked in her thoughts, tangling with memories of games in the meadow and turning beloved faces white.

She shook her head hard enough to dislodge the distraction. Focus.

She strode to the washbasin and splashed her face with tepid water. Drops slid down under the leather cuff on her wrist, and she let her fingers slide over the stitches, counting. One stitch for every day she'd searched for her father. The line wrapped in a spiral, looping her wrist over and over.

One thousand nine hundred and twenty-three of them. Five years, three months, and seven days.

She'd known it wouldn't be easy to hunt down the ex-commander of the Bladesaints. But every day that she was out here was a day that she wasn't serving on the front lines where she was needed. And another day that a heretic roamed free after placing the world in danger.

The Abdicant had passed on her duties as Judge five years ago, and now V was the only one who could deliver the Last Death to the victims on the front line. And she was the only one who could hunt down the heretic. But when she focused on one task, she fell behind with the other.

V slammed the shutters open and leaned on the windowsill, staring out at the mist hanging over the trees.

Two things. Such a paltry number. A Judge should be able to handle two things.

V took a deep breath, letting the frustration drain out through her clenched fingers. Then she yanked her pack open, rummaging for a clean shirt and pants.

She could have returned to the city. Just for a brief rest. She hadn't actually seen her mother in over a year. Not since her search had taken her near the Devastation on the city's northern border.

But her stomach clenched with the thought, and she could hear the Abdicant's words so deep in her head that disconnecting her amplification loop wouldn't give her respite.

"Where is he, Vitania?"

"We cannot let his crime go unpunished."

"How long do you plan to let him go free?"

She dropped the flap of her pack and yanked her dirty shirt over her head.

Maybe it would be better if she just went straight to the Primarch Divine. How many times had his kind words made it seem like she could go on just a little further? She could use those right now.

But the idea of returning to him with nothing to report made her stomach cramp even worse.

Better to finish and return in triumph.

She finished pulling on her clean clothes and grimaced her way back into her breastplate.

The innkeeper nodded as she left. He'd let her use the room for the last couple of months as a place to store her things when she went back to the front, but hopefully now that she was back, she'd be able to move on from this damp, smelly place.

Squallhaven sat at the edge of one of the newer Devastations. In the last five years, her father's trail had led all over the countryside. V had gotten to see corners of the continent she never would have thought to visit. But this one was by far her least favorite.

When it wasn't storming over the Devastation, it drizzled. And when it wasn't drizzling, a heavy mist hung over the swampy trees crowded so close together the moss hanging from their branches formed walls. And the surrounding area bore the aftereffects of all the moisture, making the ground sodden and noxious.

V walked the path she knew her father had taken, kicking mossy rocks out of the way. She'd only been back for less than a day, and she already hated this shade of green.

His trail was months and months cold, but this was the last place where she'd made any sort of progress. The place where every hint of his movement had just disappeared under the deluge of water.

Rain was supposed to be life-giving, but V didn't think this particular rain came from the Goddess.

She had to find something new this time. One tiny thing that could lead her forward.

By the time the sun set in the distance, she knew miracles weren't happening today. Anything that had been here had been washed away so long ago it wouldn't have mattered, anyway.

Her hands clenched at her sides, empty.

Maybe miracles weren't meant to happen to her at all.

An image of the Goddess's threads wrapped around her fingers popped into her head, and she winced. Dea, they all thought she was "the chosen" when she'd really just been as frightened as an abandoned eight-year-old, grasping someone that didn't want to hold on to her.

V tore the loop from her ears and screamed into the silence, until the rawness of her throat made her cough and hack.

The threads around her shivered, reflecting black and gold, even in the dim light. And for a moment, she wished she could disconnect her sight too and just rest in the dark and the quiet where no one expected anything of her.

But the gold strands shimmered, and the patterns nipped at her, making her drop her chin so she could stare at the network threading through the mud.

"Everything is a tool," her father used to sign while they played. "You just have to hold it right."

She'd been using Bladesaint tools. Interrogation, observation, wilderness tracking. She hadn't been using Nexsaint tools.

V dropped to her knees in the swampy road. Connections spread away from her, threads of healthy black in the ground, the brush, the birds cawing overhead.

It all looked normal. Like a healthy countryside.

But as she shifted down into the strands, focusing her vision and sifting them aside one by one, looking for anything out of place, she saw dozens of threads buried underneath.

Years worth of objects lost in the mud.

V dug her hands down, letting the mud seep past her gloves as she sent out threads of her own to catch them and pull them to the surface. They emerged in heaps and mounds, too dirty to determine details, but she recognized a shoe here, a ring there, and one tattered doll missing its head.

Her breath came faster as she stared at a treasure trove of forgotten things. She reached out for the nearest object—the ring—and lifted it free with a squelch. The light from the Nexum strands faded into background noise as she focused on the shape. She held it flat in her palm so the constant rain washed away the mud.

But she didn't need to be able to see details to see the connection that stretched away into the growing night.

Objects retained connections with their owners when there was some emotional bond, but time would erode the strands as the person forgot about it or replaced it.

This connection was still strong. And there were others among the treasure trove that still retained some thin thread of feeling leading off into the darkness.

The despair fell away, and V smiled. Despite the terrible weather and her terrible luck and the terrible memories that marred this hunt, the Goddess was smiling on her.

V had a lead.

V would never say she was having fun on this hunt, but there was something deeply satisfying about following the connections and learning the stories for each object she found along the road where her father had disappeared. Like a puzzle forming a whole, piece by piece.

Like the challenges her father had constructed for her as a child.

She did not follow that thought to its conclusion.

It took time to track down the owner of each object, but the delay felt different now. Each question was a step forward. Each answer brought her closer. And she could be patient as long as she kept moving.

V followed the second-to-last thread, the one stretching from the ring, prepared to walk forever if she had to.

But the strand led her to a house outside of Squallhaven, only a couple of hours from where she'd originally found it. Candlelight shone from the windows, and a sturdy fence surrounded a pigpen on the far side of the house.

She knocked on the door, and a man opened it. He glanced at her dark cloak and gave her a polite nod.

The man's mouth moved in greeting, drowned out by the constant shushing of the rain. V reached up to adjust the amplification loop to focus in front of her.

"Nexsaint?" he said, then his eyes narrowed in the gloom. "No, sorry. Judge?"

"Is this yours?" She held up the ring, not bothering with a softer tone. All her softness had been washed away in mud.

"I don't know what..." He squinted. Muffled voices came down the hall, ringing with quiet normality while V's heart beat in time with the question in her heart and head. *Where is he? Where is he?*

"Come inside, Your Serenity, and we'll sort you out."

V braced herself as the man opened the door wider, waiting for a trap, but he just beckoned her inside. A young girl poked her head around an open doorway and gasped, then ducked back again.

"Conner," a woman asked. "What is it?"

"A Judge," the man called. "On a hunt, looks like."

"A Judge?" A woman appeared in the doorway, eyes wide. "Your Serenity. We—we—"

"We're happy to help you," the man interrupted. "We can make you comfortable—"

"I'm not staying. I just need to know if this is yours." She held up the ring again.

The man reached out, and she dropped it into the palm of his hand. She had her answer from the way the threads sang as they came together again.

"I think...Yes!" He smeared away some of the grime to reveal the metal. "Yes, this is mine. Wherever did you find it?"

"Along the road east of Squallhaven. Do you travel there often?"

He shook his head. "Only when I take the pigs to the market. I haven't in months. I lost the ring on my last trip. Lightning scared one of the sows, and I had to wrestle it in the mud. It must have slipped off."

"While you were on that trip, did you happen to see any other travelers along the road? I'm looking for one in particular. Tall, dark hair, trimmed beard."

His grin faded. "The heretic."

V's stomach clenched, and she caught her breath. After five years, the words felt too easy. "You've seen him?"

The woman covered her mouth with her hand.

Conner rolled the ring over and over in his palm. "I have, aye. He was injured and limping along the road. I offered him a ride and some help, but he refused. Wouldn't let me near him. He said if I offered aid, you'd send me to the Last Death."

Why would Wesley care? He'd nearly condemned the world, and he wanted to protect this one family from being collateral damage? She nearly laughed in Conner's face.

He'd had no problem ruining V's life in a battle of politics.

She raised her chin and looked at Conner, who stared back at her, waiting. The man's nerve must have been made of steel to face down a hunting Judge.

"He also said if I helped you, you might spare me."

V heard it as if from a distance, but she knew her loop was secure.

Wesley had known she was coming for him. Of course, he had. It would be her or her mother, and the Abdicant hadn't left on a hunt in years.

"I'm not here for you," she said quietly. "Only for him. As far as I know, you've committed no offense." At least not one that required execution. "Do you know what direction he headed in?"

"I do, Your Serenity. He didn't try to hide it."

She spread her hand out, waiting.

"He disappeared after I got the sow under control. Into the Devastation."

Chapter 48
Concordim

It was impossible to tell how long they traveled, but according to the magpies who wheeled under the bright sun above, they'd been under the Devastation for nearly two days when they finally reached the end of the root.

Ash and Morlinna had each napped for an hour or two at most, but they couldn't afford to delay. The Malady had been growing this way for years, and it had nearly reached the walls of the dead city.

Here the root tapered to a blunt end and started growing upward, spearing toward the unsuspecting necropolis. The still-living vines that formed the walls of the tunnel writhed away from the tip even as they watched.

Morlinna and Ash exchanged a glance.

The root itself grew fast enough Ash imagined she could see it moving.

"Have you ever seen it do that?" Ash asked Morlinna.

Morlinna shook her head. "I have only ever seen the Malady spread through the threads of the Nexum. Never by growing."

Ash unslung the scythe from her back.

"We must cut it back," Morlinna said. "Keep it from reaching the Absent."

Bad enough if it reached the village. But if it reached the necropolis, there were thousands of soulless bodies there waiting for their chance to Return. If they were corrupted, then they never would. And the madness of the Malady would drive them to corrupt everything around them before they finally succumbed to the Last Death.

Ash shuddered, then surged forward and swung her blade, putting her entire strength behind it. After years of climbing and fighting in the Devastation, her arms were wiry with muscle.

But her blade stuck in the thick wood.

She yanked it free, ignoring the way the blow had jarred her shoulders. The curved blade of the scythe left behind a long scar, and the ends of the Nexum shriveled and curled.

But there were hundreds more weaving through the thickness of the root to take its place.

"How far do we have to do this?" Ash said, staring down the length of the tunnel where they'd already come. She knew the answer, but, mortis, she hoped Morlinna said something else.

"All the way back to the Underheart, if we can," Morlinna said.

Ashwyn winced. "It's never going to happen."

Morlinna straightened in the narrow tunnel and gave her a desperate look. "What else can we do? We cannot let it continue."

Ash stared upwards at the tangle of roots and vines that hid the walls and courtyard beyond. She didn't need to look through Ebonheart's eyes to remember the Absent shuffling aimlessly through the sunlight. Or Uniah carefully keeping them clothed and their hair trimmed. Rotating them every day so they each got their chance in the sun.

She didn't need to see her mother's face to remember her strong grip and Cass's voice saying, "She's down there, too, you know."

Ashwyn swore under her breath as Wraith whined and butted her hand with his head.

Morlinna had already turned back to the root.

Ashwyn joined her.

Her arms ached and her shoulders screamed with each blow to the root, but they had to cut through each inch and the strand behind it. If they tried to cut the root off closer to the buried city, they risked leaving behind pieces that could infect the rest of the Devastation.

Was this how the Malady jumped? Had it sent tendrils to creep to the surface for them to discover? They'd never been able to trace the trail back to a source, but they'd been looking for something traveling toward the Heart. Perhaps it was this root all along. Mortis, what if there were more of them, spreading from the Underheart below?

Ash blocked the thought and set it aside as a problem for another day. This was enough for now.

They hacked and sawed, and Ash could feel the blade of her scythe going dull even as she swung. Sweat trickled down the back of her neck, the heat of her exertion finally countering the chill of the air at this depth.

For hours, maybe days, Ash and Morlinna cut back this one root. Maybe it had been years now. Her blade broke loose a chip, and it flew past her, scoring her cheek. The corrupted threads had already been severed, but the chip itself was still sharp.

Ash cried out in pain and frustration and let her blade drop for a moment.

Morlinna spun, face white.

"We can't do this forever," Ash said with a groan. "We have to find a different way."

"You know as well as I do that I have no other tactic."

Ash winced. She hadn't meant to accuse Morlinna of not doing enough. That was the whole point of this excursion. She'd wanted to give Morlinna the space to find a better way to fight the Malady. And look how well that had turned out.

"I can force it to turn aside," Morlinna said. "But it will resume its charge the moment I turn my back. I would have to stay here to ensure it remained trapped."

The resignation in her voice cracked something in Ash's anger. She was prepared to live the rest of her life down here, fighting back this one branch of the Malady because she was the only one who could.

Ash shook her head hard enough to start a headache. "No. Better to kill it off. But there are more ways to cause the Last Death than just a blade."

Morlinna rested her scythe against the tunnel floor and slumped over it. "What do you suggest?"

"Fire."

"The Order has tried to burn through the Malady before. But the strands are too weak. They succumb to the Last Death before they—"

"So weave them."

Morlinna straightened and stared at her.

Ash's breath came faster as her mind raced down the possibilities. "No one makes weavings with threads of the Malady because it corrupts them at the first touch. But you could."

Morlinna stared at her hands, the air leaving her lungs on a soft, "oh."

Ash took a step toward her. "You could weave the Malady like ordinary threads. You can send heat down the strands of the Nexum just like a Mender does to burn out infection in a person."

"And the weaving would make the threads of the fire stronger. At least for a little while." She looked up at Ash, her lips set. "How have I never thought of this before?"

"Why would you? You've always focused on destroying it. Not weaving with it."

"We will try. Feed me the strands, and I will weave them with the root."

Ash's chest went tight at the wonder on Morlinna's face.

She dug in her belt pouch for her flint and steel, then jerked her chin at the wolves. "Stand back," she told them.

Ash struck a spark over the chips of dead wood at her feet, letting it catch and whoosh into a healthy flame. She snatched a wispy thread as soon as it appeared, feeling the heat of fire against her fingers. The moment she had a good grasp on it, she tossed it to Morlinna, letting the other woman feed it through her hands.

Between one finger and the next, the strand in Morlinna's palm went white and sickly, and she spun it into the root, weaving the searing heat of the fire into the corrupted strands.

The strands writhed and pulsed and then curled up, dying from the inside out. The root went black and cracked with the heat as the strands of its Nexum burned to death.

Fire swept down the length of the root, away from them, and Ashwyn whooped.

"It worked!"

She couldn't chase it down like she wanted, ensuring that the fire burned it all the way to the Underheart. She had to keep feeding the healthy strands to Morlinna. But moments later, the strand in Morlinna's hand went taut and snapped.

The cut end of the fire curled, and the flames at Ashwyn's feet went out.

"What?" Ash stared at the pile of cinders. "What just happened?"

"I don't know. Something broke the weave." She met Ash's gaze and gave her a weary smile. "It might not be anything nefarious. I've never seen such a tenuous weave last across such a great distance before. The strain was probably too great for it. We can follow it to the end and keep burning it away until we reach the city. But congratulations. This was much more efficient and effective than I imagined."

Ash flushed, the success burning bright in her belly, and she turned her face away in case Morlinna could see the effect her words had just in Ashwyn's eyes.

Morlinna put a hand to the still-warm root, her fingertips coming away blackened with charcoal, and she started down the tunnel to find how far the burn had reached.

Ashwyn struggled to her feet, her back sending pain down her waist and legs from all the chopping they'd done.

The vines under her feet trembled.

"What was that?" Ash said, but Morlinna was too far to hear her now.

She glanced at Wraith. The wolf stood with his hackles raised. Felleron had already followed Morlinna.

"Wraith?"

I smell Malady.

Ash glanced at the burned and blackened root. The Malady had been all over this tunnel until just now. But she trusted Wraith. If he said he smelled corruption, then he wasn't talking about what was obvious.

She hurried down the tunnel toward Morlinna.

"Morlinna-"

She reached the other woman, who had stopped abruptly and stood staring at the crisped root.

The burned bits of root tapered away here. This was where the weave had snapped.

But brand new shoots had sprouted crossways to the main root they'd followed here. They each plunged into the tunnel wall, infecting the Devastation with the Malady they carried.

"Oh, mortis," Ashwyn breathed. It had doubled back.

The vines and roots of the wall shivered and tried to draw back from the infected pieces of itself, but before it could move more than an inch, the wall exploded inward.

Ash and Morlinna threw themselves backward as a swarm of badgers spilled through the hole in the tunnel wall. Morlinna recovered first, rising to her feet and sweeping her blade around to form a silver barrier between the swarm of creatures and Ash and the wolves.

Each badger raised a curved tail behind it, tipped with a poisoned stinger. And each had white streaks stretching from its eyes, marring the fur of its face.

Ash followed the line of the new corruption from the root to the hole where the badgers had appeared. "Did it infect them on purpose to stop us?"

Morlinna shook her head. "The Malady always seeks to corrupt life. It saw a way forward, and it took it."

Ash opened her mouth, but the swarm of badgers had zeroed in on them and surged forward.

"Don't let them leave the tunnel," Morlinna shouted, leaping headlong into the swarm. "They'll infect everything."

Ash didn't need the warning, but she followed Morlinna without a word.

Chapter 49
Concordim

Ashwyn dove under the root and came up on the other side, swinging her scythe to behead a badger.

The first one went down, but three more surged to take its place.

Behind you, Wraith called. Ashwyn ducked, and a stinger stabbed over her shoulder. She rolled and swept her scythe around, catching the creature's legs. It snarled as it toppled over, but that wouldn't stop it for long. The Malady didn't care about missing limbs. Morlinna was right. It would find a way forward.

The corruption spread along the floor of the tunnel, racing for her feet. She spun her scythe around and cleared a space to stand.

She grabbed for an uncorrupted strand of the Nexum above her and pulled a vine loose from the ceiling. The entire tunnel warped and shifted, and she had to drop it to grab for the walls and hold them steady so the tunnel didn't collapse on them.

The badgers surged forward, taking advantage of her distraction.

Ashwyn dropped one of the strands she was holding and grabbed for the vine that she'd pulled loose. She wrapped it around the closest badger and tied it to the wall.

But while she stretched out her hand, another badger lunged for her, jaws open.

She screamed and twisted, avoiding the blow, but she overbalanced and fell, her wrist snapping under her.

The creature charged. Wraith darted between them, flapping his wings in the small space. The badger faltered, confused by the flurry of feathers.

It gave Ash just enough time to pull threads from the ceiling and make them sharper than any knife. She threw out her good arm, sending her threads slicing through the badger. One severed its heart thread, and the creature fell to dust.

"Thanks," Ashwyn gasped at Wraith.

She tucked her injured arm closer to her side and settled the shaft of her scythe against her other arm to give herself more stability. Then she flung herself back into the fray.

With the ceiling so low, she had less space to flip herself over the badgers, but she moved faster than them, pulling up strands of vines and roots to block their attacks.

Ashwyn herded them with walls of foliage, trapping three of them in a corner. She let go of the strands even as they reached to corrupt them, and as they moved, she swept her scythe around to sever their threads and their heads.

Three more badgers fell to dust.

Ashwyn spun around to check on Morlinna, where she battled the worst of the swarm, and caught a glimpse of her dark robes disappearing under the weight of several badgers at once.

"No!" Ash cried and cut a safe path to the other woman. She swung her scythe like a club, using the flat of the blade. The blow knocked aside two badgers, and they tumbled into the rest, leaving Morlinna gasping against the tunnel floor.

Ash reached with her good hand to help her up, sucking in a breath when her fingers encountered blood soaking the shoulder of Morlinna's robe.

"I'm all right," Morlinna grated out. "Or I will be."

A rising shriek cut off anything else she was going to say. Frost crept up the tunnel as displaced rage sent a shiver down Ashwyn's spine.

"A dread," she whispered. "Coming up from the city."

Even the last of the badgers seemed to feel it. The creatures froze, staring down the tunnel, their noses twitching.

Then they scattered, heading for the opening into the tunnel.

"Stop them," Morlinna gasped. She tried to straighten, but collapsed against the wall. "They can't escape."

The certainty shot through Ashwyn, too. If these got away, they'd have to hunt down each and every trail to stop the spread. And from this deep in the Devastation, they could pop up anywhere.

Ash swept in front of Morlinna, dodging to block the opening even as the rage climbed up the back of her neck and rang in her head. It spread down her limbs, making her slower.

But she pushed herself to raise her scythe and swing at the first badger to reach her. It fell in a spurt of blood and a pile of dust.

Wraith darted in to her side to snarl and keep the next badger back as Felleron wriggled under Morlinna's free arm to support her as she stood.

Ash swept her scythe and locked the blade around a badger's foot, flipping it over. Her blade sank deep into its fur, and she severed its threads. Then she swung to catch the last badger as it backed away from Wraith.

What little light still shone from her hand, flickered as the chill of the dread came up the tunnel. Ash lunged for Morlinna.

"Is that the last of them?" the woman whispered.

"I hope so," Ash answered. "Because we can't stay here. We'll come back to finish the root later."

She reached for the thread in her Nexum that said home and pulled.

Obitusim

Morlinna had no choice but to let Ashwyn lead her to one of the pews in their temple and begin the weave that would eventually heal her shoulder. The younger woman had to be exhausted after two days under the Devastation, two different Nexum jumps, and the fight. But Morlinna was in even worse shape.

"Here," Ashwyn said, handing her the bandages. "Unroll those for me."

Morlinna managed it one-handed while Ashwyn set some water to boil. Skilled menders could prevent infection with more complex weaves, but she'd never learned them. All those years spent lying in the infirmary in Vitamorn wasted because she hadn't paid more attention to what was going on around her.

"Did—" Morlinna hissed as she tried to ease her arm from her ruined sleeve. "Did everyone make it out unscathed?"

"Felleron and Wraith are fine," Ashwyn said, sitting down beside her. "And I asked the magpies to keep an eye on the Devastation and the necropolis. In case any spots crop up. It's you and me who need attention."

Morlinna hadn't missed the way Ashwyn worked one handed. But there was nothing she could do about it while she sat here losing so much blood.

She did not sit still well. Too many years where sitting still meant something was creeping up on her. Or she wasn't out fulfilling her purpose.

But for once, the anxious buzz along her limbs calmed under Ashwyn's touch. Morlinna glanced up. Ashwyn's gaze remained fixed on her work, her dark hair tucked behind her ears so she could see.

Morlinna's fingers twitched with the distracting urge to untuck the strands and let them fall.

She swallowed and turned away, shame flooding her until the thought was swept away with it.

Ashwyn had given her space and—and a peace with another person she'd never had before. She'd never wanted anything more than that.

She'd never deserved anything more than that.

Morlinna had been selected for one purpose. She knew all the things her end would be. Abrupt. Ugly. Necessary.

But now it would not be lonely.

And that was enough for her. She would not look for more than that. Not when it was Ashwyn who would have to bear the burden of saying goodbye sooner rather than later.

But her mind returned to that moment in the tunnel, where Ashwyn had given her a gift beyond space and safety. She'd given her something new. A technique Morlinna could use in the fight.

Morlinna had never thought Ashwyn could teach *her* something.

Ashwyn finished tying off the bandage.

"Now you," Morlinna said.

"I'll be fine to wait until you've rested," Ash said, hiding a grimace.

Morlinna raised an eyebrow. "I did not teach you stubbornness," she said.

"No, I came with that on my own." She flashed Morlinna a grin, but the other woman just sat there with her hand out until Ashwyn let her tend her broken wrist.

"It will need time to knit, but at least it's started," Morlinna said as Ashwyn extended the bandages to her again. "We will rest. Then we must go back to the root and—"

The forest erupted with the calls of a hundred magpies spread between the cloister and Edgefall.

Morlinna looked at Ashwyn, but Ashwyn had already risen to her feet.

"What is it?" Morlinna asked. "What have they spotted?"

"One of the corrupted badgers made it to the necropolis," Ashwyn whispered, and Morlinna's heart seized in her chest. "We didn't get them all."

Chapter 50
Concordim

Over and over again, Ashwyn had cut away the thread connecting her to Edgefall. So the closest connection they had was one Morlinna had formed with a landmark ruin somewhere to the north. But from there, they had to run.

Ashwyn led the way through the trees, using the Nexum to swing up to the pathways that would carry her in the swiftest line to Edgefall. But even as she raced toward the village where she'd grown up, a dark ferocity burned in her breast. They didn't deserve her protection. They didn't deserve her care.

But this was the right thing to do. And she was still strong enough to do it, despite the way they'd tried to destroy her.

Two things could be true.

Morlinna followed behind, no more than a black shadow against the dark foliage. She'd donned her mask and raised her hood so only the polished surface flashed white in the dim light.

Ashwyn dropped to a lower branch that sloped up the side of the crater. As the rough surface rose under her feet, she leaned forward and used her scythe to help her scale the sheer climb.

Before she was ready for it, she'd reached the lip of rock where they'd thrown her all those years ago.

She faltered and stumbled to a stop, feet rooted against the crater's edge.

She stared out across the moonlit roofs, little wisps of smoke rising through the clear air from the cracked chimneys. Little had changed. Bayna's house had new thatch, but the orphan house still sagged like a tired dog.

The heat of Morlinna's presence warmed her left shoulder as the other woman leaned close. "Are you all right?"

Ash shook her head, not as an answer but to free herself of the weight of misery that had settled over her the moment she'd dropped from the trees.

"Fine," she said shortly. "I don't hear the bells. Uniah hasn't called the alarm yet."

She exchanged a glance with Morlinna. That wasn't a good sign. Even traveling as fast as they could, it had taken them over an hour to reach the village.

"We'll go quietly," Ash said under her breath. "I don't see any Bladesaints, but they have to have replaced Rafe and Ingram by now."

Ash led Morlinna around the back of the necropolis. She'd never come at it from the Devastation side before, but that made no difference. Even in the dark, she knew this place as well as the orphan house. Sure enough, the crack in the wall where they'd spilled out five years ago had been patched, but badly.

A Nexsaint could have fixed it easily and smoothed the stone over, but someone had just filled in the gaps between broken blocks with mortar and called it good.

Silence blanketed the space, and Ashwyn held her breath as she leaped to the top of the wall. Morlinna followed her, and they came to rest in the same spot where Ash had sat with Cass through so many summer afternoons.

She'd been reluctant to come back, given what had happened with the Absent last time. But Morlinna was convinced they'd been attracted to the presence of the Goddess, not her.

Moonlight bathed the broken flagstones of the courtyard below, painting everything in silvery light. Blood splattered the ground and painted the iron-bound gate in ominously dark streaks. A stone bench lay overturned, its surface cracked from the force.

All that was left of the badger were pieces, the carnage of limbs and severed fur lined with the pulsing white of the Malady. It crept across the flagstones, streaking through the healthy strands of the Nexum, turning them white and ashy.

With no one to sever the heart thread, it hadn't fallen to dust.

"We're too late," Morlinna muttered and stood to her full height.

Ashwyn followed her gaze and found the broken and torn shadow of a body lying amidst the pieces of the Devastation beast.

She leaped lightly from the wall, using a strand of the Nexum to slow herself at the end. Her feet made no sound as she picked her way between the streaks of Malady-stricken threads to the body.

Uniah. Even after all these years, Ashwyn recognized her face. She lay in too many pieces, her Absent eyes staring up at Ash as her limbs moved listlessly, trying to pull her broken body back together.

The white of the Malady pulsed through her, infecting the strands that stretched between the torn edges of her torso, reaching all the way to her heart and the gap that formed there.

"Mother of Life," Morlinna whispered from behind Ash.

Ash's mouth had gone so dry she couldn't even form words. She stepped forward, but Morlinna stopped her with a hiss.

"Don't get close. Look how fast it's growing."

The white streaks of the Malady raced along the healthy strands, turning them ashy even as she stepped back. The gap itself yawned wide, sucking at the edges of the flagstones. Most of Uniah had disappeared behind the swath of inky blackness lined with flashes of white.

"I have to give her the Last Death," Ash said. "She's still Absent."

"There's no way, Ashwyn. She'll be gone before you even get to her."

"I can be quick."

But even as she spoke the words, the gap pulsed like a living thing and surged wider. Uniah's wide, blank eyes smeared and spread as they were sucked into Obitullas and whatever lay there.

Nausea threatened to choke Ashwyn. Mortis, she hoped the stories were true and there was no awareness after a person became Absent. If the Keeper could feel or see what was happening to her...

Ashwyn gulped, but the Malady crawled across the flagstones toward her feet, and Morlinna dragged her backward to avoid it.

"How is it moving so fast?"

"I do not know." Morlinna shook her head. "I have never seen the Malady so hungry."

The corruption crowded them back against the wall, but Ashwyn raised her head and gasped. "Morlinna, the Absent. It will reach the Santcums." And her mother.

Even now, the pool elongated on the far side, stretching for the doors that led to the towers.

"You cut it back at the edges," Morlinna said. "I will try to control the speed of its spread."

"What?" Ash gaped as Morlinna waded into the Malady. She tried to snatch at the other woman's clothes, but she was already out of reach.

"Morlinna! It'll try to take more of you. Can you afford to lose any more of yourself?"

Morlinna turned pulling the mask from her face to meet her gaze fully. "You forget. This is what I am for, Ashwyn. This is why I corrupted myself in the first place. If I am to be a sacrifice here, then I will have fulfilled my purpose."

Ashwyn growled, not hiding her frustration, but Morlinna had already grasped the threads outlining the gap.

"Fine," Ash cried and snatched for a strand of the Nexum above her with her good hand and used it to fling herself to the top of the wall. She had no time to fight against the wrongness in Morlinna's words. The strands writhed and tried to climb the other woman's legs, clinging to her robes.

Ashwyn raced around the top of the wall and threw herself toward one of the towers, using a thread to swing across the courtyard.

She skidded across the bare flagstones between the spreading pool of the Malady and the sanctum doors.

It should not be spreading so fast here. The thin cracks between flagstones had been scoured of all plant life, and even regular stone slowed the Malady's progress. But it reached, as if seeking the life it could feel just beyond.

Maybe it was the proximity of the Absent that lent it strength and speed. Like a flower that turned its face toward the sun, the Malady sought the bodies that would help it spread.

Ashwyn ruthlessly cut it back, severing the strands closest to the doors and sweeping the edge of the threat back as she moved. She could still slice faster than the Malady could spread, and she used that to her advantage, pressing forward as the dead ends curled under her feet.

In the middle of the pool, Morlinna stood, hands raised, her arms wrapped in corrupted strands as she held them, preventing them from reaching for healthy threads. The cords in her neck stood out as she strained, and the bright moonlight shone against the sweat that stood on her forehead.

Ash's hands shook, making her wrist twinge. How much of this could Morlinna take? Her eyes weren't white like they were when she connected directly with the Malady, but she had to be fighting it to keep it from stealing more.

Ash sped up, cutting through corrupted strands and leaving darkened flagstones behind her. Her arms ached with the speed and the weight of her scythe as she pushed the Malady back to the edge of the gate, where it plucked at her overcoat, trying to suck her in.

She checked the fringes of the pool, ready to call Morlinna to ease up. But even as she watched, the gap surged and bulged outward, spilling more Malady. The dead strands Ashwyn had already severed writhed, and the ashy sign of the Malady slithered down to the ends and began creeping across the ground again.

Ash gasped and skipped back a step to avoid it. What was happening? She'd never seen dead strands revived before. The Last Death was final. Always.

If that wasn't true anymore...

Bile crept up her throat.

A thump from across the courtyard caught her attention. The big ironbound gate shuddered against the overturned bench, and a muffled voice called, "Uniah? Are you all right?"

Ashwyn sucked in a breath. "Morlinna," she hissed. "Someone's coming."

Morlinna looked up, face tight with strain, her hands still wrapped in lines of the corrupted Nexum. She was trapped.

"We can't risk this spreading," Morlinna grated out.

Ashwyn was already moving. Wraith, silent as a ghost, winged over her head, and she borrowed the lightness of his bones, then grabbed a thread in the wall high over the gate. She pulled, and her body soared over the pool of Malady.

It took advantage of her distraction and crept across the flagstones, regaining the ground she'd just cleared.

But fighting it back would have to wait. Now they were under assault from two sides.

The gate jolted again before she got there, and a figure tumbled through the narrow opening. Ashwyn had time to see bright hair tamed in a braid and a hastily donned overcoat before she landed lightly by the gate.

She slammed it shut in case there were any more coming.

The intruder stumbled to her feet, just inches from the edge of the Malady.

Ash grabbed the woman's shoulder and hauled her backward as the creeping threads reached to climb up her bare feet and legs.

The woman fell back, taking Ash with her, and they landed in a tangle across the blood-stained flagstones. Ash's wrist screamed in agony, and some of the threads holding it steady tore free.

Ash swore and leaped to her feet, snatching up her scythe in her good hand. She had to get back to Morlinna, but what would she do with this interloper?

"Wraith, take Felleron and guard the other side of this gate in case anyone else gets any bright ideas."

Wraith barked an affirmative and spun in the air to dive over the wall.

The woman pushed to her elbows and gasped. "Ash?"

Ash froze, the familiar voice shooting up her spine and lodging in the base of her brain, making her heart seize. She'd heard it so often, she knew it as well as she knew her own. It had laughed at her stupid jokes; it had whispered to her across the pillow; it had condemned her to die a heretic's death.

Ash drew herself to her full height and met the woman's gaze, taking in the bright hair hanging over her shoulder, her bloodied nightgown barely covered by an overcoat.

Cass.

She shouldn't be here. Ash shouldn't have to see her. Shouldn't have to decide what to say, what to do with her.

"Ashwyn!" Morlinna's voice choked from behind her, and Ash spun, scythe ready in her hand.

Corrupted threads pulled at Morlinna, dragging her to her knees. And behind her, the air shrieked as the gap tore even wider.

Wide enough to swallow them whole without having to pull them apart first.

The corrupted strands in the courtyard shuddered and writhed as if they still lived. Then the Malady's progress halted, and so slowly Ash wasn't even sure she was seeing it, it started reversing course.

The white strands pulsed toward the gap and sped away from Ash's feet. The threads dropped from Morlinna's arms, leaving her gasping against the flag-stones. White streaks flowed back toward the gap as the Malady drew together, pooling like dew in the early morning.

Ashen arms reached over the edge, grasping the flagstones, and a figure hauled itself out of the gate.

Ash's mouth went dry.

The Malady drew together, forming a skeletal creature. Long white hair hung lank around its face and shoulders as it scrambled over the edge of the gate. It pressed emaciated hands into the stones, and threads of corruption speared away from its touch.

The Malady creature raised its gaunt face, skin stretched taut over its skull, and its eyes raked the courtyard.

"Oh, Dea," Cass whispered, half swear, half fervent prayer.

Black eyes as deep as the gap stared out of the holes in its skull. It opened its mouth and let out a moan that echoed in Ash's bowels.

"What is that?" Cass said behind her.

Ash shushed her, not wanting to draw the thing's attention.

But its gaze had passed over them. And locked onto Morlinna.

The other woman knelt on the ground, transfixed.

The Malady creature moaned again and scrabbled at the edge of the flag-stones, crawling forward then rising. Knobbly knees straightened to support it as it stood to its considerable height.

Unlike every other corrupted monster Ashwyn had fought in the last five years, this one ignored the living people in front of it. It ignored the Absent locked safe in their sanctums behind it. Instead, its empty gaze fixed on Morlinna.

And Morlinna sat there, gazing up at it.

"It calls to me. I hear it sometimes, urging me to give myself up to it." Morlinna had said ages ago. She'd always spoken as if it were a voice as real to her as the Goddess's.

Was this what she was hearing?

"Sometimes, I'm tired and...I want to let it have me."

Ash's chest finally moved, and she sucked in a breath.

"Morlinna, I'm coming!"

She raced forward, leaving Cass sprawled across the flagstones. The Malady could take her, or it wouldn't. Ash couldn't bring herself to care one way or the other.

She swept her scythe ahead of herself, clearing a path across the corrupted flagstones.

The creature surged forward, staggering across the courtyard toward Morlinna.

Ashwyn reached and wrapped her hand in Morlinna's hood. Then yanked.

Morlinna fell backward as the Malady creature's skeletal fingers closed over the space where she'd been.

Ashwyn spun her scythe in a circle and slashed the blade through the creature's wrist.

It shrieked and drew its severed arm to its chest.

"You can't have her," Ashwyn grated out.

Morlinna raised a hand to her head as if struggling to fight off dizziness.

Ashwyn couldn't wait for her to regain her senses. She spun her scythe, creating a blurred barrier between herself and the creature.

It hissed and stepped back, closer to the gap.

Could she cut it all away? Every last bone and scrap of flesh? It was just Malady, and she carried a blade that cut through the corruption.

But it stood near the gap, and if she got too close to that, she'd be sucked in.

Even now the Malady creature lurked beside the gate, glaring at her through the silvery screen of its impossibly long hair. She advanced, and the creature jerked back, its disjointed movements putting the gap between them.

So it was aware enough to use reason.

Somehow, that made it worse.

She couldn't fight it while it stood in the gap between worlds. And she couldn't be sure that Morlinna would be able to control it, if she was even willing to try. This thing didn't act like the normal Malady.

She needed a way to contain it instead.

Her eyes went to the walls. There was a reason necropoli were built out of volcanic rock. It came from deep within the most sacred places of the Goddess's domain. Volcanoes and the nutrients they left behind as they became dormant were some of the greatest sources of life in the world. The stone from the heart of a volcano was supposed to guard against the corruption of the Malady.

Ashwyn reached for the Nexum that stood out in the necropolis's wall. And pulled it toward her. She wrapped it around the figure from a distance.

The Malady creature screamed, and its skin smoked where the strand lay, but the black strand gradually went white and broke as the thing strained against it.

The creature surged for her.

Ash pulled clean strands from the ground at her feet and imbued them with the strands from the walls. There were still some uncorrupted underneath the dead threads that she could reach. She dropped her scythe so she could use both hands to yank them into place, weaving them as fast as she had ever weaved anything before.

The barrier grew under her movements, and the creature fell back with a hiss.

Ash had no time to celebrate. She worked, pulling more and more strands into place behind the gap, closing the spaces between and trapping the figure inside.

Until a dome of light wove around the figure, containing it and the gap inside.

Chapter 51
Concordim

Between the strands, Ashwyn glimpsed the sickly white figure. Through the narrow space, the Malady creature's eyes met Ash's, and pain speared through Ash, like the jolt from a static shock, only this struck the space behind her eyes and made her gasp.

The feeling spread along her limbs, racing through her veins, and her fingers spasmed.

Ash gritted her teeth and grabbed for the slipping end.

The thing—Ash shook her head. No, there was something very feminine about the creature. Feminine and angry.

She bared white teeth sharpened to points and leveled her gaze at Ash, but when she tried to move forward, the healthy black strands from the volcanic rock held, and she fell back with a hiss, holding her wounded arm to her chest.

If she pressed forward against the strands, her Malady would corrupt them and they would fall away—eventually—but how much pain would it cause her before they did?

Too much. The creature retreated step-by-step back to the gap.

"Keep going," Morlinna's voice came from over her shoulder, and Ashwyn couldn't help the rush of relief that swept through her. "She's nearly gone."

Ash gritted her teeth against the strain and pulled, forcing the weave tighter and smaller, shrinking the dome in place around the gate.

The Malady creature moaned her displeasure, making Ash's bones ache with the noise, but she finally climbed back into the gap and sank down into the abyss between worlds.

Ash stared, keeping the strands locked tight between her fingers. She didn't trust the creature not to come back out the moment she let her guard down.

Morlinna stepped up beside her. "If you hold it there," she said. "I will scour the courtyard."

Reversing their roles from before, Morlinna swept across the flagstones, clearing away the corrupted strands that remained, while Ash held the barrier against any further onslaught of the Malady.

When she'd finished the ground between them and the sanctum, Morlinna turned and gently pressed against the strands of Ashwyn's barrier. They let her through, sending a shiver down the connections and into Ashwyn's hands. She ignored the butterfly brush of feeling and held the strands until Morlinna had scoured the entire courtyard clean of the Malady. Until all that was left was the gap standing in the middle.

Ashwyn took one last deep breath and hauled the lines down, fastening them against the flagstones to create a new sort of barrier. Similar to the perimeter around the chasm, but this one would block as well as warn.

She slumped to the ground as she released them, wincing at the twinge in her hands. Rock was far more stubborn than steel, and the strands had pulled and burned against her skin.

"Are you well?" Morlinna asked, kneeling beside her.

Ash shook her head, her body tensing with a delayed reaction.

"Ashwyn?"

"What was that?" she said, voice hoarse.

"I don't know." Morlinna's words came quietly. "An attack? The Malady used the gap to breach this world. I've never seen it do that before."

Ash surged to her feet. "I meant you, Morlinna."

Morlinna's face went blank. "What?"

"You—you leapt at the chance to kill yourself! You practically gave yourself to it. It wanted you, and you didn't even try to fight it."

"Ashwyn."

"You would have let it take you."

Morlinna turned away, cheeks blazing in the moonlight. "You know that is what will happen, eventually. If it had happened tonight, then at least I provided a distraction so you could fight it."

Ash slashed her hand through the air. "No. You don't understand." She crowded forward into Morlinna's space, just short of touching her, forcing the other woman to look at her. "I'm not talking about duty or necessity. I'm saying you are not expendable. You're not some sacrifice just waiting to be made. Facing death eventually is very different from seeking it out because it's the only way you feel valuable. I will not let you just throw yourself away like that. Do you understand?"

Morlinna's eyes widened in shock, and then, achingly sweet, a smile twitched her lips.

"I understand."

Ash stepped back, her own flush painfully obvious on her cheeks. She bent to check her work, to give herself something to focus on.

"It looks like the obsidian will hold it here," Morlinna said.

"Not forever. The creature would have gotten through, eventually. That means the Malady might, as well."

Morlinna swept her gaze over the gap and the space they'd cleared around it. No threads of Malady marred the area. And the gap had stopped its growth. Now it lurked there as static as the two in the forest.

"It chose this place."

Ash glanced at her. "I thought the Malady wasn't sentient."

Morlinna shook her head, but Ash couldn't tell if it was in denial of Ash's words or as a way to shake free of the idea that they were fighting something that could plan and feint and charge.

The sound of cloth on stone made Ash stiffen, and they turned to see Cass climbing to her feet amidst the carnage. She'd completely forgotten the other woman was there.

The badger's blood stained Cass's nightclothes and the back of the overcoat she'd thrown over them. Her hair came out of its braid, hanging in strands around her face, and Ash hated that she knew what it would feel like against her fingertips.

Ash froze, waiting for the next few seconds to destroy her.

Cass stared at her, eyes drinking her in in a way that made Ash's gut clench.

"You're alive," Cass whispered.

Ashwyn's breath left her chest on a little huff she couldn't control. In all these years she'd never realized that her survival had been her own thing. Her life in the Devastation had been this bright, colorful segment painted across the gray canvas of her life. But the rest of the world hadn't even noticed. To Cass and the villagers, she'd disappeared. Just like they'd wanted her to.

Ash drew herself up, her teeth clenching when she realized Cass had grown taller than her. Where had she found those extra inches?

"Sorry to disappoint you," she spat.

Cass's open face went slack, then tight. "I never wanted you dead." She stepped forward as if she couldn't help herself.

Ash retreated a step, and Cass stopped.

"What are you doing here, Cass?" She forced herself to breathe, in and out. "It's the middle of the night."

"I like to walk when I can't sleep. I heard the fighting and came to see why Uniah hadn't rung the alarm."

She glanced at the gap where Uniah had once been and gulped.

"No one's allowed to walk at night. Remember what happened to Mikel."

Cass's lips went thin. "No one will say anything to me about it. I'm the elderman now."

"The..." A tightness swept through Ash's chest.

Cass had never wanted to be the elderman. At least, she hadn't while Ash had been here.

"I'm glad you've been doing so well without me. You know if you thought I was holding you back, you could have just said so instead of getting me Absented."

Cass's mouth fell open. "I argued for exile," she said. "Not Absenting."

"Exile to the Devastation is a death sentence, Cass."

Cass reached for her. "I thought there'd be a chance you'd survive."

Ashwyn smacked her hand away, heat beating in her cheeks. "I lived because of me. Not because of anything you did. I lived to spite you."

Cass backed away under the force of her words.

"Is that why you're back then?" Cass asked. "To punish us all? Did you bring the Malady here?"

Ash couldn't help the cry that escaped her lips. "No! My mother's still in there."

"Then why are you here?"

"We're the ones who have been protecting you. From that." Ash threw out her hand to indicate the gate and the Malady they'd already cleared away. "We're the only reason the Malady hasn't overrun Edgefall."

Cass gave her an exasperated look. "The Saints keep us safe—"

"The Saints have been lying!"

Morlinna touched Ash's shoulder, and the moment her fingers made contact, Ash saw the vines of the Devastation growing up over the walls of the necropolis, writhing in time with her anger.

Ash bit her tongue and shoved down the outrage, taking steady sips of air until her heart stopped pounding and the reaching Devastation calmed and lay quiet once more.

Morlinna's hand fell away from her shoulder, and Ash swallowed down the realization that she was watching everything, hearing Cass's words, witnessing Ash's unearthed pain.

Cass stared at Ashwyn, eyes sad. "You always felt things so big and so deep. It's...it's hard for the rest of us to keep up."

Behind her shoulder, Morlinna flinched, but Ashwyn barely noticed.

"Things like betrayal?" Ash said.

Cass huffed. "What was I supposed to do, Ash? You stole the Goddess's power."

A cold, hard knot formed under Ash's breastbone. The anger she'd shoved down wound itself into a ball of rage so tightly controlled a rampaging Devastation beast wouldn't be able to move her.

Ash swept every emotion from her face and spun her scythe to attach it to her back.

There are lights in the village, Wraith said in her head. *People are waking. Do you want me to keep guarding the path?*

No, Ash told him. Dawn lightened the sky over the Devastation. *We're leaving. It won't be safe for us here much longer.*

The magpies lining the walls took flight all at once, startling Cass. The other woman raised her arm as if to ward them off, but it was Wraith who came winging back over the wall to land lightly at Ash's side.

"*I* know who I am, at least," Ash told Cass. "I'm strong enough now that I don't have to stand here while the people I love tell lies about me."

She turned on her heel, and Wraith spun with her. "Good luck with your Malady problem," she said, jerking her chin at the gap in the necropolis courtyard.

She reached for a strand of the Nexum that would fling her back to the Devastation. Back home.

"Wait," Cass's voice came from behind her.

Ash paused. She wanted to jump into the trees and never look back, but something in Cass's tone stopped her.

For the first time in their lives, Ash heard fear. As if Cass was finally afraid of what Ash would do.

How many years had Ash worried and changed herself, making herself smaller out of fear of losing Cass?

And now that it was the other way around, a piece of Ashwyn loved the feeling. She was finally the one in control.

She turned to stare over her shoulder.

Cass passed Morlinna and stepped closer to the gap. She couldn't see the glowing barrier, but she could see the invisible wind that stirred the edge of her overcoat, pulling it toward the gap.

Ash saw her swallow.

"The Malady came here," Cass said. "It can come again?"

"Yes," Morlinna said, finally speaking to Cass directly. "Only it will be worse. The Malady wants this place. It has sent a root from underground. It will reach the necropolis eventually, and when it gets here, it will take everything."

Cass's gaze locked onto her face, her eyes noting the white streaks through Morlinna's veins. Morlinna made an abortive movement for the mask tied to her belt.

"You're the witch of the Devastation." Cass sighed. "Of course Ash would find you."

Ash couldn't control the flush that swept up her cheeks, but Morlinna wasn't watching. Her face had gone slack with surprise before her features flattened and smoothed. But Ash knew that particular blankness. The bemusement she used to cover up resignation.

"Is that what you call me?"

Ash winced, but Morlinna was speaking to Cass.

"Yes," Cass said.

Morlinna glanced at Ash. "You never told me that."

Ash raised her chin, silent. She'd never said it because Morlinna already thought of herself as some kind of monster. And Ash had never figured out how to tell her that the monster was beautiful.

Ash waited for Cass to say something stupid. To spout all those terrible tales they'd told each other when they were kids. About witches who hunted trespassers and apostates who corrupted people.

But Cass's gaze returned to the gap. "What are we supposed to do?" she said quietly. "We can't move the necropolis. All those Absent…"

Morlinna raised her chin. "Bury the gap with obsidian. Do not get close enough to be sucked in. It is worse than the Last Death. When it is buried, dig down and build walls under the necropolis. The Malady can burrow. It had no problems getting in here tonight. I would tell you that you need more Bladesaints and at least a Nexsaint to protect you, but they are useless against this."

Morlinna turned to join Ashwyn beside the wall.

"But how will I explain this to the village? To the city."

Morlinna raised one eyebrow. "You are the elderman, are you not? A job you are presumably qualified for."

Cass choked, and Ash could have kissed Morlinna right there.

"I suggest you find the words," Morlinna said. "Because the Absent can't stay here. But until then, we will continue to do what we have dedicated ourselves to. Your safety now belongs to Ashwyn. Lucky for you, I cannot think of anyone better to keep it."

Morlinna took hold of a strand of the Nexum and hauled herself over the wall.

Ash gave Cass one last look and followed her, surrounded by Wraith and the magpies.

Chapter 52
Concordim

They both needed to rest and recover, but there were too many things floating through Ash's mind to sleep well. Every time she drifted off for more than a few moments, something else sprang to the front, startling her awake with false urgency. First, it was the idea of the root inexorably growing toward the necropolis. Then it was the memory of the Malady creature's gaze, sending remembered sparks across her mind. Then it was Cass's face that loomed before her, the relief and fear and horror in her expression morphing until it wasn't Cass's face anymore at all. Just a terrible amalgam of all the worst parts of her.

Ash gave up trying to sleep and wrapped her blanket around herself, careful of her still-healing wrist. She stepped over Wraith, who lay across her doorway, legs twitching with his own dreams, and made her way to the nave. She tiptoed so as not to wake Morlinna, but when she crossed the threshold, Morlinna's thin figure already sat propped against the curve of the hearth.

Her eyes were closed, but she turned her head as Ash stepped up beside her. Ash rarely saw her in anything other than her Nexsaint black, but Morlinna had draped a soft blue robe over her nightdress. It was worn at the elbows, and the ends of the sleeves had frayed, and for a moment Ash wondered what the fabric would feel like against her fingers.

She shook her head and joined Morlinna at the hearth.

"You can't sleep either," Morlinna said as if she'd already made her peace with the concept.

"No. I know we have to go back down after the corrupted root to stop it somehow. But that doesn't make it any easier to rest before setting out."

"No, it doesn't." Morlinna tipped her head back to rest against the hearth, her eyes still closed. The neckline of her nightdress pulled enough that Ash could see the edge of the bandage across her shoulder. "Is that the only thing that's bothering you?"

Ash laughed. "That's more than enough, isn't it? Or did you really want to add the Malady's newest trick and a threatened necropolis to it?"

Morlinna's mouth twitched, but she didn't rise to the bait. She spoke into the air to no one in particular. "I can't help wondering what it would be like to return to the city. To have to face the Saints who named me apostate. To confront the ones who tried to kill me when they scoured the Malady."

Ashwyn let out her breath, all mirth gone. "Oh."

Morlinna finally cracked her eyes open and fixed them on Ash. "It's all right to not be all right."

Ash's lungs seized, and she stared hard at the low flames in the fireplace, willing the knot in her gut to ease.

"You saw your village for the first time in years," Morlinna said quietly. "And I know you did not want to. I am lucky. I live far enough away that I will likely never see my old home again. I never have to decide what to say to anyone."

"It's fine," Ashwyn said between her teeth. "I chose this. I could have left any time. Like you wanted."

Morlinna pressed her lips together as if she hid a smile. "I will not say I told you so."

"Good."

Morlinna's fingers rubbed the ends of her sleeves in a pattern that seemed more habit than conscious thought, and Ash couldn't help fixating on the movement. She would have sworn up and down that Morlinna had no such thing as a nervous habit.

"Cass is the one who went to the city to kneel before the Goddess, yes?" the woman said.

Ash's jaw clenched. "Yes."

Morlinna's gaze settled on Ash's face. "You've spoken of her before. I knew she was important to you, but not..." She glanced away. "That was not the reaction of a friend."

Ashwyn swallowed. Why was Morlinna asking? Now, when Cass wasn't just a story in her past?

"She was always my friend. Since we were little. But toward the end, she was much more. I thought we would spend our whole lives together." Ashwyn's wrist twinged with pain, and when she looked down, she realized she'd wrapped her fingers around each other so tightly the knuckles had turned white. She untangled them carefully.

"It turns out I loved Cass far more than she loved me." She blinked, her eyes stinging. The feeling writhing in her chest was familiar, recent pain echoing remembered wounds.

Had she done the same thing with Morlinna? Had she fallen in love with someone who could never return her feelings? Morlinna was bound to the Goddess the way the Goddess was bound to the throne. Tied there so tightly, she would have to tear out pieces of herself to pull away.

And Ashwyn would never ask Morlinna to bleed.

She took a deep breath, smoothing the feelings out until they slipped back into their place behind her heart where she could keep them safe and hidden.

"Do you still love her?"

The words were so far from her wandering thoughts that Ashwyn was left blinking. "Who?"

Morlinna raised an eyebrow. "Cassarah."

"No!" Ashwyn rose to her feet, her blanket falling around her.

"It was a question, Ashwyn. Not an accusation."

Ash paced to the nearest pew and back, searching for words to explain the tumult in her head and heart.

"She was so important to me for so long. I shaped my entire self around her. When she didn't defend me...it left a Cass-sized hole in the middle of my life, and I've had to work to fill it in. I've had to grow."

Her mind filled with the image of Cass standing in the same place they'd met for years, looking just like she had the day Ash had been exiled, leading the same people that had hated her.

"I grew, and she didn't." Ash crossed her arms over her chest. "I loved her once, and that will always be a part of me, but she isn't a part of me anymore. She doesn't deserve to be."

Morlinna stared up at her, face sad, and Ash gulped.

"Who deserves to be?" Morlinna said.

Ash knew the answer to that, but bit down hard on her tongue to avoid saying it out loud. "I..."

Morlinna's gaze flicked away. "Maybe she doesn't anymore. Maybe there are some things that cannot be forgiven. But no one is perfect. No one is worthy of love and forgiveness all the time."

Were they even talking about Cass anymore?

"There was something you admired in her once. Do you even remember what it was?"

Ashwyn sank back into her seat, reaching for her blanket. "She was always so calm. Like nothing ever bothered her. And when it did, she was strong enough to do something about it."

"I see that. She was strong enough to handle the idea of the Malady invading her village. She was steady enough to stand when she saw what the Malady had became in the necropolis."

"So were you," Ashwyn whispered.

Her gaze met Morlinna's almost by accident. Almost. And she glanced away immediately, her heart beating against her ribs as she realized how close she'd come.

She had to retreat. Cover it all up again. Ignore, and deny, and pretend. Or she'd lose the thing she needed more than Morlinna's love.

Morlinna's safety and comfort.

Everything else could be ignored if Morlinna felt safe.

She finally turned back to see Morlinna's outstretched hand being pulled back. As if she'd reached for Ashwyn and thought better of it at the last second.

Ash cleared her throat. "What *did* the Malady become?" She let the thought grow in strength. "What was that thing? That...woman made of corruption?"

Morlinna shook her head. "Just a concentration of the Malady. Not an actual woman. A concerted attack on us where it would hurt the most."

"But why would it choose to look like a person?"

"It cannot choose. Not the way we do. The Malady has always been mindless."

Ash's brow drew down. "But it chose the necropolis. It knows how to fight us."

"So do Devastation beasts," Morlinna said, extending a white-laced hand then wincing as it pulled the bandage across her shoulder. "So does much of nature. Disease knows exactly how to attack the body. That does not make it sentient."

Ashwyn blew out her breath in a frustrated snort.

Morlinna gave her an empathetic smile. "Plants adapt to their surroundings. Animals learn the safest routes to water. The Malady is just trying everything to see what works."

Ash wanted to believe her, but she couldn't help remembering the way Morlinna had knelt there, transfixed as the woman had climbed out of the gap.

"You said it calls to you," Ash said quietly, keeping any hint of accusation out of her tone. "Did it talk to you last night?"

"It is not words," Morlinna said. "It is feeling. A siren call that promises an end to the pain."

Ash bit her lip, eyes on Morlinna's face as the other woman leaned her head against the fireplace and closed her eyes again.

"And you'd trade yourself to get rid of the pain."

Morlinna's throat bobbed, but her face remained serene. "I know you think sacrifice is unnecessary. But I made my peace with my role long ago. You have not changed that."

The words should have hurt. But Ashwyn carried her own pain, and this felt too much like standing in the square watching Cass ride away with her dream.

"No, I haven't, because you've always been worth more than that."

Morlinna opened her eyes and met her gaze, the corners crinkling as if Ash had said something sad. Like Morlinna was upset that she still didn't understand.

She opened her mouth, but Ash beat her to it.

"Don't," Ash said. "Just..." She took a breath, trying to put it into words Morlinna would accept. So that she would finally understand what Ash had known from the beginning.

"You've spent your life fighting this thing. And I really mean spent. You've used it up. Now you're just waiting around for a chance to die in some way that's acceptable to you and your goddess."

Morlinna's brows came down. "That's not—"

"Edgefall tried to use me up. They tried to tell me what I was. A tool to fill in the gaps. That was all I was worth to them. But if your goddess is so great, then shouldn't She want more than that for you? You are more than a tool against the Malady. You're not just some trained monster She can set loose on Her enemy."

Ashwyn didn't believe the Goddess cared that much, but Morlinna did. She was the one who prayed at Her altar every morning. The one who listened to Her voice when no one else could.

If Morlinna was ever going to believe what Ashwyn believed, she had to put it into the Goddess's voice.

"Ashwyn," Morlinna said gently. "I know you don't want to let go—"

"I think it's you who doesn't want to hold on."

Morlinna jerked, and Ashwyn plowed ahead.

"You underestimate yourself. And Her. She changed the way the world works for you. You really think She doesn't have something more planned for you?"

A soft sip of air told Ash her words had struck. Morlinna's severe expression softened, and she reached out a hand to Ash, fingertips touching fingertips.

"Beautiful words. Do you believe them?"

Ash swallowed to give herself time. "Why are you asking?"

"Because She changed the way the world works for you, as well. So you could be a Nexsaint with me."

Ash blew out her breath on a sigh, admitting defeat. If she wanted Morlinna to believe the best about herself, Ash would have to believe the best about the Goddess, and she wasn't willing to jump to that yet. Maybe not ever.

"And Nexsaints fight the Malady." She cracked her neck. "I guess that means we should get to work."

"That just leads us back to the start," Morlinna said, leaning her head against the statue's base. But she didn't draw her hand away. "The root. And how to clear it."

Ash was more worried about the figure that had climbed from the pool and what it had to do with the Malady.

They still didn't know where the Malady came from. Not exactly. And Ash had the suspicion that if they knew that, they would know why it chose a female form.

"Why do we call it the Malady?" Ash asked.

Morlinna answered without opening her eyes. "Because it is a corruption of the Goddess's power. A sickness in the strands of Her Nexum that spreads death."

What would be strong enough to corrupt a goddess? Ash thought with a shiver.

Their foray into the city had only left them with more questions. The Goddess had once had a spouse. She Who Had Been He, she'd been called. And after an epic battle, the only one left had been Deavita.

And now the only evidence of their marriage was covered by the Devastation. A forest that teemed with life.

Some said the Goddess had sent the Devastation to protect them from the place where the Malady had formed.

What if She'd sent the forest to hide it?

Had the Goddess gotten rid of Her wife? Why? Because he'd become she? Or was it simply because a goddess marrying a mortal was another blasphemy?

Would the wrongness of a goddess murdering Her spouse be enough to corrupt Her power?

Deavita's face hung in Ash's mind, stunning and calm, with eyes as white as Morlinna's when the Malady rose in her body.

Ash shut down the line of thinking. She already didn't trust a goddess who refused to protect Her servants. She refused to let the deity know the awful doubts in her head.

Or Morlinna.

"If it's a sickness, why haven't we treated it like a sickness?"

Morlinna lowered her head to look at Ash.

Ash stared into the flames, teasing at the edges of the idea and which parts she could share with Morlinna.

"We've always tried to fight the Malady. Maybe we should try healing it."

Chapter 53
Concordim

Morlinna had kept a thread from the tunnel where they'd burned through the root, so returning was just a matter of one Nexum jump.

Felleron stayed above, scouting for places where the Malady might have surfaced already. In the thickness of the Devastation, Felleron still knew the forest better than anyone except Morlinna, and he had his own secret ways to move between layers quickly.

The magpies remained on guard around the necropolis. It gave Ashwyn a vicious little surge of pleasure to think of them swooping through Edgefall, terrifying the villagers with their very existence. Perhaps every time Cass looked up at them, she thought of Ash.

Morlinna linked her arm with Ash's, and Ash grabbed for Wraith's ruff. The older woman pulled, and the three of them snapped along the thread of the Nexum, the world smearing around them.

Ash kept her feet as they landed, immediately scanning their surroundings for Malady and dreads and corrupted Devastation beasts.

But the tunnel stood quiet, just as she remembered it.

Except for the hole where the badgers had broken through and they'd cut back the spreading infection.

Thick roots and vines had already grown across the gap, almost as if the forest was trying to hide the way to the corruption.

The hair along Ash's neck rose, and she had to suppress her shudder as

Morlinna touched the strands along the wall, checking for anything else that might have been coming from farther away.

"Anything?" Ash asked.

"Nothing yet," Morlinna said. "The dreads must have moved on after we fled. But they will notice we're here, eventually."

"We'll be careful as we work," Ash said. "And we'll set a guard. Wraith?"

I will keep watch at the base of the tunnel, Wraith said into her mind. *To be sure they do not come from below.*

He tucked his wings close to his back, then trotted down the path toward the city buried deep under the forest.

Ash turned her attention to the blackened shell of the dead root, which had fallen away and lay crumbling against the floor of the tunnel. It collapsed into dust as they stepped through the debris.

Underneath, a new root had grown, pulsing white with the Malady, its fresh bark lighter than the old root that stretched down toward the city.

Ashwyn swallowed as she followed the line of it with her gaze. They couldn't even see the new end from here.

"It's grown so much already," she whispered.

Morlinna silently followed the new growth. It went on for twenty feet before the root ended in a blunt point.

"At this rate, it will reach the necropolis in days," she said, eyes fixed on the white end.

Ashwyn blew out her breath. "It sped up. Like it knew we were coming to cut it back again."

"It is only reacting the way life would," Morlinna said, shaking her head. "It does not know anything."

Life was the Goddess's purview. If She was in control, then She could control the Devastation. The growth of everything.

And if the Malady was a corruption of Her power...

Ash bit her lip on her argument. Morlinna wasn't ready to hear it.

"Do you need a minute?" she asked instead.

Ashwyn couldn't help her this time. Healing required actual manipulation of strands, not just severing them. So it would be Morlinna from here on out.

Morlinna raised her chin. "No, I am ready."

She settled herself on her knees in front of the root's end, ash and dust coating the skirt of her robe. She glanced up at Ash, and Ash read trepidation behind her normally austere expression. "I...I am not skilled with healing. I never was a Mender. I don't know how long this will take."

She'd always patched Ash up just fine, but still she seemed bothered by that blind spot in her training. Ash could have told her that blind spots did not always equal weakness.

"It takes as long as it takes," Ash said, slinging her scythe from her back. "I will be here, guarding you."

They had no idea if the Malady would react the way it had last time. If they would be facing more hordes of corrupted creatures deep in the tunnels. So Ashwyn prepared herself.

Morlinna stretched her hands on either side and cracked her neck before letting her arms drop. Then she began. She wrapped strands of corruption around her fingers, carefully separating the threads from the ones she wanted. With her free hand, she then reached for uncorrupted strands in the roots around them.

Healing required weaving healthy strands with those that weren't so healthy. The healthy strands could then lay a framework for the unhealthy ones, showing them the way they were supposed to be originally.

Knitting broken bones was the easiest; bone was used to growing back, it just needed a template to do so faster. Torn muscle shouldn't have been too difficult. Morlinna usually managed it just fine, though Ashwyn found muscle stubborn. And theoretically, a skilled Mender would have been able to fix Ash's vision had they gotten to it in time. Theoretically.

The thought made Ashwyn feel squidgy. If her sight had remained normal, she might have been a Bladesaint. She would never have known the truth at the Heart of the Devastation. She would have been one of the ones perpetuating the lie.

She would never have met Morlinna. Would she make that trade?

Ashwyn refocused her thoughts on Morlinna's hands and the way she wove the healthy strands through the corrupted ones.

Illnesses of the blood were the most complex. Blood renewed itself constantly, therefore it needed consistent attention. It took time and patience to get blood to relearn itself.

The strands of the Nexum weren't exactly blood, but they were the source of power in the world. Morlinna assumed—or maybe hoped—they would react the same.

Normally a Mender would cut a healthy strand free to weave to the unhealthy strands. But if Morlinna did that, then the corrupted strand would infect the new one, and there would be nothing to teach it how to be. Instead, she had to weave the strands together uncut and fight the corruption back the entire time to allow the unhealthy strands time to learn.

Morlinna sat on the floor of the tunnel, her body going more and more rigid as her focus turned inward. Ash couldn't see anything different with the strands she held tangled in her hand, but she could see the battle Morlinna fought against the corruption in the way the white in her veins writhed, trying to climb up her arms.

Ash closed her eyes and turned her back. Helplessness ate at her insides until she regretted her breakfast, and she had to turn her attention to something else or go mad. She felt along the healthy strands around her, weaving them into her own primitive sort of perimeter to warn her in case anything came at them through the growth beyond the tunnel walls.

Hours passed, and Ash fell into her own stupor, checking along the strands for any incursions as Morlinna knelt, tangled in threads of the Nexum.

And then Wraith's voice came through their connection. *Ash, a dread!*

Ashwyn gasped and shook herself free of her fog, her mouth going dry. *Coming up from the city?* she asked silently so as not to startle Morlinna in the middle of her work.

Yes, it knows you're there. I can try to stop it if you want.

Don't you dare. Get back to me if you can.

She spun to Morlinna, but the other woman had her eyes closed, her face set in stony concentration. Her hands were bound tight in strands of the Nexum, binding her to the tunnel in this place. If Ash asked her to move now, it would undo all her work from the last few hours. It would mean Morlinna had fought down the corruption this whole time for nothing.

Ashwyn made her decision and spun. She raced down the tunnel, leaving Morlinna in the relative safety of her hasty perimeter in order to head off the dread. A thing of rage and spite that they'd never managed to fight before.

Ash! Wraith's ghostly form came out of the tunnel ahead of her, and Ash gasped to a stop.

"Where is it?"

Behind me. He skidded and ducked under the root to reach her side. *What do we do? Can Morlinna leave yet?*

"No. We have to turn it aside. It can't get to her."

How?

"I have no idea."

The waves of despair and anger swept up the tunnel, and a hideous shriek sent shivers down Ashwyn's spine. Wraith whined and pressed into her legs.

Ash fought down the feeling that she was lost before she'd even begun.

She'd felt despair before. She'd felt rage, but this uncontrollable knot of helpless anger in her chest was not hers. She pushed away the thoughts that nothing she did was good enough, that she might as well lie down and scream into the floor of the tunnel.

The floor.

"Step back," she told Wraith. "I have an idea."

I hope it is a good one, Wraith said, but he did as she asked.

She'd already clipped her scythe to her back to free her hands. She pulled her waterskin from her belt and poured a splash of liquid into her palm.

The strands slipped through her fingers, as slick and fluid as the water itself. But she twisted one around her finger and pulled until it lengthened, and she could weave it through the vines at their feet.

The air grew cold as she worked, and a shadow crawled across the wall of the tunnel, fingers of darkness reaching for her.

She clenched her teeth and stood her ground, tying off her weave as the elongated figure came into view. Dark limbs with too many joints crawled along the floor, and a gaunt face topped with jagged antlers stared at her, black eyes rimmed with white. The tips of its antlers scraped the ceiling, cutting through the vines and showering them with pieces of foliage.

Ashwyn swallowed down the mounting panic, trying to push it deep down as her legs trembled under the gaze of the dread.

It crawled inexorably closer. And the rage and despair grew so thick the edges of her vision flickered, sending a wave of darkness across the already dim light of the tunnel.

Ash didn't try to fight the darkness. Instead, she closed her eyes and felt the world through the strands around her. She saw the black strands reaching through the dread and the way they pulsed in time with its harsh rasping breath. It shrieked again, making her jump, but she anchored herself to the strands at her feet and the ones along the walls.

Ash? Wraith's voice came ragged with panic.

Not yet.

He pressed against the backs of her knees as if he longed to run but didn't want to leave the safety of her warmth. Their breath came in little clouds of fog as they panted, and she heard him snarl behind her.

Wait.

His trust flooded through her, countering the dread's throbbing anger, and she lifted her chin.

The dread stretched out long clawed fingers and dug into the vines of the tunnel to drag itself forward.

Now. Ash pulled the end of her weave, and the thread she'd borrowed from the little pool of water in her hand tightened across the floor, infusing the vines with its properties.

The vines below the dread loosened, and suddenly it plummeted downward, as if into a swamp.

Its scream echoed with shock and outrage, and it scrabbled at the sides of the trap, but Ashwyn had carved it deep and strengthened the edges.

The dread hissed and hooked its claws in the vines. Its knobbly joints heaved, and Ash sucked in a breath as it hauled itself upward out of the mire.

It had only worked for a moment. She was trapped in here with an enraged monster.

And Morlinna was just down the corridor.

The thought sent a spike of fear and determination through her, each feeling bound to the other like the tightest weave.

She had seconds and only one idea.

It would be bad, but mortis, what else could she do with Morlinna helpless and counting on her?

Any price was worth paying if it meant Morlinna could live to fight the Malady another day.

Ashwyn dug into the strands of the vines then reached into the creature's body, weaving the two together.

After the disastrous experiment with the vipers and the day she'd tried to make Felleron listen, this had felt like the furthest possibility in the world. The last resort she would never ever touch.

But this dread would kill her. It would tear through her, and then it would go for Morlinna. And that thought gave her strength.

Ashwyn screamed as she wove the strands of the vines with the strands of the dread. Its threads cut into her hands, razor sharp and strong, like fine wire.

But she held the strands tight, even as they sliced through her skin.

And the Nexum in her body burned and shriveled in response.

She yanked the weave into a secure knot and dropped the threads.

The dread lay in the middle of the floor, its face staring up at the ceiling, impotent rage burning in its dark eyes. The bark-like skin had stretched, melded with the vines and roots around it until it seemed a part of the floor and the forest itself. Its limbs reached through the vines, each one a piece of the surrounding foliage until Ash couldn't tell where the dread ended and the Devastation began.

When it snarled, the floor around it flexed with the movement.

But her weave held fast. The dread wasn't moving anywhere.

Her stomach roiled, and the world tilted. She tried to catch herself against the wall of the tunnel and missed, plummeting to the floor. She gagged and barfed up everything in her stomach. The mess steamed against the frost, and she gagged again.

A furry head slipped under her arm, but she couldn't see past the throbbing in her head.

"Oh, mortis." Her voice slipped through her teeth on a gasp.

If you vomit again, please don't vomit on me.

She couldn't even think about laughing with the entire world spinning.

"I think I'm going to die."

You do not have time to die. We have to get back to Morlinna.

Right. She dragged herself to her feet and grabbed the wall, successfully this time.

She had to get back, not because she was useful in this state. That was the best reason she could think of for never doing this again. Morlinna needed her, and she was going to be nothing but a sickening puddle for hours, maybe days.

But that didn't mean she couldn't be there.

She glanced over her shoulder as Wraith stepped delicately up the tunnel, moving slowly enough that she could creep along with him. Behind her, the dread still stared up at the ceiling, but the strands in its body pulsed with feeling, and that carried into the surrounding vines, its rage infecting the Devastation where she'd woven the two inextricably together.

Chapter 54
Concordim

Morlinna sat against the wall of the tunnel where they'd left her, but her hands lay against her sides, free of the Nexum, and she had tipped her head back to rest against the wall.

Ashwyn collapsed beside her. Her stomach heaved, and she turned her head, but there was nothing left in her stomach except bile.

Gagging made her head throb and her throat burn, but she finally turned back to blink at the other woman.

"What happened to you?" Morlinna asked.

"Dread," Ashwyn said and Morlinna stiffened.

She waved a hand that she hoped appeared nonchalant but probably came off as drunk. "Don't worry. I trapped it in the floor. It won't be coming after us. Not soon at least."

Morlinna leveled her gaze on Ash's face.

Ash winced. "How bad is it?"

"Half your strands are dead. It will take time for them to grow back."

A hand covered hers, and Ash only just avoided jumping with surprise.

"You did what you had to do," Morlinna said.

Ash choked. She hadn't realized how much she'd needed to hear that.

"Yeah," she whispered. "But let's make sure I never have to do it again. Is it done?"

Morlinna gestured to the root, and Ashwyn squinted to focus her gaze.

The root remained where it had been, reaching into the space created by the tunnel. But its bark had gone a strange gray. The white of corruption had sloughed away, leaving it darker, but something about it turned Ash's stomach as much as binding the dread had.

Under its surface, the Nexum pulsed. White still stretched down the strands, but here and there threads of black pierced the corruption, giving the whole thing an overall gray appearance.

"Oh," Ash said.

It hadn't worked. Even from here she could see the healthy strands weren't strong enough to counter the Malady completely. Eventually they would lose their fight, but as they did, the Malady changed them, creating something fundamentally wrong. Ash couldn't tell what it was exactly, but the root had taken on properties that made it something else. Like the vipers blended with the vines. Like the dread melted into the floor behind them.

"What happened?"

"I don't know," Morlinna answered. "I am not enough of a Mender to guess. It feels like...like an abomination. A thing that simply should not be." She let her head fall back against the wall and she closed her eyes. "And I cannot try again. Not today. Not for a while maybe. It took too much."

Ash didn't ask to see her arms. To see how far the Malady had climbed in her body.

Ash pushed to her feet, using the wall for balance. The root was supposed to take its cue from the healthy roots Morlinna had used as a template. And something about the pulsing strands did remind Ash of the Devastation. But that wasn't all.

"I wonder if the Devastation isn't healthy," Ash said, mostly to herself.

Morlinna sat up. "What?"

Ash shook her head. "Nothing. Just thinking." It skirted too close to that idea that had been niggling in the back of her head since the fight in the necropolis. The figure of the Malady. The Devastation covering a secret sin. A goddess who might have gotten rid of Her spouse.

But even if the Devastation wasn't a healthy example for the Malady to follow, what else did they have to use? Maybe they just needed to try harder. Or longer. Blood took time to relearn its purpose.

But Morlinna was exhausted. How much of her life had she used in this attempt alone? How much more could Ashwyn and the Goddess and the world ask of her?

"I could help," she said before she'd realized she was going to.

Morlinna pushed to her feet. "Ashwyn—"

Ash turned, settling into the decision. Morlinna had already proven she could hide from this for years if Ashwyn didn't push this.

"Corrupt me," she said, and Morlinna's eyes went wide. "Then I can help you. With both of us working together—"

"No!"

Ashwyn stepped back, the force of Morlinna's answer striking her in the chest.

"Listen," she tried saying.

But Morlinna slashed her hand through the air, cutting her off. "No. We're not doing that."

"Morlinna. We have to. You can't do this alone. If you're worried about me being able to kill you eventually, you don't have to. I'll still be here to keep my promise when it comes to it."

Morlinna shook her head, her hands clenching and unclenching at her sides.

Ashwyn blew out her breath. She'd never seen Morlinna rise to such feeling. The woman kept everything locked away behind the exterior of a Saint. Dedication and determination hiding anything deeper. But now Morlinna's face went tight with pain and something else. Something Ash didn't recognize right away.

It made her heart pound, and instinct made her want to pull back, to apologize and return to the status quo.

But another piece of her crowed with triumph. She'd done this. She'd given Morlinna a reason to react.

"Why?" Ash stepped forward, but Morlinna retreated, head swinging back and forth in denial or fear or something else.

"Morlinna, talk to me. Why won't you teach me this one last thing? You don't think I'm strong enough to survive? To push it back?"

"We have no way of knowing if you are."

"You don't trust me?" The words careened out of her, but Ash kept a tight hold on the frustration, leashing it so it didn't reach the Devastation around them.

"We are done talking about this," Morlinna said, her face shutting down.

Ashwyn threw up her hands. "Because you've said so? Mortis, you call *me* stubborn."

She spun away from Morlinna, unable to look at that stony expression one more moment, knowing there was something under it all that Morlinna just didn't trust her enough to share.

Hands caught her upper arms, and Ash froze. Morlinna so rarely reached out to her that the touch coursed through her, sending a tingle through her skin and a wave of heat through her chest. Her mind instantly went to the single moment they'd tried to connect years ago and the conflicted memory of that brief touch. The intimacy given then pulled away.

Ashwyn caught her breath as Morlinna rested her forehead against Ash's shoulder. She swallowed and stood still as stone, not wanting to knock Morlinna away.

"I've tried it, Ashwyn," Morlinna whispered into the fabric of her overcoat. "Tried to teach someone to fight it. And now he's gone."

"Who?"

"The Judge who came for me."

Ash let out her breath. The one who'd become a gap. Morlinna had said he was a friend.

"We grew up in the cloisters together. He was one of the only friends I could trust. He and Illyra. I didn't even blame him when he had to hunt me down. It was his duty. We both knew that. That wasn't the betrayal. The betrayal was that I couldn't save him."

Morlinna's voice hitched.

"Tavian was strong when he was infected. Judges are the elite of the Saints. He was the best of us. And I still couldn't walk him through it. I had to watch—" Morlinna choked.

Ash couldn't think of anything to say. She knew that pain. Morlinna had Tavian, and Ash had Rafe.

"Maybe it would be different for you," Morlinna said. "But even if you survived, I'd be able to look at your face and see... Please," Morlinna whispered. "Please don't make yourself like me."

Ash's chest constricted. "Why?" she said as gently as she could manage. "What's so wrong with you?"

Morlinna's head rose, and Ash spun in her arms, catching the other woman before she could pull away. "No, tell me. What do you think is wrong with you?"

Morlinna gave her an exasperated look, and Ashwyn flushed. She was breaking their unspoken rule, forcing Morlinna to speak the things they didn't speak about.

Ash dropped her gaze, unwilling to push. Unwilling to lose this one tiny hint that Morlinna cared more than she showed.

She kept her hands on Morlinna's arms but stepped back a pace. It felt like the destruction of her strands; it felt like cutting out a piece of herself.

But Morlinna breathed easier as she retreated, and Ash swallowed down the pain of it.

"All right," she said, softly. "I won't do it. We have other problems, anyway."

She focused her breathing and turned her mind to the root. After everything they'd learned of the Malady, it seemed unfair that they hadn't learned this one thing that would help them. If the Malady was a sickness, healing it should have done more than turn it into an abomination of nature.

Ash remembered her thought that maybe the Devastation wasn't a healthy template to follow. Maybe it wasn't the right template at all.

The root looked like the Devastation. But underneath that, they were trying to heal the Malady in the strands.

And the Malady had willingly taken the form of a woman.

"What if it's not the Devastation that the Malady needs to remember how to be?"

Morlinna cocked her head.

Ashwyn met her eyes, choosing her words carefully. "The Malady chose a human form when it climbed out of the gap. What if it's not a plant or even just a network of strands. What if it's a person?"

Morlinna's mouth thinned. "How could it be a person?"

Ash forced away the thought of an untrustworthy goddess and Her corrupted power. "I don't know," she said instead. "We don't know enough about it at all. But we have to try something. And if it thinks it's a person, then it would need a person to show it how to be healthy again."

Morlinna's eyes went distant and she turned her head as if listening. She snatched her hands from Ash's shoulders and spun, as if to hide the moments they'd stood there touching.

Ash ignored the hurt. "Is She speaking to you?"

Morlinna raised her head and gave Ash an apologetic smile. "She says it is a good idea."

Frustration quickly drowned the stab of triumph. Morlinna always drew away.

She should stay quiet. She should sink back into the unspoken rules. But something kept her at the burning edge of words. Something that said that maybe if she wasn't afraid, then maybe one day Morlinna would be courageous enough, too.

"You know, you don't have to hide behind Her."

Morlinna's glance was full of pain and Ash stifled a gasp. "If this is how I can have both of you, then please, let me keep it this way."

Ash took a deliberate step back, giving Morlinna the space she craved.

Chapter 55
Concordim

They had to wait to test their theory. If the Malady threw anything at them, neither would be in any shape to counter it.

Ash slept nearly an entire day, recovering her strands after her brush with the dread.

And when she woke in the late afternoon, she found the temple empty. Morlinna must have been off checking the Devastation.

Ebonheart sat in the rafters above, as if waiting for her.

"How's the necropolis?" Ash asked the magpie.

Quiet, Ebonheart answered. *No bad yet.*

"That's good."

Ebonheart wove back and forth as if she were shaking her head. *Not good. Bad comes. Quiet before cat leaps.* She sent Ash an image of a Devastation beast, a slinking feline with deep blue scales stalking its unsuspecting prey.

Ash shivered.

She hated the idea of the corrupted root lurking under the layers of the Devastation, growing unchecked until it burst through the flagstones and sent its sickness all through the Absent sleeping in their sanctums. Ebonheart was right about it feeling like a lurking predator.

Morlinna returned while Ash was listlessly eating some dried fruit. Her stomach still felt too sensitive to eat anything real.

"What's happening out there?" she asked, swallowing.

"Nothing. The forest is quiet." Morlinna gave her a sheepish smile. "I don't trust it."

Ash nodded and abandoned the rest of the berries. "Neither do I. I think if we're going to use a person to heal the Malady, we should try it out on something smaller before moving to the root. Hopefully, that way we can handle anything it might try to send to distract us."

Morlinna shook her head wearily and leaned against the doorframe. "There are so many factors to consider. Using a person is so much more fraught than connecting the Malady to another plant. If I fail to push back the corruption, it will infect whoever I use, and then I will have to kill them."

Ashwyn stood and moved in front of her to hold her gaze. "I trust you."

Morlinna's eyes went sad and resigned. "You want me to use you."

"You have to. There is no one else. Too many of your threads are already corrupted. We want to give the Malady the best chance to heal, and for that, we need healthy strands." Ash glanced away and then back. "And...I'm not angling for you to corrupt me when you don't want to. But if something happens, if there is an accident, I'm the most prepared to push it back in myself."

Morlinna closed her eyes, her head resting against the stone of the wall. She took one deep, cleansing breath, then opened her eyes again.

"You are not. But in the end, that is my fault. I have not explained the battleground to you. And I should have, if only to prepare you for accidental infection."

"The battleground. That's what you call the...the space created when the Goddess gifted us." Ash rubbed her chest, remembering that feeling of opening.

"It is the little bit of Her power that rests in us. I suppose everyone sees it differently, but when the Malady attacks, I see mine as a fighting field."

Ash nodded. That's how she'd always thought of it when she'd seen Morlinna wrestling with the Malady.

"It is not a physical space but a mental one that reflects our reality. Everything that happens there is true in the best sense of the word. But you will never actually leave our world while you're there."

"How do you get there?"

Morlinna pointed, her finger ending just over Ashwyn's chest. "Follow your own heart thread. It is not hard. A little like taking a Nexum jump to home."

Ash rubbed her chest, feeling it constrict.

Morlinna's frown returned. "The hard part is the fight."

Ash snorted. "Well, at least I've been practicing."

Morlinna glanced at her, pushing up off the doorframe. "Yes," she said, though the word sounded far away and uncertain. "That should help."

Ash's stomach clenched as Morlinna moved outside. But that had to just be residual from fighting the dread.

"There is one other thing you should know about the battleground,"

Morlinna said, voice serious. "It holds our connection with our Goddess. Do not follow it."

That was the last thing Ash had expected her to say. "What? Why?"

"If you thought connecting to a human or another creature was confusing, this would be far worse. Deadly even. We are not meant to know the mind of divinity. We cannot contain it."

"So She kills us if we get too close to Her? I thought She was supposed to like Her Nexsaints."

Morlinna raised an eyebrow. "I like *you*, but I would still destroy you by accident if you touched me while the Malady rose in me."

Ash gulped. "All right, point taken."

"I've agreed to try this with you, Ashwyn. But that does not mean I think it is without risk. Just that I think you can handle the risk."

Ash sucked in a breath, but before she could say anything, Morlinna held up her hand, and the white streaks pulsed and surged through her skin, suddenly alive. White crept across her eyes, and with a shiver, Ash remembered the first time she'd seen her like this.

Whenever Morlinna opened herself to the Malady, she became something fearsome and horrifying to behold. But there was also something beautiful and ethereal about the pattern of white under her skin. Her changed eyes looked right through Ash, and it wasn't fear that made her shiver.

The sheer power of her made Ash stagger.

Morlinna reached for a bush, a squat thing with purple blooms growing out of the vines at their feet. Her touch spread an ashy dust along the leaves, and the strands beneath its surface turned to white. The Malady spread through the branches, and each leaf and blossom shriveled under its onslaught.

Morlinna took the corrupted strands in her fingers. Then, she reached her unaffected hand toward Ashwyn.

Ash gulped, then spun out one of her own threads from the very center of her being, handing it over to Morlinna.

Morlinna's white gaze met hers, and Morlinna nodded.

Then she wove Ash's strands with the Malady.

A profound chill swept through Ash, settling in her chest. And instinct drove her to grab hold of her own heart thread and follow it down.

The feeling carried her down deep, like a wave across the pond when she was little, sweeping her under until she lay gasping on the shore.

She sat up, a very real feeling, even if this place wasn't physical, like Morlinna said.

Grass grew in the cracks between worn flagstones, and Ashwyn recognized a courtyard just like the one in the necropolis. Black walls rose around her, and a weather-worn statue of the Goddess stood before her, eyes closed, empty arms outstretched.

It felt so familiar, but when Ash glanced at the sky, her stomach dropped.

Silver lightning streaked across flat black clouds. Just like the gates to Obitullas.

Ash's fingers flexed against the ground, feeling the cracked stone under her fingertips. But at the same time, she could also sense the forest around her, Wraith's breath hot in her ear. Two worlds overlaid with each other, and this one was somehow more real right now than the other.

Stark white fog gathered at the edges of the sky, shot through with silver lightning. Streaks of it swept over the top of her walls and struck the ground at her feet.

Ash jumped back.

A pit formed in her stomach, and she reached for her scythe to fend off the attack. Because that was exactly what this was. A siege inside of her, and she stood as an army of one against it.

Her fingers closed over nothing, and she spun to find the space where her scythe normally hung waited empty.

The fog swept forward, stabs of lightning cracking against the stone at her feet.

Ashwyn screamed and threw up her hands, utterly defenseless.

A figure leaped between her and the storm front. Morlinna caught a crack of lightning across her outstretched arm, face and hair contrasting with the black of her robe as she met the fog's attack.

And suddenly the forest rushed back into place, the vines pressing against her hands instead of rock. She looked up from her sprawled position against the matted roots and foliage to find Morlinna standing where she'd been, hands together in front of her. She wove Ash's strands with the pulsing white threads of the Malady, nothing in her expression showing the battle that raged under the surface.

But Ash could still feel it there. She could almost see the sweep of Morlinna's hand, catching silver lightning along her limbs, keeping it from striking Ash.

Ash's heart pounded. Was that what it was like to push the corruption back? A stark, empty battleground inside where you stood weaponless against the onslaught?

Had Morlinna known she'd be able to help?

Ash put out a hand and found Wraith waiting. She buried her head in his fur.

If Morlinna failed, she'd be right back there, facing the fog by herself. All she could do was wait and prepare. Except she had no idea how.

Ash shivered and forced herself to breathe. Then, with what felt like monumental effort, she unfocused her eyes and tried to find the battle being fought just under the surface.

She looked for movement. But she found none. The courtyard stood empty within her.

And when she focused her gaze on the real world, Morlinna stood beside the bush, blinking blue eyes.

"You're back."

Morlinna blew out her breath. "I am. How do you feel?"

Ash held out her hands. They remained tanned and healthy, but her fingers shook, and she closed her fists again to steady them.

"Shaken," she said with a laugh. "You didn't tell me I'd have to fight barehanded."

Morlinna stilled. "What?"

"The battleground. It was an empty courtyard. What are you supposed to fight with?"

Morlinna bit her lip, making it turn white. "I don't know...I've always had my scythe come with me."

"But..." Ash glanced at her weapon. Why hadn't hers?

Her gaze went to Morlinna's hands, still holding the leaf. Under her touch, the white strands of the Malady pulsed and...receded.

The healthy black strands from Ash's body wrapped them, and the white faded, leaving behind more healthy black strands.

She sucked in a breath and stood, knees shaking. "Morlinna."

"I see it," Morlinna said, voice hushed.

The leaves along the branches unfurled, returning to a deep lustrous green, bits of ash and dust falling away, as if the bush shed its sickly skin.

"It worked." Ashwyn laughed. "It worked!"

She seized Morlinna around the waist and lifted the taller woman in a fierce embrace. "You know what this means? We have a way to cure the Malady. No one else has to die. Ever again!"

Morlinna let out a shuddering breath, and Ashwyn put her down abruptly.

"It could change the world," Morlinna whispered. "We could eradicate the Malady entirely."

"Eventually," Ashwyn said with a grin. "We should take care of the root first. That's the thing that's going to cause the most problems right now."

Morlinna frowned and stepped toward the bush, lifting each branch and examining each leaf. "Yes," she said. "And this is just the start of understanding what we just did. Look. It did not heal everything."

Several leaves toward the bottom of the plant remained sickly, the Malady pulsing under their surface.

Ash bit her lip and knelt to see closer. The strands of the Malady still wrapped her threads. If they were going to heal it, they would have already.

"So one person as a template wasn't enough," she said, glancing up at Morlinna. "To heal the root, we'll need more than just me."

"Many more," Morlinna said quietly.

Ash's hands clenched against her knees as the distant sound of bells carried over the Devastation. "A whole village worth?"

Chapter 56
Concordim

"I don't like this plan," Morlinna said as they swung their way toward Edgefall for the second time that week. They'd taken the rest of the day to recover, and now the sun had set below the edge of the Devastation, plunging the forest into deep night. Wraith flew along above, watching their route from the air while Felleron traveled along the lower layers, guarding them from any creatures that might come up from below.

"Which part?" Ash said, landing lightly along a branch and borrowing a thread from Wraith in order to see in the gloom. "You don't want to use the villagers?"

"I do not want to use them without their knowledge. It is important that they know what they're agreeing to."

"If they knew, they'd never agree. It's heresy. It will be bad enough to convince them to work with us at all."

"I'd prefer not to earn my name as the witch of the Devastation."

Ash stared at Morlinna incredulously. "You kill people who stray into the Malady. You threatened to kill me before I'd even been corrupted."

Morlinna cocked an eyebrow at her. "But I always make sure they understand what is happening. They may not agree with it, but my motives are always plain. I always do them that courtesy."

"You always do what you have to to keep the world safe," Ash said pointedly. "Even if no one else agrees."

She took a step closer to Morlinna. "We're telling Cass, and she can convince them to work with us. This way we're not forcing them. What would you do if the root reaches them and they're all corrupted?"

Morlinna sighed. "I would kill them."

"So keeping them alive is better, yes?"

"Yes."

"Then let's go."

Ashwyn led the way up the steep slope of the crater, using strands from the big trees to climb upwards. Felleron joined them just as they reached the top, and Morlinna paused to listen to him.

What is it? Ash asked Wraith, who swooped overhead toward the necropolis.

There are a number of areas where the Malady has jumped or spread. A corrupted creature ranges beside the gap on the eastern side of the Devastation.

Ash blew out her breath. "We'll have to take care of them after we've healed the root. I don't think it's a good idea to split up on this," she said aloud, and Morlinna nodded sharply.

Morlinna followed as Ash dropped to the ground just behind the orphan house. She borrowed Wraith's ability to move smoothly and quietly across the ground and slipped between houses. Several more had been built in the intervening years. They stood crowded as close to the town center as they could get, away from the edges where the Devastation clawed its way closer.

Ashwyn crept up under Cass's window and stacked four flat stones against the sill. Then tapped sharply against the windowpane so she'd be sure to notice.

Morlinna raised an eyebrow.

"She'll know what it means," Ash said, a trace of bitterness creeping into her voice. "Come on."

They slipped away to the necropolis and swung up to the top of the wall, where a chorus of magpie chirps greeted them. Morlinna settled against the broken gap where Ash had tried to fix the wall all those years ago. Ash chose to pace. The blood had been cleaned away, and the broken flagstones replaced. But the gap where Uniah had died still swirled under its dome of strands. The villagers hadn't gotten around to burying it yet.

Ash tipped her head back and closed her eyes, feeling the night air against her face. It always felt so different out in the open than it did deep in the Devastation. It was chillier here, where a breeze was free to move across the open. Ash spread her hands, letting the wind pluck at the edges of her overcoat.

A step on the wall made her stiffen, and she took a bracing breath before turning and opening her eyes.

Cass climbed up onto the top of the wall, still lithe and limber but not as practiced at the climb as she had been once.

She stood and stared at Ash, her gaze wary as she waited.

Ash needed to find words, to arrange her argument so they could get what they wanted and everyone would be safe. But her tongue stuck to the roof of her mouth, and she struggled to swallow.

Cass's fear, which had been so intoxicating just days ago, now sat like a pit in Ash's stomach.

"What is it?" Cass asked. "You wouldn't have asked me to meet you here for nothing."

"No," Ash said. "I wouldn't. I would rather have left you all to rot."

Cass winced. "Well, thank you for not doing that. It's been bad enough keeping everyone from panicking when they saw that." She gestured to the gap swirling below them.

Ash huffed a mirthless laugh. "How'd you do it?" She didn't want to care. But she couldn't imagine what it had been like to convince the others to clean up the necropolis with that thing lurking just feet away.

"I told them all this was our Goddess-given duty. Father Liman backed me up."

"He would." Ash remembered his straightforward piety with anger tinged with fond regret. "Did they recognize it as the Malady?"

"No," Cass said.

"Good."

"Why is that good?" Cass spit out. "Why shouldn't I tell them? We should call the Order. We could have Nexsaints here in a matter of hours, and they'll help us."

"They won't."

Cass jumped at the sound of Morlinna's voice. She must not have seen the other woman where she was tucked against the wall, her dark robe blending in with the volcanic stone.

"What?" Cass said.

Morlinna rose gracefully. "The best they can do is evacuate Edgefall. But you will lose your homes, your livelihoods. You will have to start over somewhere else and never come back. There will be nothing here to return to when they are done scouring it."

Cass took a deep breath as her eyes raked up and down Morlinna's form. "You were a Nexsaint," she said. "I found your name on the Saints' record. But it's been crossed out."

"Because they didn't believe what I had to say either."

Ash tilted her head. "The Order thinks the only way to fight the Malady is to kill everything it feeds on."

"Kill…"

"The Last Death, Cass. Everything in the area will be scoured until nothing lives. Plants, livestock, even people."

"But you think you've found another way?" Cass said with an incredulous glance at Ash.

"We can heal it, Cass. Return the corrupted strands to the way they were. It just takes more work than the Order is willing to do."

"And risk," Morlinna added. "Some of us are willing to risk our souls in order to keep the rest of you safe."

Ash gave her a sad smile, and when she turned back, Cass was looking at her looking at Morlinna. Ash flushed.

"We have a plan," she grated out. "But we need your help."

Mortis, that hurt to say.

Cass raised her chin. "What do you need?"

"We need the villagers in order to heal the Malady. We'll need to have them here all together."

Cass shook her head, her eyes widening. "They'll never agree to that. They don't want to have anything to do with this place. I couldn't even get them to bury that-that spot. They want the next Keeper to do it."

"They have to. Cass—"

"You want me to force them?"

"I want you to convince them. For their own good."

"Because you say so?"

"Yes!" Ash threw up her hands. "For once in your life, Cass, can you just believe me?"

Cass took a staggering step back, and Morlinna put out her hand to keep the young woman from stepping off the wall entirely.

"It's not about trusting you when you ask for the most outrageous things," Cass said quietly. "You make it into a yes or no question, but it's not as simple as that."

"It is," Ash said, shoulders slumping. "I'm not the one who complicates it."

It was the same argument, and suddenly Ash was twenty years old again, reaching out to Cass, asking her to love her.

"I'm sorry," Cass said softly. And the worst part was that she sounded sorry. "I'm not going to force my people to do something they don't want to do."

"And we can't make you," Morlinna said with a pointed glance at Ashwyn.

And just like that, Ashwyn had lost the argument again. Had Cass ever trusted her in anything? Or had she just deluded herself for twenty years, thinking they were friends, lovers? Equals?

"No," Ash said.

"What?" Cass turned her head to eye Ash warily.

Morlinna's voice dipped in warning. "Ashwyn…"

"No. I can't force you," she said. "But I will convince you."

Ash grabbed Cass's hand before she could pull back and reached out along the connections that she kept with the Devastation. There were the ones she'd formed deliberately as a touchstone to the various parts of the forest. And there were the ones that she couldn't get rid of if she tried. The ones so deeply burned into her that even when she cut them, they grew back over and over.

She held tight to Cass's fingers as the connection swept over her and pulled her along its length, like a thread wound around the shaft of a spindle.

She was used to the feeling and came out the other side light on her feet, her overcoat whirling around her.

But Cass stumbled to the mat of vines and retched.

Ash let go of her fingers and swung the scythe from her back, falling into an attentive stance. The Devastation might have been her home, but it would never be safe.

"What just happened?" Cass gasped. She stared around her with bleary eyes. "Where did you bring me?"

"The Devastation," Ash said shortly.

The tall, thick trunks of sentinel trees surrounded them, interspersed with the shorter, squat shapes of others. Vines strung between the branches, moss hanging down to obscure the spaces between, closing everything in until it felt like standing under a bowl of growth.

Cass gaped. "Why would you—Dea, this place is forbidden."

"For good reason," Ash said.

"It's sacred."

"It's deadly. But I won't let you be hurt. I brought you here to prove a point."

"You lived here?" Cass said. "Alone?"

Ash gave her a pointed look. "It was better than the alternative. But as dangerous as the Devastation is, this isn't the threat you should be worried about."

She raised her scythe to point at the gap tearing at the base of the wide sentinel ahead of them. The gate to Obitullas yawned, licking at the edges of the world, sucking pieces of it in so it could grow larger. Strands of Malady poured from its sides, pooling against the mat of vines and reaching for freedom.

Ashwyn stepped forward and slashed at the corrupted strands, severing them.

"You've seen the gap where Uniah died," she said, not looking back at Cass.

This gap called to her, and she dared not look away. "This one was once Rafe. And Ingrim."

The two had combined into one large abomination, spilling corruption into the world.

Cass made a noise, but Ash didn't turn to look. She wasn't sure she'd be able to stand it if Cass cried over Rafe's remains.

"The Malady tries to spread from here. Every few months we come and clear it away, make sure it doesn't get any farther."

She made her way around the pool, slicing through the strands of Malady until the gap stood clear.

Then she finally turned back to Cass, who knelt with her hand against the trunk of a sentinel, as if it was the only thing keeping her stable. Her face had gone pale, and she swallowed over and over.

"Rafe came to find me. I don't know if you knew that. He found me here, but not before he'd been corrupted." She didn't let Cass's obvious horror stop her from telling the story. "He went Absent. I watched as everything he was drained out of him. And then the Malady took over his body. He tried to kill me, corrupt me, turn me into another infected shell that would walk around and doom the people I love.

"The root that's growing toward the necropolis will do the same thing. It will corrupt them all. My mother. Your father. Your grandmother. All of them. Turn them into mindless vessels to spread itself until everything in the world faces the Last Death."

A snarl shook the branches around them, and Cass screamed, short and sharp, before she slapped a hand over her mouth.

Ash just turned to meet the rush of the large cat lunging from the overgrowth.

She swung her scythe and leaped over the creature, slicing through the scales along its back. Blood splattered the leaves, and Cass flinched back. But Ash had distracted the thing, leading it across the clearing.

She ducked a clawed paw as it swiped at her and rolled to the other side.

"Do you see the white around its eyes?" she asked Cass calmly. "And the way it comes for me, despite the danger I pose?"

She sprang to her feet and swung her scythe blade, latching it behind the creature's neck. Then she yanked, severing its head from its body and its strands in the process.

The cat fell to dust, and Ashwyn straightened, flicking the blood from the blade of her scythe.

"That is what's heading for the necropolis," she said. "I'd take you down to the root to show you firsthand, but it's too dangerous. I can't handle it by myself."

Cass's wide eyes darted between Ashwyn and the pile of dust that had once been a living, breathing Devastation beast.

Had Cass ever seen the Last Death before? Ash couldn't help the twinge of memory. She'd stared out between screening branches as Morlinna had ended a man's life and his suffering before her eyes.

Slowly, Cass used the sentinel's trunk to climb to her feet. She swallowed and cleared her throat.

"You're sure you can protect them from this?" she said.

Ash opened her mouth, and Morlinna's honesty snuck past Ash's logic. "I'm sure I have to try."

Cass scrubbed her hands down her face. "How do I get them to do it? You can't drag all of them in here to force the point."

Ash raised her chin. "Lie," she said simply. "Tell them whatever you have to for their own good. If you get them to the necropolis, Morlinna and I will help cover the gap. And if they don't want to work with us, well then just remind them that everyone has to pull their own weight. Even heretics."

Cass glanced at her sharply, and Ash gave her a sickly smile full of memory and bitterness.

"That won't be as hard as you're imagining," Cass said.

"What? Why?"

"You survived the Devastation. They might not like you, but they can't argue against the Goddess's favor."

Ash stared at Cass as the other woman turned back toward the village.

The temple bell was tolling the midnight prayers by the time they returned, and Ash deposited Cass back on the wall. Morlinna waited there, as if she'd been prepared to wait all night if she had to.

She said nothing as they reappeared, only raised an eyebrow in Ash's direction.

Ash just nodded toward Cass.

"We'll meet you here tomorrow afternoon," Cass said. Then she glanced at Ash. "You're sure this is the right thing?"

Ash nodded. "The Goddess speaks to Morlinna, you know. She's said this is a good idea."

Cass sat and swung her legs over the edge of the wall to climb down, her face going pensive. "That's as reassuring as anything else," she said. "Since she's never spoken to the rest of us."

She slipped down the wall and back toward the village as a shiver went down Ash's spine.

Was there a reason the Goddess spoke to Morlinna and not to the rest of them? Ash had always assumed her own faith wasn't nearly strong enough to attract Her, but what if it was something else? What if it was easier to hide things from Morlinna? They had no guarantee that the voice was even the Goddess's.

Only Morlinna's conviction.

Chapter 57
Animatim

Vitania stalked through the Devastation, murky water rippling away from her boots no matter how hard she tried to keep her movements slow and silent. Sprawling trees with gnarled branches blocked her way, their roots reaching from the shallows to trip her as the lowest limbs curved toward the water's surface. An island of algae floated by, bobbing on the waves of her passing, as if mocking her ability to move silently.

V held aside a handful of moss hanging from the lowest branches and climbed underneath. A drip hit the back of her head and slid down her neck, under the edge of her shirt and armor. She suppressed the urge to shout in disgust and hunched her shoulders instead, getting her shirt to absorb the offensive drip.

Each Devastation had its own personality and its own designation to differentiate it. Boring names like Dev Alpha One and Dev East By Two. V would have called this one the Damp Hell if she'd been given the chance.

She paused and knelt, water seeping past her shin guards and pooling in her boots. The trees blocked the light, leaving everything dark and green, the occasional shaft of dim light spearing down like broken columns in a ruined temple.

Threads of the Nexum wove through everything: the trees, the moss, the water pooling under her feet. All of it formed an overwhelming network of interconnected parts.

She couldn't track anything here. The water hid any footprints or scuffed roots. Even broken branches and cut moss regrew in a matter of hours.

Her father had known exactly what he was doing when he'd come here.

But she wasn't completely without tools. The connections gathered under her feet, and she swept her eyes across, looking for patterns. Here, a jumble caught her eye. She plunged her hand into the water, stirring the silt of the forest floor, searching...

She pulled up a piece of rope attached to a tent peg.

And smiled. Everyone left a trail to follow. Even the most careful ex-commander of the Bladesaints.

She grinned at the evidence, then her eyes followed the twisted end, unraveling under her fingers.

It had been severed, cut by something strong but not sharp. Like the aftermath of a fight.

V dropped the peg and stilled.

She had never hunted in a Devastation before, but she was learning to translate her skills here.

The noise of the sodden forest crowded her ears. Water splashed and melded with the harsh cry of a heron overhead, and the branches creaked and groaned under the weight of their greenery.

She couldn't rely on what she heard.

She held still, ignoring the itch under her armor and the pain of a stone in her boot to become just another immovable object in the forest.

Across from her, the water rippled along a root, waves echoing from something larger moving ahead.

A shape sprang at her from the depths of the forest, and she brought her blade up to meet the threat, ready.

The enormous weight flew at her, straight for her chest, but she turned her shoulder to meet it. It struck her, and she turned, using the momentum to fling the creature away. She slashed as it went and heard a snarl.

Vitania spun to face the Devastation beast, taking in its long snout, lined with teeth. Leathery skin stretched over long knobby legs like a crocodile built to run instead of swim.

More splashing made V tense, but when she turned her head it was only a fall of moss.

The crocodile creature used her moment of distraction to charge. V ducked the teeth and swiped for the legs. It tripped with a roar and splashed to a halt.

Another weight hit her, and she sprawled in the water, a root wedging into the space just below her breastplate.

V held her breath, so she didn't inadvertently breathe water, and heaved against the weight across her back.

There *had* been a second creature. She just hadn't trusted her ears because of all the water.

Dea, she hated this place.

The crocodile creature thrashed on top of her, trying to bend its long head to get a bite in. The first one lunged to its feet, holding its injured leg gingerly.

That wouldn't necessarily slow it down. Injured creatures were angry creatures.

V dropped her sword and spun to grab the snapping jaws; she didn't have room to get her blade into its soft belly, anyway. It was too close.

She wrestled with it, its teeth digging into the leather covering her hands. V toughened her skin with the bark from the trees and pulled the strength of steel into her legs, then planted her feet against the creature's chest and launched it into the first one.

They tumbled in a pile of limbs, and V leaped to her feet, shedding a cascade of muddy water. Her blade came easily to hand, called there by the thread she kept connected to her palm. She grabbed another thread from the tree behind them and yanked. Her blade slashed out, cutting throats as she streaked through the air.

She skidded to a stop among the roots of the tree and spun to see the two creatures freeze and then topple into the water.

They disintegrated before her eyes, returning to dust that sank into the swamp.

V straightened and reached for the cloth in her belt to clean her sword, but muddy water had soaked it through.

Her shoulders sagged, and she heaved a great sigh instead of screaming into the forest like she wanted to. Then she used the cloth to swipe at the water running down her breastplate, mopping up the worst of it and leaving the muck to deal with later. She kept the blade in her hand as she leaned against the tree and breathed deep. In and out, ignoring the dank scent that somehow managed to smell green.

Her sodden braid snagged against the buckle of her breastplate, yanking at her scalp, and she yelped in pain.

She tore the hair free and held the end of the braid in one hand. For so long she'd kept it like this, trying to look like someone she wasn't, trying to earn the approval of a woman who never showed anything.

The rage shifting under her skin had everything to do with the situation and this damp hell. But a little piece of it speared directly at herself. Before she could think too hard about it, she raised her blade and sliced through the braid just below the base of her neck.

It was definitely not what the obsidian-lined sword was for, but her head immediately felt lighter, and she could turn it without the wet chunks of hair getting caught. The end of the braid sat heavy in her hand, the dirty strands not matching her mother's at all right now. She turned her hand and let it drop, trying not to imagine what the Abdicant would say.

Something in the connections at her feet caught her eye—a thread traveling away in a straight, unnatural line.

She knelt and sifted through the silt and sodden dust of the Devastation beasts. Her fingers caught against the sharp edges of an arrowhead.

She lifted her hand and let the water and silt drain away from the metal in her palm. The razor-sharp head of a crossbow bolt glinted in her hand, standard issue for Bladesaints, and from its markings, forged five years ago.

A connection stretched away, thick and glossy, leading to its former owner.

Her breath caught. Her father had been here. He'd camped here in the mire and been surprised by these creatures. And he'd left behind debris she could use.

She started forward, following the easy trail through the trees.

Then stopped.

The thread *was* easy to follow, thick and straight like an object that had been with someone so long the memory of them had been imprinted into the metal itself, forming a true connection.

Which was odd for something as disposable as a crossbow bolt.

He would have had to carry this in his pocket, would have had to reach in and touch it occasionally, think of it constantly.

Who would do that with a crossbow bolt?

Unless on purpose.

She'd found the discarded tent peg here, the only remains of a camp that had been meticulously cleared otherwise.

And before that, Conner, who had been able to tell her exactly where her father had been heading next.

V squeezed her eyes shut, envisioning the last five years of her life, traveling around the country finding clues, following leads, interrogating witnesses.

Every moment feeling like the games she'd played as a child.

He'd designed every puzzle in her childhood to train her, to teach her to be a better Bladesaint, a better Nexsaint, and eventually a Judge.

Mortis, he was doing it now. Using this hunt to train her, to make her better, to make her reach harder and further than she'd ever done before.

Her breath stuttered, hot and cold sweeping over her in turn, making her chest tight and unbearable. She gripped the top edge of her breastplate, trying to catch her breath, the anger in her chest tied up in a warmth she hated. Everything tangled until she had no idea what to feel first.

She landed on rage as the safest thing.

He'd been playing with her. Setting up silly games while she'd spent five years trailing along behind him instead of on the front lines, serving against the Malady where she was actually needed.

He'd created this connection deliberately for her and left it in a creature he knew she would find.

The hunt was over.

She could stalk him, using the stealth and cunning he'd trained into her. Or she could use the tools her mother had given her, bypassing his game. Ending this forever.

She reached for the cord connected to the bolt. And pulled.

The world smeared as she traveled along the connection. At the other end, she stepped into the empty air of a stronghold. A ruin deep in the Damp Hell with tumbled walls open to the sky.

A figure straightened at the fireplace opposite her, the fire lighting him from behind.

But the shadows across his face did nothing to obscure him from her. She knew him too well.

Vitania's hands clenched as she faced her father.

Chapter 58
Concordim

Ashwyn arrived at the village first. Morlinna had stopped to take care of the spots of Malady Felleron had identified earlier while Ash went on ahead.

She had just wanted to get this day over with.

Below her, the villagers bustled through the big gates of the necropolis. For the first time Ash had ever seen, they'd been thrown open to accommodate everyone, not just the Keeper, or the occasional Returned Divine.

A couple of figures bent to clear the weeds between the walls and the Devastation, but most gathered big blocks of obsidian in the necropolis itself. The village must have a stockpile squirreled away to repair the walls.

Ash snorted. If that was true, they'd never used it before, letting the walls sit broken. It wouldn't surprise Ash if the former elderman had been too miserly to bother.

Even from here, Ash could hear the grumbling as the villagers complained about the work.

Everyone needed to pull their own weight in Edgefall, but some had more of a debt than others. Which meant that the rest felt they had no debt at all.

How long had she believed those lies? The ones that said she had to earn her food, earn her clothing, and earn her place in the orphan house? The one that said she had to earn their love. And the one that said she would never be enough.

She'd always thought it was her fault. If she had just tried harder, the elderman would have wanted her to stay. If she'd kept her mouth shut better,

Bayna wouldn't have hit her. If she'd just been a different person, Cass would have loved her enough.

But that was all part of the lie they'd spun around her life, keeping her too afraid to fight back.

And now they worked beneath her, their lives in her hands.

Greta, the herbwoman, was now stooped with age, but her gnarled fingers still pointed out the blooms between the roots of the Devastation to her newest apprentice.

Father Liman pulled weeds by hand, his lips moving in silent prayer as he dug.

The Fairhands spread out from here to the far corner of the necropolis. There were a few more in their brood than Ash remembered. The oldest brothers must have gotten married and started procreating since she'd last seen them.

Ash didn't see any telltale black of the Saints. She'd worried all morning about how she'd get around them, but Cass must have gotten rid of them somehow. Sent them off on an errand to keep them out of the way of the heretic they would have gladly chased away.

Ash was almost disappointed.

A weight landed lightly on the branch beside her, and Ash put a hand out so Wraith could press his head into her palm. She scratched him around the base of his horns where she knew it was always just a little bit itchy.

"You should stay here," Ash told him quietly. "I don't know what they'll do if we bring Devastation beasts out of the forest with us. We need this to work, and that will be easier if they aren't so afraid."

His nostrils flared. *Too late. They already stink of fear. But yes, I will stay here in case you need me.*

She squeezed him in a tight hug. "Thank you."

Ashwyn stood, flapped the tails of her overcoat once to knock aside the twigs and leaves, and then she dropped from the trees.

She landed heavily at the edge of the crater, feet sure among the roots.

Greta was the first to look up, and Ash could hear the sip of breath when the woman saw her face.

Ash spared her a glance and was struck with the last memory she had of the woman. Greta bent over Uniah's bleeding form. She hadn't watched as Ash had been dragged away.

Ashwyn raised her chin and stepped out across the broken ground where the Devastation had already sent roots and vines to encroach on the necropolis.

She spotted Cass already inside the walls, her hair bright against the black stone. But someone bulky blocked her way.

One of the Fairhand boys. Mortis, he'd gotten big. Ash drew her gaze up his form, expecting a spike of fear, but it never came. Instead, she managed a lazy smile.

"Nial," she said, dredging his name out of the recesses of her mind. She and Cass hadn't played with him much as kids. He'd been four years older and uninterested in "girl games." Years later she'd saved him from getting dragged into the Devastation during an incursion.

He cracked his knuckles. She knew what his hands had felt like as he and his brother had thrown her over the edge of the crater into the Devastation.

"Shouldn't be here, Ash," he grated and spat on the ground at her feet. "We threw you out once. We can do it again."

She tipped her head back to meet his eyes and bared her teeth. "Try it."

She didn't even reach for her scythe. When he took a step forward, she snagged a strand of the Nexum from behind him and pulled.

Her body snapped forward, traveling through him as she jumped to the space she'd selected.

He overbalanced in her absence and stumbled forward. He turned to glare, but she sniffed and kept walking.

It had finally happened. She was strong enough now. None of them could control her. None of them could manipulate her.

Ash stepped through the gate of the necropolis and swept toward Cass, who was speaking with someone else.

The other woman turned, and Ash fought to hold on to her calm.

Bayna. There'd been a part of Ash that had hoped Cass's mother was dead and gone.

But of course, Ash was never that lucky. She traveled with magpies, after all.

Bayna's gaze swept over Ash, and she had to suppress the need to check her clothes, smooth her hair, and remember if she'd washed her face that morning. Any flaw would result in a lecture at best or a smack at worst.

The corners of Bayna's mouth drew down, the lines at the corners deepening to endless crevices. The woman had not aged well. Her hair had gone wispy white under the blonde, and her cheeks were falling to jowls.

She spun back to her daughter. "You can't do this, Cassarah. You risk all of our souls with this madness."

"What madness?" Cass asked as if she'd been living this argument for hours already. And Ashwyn had the sudden urge to catch Cass's gaze and roll her eyes behind Bayna's back.

She suppressed it ruthlessly.

"I don't think it's madness to protect ourselves," Cass said. "They're here to help us do that. If that gap grows, it could swallow all the Absent in the necropolis and then come after us, too."

"We only have her word to tell us that's going to happen. And I've never trusted her."

"Her word and that thing in the middle of the necropolis. The thing that's eating into our world." Cass stepped up to her mother and frowned down at her. "I won't let it take anything more. And neither will you."

A little shiver went down Ash's spine. She'd yet to see Cass in her role as elderman. Soft-spoken Cass, who had never raised her voice to anyone, let alone her own mother, still lived in the back of Ash's head. But Ash had always guessed at the core of steel underneath it all. And apparently, she'd wasted years of her life not imagining it in the dark of her room at night.

Ash coughed.

"We all have to pull our own weight, Bayna," Ash said sweetly. "Shirkers don't eat around here."

Bayna glared at her, mouth working with outrage as Ash took her scythe from her back and spun it idly to slash through the weeds that had crept through the cracks in the paving stones.

"Get back, girl, or we'll throw you back in the Devastation."

"Now, Bayna." Father Liman had followed Ash into the necropolis. Streaks of silver shot through his dark hair now, and his limp had grown more pronounced. But he met Bayna's gaze squarely.

"She survived the Goddess's domain," he said. "The Gentle Mother judged her, and she has come out alive. It is not for us to question Her Holiness's decision."

Bayna looked like she wanted to argue, a muscle in her jaw flickering as she clenched her teeth, but when her glare changed nothing, she spun to stalk away down the path. She carried an axe, but she only used it to poke half-heartedly at the vines outside.

In the last few years, Ash had assumed there was something about Bayna, something in her past that had made her into the woman who'd hated a particular war orphan. Something that would make Ash understand why she'd singled her out.

But even looking at her now with the wisdom of adulthood, Ash couldn't imagine what justified Bayna's words.

Father Liman shook his head in Bayna's direction, then tilted his head to look Ash in the eyes and placed his hand over his heart in a sign of blessing. "Welcome home, Ashwyn."

"Not my home anymore, Father." Ash gave him a flat smile. "You all made sure of that."

Ash almost felt bad for the stricken look in his eyes, but he had been one of the ones who could have defended her. His words would have made a difference then. Not now, when it was five years too late.

He ducked his head and stepped back, limping toward the next patch of green in the pathway.

"Well, that was fun," Ash said, keeping her voice light. "What other chaos can I cause? I can paint rude words across the necropolis. Ooh, I could desecrate the temple."

Cass sighed and closed her eyes. "Please don't. It was hard enough to convince them to work with you. I'd rather you didn't ruin all of my hard work."

Ash rubbed her forehead. "All right, fine. You know, it makes perfect sense that you'd be no fun anymore."

Cass sucked in a breath and scowled. "I'm plenty of fun."

"You never were. I was everything fun about us."

"Just because someone had to remember our responsibilities—"

Ash laughed short and sharp. "Right, I never did that. I can't believe you still don't see that I had to work twice as hard as you, Cass. Every day. Just to deserve my bread. Just so no one would kick me out of my only home." She jerked her chin up as Cass's eyes went wide. "Well, no need to worry now. I have a home no one can take away. And you have to hope and pray I do my job well enough so you can keep yours."

Cass groaned. "Can we not argue about this? Everyone is watching and—"

"And you don't want them to think you can't control me?"

"I need them to think you can do this," Cass hissed.

Ash's mouth snapped shut.

Cass sighed. "I have to make you look strong so they don't panic. You can't see it, but they're barely holding it together, Ash. They're frightened. They don't know what that thing is." She gestured to the gap. "The Devastation gains a foot of ground every month now, instead of every year. And there's nothing to keep out Devastation beasts if they come calling."

Ash gritted her teeth and swept her gaze over the workers. She'd expected them to be wary, but now that she was looking, most kept their gazes on the Devastation just outside.

"Where are the Bladesaints?" Ash said. "They should be watching for any beasts while you all are out here."

"There are none, Ash."

Ash jerked. "What?"

"The Order never sent us replacements for Rafe and Ingrim. At first they promised more, but they kept putting it off. There was always some excuse for the delay. Now they've stopped even giving us that much. They told us Edgefall wasn't important enough to warrant Bladesaints. We keep their Absent, and we fight the Devastation back, and they dared to tell us we weren't important enough."

Ash stared at her, and Cass gave her a rueful smile. "Your friend said we shouldn't tell the city about the Malady because they wouldn't care. She was right. As soon as she said it, I knew she was right."

Ash stood silent for a moment until Cass cleared her throat.

"What do we need to do here?" Cass asked. "What do you need us to do so you can heal the Malady?"

Something stirred at the edge of the forest, and Ash shook her head.

"Just keep them all here. We'll do the rest."

Across from the open gates, Morlinna stepped out of the Devastation, her robe flaring as she walked alone. Wraith must have warned Felleron away.

Standing near the gate, Ash watched as each villager between them raised their head to look at her. Whispers rushed across the crowd as they took in the streaks on her face and her Nexsaint black.

Her mask hung from her belt.

Morlinna stared back at them, and Ash knew exactly what that resignation with a hint of guilt meant. She'd served these people for over a decade, keeping them safe from the Malady. But if they failed here, she would have to kill them all eventually, anyway.

Ash stepped forward, and Morlinna's gaze snapped to her. The tightness around her mouth eased, and she angled herself toward Ash and Cass.

The villagers scrambled out of her way, stumbling over themselves in their haste to leave room. Fear lent weight to their voices, and Ash could finally make out words in the commotion.

"Witch," they said. "Witch of the Devastation."

"Heretic."

"Apostate."

"Monster."

Ash whirled, trying to find the speaker of that last one, but they all ducked away from her and bent to their work.

Ashwyn abandoned Cass and met Morlinna halfway between the forest and the gate.

"This is..." Morlinna faltered. "Much as I imagined."

"I'll handle them," Ash said. "You don't have to interact with anyone if you don't want to."

"I do not require a shield, Ashwyn." Morlinna's smile took the sting from the words.

"No, but I'll give you one, anyway." She turned back toward the necropolis. "I'll feed their connections to you while we bury the gap."

As Morlinna passed Cass, the elderman gulped and flinched. Morlinna didn't even cast her a look, and Ash held tight to the fierce pride that beat in her chest.

The villagers had piled their blocks of obsidian against the wall of the necropolis, waiting for the Nexsaints to come finish the job.

Morlinna raised her arms, pulling the threads in the blocks to guide them into place around the gap.

Ash moved between the gawking villagers and Morlinna, teasing a strand from each and passing it to Morlinna.

The action didn't make Ash sick. Whatever Cass had said must have convinced the Edgefallers to trust Ash and Morlinna. At least enough for this one thing.

Morlinna took the strands with a practiced twist and wove them under her arm to keep them separate and organized until they could carry them to the root.

And all the while, she built the wall around the gap, weaving the strands with the fluidity of water until the edges melted together and formed a smooth, sleek barrier.

The moment she had the shape she wanted, Morlinna pulled the weave apart, and the blocks solidified into their new configuration.

When she lowered her arms, a murmur went through the villagers. But no one approached. Even Father Liman took one look at Morlinna's white-streaked face and spun on his heel instead of confronting her. Ash had no idea what he would even say to an apostate. She doubted his argument about Ash having survived the Goddess's judgement would mean anything when applied to a woman whose name was slashed through on the Saints' record.

Not everyone was afraid. The moment Morlinna turned, Bayna angled to intercept her.

Heat crept into Ash's cheeks. She grasped a thread from the flagstones and yanked. The other woman tripped over the rising edge and landed on her hands and knees.

Ashwyn stepped forward with a satisfied smirk and knelt to help Bayna up.

"Oh, what did you trip on? There's nothing there."

Bayna shook off Ash's hands and glared at her. "Don't touch me, girl."

Bayna tried to move around her, and Ash sidestepped to block her way.

"Sorry," she said. "It looks like you were trying to speak to my friend. That wouldn't be a good idea."

"Get out of my way, Ashwyn."

"No."

Bayna's hand twitched as if she wanted to box Ash's ears and then thought better of it. Ashwyn smirked.

Bayna finally spat, her spittle staining the dry flagstones. "Doesn't matter what Father Liman says. You're as damned as that one."

Ashwyn's lips twitched. "I'd rather be damned with her than back in the orphan house with you," she said quietly.

Bayna huffed and turned to stomp away.

"I think we have enough threads now," Morlinna said over her shoulder.

Ash turned as Morlinna raised her mask to cover her face.

It was supposed to be a barrier. Armor to protect her identity, but the whispers behind them only grew, and Ash knew Morlinna was using the delicate porcelain as a way to hide herself from those who didn't understand.

"Morlinna."

The other woman paused, and her eyes caught at Ash's behind the mask. But Ash wasn't even sure what she was trying to say.

"I'm sorry." For bringing her here. For the reactions of people Ash hated. She knew this would happen, but it had been her idea that had made them both face it.

Below the edge of the mask, Morlinna's lips tipped in a tight smile. "I know, but it isn't any more than what I was expecting."

And that was the problem. Morlinna saw herself as a monster.

Ashwyn had returned to the village, older and wiser, with a clearer vision of everything that had happened to her here. She knew what she was worth, and the memories here just lit a fire in her chest.

Morlinna didn't have that buffer.

"Morlinna," Ash said quietly, for her alone.

"It's fine, Ashwyn," Morlinna said, and Ash could hear the sad smile in the words. "I chose this, remember?"

"That doesn't mean you deserve it."

Morlinna sucked in a breath.

"You are strength and power and a fierce kindness I will never be. You protect people who spit on you for it. And you grant mercy to those too stupid to see their danger. You've given so much of yourself to them." Ashwyn gestured to the villagers who lurked just beyond earshot. "Maybe you are a monster. But you are a good one."

Morlinna's eyes went wide, but behind the mask, Ash couldn't read more than her sudden flinch.

Mortis, she'd gone too far.

Ash stepped forward, reaching for her, but Morlinna shook her head.

"We're done here. Stay if you would like. But I wish to be alone in the quiet of my cloisters."

Ash's shoulders dropped as Morlinna stepped smoothly to the edge of the Devastation and swung into the trees.

It was fine. They had enough threads. One from nearly every villager except for the children and the elderly who hadn't come. And Cass. Ash hadn't been able to bring herself to touch Cass's threads.

But Ash couldn't help feeling that something else had stayed broken. Like a chip on the edge of a bowl. A missing piece she'd never be able to fill.

Cass moved up beside her. "That was abrupt. Is it done?"

"Yes," Ash snapped. "It's done. You can go back to hating us now."

"Why are you upset? She's the one who ran."

"Because you all made her feel wrong." Ash made a throwing-away gesture, trying to shake off the anger. "I don't know why I expected better. This place was always good at that."

Chapter 59
Obitusim

Morlinna swung through the trees before reaching for her connection with her home and pulling the thread taught. She whirled through the air, the greens and reds and browns of the Devastation smearing into a jumbled mess as the world slashed by.

Her feet hit the worn flagstones of the nave, and she took a step to steady herself as everything righted around her. The comforting features of her home settled into place. The banked fire in the hearth glowed; the rug she'd woven years ago lay with one edge flipped over, pulled by Ashwyn's coat as she'd passed.

Morlinna lit the candles in the sconces and breathed in the scent of tallow and smoke.

It all should have soothed the desperate jitters that rang along her nerves. But her heart still raced, and when she raised a hand to press it against her chest, her fingers trembled.

Witch. Apostate. Monster.

The names echoed in her head, but they drew no answering echo in her heart. She'd accepted them years ago and lived with them every day.

It wasn't the villagers who made her hands shake today.

Different words replaced the ones in her head.

Kind. Brave. Selfless.

Morlinna's fingers crept to the edge of her mask, grateful it had concealed the things she felt but couldn't hide.

For once, her stone walls weren't the sanctuary they'd always been. She could hear Ash's voice ringing against them. She could hear the younger woman's words as clearly as if she stood there.

"You can keep using the worst ways to describe yourself. But I'm not leaving you."

"You are more than a tame monster."

"Why wouldn't I love you?"

Ashwyn had given her everything she'd ever wanted. She'd given her safety and space. Friendship. And a love that demanded nothing in return.

But even within that safety, Ash's words had battered at Morlinna's walls. Year after year she'd torn them down and had somehow made the destruction soothing.

Every beautiful phrase had worn away Morlinna's resolve and her self-loathing until she stood naked and shaking, facing the truth of who she was.

And who Ashwyn was to her.

The realization left her breathless for one bright moment before a wash of cold shook her to her bones.

Morlinna staggered to the statue of the Goddess and rested her head against the chilly stone feet.

"Forgive me," she whispered. "Forgive me, please don't leave me."

Morlinna could still feel Her there. The promise of Her gift still filled all the empty spaces in her chest.

She was the Goddess's tool. Her weapon in the dark places of the world. It was still true. She had not given that part of herself up. In fact, she held it so tightly she should have bled with it.

The Goddess's voice rarely felt like actual words. Sometimes it came as the soft sigh of wind through the trees. Sometimes like the murmur of a conversation drifting through a thick curtain from a far-off room.

This time she couldn't be sure the words belonged to Her or if they were an imagined echo in Morlinna's mind.

...what are you afraid of?

Morlinna's breath stuttered.

"I'm afraid..." she whispered. "That if I love her, I would be giving you up."

So soft and so far away, and yet the next words hit her like a charging Devastation beast.

...it is possible to love more than one thing.

Morlinna's knees shook until she slid down to sit against the base of the statue.

So many years ago, she'd watched her fellow Saints pair off. She'd watched them, and she'd known she hadn't wanted what they had, and it had made her feel broken.

She could still see Illyra on the steps of the Greater Temple, offering her a hand. The sun had glinted off the silver chain braided into her dark hair.

She could still remember that wash of shame as she'd stepped back. "I belong to Her."

She'd never wanted what the others had because she'd already been fulfilled.

For the first time in her life, Morlinna could see herself wanting more. Why? Because Ashwyn had given her the space to want it?

"I think it's you who doesn't want to hold on."

How long had she been living only for death? Morlinna's breath came faster, in great heaves as the tension slipped from her neck.

"More than a monster. More than a sacrifice."

When Morlinna laughed, it came out broken, and she swiped at her wet cheeks.

The nave glowed, lit with the softness of the candles and the promise of tomorrow. It wasn't just something she would have to say goodbye to, eventually. It was a place to live and breathe and be.

Her home was here with Ashwyn, and for the first time, she could see it without a twinge of guilt.

She was so tired of shame.

She raised her hands and stared at the white lines of the Malady traveling through her skin. She'd hated her power even as she'd taken it into herself. A holy atrocity.

But Ashwyn had never seen her that way.

She'd seen the monster and called her beautiful and kind and worth loving.

Morlinna swallowed back tears. Ashwyn had given her her name back. She'd given her this view of herself that was wrapped in so much light it burned.

Illyra had offered love once. And Morlinna had lost so much by saying no.

How much would she lose by saying yes?

Chapter 60
Concordim

Ashwyn swung up to the temple, landing on the doorstep. She pushed through the door, heart in her throat.

Ash's gaze swept the dim interior of the building. The pews had moved over the years, standing along the walls instead of lined up in the middle. But the altar remained in its place at the end, the statue of the Goddess looking down from the shadows.

It took Ash a moment to pick out Morlinna at the foot of the altar, her dark robe hidden in the blur of Ash's ruined vision.

The other woman knelt as she did every morning, her hands clasped in her lap, her face tilted back to stare up at the face of the Goddess.

Ash blew out her breath and closed the door behind her. Then she rested her head on the rough wood, avoiding the sight of Morlinna, content with a piety Ash had never felt.

Which goddess was she speaking to now? The one who was depicted with a benign smile and an open, welcoming hand? Or the one who had murdered Her wife?

The one whose corrupted power was killing them all. Was it Her voice Morlinna heard in her ear urging her to corrupt herself, urging her to give herself up to it?

What could Ashwyn do to drown out the voice of a goddess?

Ash stepped away from the door and moved up behind Morlinna.

Morlinna closed her eyes and breathed deep.

"Is it all right if I'm here?" Ash asked.

Morlinna glanced up at her, red tinging her cheeks. "Of course it's all right."

"You said you wanted to be alone."

Morlinna bit her lip. "I did say that. Didn't I?"

"I just wanted to be sure you were all right. After..."

"After seeing the way your people react to me?"

Ash's lips thinned. "They're not my people," she said. "And you can ignore them. They don't know you."

Morlinna's gaze went distant. "I thought they did," she said quietly.

"What?"

Morlinna's hands chafed each other in her lap. "I spent my life thinking their fear was justified. I was the monster your people whispered stories about. They weren't wrong. I did the things they accused me of. I corrupted myself. I killed anyone who came into my forest. I made myself into something wicked and terrible."

She looked up at the face of the Goddess above her. "All because my lady called me to do so."

Ash opened her mouth, but all the doubts crowded forward, choking her so none of them could come out first.

"That sustained me," Morlinna said and glanced back down to meet her eyes. "You need to know that was enough for me. Until you."

"Oh." Ash swallowed and tried for a smile. "Should I...should I apologize?"

Morlinna's lip twitched. "Maybe. At first I thought it took something away from me. But now...I think you've opened me, and I can't close the door again."

Ash sucked in a breath.

"I've never cared how other people felt about me. I do what I have to do, and that's all. But you've always been an enigma. You saw me so differently than I saw myself that I thought you had to be confusing me with some ideal. I couldn't trust myself to know how you felt."

Ash's chest seized, and she swallowed. It took her two tries to be able to speak. "I think you know how I feel," she said slowly.

Morlinna's gaze was steady. "It hasn't changed?"

She knew. All the years Ash had buried it, hidden it deep so as not to scare Morlinna away, and now it sat between them like a shout.

"It's grown. It's deeper and wider and more patient."

"Some might call that stubbornness."

"I think most people would call it love."

Morlinna closed her eyes, almost as if the words pained her, but Ashwyn couldn't bear the thought of taking them back. They were moving forward. There was no other choice now.

"I've never been confused about who you are or how I feel about you,

Morlinna. I might have been your student once, but I haven't been for years. I know what I want, and what I want is you."

Morlinna closed her eyes.

"If you're worried about my promise, then you should know that loving you will not keep me from killing you when the time comes."

"I'm not worried."

The words came quiet, but they lodged deep in Ash's chest. "You're not?"

Morlinna's eyes met hers. "I trust you."

Ash waited, her breath stuck in her throat. She had said these words before. Her feelings changed nothing, because they'd always been there.

Morlinna had to be the first one to move. The first one to step them forward into the unknown.

But Morlinna sat, hands clenched in her lap, her eyes trained on Ash's face, and Ash didn't think it was her imagination that they seemed to plead for something. A way forward, perhaps.

"I'm sorry," Morlinna whispered, and Ash's heart fell.

She took a deep breath, resolving to build the wall around her heart higher next time. She could keep this all inside, but only if Morlinna didn't test the boundaries. Didn't make them swell with hope.

She turned to hide her expression.

And Morlinna grabbed her wrist.

A flicker of light caught Ash's eye, and she turned to see Morlinna extending a thread toward her. Asking for a connection.

Ash's mouth went dry, and she fumbled with her free hand as she pulled a strand forward from her chest and handed it to Morlinna.

Neither of them had to work to fix them together. The ends twined around each other, as if recognizing each other.

This time, Ashwyn kept the thoughts from pouring down the strand like water down a drain. Instead, a flood of feeling came through the connection, surging through Ashwyn until she lost herself in the tidal wave of Morlinna's thoughts.

The guilt and shame she'd seen five years ago still lingered on the surface, but Morlinna pulled her under to see the events that had built them into a crystalline barrier.

Flashes of memory laced with emotion flitted past. Ash caught a glimpse of a little girl who sat in the cloisters of the Greater Temple as other initiates talked and laughed over her. No one noticed the loneliness in her stillness.

She saw the same little girl, now a woman, kneel before the throne of the Goddess. She felt the flush of a life accepted for one purpose, a voice in her head that promised never to leave her alone again.

A woman with dark hair braided with a delicate silver chain looked at her in deep disgust and turned to twine her fingers with a man who wore the circlet of a Judge. Leaving her behind.

The man lay against the vines of the Devastation, circlet rolling away from his head as the gap ate into his chest.

She saw herself and her clumsy confession. Morlinna's fear swept through her. Fear that she had no idea what to do with what was being offered. Fear that if she said no, she'd be left alone again. Fear that saying yes would mean the Goddess would pull away.

All the pieces faded back into memory. None of them was the present, just the things that had led to this moment.

Ash staggered, the wave of Morlinna's experience washing everything aside to leave one single thing in its wake. The overwhelming sense of safety. Of belonging.

Ash came back to an awareness of her own body and the sense that her eyes were wet.

Everything Morlinna hadn't been able to put into words lay before her, a gift freely given.

Morlinna still gripped Ash's wrist, but now she slid her fingers down to twine them with Ash's.

"I'm sorry, I don't know how to say what I'm feeling. I don't know how to love someone else," she whispered. "But I'd like to learn."

Ash choked on a laugh. "Well, I can be your Rector. But then we can't be in love. There's this whole power imbalance there. And I could never take advantage of you that way."

Morlinna huffed, but her fingers stayed locked with Ash's. "I suppose it's my own fault to hear my words coming back at me."

"Yes, but I'll try not to make us relive the past. As long as you're here with me now."

"I'm here," Morlinna said, words low and pained.

"What's wrong?"

"I've already given so much of myself to the Goddess," she said. "I don't know how much is left over for anyone else."

Ashwyn shook her head. The Goddess was a part of Morlinna. With Morlinna's thoughts twined with Ash's and her past hurts and triumphs laid bare, that was more apparent than ever. Ash's own doubts remained hidden in the back of her mind, buried under the immediacy of the moment. And they were a part of her, too. But it didn't mean she couldn't accept what Morlinna was offering.

She cleared her throat. "I'll take anything you're willing to give me. Every piece of you is a treasure." She pulled on Morlinna's hand, drawing her closer. Morlinna ducked her head to lay her temple alongside Ash's.

"Which piece would you like to start with?"

A shiver went through Ash, making her mouth water. She tipped her head the barest bit and captured Morlinna's mouth with hers.

Like a hand reaching under the covers, the warmth of it went down Ash's spine. She spread her palm across Morlinna's cheek, then curled her fingers around the other woman's neck, pulling her closer, harder, until Morlinna gasped against her skin.

Ash pulled away, giving her space even as her own breath tore at her chest and her arms ached to draw Morlinna down into her, deep enough they'd drown in each other.

"I'm sorry," Ashwyn said, breathless. "Let me know if I go too fast. I've been told I feel things too much for other people."

Morlinna took Ash's face in her hands, the tips of her thumbs brushing Ash's eyelashes. Her voice went fierce and husky.

"Never apologize for loving me."

Chapter 61
Animatim

Vitania's chest heaved as she stared across the ruins at her father.

His hair had grown long around his face, cut in a ragged line with a knife that wasn't nearly sharp enough. The beard did nothing to hide his sad smile as he stared back at her, blue eyes steady.

V's hands shook as thoughts careened through her head, too fast to catch. Something thick and bitter crept up her throat, threatening to choke her, and she had the horrible feeling it might be tears. A chasm opened inside her chest, bleeding and festering and spilling its bile all through her veins.

Would it hurt this much if she didn't still love him with some long-buried piece of her heart?

No. V shook her head. She didn't want to love him. He'd hated the Abdicant so much he'd used V as the agent for her destruction. He'd set her up to fail and to pull the Abdicant and the Primarch Divine with her.

What kind of monster would do that? What kind of monster would still love someone who did that?

And somehow the rest was worse. He'd abandoned V there in Vitamorn. He'd left her alone with a mother who hated him. A mother who'd been angry and frustrated and refused to sign no matter how helpful it would have been.

Rage simmered within the chasm, bolstering the chaos, and she clung to it, willing it to make her strong. She couldn't even tell which part of her childhood she should be the angriest about. The sabotage or the abandonment.

He raised his hand, and she tensed, her grip tightening on the hilt of her sword.

Then he signed her name. The shape of a V across his chest.

And something in her heart tore open, another gaping hole leaking its hot filth into her.

He'd given her language and understanding, and her heart craved it, aching for more. But the craving only made her sharper, strengthening the edges of her anger.

"I don't need those anymore," she spat, keeping her hands clenched hard enough to ache. The words wanted to come thick and slow, and she concentrated on making them as clear as her mother's always were. "I have this now. I don't need something that makes me look weak."

She touched the amplification loop around her ear. He couldn't see it, but he had to know what she meant by it.

The air left his lungs in a surprised puff, and his eyes went wide, then deep and soft. "You've never looked weak, V-girl."

His voice sent a jolt through her, making her stagger. It was rougher than she'd remembered. Most of her memories of him were so gentle around the edges. The sound of it rang in her head, comforting and deeply wrong at the same time.

"Because I made myself strong."

"Yes. That has always been true. The things Sahvia said, the things she tried to make you believe... Well, it's done now. I knew she would take you to a Mender," he said. "But only when she wanted to."

"Because she wanted me to learn my own strength beforehand." V found her hands moving with the words, signing despite her resolve not to.

"No." He shook his head. "Because it made her look like a hero to you."

V drew in a sharp breath. "Mother is not the manipulative one."

He raised his hand in a slashing gesture. "I don't want to waste this time arguing about the Abdicant."

V shook her head. For five years she'd tracked him, and she'd avoided thinking of this moment. Every word, every question remained tangled inside until she had nothing to say to him.

But he didn't seem to need her to speak. He stepped forward, hands out. "You've grown so much. Learned so much. I'm so proud of you, V."

"I can't say the same about you," she snapped.

He stopped in the middle of the room, the corners of his mouth turned down, pulling at the lines made from laughing so they seemed deep and out of place.

"I knew you'd be the one to come for me," he said, hands moving with his words, as if he also couldn't keep from signing. "I knew I had to make this moment count. And yet I barely know what to say to you. You are a different person from the one I raised. You've grown up and grown away. And I'm afraid I can't wrest you away from them now."

Her mouth tightened. He was still trying to betray the Abdicant. "I'm right where I'm supposed to be. Where you and Mother trained me to be. Hunting a heretic."

He spread his hands. "What do you think I've done?"

"You untethered the Goddess."

He froze, and for a moment, for one second, she thought they'd made a mistake.

Then his hand ducked into his pocket and came out holding the grass bracelet.

"I tried," he said.

All the breath left her lungs, and she realized she'd been waiting for him to prove her wrong. She'd wanted to believe that the man she remembered wouldn't have struck a Bladesaint. Wouldn't have risked their entire world for heresy.

But she'd stopped believing in fairytales the moment she'd walked away from him in the Greater Temple.

And she only had one thing left she needed from him. One answer.

"Why?"

Chapter 62
Concordim

Ashwyn woke when the weight beside her shifted and the bed went cold.

"Morlinna?" Her voice came out gravelly and thick with sleep. Her good eye was still pressed to the pillow, so all she saw was a dark blur. The mattress dipped, and then Morlinna's lips pressed her forehead.

Ash turned her head to blink the room into focus. She ran her hand up Morlinna's arm, ignoring the white streaks that stretched toward her shoulders.

She smiled and pulled Morlinna down. The other woman resisted for half a breath before huffing a laugh and leaning in for a proper kiss this time.

By the time they surfaced, Ash had almost had her fill. Almost.

Morlinna pushed upright with a smile and shook her head. "We must go. Our work could take all day."

Ash groaned and stretched. "Is it morning already?"

"Dawn will come soon."

Ash let herself fall back as Morlinna stood and stepped across the cold flagstones to the chair where she'd draped her robe the night before. Even in the midst of everything that had happened last night, Morlinna took care with her things.

Ash lay there for one more moment, admiring the fall of her hair down her straight, thin form.

Morlinna raised an eyebrow as she fastened the buttons that marched down her sternum. "Are you going to help me or not?"

Knowing Morlinna, it wasn't a suggestive question, as much as Ash wanted it to be. She was readying herself for their task. Their nearly impossible task of healing the Malady, which had never been healed before.

"Always," Ash said and finally slid out of bed.

They didn't bother climbing down through the layers of the Devastation today.

Ashwyn wrapped her arm around Morlinna's waist while Morlinna buried her hand in Wraith's ruff. Then Ash reached with her free hand for the thread that connected her to the city below the Devastation.

In the last moment before she yanked them along the strand, Ash felt claws latch onto the back of her overcoat.

The world smeared into streaks of color, and for once, Ash was sure everyone had the same blurred vision she did.

Then, the ground appeared under their feet, and she took one step to steady herself. The air grew close and stale and much colder than even the morning air in the cloister had been.

Ash blinked, bringing the world into focus, and the city rose in front of her, ruined buildings marching away from her toward the center where she could just imagine the white pillar of the Underheart rising over it all.

Ebonheart untangled her claws from Ash's collar and flapped to her shoulder. Ash cast a smile at her. "Didn't want to miss out on the fun, eh?"

Nestlings need looking after, she sent down their connection.

Felleron had taken the long way down, through the layers of the Devastation to scout the root's progress. Morlinna had wanted to try healing the Malady from here where it was the most potent, but they needed to know how much time they still had before the root reached the necropolis.

Morlinna stepped toward the base of the root where it burst free of the ground. She knelt as if to examine it.

"We must prepare quickly," she said. "The dreads will not leave us alone for long once they sense we are here."

"I'll start now," Ash said.

She trotted away along the edge of the dome made by the Absent roots of the Devastation in order to set her traps. They hadn't tested the theory her plan was based on, but they needed something to help them against the dreads. Morlinna would be working for too long to avoid them completely.

Ash worked backward, and it was nearly an hour before she reached Morlinna again.

"Felleron says the root has nearly reached the necropolis," Morlinna said, standing and brushing off the skirt of her robe. "We must do this now, or we will never have another chance."

"I'm ready," Ash said.

Morlinna had the connections to the villagers wrapped carefully in her chest, their strands extending back up and north toward Edgefall, glinting thin and black in the dim light.

Morlinna tipped her head as if listening to someone, and a spike of worry slashed through Ash's mind.

She bit her tongue and glanced down, fists clenched at her sides, but her gaze was drawn to the buildings behind her, the signs of battle written on their walls.

She couldn't let Morlinna go through with this without telling her what she suspected. She couldn't let the Goddess continue to whisper in her ear, knowing what might have happened here had changed the world forever.

"Morlinna."

The Nexsaint turned. "What is it? We must be swift."

"Is She speaking to you? Is She telling you this is the right thing to do?"

Morlinna's mouth went tight. "Her words are faint and far away. I can hear Her but not clearly."

"So this might not work."

Morlinna glanced at her sharply. "I know you do not trust Her yet but-"

"Morlinna. I think She might have killed Her wife."

Morlinna jerked. "What? Why would you say that?"

"I think She killed Her wife, and it broke the world."

"That's-"

"Blasphemy? Like everything else She's told you to do?"

"Ashwyn."

"I know you don't want to hear it. I didn't want to be the one to tell you, but I can't let you do this without you knowing."

"You don't know anything. You are speculating."

"Based on everything we've found here. This was Her wife's city. And look at it. It's in ruins. It's been destroyed in battle. And sometime after that battle, the city sank, the Devastation grew to hide it, and there was only the Goddess left."

"This does not make her a murderer."

"What would corrupt a goddess's power?"

Morlinna stilled. "What?"

"The Malady is a corruption of Her power. What would be strong enough to do that if not Herself? If the Goddess killed Her spouse, subverted Her entire purpose as the Gentle Mother and Giver of Life, wouldn't that corrupt Her power, sending death through the Malady?"

Morlinna remained silent, staring at Ash, and Ash's heart twisted to see the hurt in her eyes. She'd promised herself never to bring Morlinna pain. But this had to be said before it festered inside Ash.

"We saw Her, Morlinna. In the necropolis, climbing out of the gap She made."

"She speaks to me," Morlinna said, voice hushed.

"So does the Malady. How do you know they aren't the same voice?"

"Because I know." Morlinna's voice raised in a shout that rang against the nearest buildings.

Ash swallowed.

Morlinna took a deep, bracing breath. "The Malady calls to me. And the Goddess called me to the Malady. But they are not the same. They are two separate feelings. I trust the voice of the Goddess. Even if you do not."

Ashwyn winced, but instead of pounding her point home, Morlinna stepped forward and laid her hand on Ash's cheek. Ash's breath shuddered.

"Her voice led me to the truth about the Malady and the Order. She led me to the Devastation, which has become my home. She led me to you."

"Morlinna—"

"All of this has been hard. But everything good in my life has come because I listened to Her when no one else could hear Her. You have been the best of these good things. I will not lose you because you do not understand."

Morlinna smiled and stroked her thumb down Ash's cheek. "I will just have to prove that She is who She says She is. Uncorrupted and good."

Before Ash could reply, a wash of cold swept from the city, leaving Ash chilled to her heart. It stuttered in her chest, the pain and despair rising.

A dread was coming. Possibly more than one. They were out of time.

She had to trust Morlinna. Long, long ago, Morlinna had believed Ash when she said the Goddess had gifted her. And Ashwyn had chosen to believe Morlinna could hear the Goddess. She just had to keep holding on to that belief. For a little longer.

She reached up to squeeze Morlinna's hand. "Go," she said. "I will keep them off of you for as long as it takes."

Morlinna gave her one last worried look before Ash spun and headed for the feeling of rage creeping down a debris-strewn alleyway.

She pulled a thread from above and sailed to the roof of the nearest building, stumbling when the supports collapsed under her feet. She tripped across to a more stable section and knelt to get a good view of the approaching threat.

A white shape flew past her shoulder and flapped to gain height. Wraith immediately let her in through their connection, and she saw the city spin below, washed in the grays he could see.

It was harder to discern movement when everything careened below him, but a flicker of long limbs drew her eye toward the north edge of the city. The long, loathsome creature skittered and jolted in a straight line, as if drawn by something in particular.

"It's working," Ash said.

Wraith wheeled to follow the creature, darting down to bound along the rooftops. Ash could feel the creature's wrath creeping into the wolf's mind and along his veins, and she bolstered him, sending him strength and encouragement to counteract the misplaced feelings.

The dread jerked past the last buildings toward a bright beacon that waited beside the dome of the Devastation. A figure wreathed in glowing black strands of the Nexum.

It stood on two legs, shrouded with a shadow that could have been an overcoat.

The dread screamed, a high-pitched shriek that traveled down Ash's spine even across the city. It surged forward.

And fell into the pit Ashwyn had formed earlier.

Wraith swooped low and pulled the vine that Ash had placed exactly. From her position on the roof, Ash tugged the connection she'd left with the pit, and the rest of her trap fell into place, a thick net of Absent vines and roots that tangled with the creature's limbs.

It thrashed at the bottom of the pit.

Ash let out a satisfied huff. It wouldn't keep the dread forever, but she was just trying to buy enough time for Morlinna to finish healing the root. In preparation, she'd placed bits of her Nexum in decoys around the perimeter of the city, knowing they'd follow the feel of a Nexsaint right into her traps.

"All right," she told Wraith. "Let's find the next one—"

The startled squawk of a magpie somewhere near her ear jolted her out of the connection with Wraith.

Awareness of her body swept through her, as did the realization that the air had grown cold and frost formed against her fingertips. Her breath puffed between her surprised lips, and instinct made her throw herself across the roof.

A dread's claws swiped through the air behind her, raking the edge of her overcoat.

Panic stabbed through her, and an answering fear echoed through her connection with Morlinna. She stomped down on it, trying to send reassurances that she was fine. Everything was fine. She wasn't about to get grabbed at all.

Apparently, she had to be careful about that. Morlinna couldn't feel everything she felt through their connection, but the strongest emotions would travel between them easily and be just as distracting on the other end.

The dread clambered onto the roof, its impossibly long elbows bent in two directions to fit. The fearsome points of its antlers cast stabbing shadows across the shattered shingles of the roof.

Ashwyn's heart thudded in her throat, making it impossible to breathe or swallow. Rage came off the thing in waves, making the hair on her arms stand up. The feeling locked her in place, as her knees refused to bend and her arms trembled at her sides.

Wraith struck the dread from the side with an audible thump, and it staggered under the blow.

It knocked Ash loose from whatever spell it had had her under, and she stumbled back.

Now, Wraith cried.

Ashwyn snatched her scythe from her back, and as the creature staggered to right itself, she swung for its knees.

But her scythe stuck, as if she'd hit the thick trunk of a sentinel. The treated blade didn't even touch the threads running through the creature's body.

Ash gasped and yanked, freeing her blade, but it also pulled the dread closer to her.

She ducked its spidery arms and rolled past it. Instinct urged her to slash again, but she pulled back, worried that if she got the scythe blade stuck again, she'd never get it free.

The dread stumbled forward, its momentum carrying it to its knees, and Ash used the moment to leap to the next building.

"This way, you big, ugly stick," Ash said and swung to the ground, knowing the dread would follow.

Morlinna remained kneeling beside the root, hands pressed to the corrupted surface.

Ashwyn sped past her and spun.

The dread followed, and Ash took hold of the threads at its feet and pulled.

The Nexum buckled and caved under the dread, revealing the pit she'd formed before. As the ground opened under it, the dread plummeted.

Ash pulled the net of vines and roots over top of it, but the dread slashed at the bindings, its claws going right through.

Ash gasped. The creature shed the shredded net and clawed its way up the wall of the pit.

Just behind her, Morlinna cried out, and Ash spun to see the ground mounding around the other woman. White-streaked noses poked through the broken ground, seeking Morlinna.

"Mortis!"

She couldn't get to Morlinna with a dread on her heels.

The dread's hand snapped out of the hole and wrapped her ankle. Ashwyn cried out, and Wraith swooped in. His teeth closed over the dread's wrist and his weight sailed by, yanking the creature's arm with him.

It bent at an unnatural angle and snapped with a violent crack.

But the dread kept climbing.

It stood to its full height at the edge of the pit, its arm hanging by a bit of broken bark, and Ashwyn gulped.

Well, it looked like dead wood, so she would treat it like dead wood.

She grabbed her flint striker out of her belt and struck a spark, pulling the threads from the flames the moment they appeared.

The dread reached for her. Ashwyn ducked under its arms and wove the strands of fire around the thing's limbs, coaxing them to grow hotter and spread.

The dread screamed as its limbs burst into flame and smoke rose up around its angry black eyes.

Ash jumped back, flinging a hand up to protect her face from the heat.

The dread staggered forward a step. Ash kicked it square in the chest, and it stumbled back and over the edge. Into the pit.

Ashwyn turned, breathing heavily, to find Morlinna in the center of a circle of corrupted creatures with long sinuous bodies like weasels and talons like eagles.

They stood stock-still around her, their feet buried in the dirt.

Ash rushed forward and realized the ground had gone cracked and broken. Like Morlinna had made it soft and then solidified it around the weasels' feet.

"Just a little more," Morlinna murmured.

Ashwyn leaped as the nearest weasel wriggled and tore free. It fell even as it tried to rush forward, its head severed neatly from its spine.

But the next weasel was already moving, its body sliding sinuously across the floor as it raced for Morlinna.

Ash slid and slashed, taking its feet so it fell. The creature shrieked, and Ash winced as she killed it.

But the others had broken free now and recognized the new threat. Morlinna had been their goal, but the life in Ashwyn called to them, and they fell over each other, swarming toward her.

Ash pulled one of the threads behind them and snapped to the free space, avoiding their long, thin bodies.

Ebonheart dove, a flash of white along her wings as she swooped in front of one of the weasels and croaked a challenge. She flapped away, leading her distracted prey with her.

Ashwyn struck out as the group of corrupted creatures turned as one to find their quarry.

There were too many. A claw raked down her coat, catching it and yanking her off her feet. Ash struggled out of the fabric, leaving the garment on the floor of the cave as she rolled out of the way of the weasels.

"Morlinna!" she cried.

But Morlinna didn't reply. She was too far into the healing to hear.

The weasels surged forward, and Ashwyn slashed, pulling herself to her feet at the same time, trying to clear space for herself to stand, but the Malady spread its white fingers through the ground at her feet, and when she danced back a weasel lunged to catch her off balance.

Ash, behind you! The dread! Wraith's voice rose in panic.

Burning claws closed around Ash's arms, and she screamed as the dread picked her up off her feet. She twisted in its arms, trying to get her scythe free enough to fight the creature, but her arms remained tightly clasped.

The dread stood, blackened and streaked with soot. Embers still glowed in the cracks along its surface, sending eerie light through the cavern.

She couldn't fight this thing. Morlinna had been right years ago when she'd said they didn't fight dreads. They ran from them.

All she could do was bind it to the ground again, but she couldn't afford to be sick when she had to guard Morlinna.

The weasels clamored at the dread's feet, scrabbling at its bark as if trying to climb to her. And a distant portion of Ash's mind noted that the Malady wasn't spreading from their touch. As if they scrabbled at the walls of the necropolis.

The dread's fingers clenched and its claws dug deep into her skin. She cried out. How did dreads kill their victims? Its claws could rip her apart, or it could just wait as the rage and the terror rose in her chest until her heart burst with it.

Another shriek from close by told Ash the other dread must have climbed free of her trap. As if one wasn't bad enough.

Morlinna had to be close. If she could just hold on until the other woman was done...

She needed her hands free to do any weaving, if there was even anything that would help. What could possibly distract it?

What were dreads anyway? A bunched-up ball of hate and rage that sought out Nexsaints. It had certainly been distracted by her decoy before.

She could still move her fingers and bend her arms at the elbows.

Perfect.

She reached for her leg and pulled out a strand of her own Nexum, cutting it free with a yank. The dread drew her close, and Ash used the movement to slap her hand to its chest.

She stuck her strand to the dread's chest, and it hung there, glowing like a beacon.

The dread's movements halted. Its papery lips drew back from pointed bark-like teeth, and it glanced down at its chest with a hiss.

Its claws retracted from Ash's arms, and it dropped her in order to claw at its chest.

Ashwyn yanked a thread close to Morlinna and tumbled across the ground beside the Nexsaint.

The weasels paused between one breath and the next as the dread stumbled back, its claws raking into the bark of its chest.

Then the corrupted creatures renewed their attack, clawing their way up its legs.

Ashwyn groaned and pushed to her hands and knees, and beside her, Morlinna shuddered. The other woman's eyes fluttered open, and relief swept through Ash as she realized they were their normal blue.

"I am done," Morlinna said, her words slurred.

And Ash finally glanced at the root. The bark remained the gray of an Absent root, but no trace of white stretched through its surface or its strands.

But there was no time to appreciate the feat.

"We have to get out of here," Ash gasped. She pushed to standing and dragged Morlinna up with her.

Morlinna stared over her shoulder at the dread that staggered in a circle, weasels climbing its limbs. And the second dread that had appeared in the distance. It made for its fellow, shrieks filling the air.

"What did you do?" Morlinna asked.

"Tell you later." Blood seeped through the sleeves of her shirt, and dirt stained her knees. There was no time to go back for her overcoat where it lay trampled under the weasels' talons.

"Ebonheart, Wraith!" Ash called, and the animals sprinted for her.

Ash wrapped an arm around Morlinna and reached for the strand of the Nexum that connected her to the cloisters.

Home, she thought to herself, and the moment she felt claws on her shoulder and the grip of teeth against her wrist, she pulled.

The world smeared, and the last thing Ashwyn saw was the two dreads converging on each other with shrieks of rage.

Chapter 63
Animatim

"It was supposed to show you," V's father said, gesturing to the bracelet she now held. "I had to give you the chance to see."

Her mouth went dry. "What are you talking about?"

"I planned it from the start. The moment she took you from me, I worked to make you see the truth."

V shook her head, the drip drip of the swamp outside drilling into her skull.

"The truth? The truth is you wanted me to fail. You wanted to sabotage Mother so badly that you sabotaged *me*."

He shook his head, a short sharp jerk. "No. I gave you everything I could so you could become the best Judge in the history of the Order. We—I needed someone with power to know the truth. I put you there at that time and place to see Her free."

She'd known he'd orchestrated it. The heresy, the untethering. Even the woman who gave birth. He must have been the one on the street who'd directed a laboring woman to the temple.

But...he'd done it for V? He'd planned for her to be there?

The remembered terror of that moment flooded back into her. The realization that She was leaving. The knowledge that had come after when the Primarch had told her of the real danger.

He could have destroyed the world, and it would have been V's fault.

She'd thought he had set her up to fail and bring her mother down with her. But the truth was so much worse.

"What have you done?"

His face smoothed out, the earnestness dropping away to reveal resignation. "I did what I had to. What my family has been bred to do. What you were bred to do."

"What?"

"Ranimas. Anima means life. We've belonged to Her for centuries. Even when the Primarch tried to silence us, we've been waiting. I'm the last one left, V. They killed the rest of us to keep us quiet. That's why I petitioned to breed with the Abdicant. To get close to Her. You were our chance, V."

Oh, Dea. There...there was an entire family of them? She knew she'd come from somewhere, but after her father's disgrace she'd never thought about them. Did heresy run through the entire paternal line? How long had they planned to ruin her life for her?

He said they'd been killed to keep them quiet. They'd been killed as heretics. Which meant her mother must have wielded the blade.

Under the questions, one sharp realization left a bitter taste at the back of her throat.

She'd just been a contract to him. Even beneath the heresy, she'd still believed in the softness of her childhood. Believed in the safety and the care he'd given her along with the flaws. But all of it had been a lie.

Her eyes burned.

Mortis, she felt like such a child. And the feelings pulled her away from what was important. She still had a hunt to finish and loose threads to track down.

"And this," her voice grated out as she held up the bracelet. "I was the target and this was the vessel. But who does it belong to? Who made a connection so strong? Not that girl who left it. She wasn't even a Nexsaint."

He shook his head. "Whose it was makes no difference. I saw the Goddess react when it was laid at her feet. So much love wound into it that She couldn't help but respond. If anything could have severed Her ties, it was that. And if anyone could bring her back, it would be you."

Nausea rolled in her gut. He'd had no idea she would be able to pull the Goddess back. What if she'd been blamed for it?

"You could have just talked to me."

"Would you have listened? Are you listening now?"

"No. Because everything you've said so far goes against what I've been taught. What I *know*!"

"You know only what the Abdicant lets you know. What the Primarch chooses for you to know."

And he'd chosen for her to know the truth about the danger. He'd trusted her. When her own father hadn't.

"Renounce it," she said. "Repent, and maybe I can save you."

"You know you can't do that." His voice came, quiet and sure.

She wished he were insane, so she could blame the decay of the father she'd known on some illness. But this quiet logic and conviction came from stark intelligence and choice. He'd chosen to betray everything they'd been taught.

And now she had to choose, too.

She tucked the bracelet into her belt, straightening her spine. And as she stood to her full height, she realized she could look him directly in the eye now.

"I'm taking this as evidence," she said, and the hope in his face crumpled, sending a stab of pain through her.

"Wesley Ranimas," she said, her voice thick. "I've judged you guilty of heresy, and I'm authorized to carry out your sentence. Immediately."

His lips curved in a smile, and she wondered how many times in her childhood his mirth and joy had covered a deep well of sadness and dissatisfaction.

"Let's make a game of it, then. One last time."

Her jaw clenched as her eyes went hot and blurry. How dare he? How could he even say the words?

She sprang at him with a cry, pulling her blade free.

He spun back, his own sword suddenly in his hand. She hadn't even seen where he'd been keeping it while they spoke.

She slashed, and he caught her blow against his blade, the metal shrieking against obsidian as their cross guards met and locked. He lowered his shoulder and shoved forward. His greater weight should have knocked her off her feet, but she'd trained harder and longer than any Bladesaint against men larger than him. She shifted her weight, and he staggered forward, unbalanced. As he passed, she kicked the back of his knee.

Vitania turned with him, keeping the distance close, but her father turned his fall into a roll and sprang away. She followed as he ran up the wall to the broken top and balanced there.

Forcing her to use the terrain to keep up.

She pulled a thread from above, soaring up and across to meet him. A sharp sting caught her midair, and she cried out, staggering as she landed on the top of the wall. Blood dripped from the slash across her thigh, where the metal of her greaves didn't quite meet.

She hissed in pain, her glove pressed against the wound.

Her father shook his head. "I've trained plenty of Nexsaints. Fought a couple, too. You leave yourself open when you fly around like that. Keep your limbs tucked next time. And tighten your greaves."

She growled and lunged, and when he jumped back, she caught him in the chest with a kick, knocking him onto his back on the narrow top of the wall.

Vitania leaped, her blade point coming down straight for his chest. He rolled and fell off the wall, hitting the stone below with a thud, but he only grunted, then he was moving again before she'd even caught her breath.

With a leap, she landed beside him, slashing. He parried, sword sliding under hers so she couldn't lock in with him again.

Every duck, every slash drew out old skills remembered from the training yard and even the days before that.

It really was a game. Another one where he tested every skill she'd learned.

But a Nexsaint always had an advantage over a Bladesaint.

She drove him against the hearth, and he used the crumbling mantle to climb up the wall again, straightening up to stand above her. A tempting target.

She threw her sword like a spear, straight for his unarmored chest.

He sidestepped and tsked.

"Never throw away your only weapon—"

She pulled the thread that connected her with her blade and it flipped end over end, returning to her. It slammed into his back, hilt-first, and he fell to the floor of the ruins.

As he gasped, wind knocked from his lungs, V reached out and yanked on the threads of the wall. The stones rumbled and fell around him.

He rolled, but a square block struck his shoulder, and he grunted, staggering to his feet again. His left arm hung limp at his side.

V reached for the stones at his feet and pulled up, hauling them into positions to trap him. He danced aside, and finally she felt like she was on the offensive instead of a schoolgirl reciting her lessons.

The power of it flowed through her, giving strength to her fury, and she wove strands of the Nexum, melding the water of the swamp with the stone at his feet.

Her father fell into the pool of liquid rock she'd made, and she unraveled the weaving as quickly as she'd made it.

He stuck there, half in, half out of the stone floor, his sword hand trapped.

His chest heaved as he caught his breath, and the sharp sting of satisfaction drove away the last of her frustration, leaving only anger and the same deep hurt.

"Fight me," she hissed, willing him to be larger than life, the way she remembered him. "Keep going."

"No." His words rasped. "This is it. My final act. The only way I can convince you now. Take it, V, and see for yourself."

She shook her head. She didn't want to hear any more of it.

"You lied to me," she cried. "My whole life. You raised me and trained me and taught me and loved me. But it was all a lie. You didn't care about me at all.

You tricked me into believing you loved me. That you wanted the best for me and all the while this rot was underneath."

He raised his eyes to hers, and still there was no anger in his face. Only acceptance. "I lied to you exactly once, V," he said. "I told you I ruined you."

Her hands clenched, fingers digging into the hilt of her sword. She remembered.

"I told you...to protect you," he gasped out. The stone pressing his chest must have made it hard to breathe. "You were already in your mother's clutches. She had control of you. I had to give you to her, and I wanted you to be safe. So you had to believe her."

He reached for her with his free hand, but she stared at it as if it would grab her and pull her down with him.

"But I didn't ruin you. I made you smart. I made you strong. And wise and funny. I made you all of these things."

Angry tears streaked her cheeks as she stared at him.

"I made myself," she said, voice hoarse.

And she ran her blade through his chest.

Chapter 64
Concordim

When they reached the cloisters, Ashwyn fell to her knees with a gasp, and Morlinna staggered to one of the pews and sat heavily. Wraith snuffled her ear as Ash's fingers flexed against the worn flagstones.

It was over. The root was healed. It was *healed*.

The village would be safe. The necropolis safe. But it wasn't just that. They'd changed the world. They'd proved there was a better way to fight the Malady than killing everything in its path.

They still had to deal with the gap in the necropolis, and Ash was sure that wouldn't be nearly so easy. But at least now they had time.

Pain stabbed through her arms where the dread's claws had pierced, and Ash winced as she sat up.

She squinted, and Morlinna came into focus, the threads of her Nexum glowing black and white under her skin. The connections she still held from the villagers stretched away through the wall and back toward Edgefall.

If they'd healed the root with those connections, then that meant the Malady was more human than anything.

Ash wasn't going to point it out to Morlinna. The other woman knew. And it was connected to the voice, and Ash didn't think she was ready to admit what it might mean about her precious goddess.

Instead, Ash climbed to her feet and went to catch Morlinna's hands and help her up.

Morlinna's fingers hovered over the blood soaking through Ash's sleeves.

"You're hurt," she said.

Ash huffed a laugh. "It's all right. It will only take a lighter weave. We can do it after we've rested. Then we can check on the village. But you're exhausted."

"I'm exhausted?" Morlinna raised an eyebrow. "You fought two dreads."

Ash snorted. "That was nothing. While you were solving the crisis of the world, I figured out you *can* fight dreads. You just have to make them think they're Nexsaints."

"Oh, just that?" Morlinna laughed, and Ash reveled in the fact that there was no worry or fear behind it.

"Don't worry, I'll teach you."

Morlinna smiled, and Ash leaned into her, expecting the brush of lips against hers.

Instead, Morlinna sucked in a breath and thrust her back.

Ash stumbled and landed on her back with a cry.

Below Morlinna's feet, white swirled through the flagstones. Like a pool of corruption.

Ash knew the Malady could jump, but she'd never seen it happen so fast before.

The pool opened and gaped, just like a gap, and strands of Malady snapped out to wrap around Morlinna.

Morlinna cried out and reached for Ashwyn.

Ash leaped to her feet and lunged to grab Morlinna's hand. But the strands tightened around Morlinna and yanked her into the pool. She disappeared beneath the surface like a sinking stone.

Ash's fingers closed on open air, and her heart clenched.

White fingers of the Malady surged up the connection between Morlinna and Ashwyn, seeking her heart.

Ashwyn gasped and pulled back, but the Malady grew.

And suddenly the strand snapped back, as if cut from the other end, and Ash knew in her chest that Morlinna had cut it to save her.

Strands from the pool snaked out, wrapping the end of the severed strand and yanking. Ash fell forward, hands just inches from the pool as it tried to suck her in, take her wherever it had taken Morlinna.

And for one moment, Ash wondered if she should let it.

Then Wraith's teeth closed on the back of her shirt and yanked. And Ash cut through the strand holding her to the pool and scrambled back so it couldn't reach her.

The strands flailed and then fell still and disappeared back into the pool, as if someone had pulled them from the other end.

The pool swirled and narrowed and suddenly collapsed in on itself until nothing was left. The flagstones stood as pristine as they'd been for the last five years, and Ash was left alone in the nave with Wraith and Ebonheart circling her.

Animatim

V stared at her father's body, stuck in the stone at her feet. She pulled her sword from his chest and stopped.

His free hand lay against the stone, two fingers curled awkwardly, leaving the others splayed out.

In the sign for "I love you."

V choked and dropped to her knees.

The grief and the rage pounded in her chest and her head, throbbing in time with her heartbeat. How odd that she still had a heartbeat.

She took his hand in hers, feeling the sign against her palm. As she had when she was a little girl. Before he'd given her to her mother.

Before either of them had made their choices.

Around the ruins, the Devastation groaned, the moss curling in the trees and the roots splashing out of the water, as if they were going to march on her where she sat in her misery.

She'd always heard the Devastations reacted to negative emotions, but she'd thought it was a myth designed to scare people into staying away.

V gulped. And took deep breaths, trying to clear away the feelings crowding her chest, forgetting who it was who'd taught her to be calm when the muffled world had seemed so frustrating.

The forest subsided, and she swiped her glove across her face, leaving a smear of something thick and wet. But at least the tears were gone.

The hand in hers twitched.

V gently tipped her father's head back, and his Absent eyes stared back at her.

She hadn't finished. He was Absent, not dead. She still had to deliver the Last Death.

Still had to do her duty and execute the heretic.

She drew her hand from his and climbed slowly to her feet. She leveled her blade at his throat, poised for the last strike.

It should be easy.

Obitusim

The air around Morlinna shrieked with her passing, colors fading to a sick, ashy white. The color of infection. Of corruption.

It no longer turned Morlinna's stomach, but the dread that surged through her was a real force that raised the hair along her arms.

The Malady formed a tunnel around her, the same way the strands of the Nexum did when she used them to travel.

A presence pressed in on one side and another crowded close on her other. Their fear traveled through her, and she realized she wasn't alone.

The connections to the villagers. She'd tried to cut them when the Malady had grabbed her, but it had been too fast. She'd only managed to cut the ties with Ashwyn and Felleron.

Dea, if they were here with her, they were in danger of being corrupted, too.

Sickly strands of the Malady surrounded them as they dove, and Morlinna spun in the middle of her fall, using her bare hands to grab them and yank them back. The threads seared her skin, cutting into her palms, but still she pulled.

The tunnel of Malady opened, and Morlinna slammed into something rough and unyielding. Solid ground. Not the forgiving vines of the Devastation.

Around her rose cries and moans from the villagers who'd made the journey with her.

Morlinna surged to her feet, fighting for focus in the disorienting spin of the world.

All she could see clearly were walls of stone broken only by frescoes painted to look like colored glass. An ancient temple plunged into the blackness under the Devastation.

This had to be the Underheart. The temple behind the wall of the Malady, where she'd heard the Goddess calling to her.

Her eyes fixed on the Malady pooling before the altar, a gap wide enough to swallow a house, filled with the aching emptiness of a broken world. Obitullas.

White strands of corruption raced toward the villagers.

Morlinna surged forward, knocking them out of the way and reaching for the Malady to slice it back, keep it from grabbing anyone else.

More strands speared straight for her, wrapping her arms and legs. She slammed to the ground, and the Malady dragged her back toward the gap.

Morlinna screamed as corrupted threads tried to grow past her and reach the villagers.

Each thread that passed under her fingers, she hauled toward her and wrapped around her arms until she couldn't tell where her strands ended and the Malady's began. But if the corruption was tangled with her, then it wouldn't go for the villagers.

The battle inside her raged, the white lightning of the Malady streaking through her, climbing higher and higher in her chest, reaching to find her heart.

And somewhere in her head, the Goddess was screaming.

Chapter 65
Concordim

Ash's fingers flexed against the smooth stone of the floor as her breath came in quick, short gasps.

"Morlinna?" she whispered, mind spinning in circles, refusing to latch onto any concrete thought.

Silence rang through the space broken only by the soft flap of Ebonheart's wings as she settled on Ash's shoulder.

"Morlinna?" Ash struggled to her feet, feeling for the connection that had traveled between herself and Morlinna just moments ago. But the frayed end swung like a broken thread

She's not here, Wraith said.

An anguished howl rose from somewhere beyond the walls of the nave, and Ash winced.

"Felleron."

The old wolf burst through the doorway, head swinging as he took in Ash standing alone with Wraith.

His lips drew back in a snarl, and he scrabbled across the floor, nosing into the corners and knocking aside pews as he searched for someone who just wasn't there.

Ash wanted to do the same thing. She wanted to flip the table over and tear back the curtain to Morlinna's room and let the panic rise in her chest as the realization slowly settled in that Morlinna was gone.

But the wolf's movements snapped her back from the precipice of feeling, and she reached for him.

"Felleron, stop."

His breath came in heavy pants, as if he was in pain, and Ash remembered the first thing Morlinna had told her about connecting to creatures. It changed them. And the longer the connection stayed the harder it would be on them to break it.

Ash held out her hands to calm him.

White showed around his eyes, and his lips pulled back to show his fangs.

Ash pulled out a thread and held it in front of him, asking for permission and holding her own terror and panic at bay while she waited for his answer.

Finally, he bowed his head and allowed her to wrap her thread with his until the sensation of fur across her shoulders and stone under her pads mingled with the feel of her own skin.

Where is she? He growled into her head before she had a chance to send anything.

"I don't know. The Malady took her." The words felt impossible and terrible in her mouth.

How?

"I don't know!" She straightened and paced to the door and back. "I didn't even know a person *could* travel through the Malady. Like we travel down lines of the Nexum."

It wanted her, Wraith said. *The pool started under her feet. Like it was looking for her.*

"Like it was thinking," Ash whispered. "It's sentient. I knew it had to be intelligent. And it was after Morlinna specifically."

Ash sucked in a breath as she remembered the thread of Malady reaching for her, the snap of it as it tried to grab for her threads.

"And anyone connected with her."

The shudder took her by surprise as her mind raced down the list of everyone with a connection to Morlinna.

She and Felleron were at the top of the list, but they stood here free, so Morlinna must have cut the ties to them in time.

But what about the villagers? The ones Morlinna had used to heal the root. She'd still held their threads within her.

Had they disappeared into pools of Malady like Morlinna? Were they corrupted now?

"Oh, mortis."

Over and over, she'd cut the thread connecting her to Edgefall, rejecting the part of her that still longed for that place to be home. So she couldn't jump there. But she did have a thread to the root's tunnel. She pulled herself and the animals to the base of the cliff where it had broken free of the worst of the vegetation. The healed bark seemed stark between the mangled vines, and it hurt that she couldn't stop and appreciate it for even a second.

From there, she just had to go up.

A cacophony of calls rose around her. The magpies she'd left stationed in the village. They'd come, hearing the urgency of her thoughts through Ebonheart.

She'd never be able to climb fast enough to satisfy the burning urge in her chest. But the magpies swooped around her, their movements asking how they could help.

She drew threads from the knife at her hip and imbued their wings with the sharpness of steel.

The flock swarmed upward, their wingtips slicing through the leaves and branches, leaving a clear path for her, and Ashwyn erupted from the Devastation in a flurry of black and white feathers.

She landed at the edge of the crater amid a fall of torn leaves. She blinked against the blur and turned her head to see through her good side as a figure coalesced out of the chaos around her.

Cass pounded up, face white.

"I saw the magpies," she gasped. "Are you here to fix it?"

Ash met her gaze. "The villagers?"

"They were pulled into puddles of white. Like the gap in the necropolis. Except these yanked them in and then disappeared." She stared down at her hands, her fingers clenching and unclenching. "I couldn't stop it."

"All of them?" she asked.

"All but the children and one or two adults. The ones too old to leave their homes."

The ones Morlinna hadn't formed a connection with.

Ashwyn gulped. This was their fault. They'd done this. They'd put the villagers in danger. They'd gotten them abducted.

And Morlinna was the only one who could save them from the Malady.

Now the panic rose, rushing through her veins, leaving her cold and shivering.

Morlinna wasn't just the most important person in Ash's life. She was the only one who could fix this. She was the only one who could handle corrupted threads and heal the Malady.

Ash knew what to do...theoretically. She'd been taught. She knew the right words to say, but she didn't have the power to do any of it.

Morlinna had never let her try.

Morlinna was the one the corruption feared. And that's why it had taken her.

A hand pressed the space between her shoulder blades, and Ash realized she was bent over, hands clutching her chest as her heart pounded against her palms.

"The thing you tried," Cass said. "To heal the Malady. It didn't work, did it?"

Ash shook her head and pushed back the tide of fear and nausea. She straightened, and Cass's hand fell away once again.

"It *did* work," Ash said. "It worked too well. The Malady is fighting back, taking the people that hurt it the most."

Cass's light brows came down in a frown. She glanced behind her at the line of children that waited on the orphan house porch, staring at them.

"What do you mean?" Cass said, lowering her voice so they couldn't hear. "Why would it want us? Edgefall has nothing to do with the Malady. At least we didn't until..."

Her gaze met Ash's, and Ash felt the stab of accusation.

"It took Morlinna," she said, the words sounding gravelly and rough to her ears. "She's the one it wants. But it also managed to grab anyone with a connection to her."

"A connection? Just because we worked together once?"

Ash shook her head. "It's more than that. It's the Nexum. We connected them all with Morlinna so she could use them to heal the Malady."

At least, all the ones who'd been there clearing. The children Morlinna had avoided and the old folk hadn't been present. And Ash had avoided taking a thread from Cass because...she didn't even know why. She hadn't wanted to get close and alert Cass to what they were doing. But there was something deeper than that. She hadn't wanted to owe Cass for anything.

"You made me lie to them for this?" Cass hissed, eyes narrowed. "Why wouldn't you tell me what you were doing? Don't you trust me?"

Ash laughed, short and bleak. "What has happened in the last five years that would make me trust you?"

Cass's mouth snapped shut, and she glanced away. When she looked back, her eyes raked up and down Ashwyn. "Why didn't it take you? Don't try to tell me you lived with your idol for so long and never formed some sort of attachment."

Ash raised her chin. Her relationship with Morlinna was none of Cass's business. "She cut the connection to save me. She probably tried to do the same for the villagers, but it happened so fast, she might not have had time." Ash's eyes narrowed. "Or she did, and it grabbed them anyway," she said, remembering the thread that had whipped out to seize her. "That's what it tried to do with me. It planned this."

Cass swallowed. "You're sure it's intelligent?"

Not just intelligent. Ash was sure it was divine. A rogue piece of the Goddess's power, corrupted because of Her secret sin. And it wanted Morlinna for something.

Ash spun just as Wraith landed lightly beside her, and she strode toward the creeping roots of the forest.

"Where are you going?" Cass said, stumbling after her. She steered clear of Wraith, but in her defense, she still kept up.

"I'm going to find Morlinna. She's the only one that can stop this." Ash's lips pressed together. "This is our fault. Your people wouldn't have been pulled into it if it weren't for us. I have to fix it. I have to save her."

Cass jerked to a stop. "Do you even know how to find her?"

Ash blew out her breath. Without a connection to Morlinna, she would have to do this the old-fashioned way.

"I have a very good idea."

Cass followed Ash's gaze to the edge of the crater and the Devastation clambering its way up the side. If she noticed Felleron lurking in the shadows beneath the branches, she gave no indication.

She sucked in a breath and squared her shoulders. "Right," she said. Then she spun to call out to one of the children standing on the porch of the orphan house. "Niko, you're in charge until I get back."

The tallest boy stood up straight. "Yes, elderman."

"Take care of the children and the oldfolk, too. Ask Goodwoman Myrtle for help if you need it. Keep them fed and keep everyone away from the Devastation and the necropolis. No one has clearing duties until I'm back. I don't want anyone snatched."

"Yes, elderman," the boy said, eyes wide.

"What are you doing?" Ash hissed as Cass turned and strode toward the forest.

"What does it look like I'm doing? I'm coming with you."

"What?" Ash had to skip to keep up. They were nearly to the edge, and what did Cass think she'd do when she got there? Step off of it?

"You're going to need help."

Ash laughed. "What could you possibly do to help me?"

Cass's pale cheeks flushed a painful pink. A muscle in her jaw clenched as she rounded on Ashwyn. "Someone of mine was thrown into the Devastation a long time ago. I had the chance to go in after her, and I didn't take it. I regretted it for the rest of my life. I refuse to regret this."

Her voice had gone sharp and savage by the end, and Ash fought the urge to stagger back a pace at the force of her words. Emotion? From Cass? Who had always been so concerned with not doing the wrong thing that she'd failed to see what was *right*?

She'd thought she'd known Cass better than anyone. She'd thought Cass was the calm one. The clearheaded one. Maybe she was just as volatile as Ash and much, much better at hiding it. Maybe she hadn't faded into her life after Ash had vanished as easily as Ash had thought.

Ash hated the swell of emotion Cass's fierce look gave her. She didn't want to think about what it meant or see Cass as anything other than the one who'd betrayed her.

It was Morlinna's fierceness she needed now. For herself and for the world. And if getting her back required Cass's help...then so be it.

She spun toward the forest. "Fine. You can come. But you'll have to keep up."

Chapter 66
Concordim

The air swirled around them as they appeared on the steps of their temple home, and Cass stumbled away from Ash and the wolves, her face pale and shining with sweat.

"Oh, Dea," she said, her throat bobbing as she swallowed, over and over.

Ashwyn didn't have time to coddle her. She stepped across the threshold and rummaged through the shelf over the hearth, tossing aside boxes and containers in her haste. A jar of preserves crashed to the floor and shattered, leaving a dark, sticky smear across the flagstones.

Felleron paced the length of the nave, his mouth open as he panted out his stress. Wraith whined, but he didn't have to say anything. His concern was written in the way his eyes locked on her movements, and he stayed at her side, following her with his body.

Ash tried to breathe past the knot in her throat, forcing her hands to take more care, suppressing the shivers caused by over-tight muscles.

The retching behind her stopped, and she heard Cass's hesitant step as she entered the nave.

"This is where you've been living?" the other woman asked.

Ash bristled, reading judgement in the words. "It is," was all she said.

"I didn't expect buildings in the forest," Cass said. When Ash glanced back at her, she was staring out one of the empty window wells at the vines creeping up the walls.

Ash paused to rub her forehead. "There's...a city underneath it all. The vines and branches push things up as they grow. The buildings float around almost like boats in the sea of the Devastation."

Cass stared at her, mouth hanging open as Ash disappeared into the cloister and her room. She didn't have much, but her overcoat had been left behind in the city, trampled by dreads and Devastation beasts. And she hated to go into a fight without one. The extra layer of fabric lent a little more protection than just her shirt.

She snagged her old overcoat, the one that had been tattered and worn when she'd fallen from the edge of the crater. She hadn't worn it in years, but it was better than nothing.

As she hurried back into the nave, she tried to pull it over her shoulders and hissed in pain.

Cass stepped toward her. "You're bleeding."

Ash glanced down at the stains spreading across her shoulders. The wounds from the dread's claws still seeped, making a mess of her shirt.

She twitched away from Cass's concerned touch and pulled the overcoat on, gently this time.

"Can't you fix it?" Cass asked. She waved her fingers in a vague gesture, perhaps trying to imitate a Nexsaint's movements. "With...with the Nexum?"

Ash's lips tightened. "We don't have time to mess with a weave." And she only had one healthy body around to use as a template, and her mind shied away from the very idea of using Cass.

"If we don't have time, then why did you stop here?" Cass said with a huff. Her eyes narrowed as they followed Ash's hurried steps. She ducked into Morlinna's rooms and turned back the covers with a curse.

"What are you looking for?" Cass said.

"I need something to track Morlinna," Ash said. "And if we're going against the Malady, I want every advantage we can get. If it's what I think it is, then it's far more powerful than me."

Cass's lips pressed thin. "What do you think it is?"

Ash's movements stilled for a moment. Her eyes traveled to the Goddess's statue at the end of the nave.

"Did you know She was married once?" Ash asked quietly.

Cass followed her gaze. "What? No, She wasn't."

"She was. We found evidence. But She's not anymore. Her wife isn't around. She's been erased." Ash turned to meet Cass's eyes. "I think She killed her. And that's where the Malady came from. It's a reaction to Her crime."

Cass sucked in a breath, her eyes flickering between Ash and the statue. "You're serious."

"It's...it's a theory. But it's the only one I have right now."

Cass laughed, its nervous edge cutting through the air between them. "And I thought you were blasphemous before."

Ash slashed her hand through the air. "I was never blasphemous. Not until the Goddess failed to defend me. Just like I wasn't a liar until you made me one."

Cass cried out, her wordless protest going down Ash's spine. But Ash shook her head before Cass could gather the words to argue.

"I'll be your villain if you need me to be," Ash spat. "But let there at least be truth between the two of us. You don't know what happened in that necropolis. I do, and I told you. But you chose not to believe me. You chose to call me a liar and a heretic. And make everyone else believe it. That's what happened. And you can't make that right, Cassarah. But you can at least do me the courtesy of using the truth with me."

The muscles in Cass's jaw worked, like she ground her teeth. "You're right. I don't know what happened in the necropolis. I only know what I believe. That's all I can give you. Is it enough for now?"

Ash snorted. It was exactly nothing. But Morlinna was more important than this argument.

"It's fine."

"Then let's get moving," Cass said, shoulders relaxing as if they'd come to some sort of understanding, though Ash was still wound tight with everything between them. "Why do you need to track her? I thought you said you had a good idea of where she is."

"I do." Ash turned back to her search. "But we're not going down there until I'm positive."

"Why?"

"Because it's the worst possible place they could be."

She just needed to find the one thing, the one object that had a strong enough connection to Morlinna that it wouldn't have been severed. She just hoped Morlinna hadn't had them in her pocket.

"Ha!" She spied them behind the statue, as if Morlinna had set them there as she stood and forgotten to take them up again.

"Prayer beads?" Cass said.

"They're Morlinna's. They should at least give me a direction..." Ash trailed off as she followed the thick thread toward the east. The Malady would be crawling up the end from Morlinna, and she didn't dare use it to Nexum jump, but she could at least note the direction.

"What's wrong?" Cass said. "You've gone white."

"She's in the Heart. Like I thought."

"The heart of what?"

"The Heart of the Devastation. It's where the Malady began."

"And it's dangerous." Cass didn't even bother to frame it as a question.

"Deadly. Even Morlinna has never gone down. And she can control the Malady."

"Then how will we get there? Can you...can you control it too?"

For a moment, she considered it. She could corrupt herself. Push it back like Morlinna had. She could become the second Nexsaint to control the Malady.

But the memory of that empty courtyard in her heart and the flickering white lightning consuming the horizon surged through her.

She had no idea if she could survive it. She'd thought she would have time to ask Morlinna how she'd done it. What her secret had been. But one thing had followed another, and she never had. And if she didn't fight it back, if she succumbed, she would become a gap in the world. Like Rafe. Like Ingrim and Uniah.

And Morlinna wasn't here to kill her to keep that from happening.

She shook her head. "I can't," she said, hating the answer enough to burn. "But that doesn't mean we can just give up."

She thrust the prayer beads into her pocket, and her fingers brushed something dry and a little prickly.

Ash pulled out her hand and stared at the dried strands of grass between her fingers. Blue and purple lay side by side on her palm, crinkled where they'd once been tied together into clumsy knots.

Her eyes met Cass's over the remains of their ancient commitment.

"That's..." Cass said on a breath. "But I left mine at the Greater Temple. How did you..."

"She gave it to me," Ash said. "In the necropolis."

And Ash wanted to throw it into the fire. So much of herself was wrapped up in those strands of grass, and she wanted to forget all the pieces at once. But the fire in the hearth had died long before, and all that remained were cold coals.

She pushed the strands deep into her pocket, burying them under Morlinna's prayer beads.

"Let's go." Ash gestured Wraith and Felleron ahead of her through the door, leaving Cass silent and stricken behind her.

Obitusim

For years, Morlinna had heard the Goddess as if through a veil, the Malady keeping her from hearing Her clearly. Like a whisper from another room or a shout from a league away.

But here the voice of the Goddess keened through her thoughts, as if She stood in the room with them.

The pain of Her voice made Morlinna double over, the strands of the Malady tightening around her limbs.

And at the same time, the Malady buzzed, the hum of its call rising to drown out the rage in the Goddess's voice. The two wove over and around each other until they seemed to be one sound that set Morlinna's teeth on edge and made her ears ache.

Was Ashwyn right? Were they one somehow?

Morlinna moaned. No. No, she knew the Goddess's voice better than she remembered her own mother's. And the Malady was different. It wasn't the same. They were separate. She knew that. It wasn't just faith. It was knowledge.

And now that she was here, she could hear both and how dissimilar they were.

But something was wrong. Morlinna knew the sound a heart made as it shattered in anger, and hers echoed it.

Within her, along the battlefield, the white lightning streaked past, giving way to a shaft of soft silver light.

And it hummed with the same tone as the Goddess, even as She shrieked in Morlinna's head.

Her connection. Every Saint had one with the Goddess who'd gifted them with Her power. Like a hand extended within a battle. An offer of help, or a plea?

No one had ever followed it and lived. Not even the Primarch Divine. Connecting two human minds was dangerous enough, as they'd proven over and over. Connecting a human mind with pure divinity would drive someone mad. Or send them Absent.

But the screaming was getting closer. And Morlinna needed the answers to the Malady now. Before it dragged her in.

Ashwyn's face shot through her thoughts. Not as she was when she told Morlinna she was being stupid. She wore the same quick grin as she had that morning when she'd woken to find Morlinna dressing. That quirk of the lips that made Morlinna's heart seize.

This is not a sacrifice, she promised, though Ashwyn wasn't here to acknowledge it. *I'm worth more. I'm worth answers.*

And before she could imagine Ashwyn's response, she reached out with one of her threads and pulled herself along the shaft of silver light, her ears ringing with the Goddess's screams.

White lightning speared toward her, pulling her under, and her thoughts collided with a consciousness as wide as the world, and an abyss opened beneath her feet.

Morlinna fell into the whirling thoughts, each one swallowing her so there was nothing left.

For that one moment hanging in the black, she knew everything. She knew the answers she'd sought, but the questions that replaced them grew to fill the space, swelling until they threatened to tear through her, leaving her open and spilled across the spaces of the world.

Then arms circled her, lifting her out of the abyss, and she saw.

Sense returned to her thoughts as she stared into a face distorted by pain and anger. And then the world spun again as the Goddess threw her back.

Chapter 67
Concordim

Ashwyn led Cass through the dense forest, taking her down the wide avenues of vines and branches, mostly because Cass couldn't pull strands to leap between layers. But it had the added benefit that Felleron could keep up.

The old wolf panted hard as he trotted behind them, his head hanging low. He said nothing, but Ash could tell from the way his stride went short on his back leg that his joints were hurting him. But she didn't dare suggest that he stay behind. When he did raise his head, his gaze was always focused forward. Toward the Heart.

Ash touched the top of his head. "Don't worry," she whispered. "We'll get her back."

He finally met her eyes. *How?*

"I don't know. But I won't stop until we do."

A little whine escaped his throat, but he kept moving.

Cass's eyes followed him, and she glanced up at Wraith, who swooped past, scouting their path along the vines.

"What?" Ash snapped.

"I always thought Devastation beasts were mindless predators. I wouldn't have thought any of them tame."

"They're animals. They're just trying to survive, same as all other life."

"Some seem to be more aggressive about it." Her eyes darted to the screening foliage, as if trying to see past it to the dangers that lurked beyond.

"They inherit things from their parents. It's like Father Liman always thought. The Goddess's power here allows for life to thrive in so many ways. Crosses happen that would never be possible anywhere else. But it means their offspring can inherit nearly anything from the ones who made them." She gestured to Wraith, who alighted on a branch up ahead and raised his snout to sniff. "Intelligence, flight, and yes, mindless aggression. There are plenty of things here that are just trying to survive. There are also plenty that I would never want to encounter on a dark night without my weapon."

"You almost sound like you like it," Cass said with a sidelong look at her.

Ash raised her chin. "I love it. I belong here, more than I ever did in Edgefall."

She passed Cass and lifted a curtain of vines to step through.

Wraith barked a warning, and Ash froze, her hands full of vines. She sucked in a breath when she saw what he had seen.

A river of white surging through the growth of the Devastation, bits of ashy residue floating free as the Malady swept along, carrying vines and roots in its wake.

Ash's mouth went dry, and she stopped Cass with a hand across her chest as the other woman tried to push forward.

"That...that's the Malady," Cass gasped. "Just like in the necropolis."

Ash gave her a sharp nod. "This space was clear just a day ago," she said.

It's coming from the direction of the Heart, Wraith said, jumping from his branch to land on the other side of the Malady's path.

"That's a problem, isn't it?" Cass said.

Ash's teeth clenched. "I've never seen it move so fast. It's...evolving. Changing the way it works. Because it eliminated the one person who could control it."

Cass's brows came down in an unhappy scowl. "Don't say that. We'll get them back."

Ash shook her head but didn't have the heart to deny the words out loud. "We'll have to go around," she said.

She picked up the pace and led Cass on. Everywhere she looked, she saw bits of Malady traveling through the forest, rivers of white spiderwebbing their way across the layers of the Devastation.

Her head hurt from clenching her teeth. She didn't dare voice her worries to Felleron, and Wraith kept his thoughts to himself, ducking and weaving through the trees to warn her when their path was cut off by a stream of white.

They reached the massive clearing in the center of the Devastation, and Ashwyn dropped to land on the mat of vines. Cass scrambled down after her, tripping and falling to her knees amid the dead roots and leaves of the firebreak.

She stood and brushed off her pants before she raised her head and finally saw the Heart of the Devastation for the first time.

Her mouth went pinched, and she raised a hand to press it to her chest. "This has been here the whole time?" she whispered.

Ash stepped to the edge of the Malady, crossing the perimeter they'd spent so much time erecting. It had been shattered in several places, where the wide streams of Malady flowed from the Heart, plunging into the forest all around them. Ash hadn't even noticed in the chaos of the last two days.

So much of their work ruined. When all this was over, they would have to start anew, clearing the forest and pushing the Malady back to its carefully maintained cage.

She felt exhausted just thinking about it.

"The Order said it was defeated," Cass said. "They said there were only pockets left. Little fronts where they fought the Little Wars."

She raised her gaze to Ash's. "What else are they lying about?"

Ash shook her head. She'd been through this all herself years ago, but they didn't have the time for Cass to come to terms with her entire worldview crumbling before her eyes.

Ash swung her scythe, clearing a path through the Malady to the edge of the chasm. Here the roots and vines plunged down, forming a break in the floor of the Devastation. A hole that pierced the heart of the forest.

Cass followed her, leaning forward to peer down. "How far down does it go?" she asked.

"All the way. We found the floor of the crater. Almost thirty layers down. There's a city down there that the Devastation is hiding. It's where this all began. The Malady, the fight, the Order. All of it. But at the very center is a pillar of Malady." Ash gestured to the ring where they stood. "It's hiding the heart of the city and the truth of whatever happened there."

"And you still don't know what it is?"

Ash's lips thinned. "We couldn't get through."

Cass stared into the dark hole, wide enough to fit the entire Lower Temple of Edgefall. "And you think that's where the Malady took our people?"

Ash's fingers closed around Morlinna's prayer beads.

"Yes," she said.

"All right," Cass said and straightened her shoulders. "You can't just yank us there like you did before? One second here and the next second there?"

Ashwyn eyed her. "You actually want to do that again?"

"Well, no. It makes me violently ill. But it *is* much faster."

Ash snorted. "As fun as it is to make you sick..." She ignored Cass's glare. "I can't travel down a thread to a place I haven't been. The one that I have leads to a space outside the Underheart. It wouldn't do us any good. We'll have to get down the hard way."

Cass made a face. "And what's the hard way?"

"Climbing. I'll cut us a path."

Ash raised her scythe.

"Wait," Cass said. She hurried back to the edge of the forest while Ashwyn blinked at her. Cass tore a couple of branches from the surrounding foliage, tucking one into her belt and hefting the other in her hand.

Ash raised her eyebrows as Cass joined her again.

"What?" Cass said. "You said we wouldn't want to be without weapons."

"I did," Ash said weakly. What else was she going to say? *Sticks aren't going to do you any good in here?*

That feeling reared its head again, the one where she just wanted to see Cass frightened. But it wouldn't do either of them any good and might get both of them killed.

Ash cut away enough of the Malady from the edge that she could reach down and start on a pathway. She could just see a wide enough root winding its way down the sheer wall of the chasm. That would be enough for them to walk on.

It would have to be.

A flutter of black and white wings made Ash glance up, and Ebonheart landed on her shoulder.

"Are you sure you want to come?" Ash said. "I can't guarantee I can protect you. I don't even know what's down there."

Others stay. Ebonheart said. *Others watch. I come to see you safe.*

Ash blew out her breath as the other magpies alighted in the trees around the chasm. She gave the leader of the flock a scratch.

"Very well. Wraith, scout ahead. Felleron, keep watch behind. Make sure nothing follows us down."

Ash stepped off the edge of the chasm and started her descent.

The way down was narrow enough that they had to travel one at a time. Wraith swooped in sharp circles, following the curve of the chasm into the depths and flapping back up to check in with them. He never went out of sight, though he could have floated the entire way to the bottom.

Ebonheart stayed on Ash's shoulder, her claws gripping the rough cloth of her overcoat while Cass hugged Ash's backside, traveling close enough that she stepped on the backs of Ash's boots more than once. Felleron trotted last, keeping a sharp eye behind them.

The bright sky narrowed inch by inch as the chasm walls closed in around them. Ash swung her scythe to clear the next bit of path, and her elbow jostled into Cass, who stood too close.

"Could you not do that?" Ash snapped.

"Sorry," Cass mumbled and stumbled back a step. She reached a hand out to steady herself against the chasm wall. Which still pulsed white with the Malady.

"Don't!" Ash smacked her hand away from the wall, making Cass overbalance so her arms windmilled over the edge of the drop.

Ash grabbed one of her flailing arms and pulled her so she sprawled at Ash's feet.

"What was that for?" Cass cried.

"Don't touch the walls," Ashwyn gritted out between her teeth. She couldn't even believe she had to say it. "Anything white. It's corrupted. And it will corrupt you the moment you touch it."

Cass eyed the wall. "And then what happens?"

"You die, Cass." Ash made sure to speak the words slowly and clearly. "But not before you try to infect everything else around you. Not before you become an agent for the Malady, spreading it to everyone and everything you can."

Cass's eyes darted past Ash, probably noting the fact that Ash and the animals were the only things around to corrupt.

Ash wondered if Cass was calculating just how long she would last in a fight against Ash. Because Ash certainly was.

She turned and kept walking, clearing the way in front of them.

They could still see a good portion of the sky when a shriek made Cass jump and step away from the edge.

A shadow stooped through the opening far above them, diving through the narrow space.

Ash had too much to keep track of between Cass and Ebonheart and Felleron and figuring out where they could place their hands and feet. She reacted too slowly to the impending danger.

The Devastation beast swooped close enough that Ash got a blurred image of feathers and talons and a whip-like tail before something thudded into it from the side, knocking it off course.

"Wraith!"

It must be really hungry to hunt down here, he said, flapping his wings to right himself in midair.

The predator shrieked again, baring crooked teeth set in a wide jaw. It made a tight turn, talons outstretched, and Cass threw herself to the cleared walkway to avoid them.

Wraith yipped and barked, trying to keep up, but something about the

Devastation beast's narrow body made it maneuverable in the air, and it outstripped him.

Ash sucked in a breath, but she had no room here, and when she reached out, all the strands in reach were corrupted, pulsing with white light.

She growled in frustration.

The thing stooped again, and Ashwyn swung her scythe around, awkward in the small space.

But something else struck the creature's wing, knocking it off course.

Ash gaped at Cass, who stood with her branch held between two hands, ready for another attack. She swung, and her club struck with a meaty thunk.

The creature spiraled away, careening into the opposite wall. It bounced, its wings flapping frantically to keep it in the air.

White crept across its face, spreading from the corners of its eyes and spearing down the veins in its muzzle.

"Mortis," Ashwyn muttered. "You know what's worse than a Devastation beast?"

"I'm guessing a corrupted Devastation beast." Cass said.

The beast made a tight turn, and Wraith back-winged desperately, staying out of its reach.

"Wraith," Ash called. "Drop."

Without questioning it, Wraith snapped his wings closed and dropped in the air.

Ash reached for one of his threads and stretched it across the space between them. It caught the beast in midair.

Ash cut the strand before it could corrupt either her or Wraith, but the impact of it knocked the beast toward her. Before it could recover control, she slashed through both wings with the corrupted end of her scythe.

The beast plummeted with a scream.

Ash followed its path with her gaze, her hands clenched around the shaft of her scythe. Corruption happened so fast. It always happened so fast.

Cass bent over, hands on her knees, wheezing. But Ash took only a moment to be sure Wraith was still all right before continuing down the pathway.

"Wait," Cass said. "Can't we take a second?"

"Every second is another second we have to fight for," Ash snapped. "And the fight is taking too long."

"Ash."

"What?"

"At least slow down. We need to be watching for more of those things."

"We can't slow down. Did you see how fast the Malady spread through it? That's what it's trying to do to Morlinna right now."

"Ash."

"No!" Ash said, spinning. "I told you you could come as long as you could keep up. If you can't do that, then go home. I'm sure you can survive the Devastation. You had no problem throwing me in here."

"I *am* keeping up, Ash. But it's a long way down. We have to pace ourselves."

"Can Morlinna pace herself?"

"Ash, look at them!" Cass flung her hand out to indicate Wraith, doing his best to hover, and Felleron, taking advantage of their argument to lie down on the cleared path behind them.

Ashwyn winced. She slashed through corrupted strands, giving them a bigger space to stand and sent a silent welcome to Wraith. The wolf landed to let his wings rest, and the twinge of guilt stabbed deeper.

Ash knelt and buried her hands in the fur at Wraith's ruff, where the first feathers of his wings brushed her fingers.

I'm sorry, she sent to him.

He turned, the ridged surface of one black horn knocking her cheek. *I am fine. I can handle far rougher conditions. It is Felleron I'm worried about.*

He's pushing himself too hard?

He shook his head. *We all are. But I, too, want to reach Morlinna. As does he.*

"Why are you in such a hurry to save Morlinna?" Cass asked as Ash stood. "We should be worried about the rest of the villagers."

Ash glared at her.

Cass took a deep breath. "Look, if anyone could fight the Malady, it's her, right? That's what you keep saying. She's the only one who can control it."

"I have to be there," Ash said, slashing through more strands of the Malady, inching forward.

"Why?"

"If she can't fight off the Malady, if it consumes her..." Ash squeezed her eyes shut, refusing to picture it in her mind. Refusing to see Morlinna's face turn into a rictus of pain and hate. Refusing to see the gap where her heart had once been.

"I have to be there," she said, voice harsh.

"Because you love her?" The accusation speared over Ash's shoulder.

Ash stopped and let her head tip back, neck muscles screaming.

"Because I have to kill her," she whispered.

Cass's breath came out on a surprised exhale. "What?"

"I promised." Ash swallowed and scrubbed a hand down her face, rubbing her good eye but not her bad one. "I promised her a long time ago that she wouldn't be alone. I promised that if the Malady ever took her completely, I would deliver the Last Death before she became the thing she's been fighting all these years."

"Oh, Dea."

If she said anything else, Ash didn't hear it. She swung her scythe and let the blood pound through her head in time with her movements.

On and on they descended. Wraith and Ebonheart took turns flying down a ways and coming back to report on the winding trek. Slowly the hole above them narrowed until the last pinprick of light disappeared, leaving them buried under layers and layers of Devastation.

A creeping feeling crossed the back of Ash's neck and made her turn. Corrupted vines snaked across the path behind them, blotting out the walkway.

There was no going back. Unless Ash cleared it again. And she refused to think of anything except forward.

The layers changed, like they had when they'd first climbed down to the city. The lush, verdant vines and roots of the surface receded, giving way to brittle, cracked foliage. Absent vines and roots tangled over and over each other, choked off from light and air and life itself.

The growth moved, writhing in the shadows at the edges of Ash's vision, and Cass grew quieter and quieter behind her.

A branch stretched across their path as if to deliberately block them, and Ash gulped, stepping back into Cass.

Cass yelped.

"It's not supposed to do that," Ash said, mostly to herself. "It's Absent. The growth is Absent."

"Absent people still walk around," Cass said. "Maybe this is the same thing."

"No, it's controlled by the Malady. It doesn't want us here. We must be getting close."

A vine slithered up, lifting as if to wrap around Ashwyn's boot. She drew back her scythe and slashed it so that it fell onto their pathway, shriveled and falling to dust.

Cass made a noise and bumped into her, trying to avoid a pair of branches that creaked across behind them, cutting her off from Felleron. The old wolf lifted his lip.

Cass smashed at the branches with her club, knocking them back enough for Felleron to slink under them.

"Stop," Ash said. "That won't work. You'll just have to lose the branch."

Cass watched the white slither across her club with horror. Then she braced the end against the ground and stomped on the dried stick.

It broke cleanly, leaving her with a much shorter but healthy club.

"I didn't come down here to watch you do all the work," she said.

"Just stay out of my way," Ash said, stepping forward to free some space so she could cut down the next vine to try to grab her.

"Watch out!" Cass cried.

Ash slashed through the vine and found another looming over her shoulder, too close to bring her scythe up between them.

Cass threw her stick at the vine, as if that would do anything useful.

But the vine closed around it as if in reflex, giving Ash a chance to step back and cut the thing back at its base.

It left them room to breathe.

"I told you to stay out of my way," Ash snapped, rounding on Cass. The other woman's face was white in the dark.

"And I told you I'm not going to just stand here. It worked, didn't it? Why can't you just trust me?"

"Why?" Ash cried. "Why can't I trust you? You abandoned me, Cass. Five years ago, when everything happened, and it all could have gone differently. You betrayed me when I needed you most."

Cass flung out her hands. "Because you betrayed me first."

Ash jerked back. "What?"

Cass made a noise that sounded suspiciously like a sob. But that wasn't right. Cass never showed anything ugly like grief or regret.

"We were supposed to be together forever," she said, voice breaking. "And you went and got yourself made into a Nexsaint. You went somewhere I couldn't follow."

Ash opened her mouth, and Cass held up her hands, shaking her head.

"I know...I know you didn't do it on purpose. I know that now. But back then, I just saw that we had the life we wanted. Together. And you were so miserable. Miserable enough that you went and changed it all."

"It didn't have to change anything."

Cass gave her an exasperated look. "You would have had to go to Vitamorn to train. You would have left me behind." Her voice rose. "And you acted like it was a good thing. You took the thing that we'd built together and broke it. You hurt me." Cass swallowed and met Ash's eyes. "So I hurt you."

Ash kept a rein on her temper but only because the Devastation would have overrun them otherwise.

"You tried to kill me. That's not the same as leaving you. Exile is a death sentence. You know that."

"You survived."

"What if I hadn't?" Ash threw her hands up.

Cass's mouth twisted in pain, and she looked away. "I know you don't believe me, and it doesn't matter anymore, anyway. But I didn't want you to die.

I was just so angry. We had what we wanted, but it wasn't enough for you. *I* wasn't enough for you."

Ash's mouth went dry hearing the words. Hearing the pain in them.

She remembered those months where she'd pretended to be happy living with Cass, but she'd been screaming inside.

She'd thought Cass hadn't loved her enough to defend her.

But maybe she hadn't loved Cass enough to be content in a life she hated.

"I thought it would be," she whispered. "I thought it would be enough to love you. But I had to fight for everything I had in Edgefall. I had to prove I was worth something. Even just survival. 'Life is hard, but we're harder?' More like life is cruel, but we're worse. I had to prove I was worthy of Edgefall. In the end, I couldn't fight for myself anymore, Cass. I was so *tired* of having to fight for myself."

She left the part unsaid that Cass could have made it easier by fighting for her, too.

"Is it easier with her?"

Ash didn't ask who she meant. And she didn't have to think about her answer.

"Yes."

"Even where you still have to fight things every day?"

"I'm not fighting people who believe I don't deserve to exist."

Cass pressed her lips together, glancing at the floor. The vines still writhed around them, growing across their path, but they were slow enough for Ash to follow and cut back.

They made progress. Little by little, and finally, Ash could see the base of the chasm widen. Enough that the wide roof and thick nave of a temple rose before them. The light in Ash's hand flickered against the tile roof, patches of white showing along its crest.

"We're almost there," Cass whispered. "We've done it."

"Not yet," Ash said. "But I like your optimism."

Maybe they could have made it work together. If Cass had been willing to bear some of the battle. If Ash had been more patient with her. Maybe they could have been worth it for each other.

But not now.

Not now that Ash knew what the alternative was like.

Cass shook her head, giving Ash a sidelong grin. "You've changed, you know."

Ash snorted as she swung her scythe. The going would be a lot tougher as they traversed the last of the chasm. It sloped the wrong way, like climbing up a cliff that arched above.

"I know. Living in the Devastation does that."

"I mean, you're loud."

Ash made a face. "I've always been loud."

"But now it counts for something. You know how to make yourself heard. And you make people listen."

Ash scowled. "Maybe people should have been listening all along."

"Some of us were trying. We just weren't very good at it."

Ash bit back a mean retort and really looked at her in the dim light. "You've changed, too."

Cass rolled her eyes. "No, I haven't."

"You never wanted to be elderman when we were growing up."

The other woman's eyes flicked away. "Maybe I just wanted to feel in control after you...when you were gone."

The familiarity struck her, settling over her like a blanket. She'd felt that. She'd been there. And suddenly it made everything slot into place a little better.

"Are you really going to kill her?" Cass asked quietly. "When you find her?"

"If I have to." Ash raised her head, her arms and back and shoulders aching. "It's the only thing she's ever asked me for. Everything else...everything else I've made her give me."

"What do you mean?"

"She didn't want to teach me," Ash whispered. "I made her. She didn't want to let me stay. I made her. She didn't want to love me."

Cass was quiet for a long moment as the floor of the chasm drew nearer and nearer. Ash could make out crumbled walls and the blackened steps to the door of the temple.

"If she's as strong and kind and brave as you say," Cass said. "Then there's no way you could make her give you anything. She gave you those things because she wanted you to have them."

Ash swallowed. Cass knew nothing of Morlinna or their years together. But the words rang true anyway, and she clung to them.

"I'm sorry," Cass said as Ash set foot on the floor of the chasm. "For everything I've done to you."

Ash glanced back at her. It was too little too late, and they both knew it. But it needed to be said anyway, and Ash was grateful for it.

"Me too," she said. Then, squared her shoulders and faced the temple.

Chapter 68
Concordim

Ash and Cass stared at the temple buried under the Devastation. Behind them, the walls of the Underheart plunged beneath the dirt and the broken cobblestones, sending out roots and tendrils to infect the forest above.

The root-woven walls curved around them in a pulsing white circle, trapping the temple at the heart of the city.

"What is this place?" Cass whispered.

"Mournefast," Ash said. "The Goddess's wife loved this city. This is where it all started."

This was where the Goddess's power had been corrupted. Where whatever She'd done to Her spouse had broken the world and created the Malady.

With the city set up like a temple, this would have been the altar. The seat of holiness.

Not everything within the Underheart was corrupted. Streams of Malady flowed from the walls toward the temple, but there were some gaps between them where healthy black strands still showed.

No. Wait. Ash squinted at the pulsing threads just beyond their feet.

The Malady wasn't coming from the walls of the chasm. It was flowing in the other direction. It was coming from the temple. Corrupted strands of the Nexum crept between the stone blocks, oozing out from the ancient mortar.

"Are you okay?" Cass asked.

"What?"

"You're shaking."

Her throat was dry too, and the only reason her hands clenched on the shaft of her scythe was to keep them steady.

"I'm fine."

They'd left their pathway at the very foot of the temple steps. Ash took the first step now, climbing toward the doors.

White strips of Malady seamed the ancient wood, the strands crisscrossing and forming a barrier she couldn't even touch.

She brought her scythe around and slashed through the strands, clearing a patch of death through the center of the door.

She placed both hands on the handles and tugged.

But nothing happened.

It didn't even rattle, as if it had been sealed into place long ago, and it wouldn't budge for anyone, especially some brand new Nexsaint.

"Is it locked?" Cass asked.

"Something like that," Ash said, then bit her tongue as strands of corrupted Nexum snaked through the door again, replacing the dead threads.

"Mortis," she whispered, the hair on the back of her neck standing up.

It was trying to keep her out. The same way it had on the pathway down.

Not it. *She.* She was trying to keep Ash out. She'd stolen Morlinna and now She was keeping Ash from getting to her. What did She want with the other Nexsaint? Was She looking for a replacement for Her dead wife? Or was Morlinna the threat She needed neutralized?

Ash gritted her teeth and planted her feet. She yanked healthy threads from beneath the ground with one hand and pulled her flint from her belt with the other. Then she struck a spark against the blade of her scythe and wove the essence of its flame into the new strand.

She might not be able to manipulate the Malady. But she could bait it. She could lure it and trap it and do whatever it took to get past the barriers it put in her way.

She expanded the thread with a sharp pull, like spreading a woven strand into pieces, and threw those pieces at the door.

The Malady snatched up the healthy threads, and corruption began spreading through them. But not before the fire's heat infected it in turn.

The door went up in flames, and Ash flung up her hand to protect her face.

Cass cried out and stumbled back.

Flames seared her skin, but instead of shrinking back from the conflagration, she stepped into it and threw more strands into the mess, weaving them with air to feed the fire.

The door exploded away from her, leaving a yawning opening.

Cass swore, using words Ash hadn't realized she knew. Ash just stepped into the temple, keeping her rage held just under the surface.

Shadows clung to the inside of the temple, alleviated only by the simmering embers left over from the door.

Ash wove the last bit of the fire's light into Ebonheart's wings, and the magpie launched herself into the air.

The light bounced off the walls, revealing frescoes stained with ash and soot. Triangular magpies, like in Morlinna's temple, lined the tops of the walls and down the open doorways. Cold braziers stood on either side of the opening, as if this had been some sort of foyer long ago.

Ebonheart swooped through the doorway, taking the light with her.

Felleron growled just behind Ash and with a howl, he darted after her.

"Wait!" Cass cried.

But Ash was as done with waiting as the wolf was. She stalked through the doorway, Wraith at her side, her scythe held ready.

And then her steps faltered.

The nave of the temple opened before her, big enough to house the entire Lower Temple of Edgefall under its roof. Frescoes designed to look like windows stretched up the walls. An ancient fire had stained the bottoms, but the rest still shone with colors and gold paint. Ash could just make out two figures in each window, standing with their arms locked around each other.

Then her eye was drawn to the far end of the nave. A painting rose behind the altar dominating the space, all done in silvers and stark black lines.

Ebonheart flapped higher, lighting up her face and sparking light in the silver paint.

A tall, thin woman towered over the temple, her silver hair a halo around her head. Her eyes were closed, but her arms were spread as if to embrace the viewer, welcoming them in.

"That's not the Goddess," Cass whispered behind Ash.

"No, it's not." Ash recognized her. Recognized her coloring and the stark angles she'd been portrayed with. The almost painful thinness and the straight planes of her torso.

Hundreds of stylized feathers fluttered around her like leaves on a breeze, concentrating around her head and her hips.

And Ash's mouth went dry at the sight of her. Because she was the reason for all of this.

Below the wall, where the altar should have been, spread a pool of Malady. A gap torn into the world, except this one stretched ten times as big as the one in the necropolis, covering the floor from wall to wall across the nave.

The villagers cowered against the doorway they'd just come through, trying to stay as far away from the creeping corruption as possible.

Morlinna knelt between them and the pool, arms stretched on either side of her. Strands of Malady wrapped her wrists, pinning her hands to the floor. They sent tendrils up her arms to wind around her neck and torso.

But Morlinna was still upright. Still holding the Malady back from the villagers. It fought her control, strands writhing across the floor, reaching and plucking, searching for freedom to spread and kill.

Ashwyn gasped and sprinted for Morlinna, only a step behind Felleron. She swung her scythe, cutting through strands of the Malady so they would have a place to stand.

She fell to her knees in front of Morlinna, her hands burning from not being able to reach for her. To tear the strands of Malady away from her and carry her from this place.

Felleron paced beside them, whining his own frustration, and Ashwyn could hear Cass murmuring to the villagers, taking a headcount and reassuring them that this would all be over now.

But Ash only had eyes for Morlinna.

"I'm here," she said, and her voice came out a croak. "I'm here, Morlinna. Morlinna, look at me."

Morlinna raised her head, movements slow and weary. Her gaze met Ashwyn's, and Ash gasped.

The white streaks through her face were lined with red, as if the Malady in her veins had dug deeply into her skin. Her pale blue eyes still shone clear, but Ash could see the white creeping into her pupils, gaining ground in the war for Morlinna's body and soul.

Ash gulped.

The neckline of Morlinna's robe gaped, torn edges falling away from her neck and collarbones to reveal white streaks spearing toward her heart.

Ash stared, waves of cold washing through her at the sight.

Then she raised her gaze again, meeting Morlinna's eyes.

Morlinna remained silent, her lips pressed tight so that creases formed at the corners.

She knew she was too far gone to be saved.

Ash's eyes went hot and wet, and she viciously fought back the tightness in her throat so she wouldn't break down, she wouldn't lose control here at the Underheart where the Devastation would take every advantage.

But, mortis, her entire body ached with the strength of her grief.

There was a step behind her, and Felleron snarled. But a thought from Wraith told Ash it was only Cass.

"I'm here," Cass said. "But how do we get them out? Can you free her?"

"I'll cut her out," Ash said, bracing her scythe against the floor so she could pull herself to her feet. "It won't...It won't save her. But I can at least take her from here."

"No," Morlinna's whisper barely made it past her lips, but it lodged in Ash's bones, anyway.

She sank back onto her heels. "What?"

"Can't leave. She needs..." Morlinna's voice cracked, and she sagged against her bonds. The strands of Malady tightened and cut into Morlinna's threads.

"Morlinna, it's killing you," Ash said, trying to figure out what the other Nexsaint was trying to say. Why wouldn't she want to leave?

"She's not...It's not what we thought." She strained against her bonds and managed to raise one hand an inch to indicate the pulsing strands keeping her in place.

"The Malady?" Ash said.

"It's Her power...out of control."

"I knew that," Ash cried. "I told you that."

Morlinna shook her head. "No. Not—" Morlinna shivered and bowed her head.

"Morlinna!" Ash cried. "What is it?"

"She's screaming."

Cass sucked in a breath and whipped around to see who might be crying out, but Ash knew she was speaking about the Goddess. The voice Morlinna had been following all these years.

"I've heard it before," Morlinna gasped. "In the temple. Before the throne. In the Devastation. Lady...lady, I'm coming."

"Morlinna, stop!" Ash cried. But she'd never been able to pry Morlinna from her faith. Her belief was tied into her so deeply Ash was sure she'd perish if they ever cut it out.

And now, her belief would be the thing that killed her.

Chapter 69
Animatim

Vitania pushed open the doors of the Primarch Divine's room, startling him and the Abdicant, who sat in the chair in front of his desk.

The two looked up, their surprise mirrored between them.

The Abdicant stood slowly, her gaze traveling down V's long body, taking in the muddy armor and the blood staining her cloak. V's dirty hair hung around her face, the shoulder-length strands jagged from her impromptu haircut. But for once the Abdicant didn't seem to care about the obvious imperfections.

Her eyes landed on V's face.

V wasn't sure exactly what her expression was doing. Her face had been numb for miles.

"Is it done?" the Abdicant said.

V clenched her teeth and stalked forward, reaching into her pocket to draw something out and toss it on the desk.

A vial of dust rolled across the surface, coming to rest between the Primarch Divine's hands. Just like the ones that lined the Abdicant's hall, filled with the dust of heretics.

He picked it up and held it in his fingers, the light catching on the glass.

He raised his eyes to V.

She bowed from the waist, pressing her hand over her heart, then turned and left before either of them could say anything more.

V's jaw ached as she made her way back down the great central street. Stars shone above in the clear night sky. Something in her longed for the comfort and safety of the manor where she'd grown up. But that place was just a memory now. Even if she made it back there, it would hold none of the remembered comfort.

Instead, she mounted the steps of the Greater Temple and pushed through the doors.

Her steps rang across the empty nave. No one gathered here this late, and all the priests and priestesses and attendants were asleep in their cloisters.

The silence pressed into her like a blanket, and she almost cut the connection to her ears so she wouldn't have to hear her footsteps either.

But she didn't.

Four Bladesaints stood at the four corners of the Goddess's throne, with one off to either side.

She looked at the new lieutenant in charge. "Leave us," she said.

His eyes widened, and he glanced at her armor as if he didn't recognize the face of one of only two living Judges.

To his credit, he stood up to a superior officer well.

"With all due respect, Your Serene Highness," he said with a slight stammer. "We're on duty tonight. It would be against our regulations to leave Her alone."

"You're not," V said, cocking her head. "Or are you saying the Goddess isn't safe with me?"

She saw the movement in his throat as he swallowed. He exchanged a glance with his fellow Bladesaints and then his eyes flicked to the blood on her cloak.

She saw the moment he realized she'd just returned from executing the man responsible for the last problem in the Greater Temple.

"The temple is yours, Serenity." He saluted her, then gave a hand gesture to the others that meant move out. "But I will have to report who I handed command to."

"Of course," she said, her voice as calm as a pond on a still day. Her eyes were already on the Goddess, as if she'd dismissed him from her mind.

She didn't turn her head as they left, using the sound of their boots on stone to gauge when they'd all filed out.

She stood in the darkness, looking up at the Goddess, whose face remained obscured in shadow. Words abandoned her. She'd thought she'd come here to pray. To ask for answers the Goddess would never give her.

But the one she needed answers from was gone.

"Why?" she'd asked her father, and her voice had broken on the word.

He stared at the bracelet in his palm. "Because She's trapped, V. We've imprisoned Her here."

"I've heard that lie before," she said with a shake of her head. "Our need made Her stay. If it weren't for us, She wouldn't have to tie /herself here."

"No. I mean, She's not supposed to be here. She needs to be freed."

V's eyes widened, then came down. "Pap—" She snapped her mouth closed. She couldn't keep calling him that; it was the word for someone closer and dearer than he'd become. But Father sounded wrong in her ears. Too close to Mother, and the thought of Sahvia sparked so much turmoil inside her.

"Dad," she tried again. "The reason She's here, the reason She's bound, is that if She were untethered, Her power would destroy us all. She's too dangerous."

"That's a lie," he snapped, his signs going sharp and jagged. "Open your eyes, V. Think for yourself."

V's breath came faster. In years of training, he'd never snapped at her. Never given her more than a gentle correction.

Her jaw clenched. "I *am* thinking for myself. The Devastations are proof of Her power." She raised her hands to indicate the Damp Hell around them. "This is where Her power goes unchecked, and it's where people die. Not just go Absent."

She drew in a deep breath to calm herself. "If the Goddess is untethered, Her power will be unleashed, and we'll be overrun with Devastations. We'll all fall to the beasts that grow here, and without Her, every death will be the Last Death."

He stood, chest moving but mouth shut tight enough to turn his lips white.

"You know it's true," V said.

"I know that She is powerful," her father said. "But that doesn't mean She would kill us. And it doesn't mean we can keep Her here."

"She chose this," V said.

"What makes you believe that? Has She told you?"

"You know She doesn't speak."

He shook his head and stepped forward. She braced her feet, hand going to her hilt, but he just thrust the bracelet at her chest. She caught it against her breastplate.

"Take this to Her," he said, voice tight and intense. "See what happens—"

"I was there the first time—"

"Then you saw. You saw the proof yourself. If She wanted to be here, then the connection to Her throne would be stronger than anything else. No stray connection in some random sacrifice would be enough to tear Her away."

V's fingers tightened around the grass strands. She'd seen it. She'd seen the Goddess fade and flicker and wink out completely. She'd felt that terror as she watched their defense against death leave them all behind.

Her father couldn't be right. He couldn't be because She'd come back. She'd...She'd come when they'd pulled Her. A goddess wouldn't be swayed by a mortal unless She wanted to be.

He couldn't be right, because if he was, V was one of the ones keeping Her here.

Her breath faltered. "She came back for Vitania!" the Primarch had said.

"You see," her father said in her memory as she stood before the throne. "We're the ones keeping Her here."

A noise escaped V's throat. A small guilty groan.

"It was supposed to show you," V's father had said, gesturing to the bracelet she now held. "I had to give you the chance to see."

V stared at the Goddess on Her throne. The woman who sat with Her eyes shut tight, as if She couldn't bear to see the world in front of Her.

"Is it true?" She signed the words, knowing the Goddess couldn't see. But the words were heresy, and she couldn't afford to let anyone else hear them. Surely a goddess would hear the words in her heart. "Are we the ones holding you here?"

There was no answer, but then she wasn't sure she'd actually expected one.

"Please. I need to know if he was right. I need to know if I-"

She froze and let her hands fall back to her sides. The silence pressed in on her, and for once it felt wide and uncomfortable.

She shut her eyes as her hand reached for her belt.

And she pulled the grass bracelet free.

It sat on her palm—a challenge, a risk, a question with an answer.

If her father was right and the Goddess was trapped, this would set Her free. If V was right and She'd chosen to be here, then the Goddess's connection with Her throne would be enough to draw Her back. Perhaps they just hadn't waited long enough last time.

V was sure...no, she trusted...no, she *believed.*

She stepped onto the dais. And placed the bracelet on the Goddess's lap.

V took one breath, then two.

And watched as the Goddess's form flickered and flashed out. Leaving Her throne empty.

V waited, holding her breath.

Concordim

Heat burned into Ash's leg, and she fell back with a cry. She plunged her hand into her pocket, finding the source, and she pulled out the strands of grass. The remains of the bracelet she'd made for Cass.

They seared her fingers, and Ash flung them away across the flagstones.

The dried grass caught fire and went up in a spout of flame.

"What was that?" Cass cried.

A wind flattened the flames, bringing a swirl of sparks, green and gold and pink, spiraling into a woman.

She stood, lit as if the sun had reached a single ray through the layers of the Devastation just for her. Her thick hair pooled against the flagstones, melting into the folds of Her gown, the red strands contrasting with the green. It shone like fire, flowers trailing down as it grew longer and longer under their gaze.

"You," Ash breathed. She lurched to her feet.

"Ash," Morlinna croaked, and the word made her falter. She'd never heard Morlinna shorten it before.

But she shook her head. "No. She's the reason for all of this. She didn't speak for you. She didn't speak for me. Her power has caused all of this, and it's Her silence that's tried to kill us all!"

Ashwyn stalked up to the Goddess who had abandoned her.

"Say something!" Ash cried. "Say anything. Tell me why at least."

Deavita, the Gentle Mother, just stared at her, eyes pained.

How dare She look like Ash was the one hurting Her? How dare She act like She didn't have to answer for Her actions?

Ash screamed, a wordless cry that echoed up the walls of the temple.

The Goddess stepped forward, movements fluid even in Her haste, and She grabbed Ashwyn's hands.

Her gaze bored into Ash, pushing past the rage and the disappointment. Then the Goddess held Her wrists out in front of Her, like a prisoner waiting for shackles.

"What?" Ash said because she couldn't think of anything else. No other words to describe the bafflement and the creeping sensation of dread crawling through her.

The Goddess held her gaze.

And opened Her mouth.

The breath left Ash's lungs, leaving her gasping. Behind her, Cass moaned.

Ash tried to swallow through a dry throat and only ended up choking.

She'd been angry for so long, thinking the Goddess didn't speak for her. But that was wrong.

The Goddess of Life *couldn't* speak. Because She had no tongue.

Chapter 70
Concordim

The voice speaking to Morlinna wasn't the Goddess.

But then, who had she been talking to for all these years? *What* had she been talking to?

Ash turned, looking for one safe spot in the chaos that was her thoughts, and her eyes locked on Morlinna.

"What is the Malady?" she whispered.

"A corruption," Morlinna gasped out. "Of power. Like you thought. But not Deavita's. Hers." Morlinna craned her head around. She couldn't turn completely with the Malady wrapped around her neck, but Ashwyn followed her gaze to the figure in the painting.

The Goddess's wife.

She Who Had Been He.

The air across the chamber changed, growing heavy and thick. Beside them, Cass coughed and Ash cleared the knot from her throat.

The Malady flowed from the pool up through the cracks in the walls, but as she watched, it slowed and pulsed and very, very gradually shifted course to flow backward.

The corrupted strands gathered, linking over and over, and the gap swelled, stretching toward their feet.

Morlinna hissed as it passed her, and Ashwyn grabbed Cass to yank her out of the way.

A white, skeletal hand surged out of the pool and scrabbled at the edge of the stained flagstones.

The Goddess seized Ash's wrist, and Ash's gaze darted to Her, but Deavita's eyes were fixed on the figure climbing out of the gap.

The creature unfolded its long, gangly limbs, strips of Malady hanging from its skull in dull strands.

It stood to its full height, black eyes sweeping the people gathered there. Its gaze fell on Deavita.

And the figure screeched.

Beside Ash, the Goddess moaned, a guttural sound that sent a shaft of ice down Ash's spine. Deavita reached for the figure, tears streaming down Her face, fingers flexing as if remembering the feel of a hand in Hers.

Ash gasped.

She had no idea what would happen if the Malady corrupted the Goddess Herself, but it was probably a really bad idea to find out.

She threw herself across the Goddess's path and held Her back, keeping Her away from the figure dressed in ragged strips of corruption.

"Is that her?" she asked. "Is that your wife?"

Deavita's face contorted with pain, and She clung to Ash's shoulders as if Ash's strength was the only thing keeping Her from running to the figure. Then She nodded.

"She's the source of the Malady?"

Deavita nodded again, then shook Her head, Her eyes pinching closed in frustration.

"Not just wife," Morlinna gasped. "Goddess. She was banished. Exiled. Carved out of Her place in the world and the world is broken now. Her power rushed to fill the gaps, but it is untamed. Uncontrolled."

Ash's chest seized. Who could hope to control a goddess?

"She is Life's partner," Morlinna said. Her whole body sagged in her bonds. "The balance opposite Her. The Goddess of Death."

If that was true, then She was as much a part of the world as Life. Without Her...they had the Malady.

She was the one who'd been speaking to Morlinna this whole time. She'd been the one to tell her to corrupt herself. The one to lead her to the secrets of the Devastation and the city underneath it.

But the Malady also spoke to her. Whispered in Morlinna's ear to give herself over to it.

Could they trust anything She said?

The Malady creature surged forward, as if to embrace or attack the Life Goddess. Either would amount to the same thing.

And it looked like Deavita would let it.

Morlinna screamed, and the Malady creature lurched back as if tethered. It spun and glared at Morlinna, who held its strands in her hands.

"Morlinna!" Ash cried.

Morlinna grunted as if struck and collapsed against the flagstones. "I can't..." she gasped. "I can't hold Her."

Ash took a step forward, but what could she do? Morlinna lay bound in a pool of corruption that just kept growing back. Ash couldn't get to her. She couldn't control it. Not without corrupting herself.

"Ash," Morlinna gasped. "Help Her."

"What?" Help the angry Malady lady who just wanted to kill them all?

"She's a victim, Ash...She was exiled."

Even all these years later, the word sent a flare of heat through her. Ash shuddered.

The Goddess beside her made a pleading gesture, Her hands folded over Her heart as Her gaze dug into Ash.

"Strip it away, Ashwyn," Morlinna said. "She's in there somewhere."

Morlinna lay dying under this creature's power, and still she fought for it. She argued for the thing that would save the most people, do the most good, even if it didn't make sense at the time.

Ashwyn sobbed, knowing what Morlinna wanted her to do.

Without Morlinna, there was no one to control the Malady. There was no one to fight the corruption that spread through the Devastation. No one to save the miserable little villagers who huddled against the wall. No one to free Morlinna and kill her before the Malady took her.

No one who could stop an out-of-control goddess.

Unless Ash did it herself. All she had to do was trust that Morlinna knew what had to be done. Trust that Morlinna was right.

Trusting Morlinna had never been hard.

Chapter 71
Concordim

Ash peeled the Life Goddess's hands from her arms and transferred Her grip to Cass.

Cass's eyes went wide as Deavita sagged into her arms, but she took Her weight and gave Ashwyn a nod.

"I have Her," she said quietly. "I'll keep Her back."

Ash didn't think too hard about whether that was even possible. She had to trust Cass as much as she trusted Morlinna in this moment.

The Malady creature strained forward, falling to its hands and knees and clawing its way across the ground toward them. It had wanted Morlinna enough to steal her away here. But whatever purpose she'd had for the Nexsaint had been superseded by the appearance of the Life Goddess. All of the corrupted Death Goddess's attention was reserved for Her wife.

Ashwyn braced herself and stepped into the creature's line of sight, blocking its view of Deavita.

The skeletal figure shrieked, a high-pitched scream that sounded just like a dread, and Ash had to fight not to jump and look behind her.

She forced herself to meet the Malady creature's eyes. Forced herself to take a step forward.

The Malady creature screamed again and reached out a hand, nails curled like rending claws.

Ash held her breath and took the creature's hand in hers, wrapping her fingers around the claws.

The Malady creature's fingers felt like bone against Ash's skin, cold and smooth and impossibly thin. And then they seized on Ash, crushing her in their grasp.

Ash cried out as the Malady surged up the threads in her body, filling her veins with a terrible heat.

White lightning flickered behind her eyelids, and Ash felt herself falling toward the battleground, that empty courtyard of the necropolis where the Malady waited to overtake her.

She opened her eyes to see the cracked flagstones, the obsidian walls, and the statue standing calm and weathered against it all.

And white lightning flashed against the blackened sky, racing across the clouds toward Ash.

A black robe flared around her legs. The clothes of a Nexsaint. But her hands flexed, empty. Wherever she was inside her own mind or body, her weapons hadn't come with her. She faced the Malady empty-handed.

Thunder rumbled behind her, and Ash whirled. The lightning came at her from all sides. There was no front or back. Only the empty courtyard and the rush of the oncoming Malady.

It was just like that moment in the Devastation when Morlinna had healed the Malady using Ashwyn's threads. But Morlinna wasn't here to defend her. She wasn't here to tell Ash how to fight it off.

It didn't matter. She could do this. She *would* do this. Morlinna trusted her. Ash knew she was strong enough.

Morlinna had always described it as a fight. A battle to hold the Malady back.

Lightning crackled over the ground at her feet, moving impossibly fast, and Ashwyn braced herself, raising her hands.

The lightning flashed, striking the backs of her hands, and she cried out before striking. But all she hit was empty air.

She'd never fought with her fists before. She'd always had a blade or a scythe to wield.

The white lightning cracked, streaking through Ash's shoulders and down her spine.

She screamed and fell to her knees.

How could she fight this thing that took no shape with hands that held no weapon?

Morlinna had had her scythe. But Ash had come empty-handed. Maybe that was what made Morlinna special. Something inside her had given her a weapon to fight the Malady when everyone else faced the threat alone.

The lightning sang across her limbs, making her bones ache and her skin sizzle.

She was going to die here, under the onslaught of the Malady. Would she even wake to find herself corrupted and dying, like Rafe and Ingrim? Or would she just slip away from here as her body turned on her friends?

The rock under her hands shook with thunder.

Who was Morlinna really? What had made her into the weapon that fought the Malady?

Nexsaint. Apostate. Friend. Lover. The witch of the Devastation. Ashwyn was all of those things as well. Except there was one identity they'd never shared.

Devout follower.

Ash tipped her head back and braved the lightning to stare at the statue of the Goddess.

She held a double-headed scythe in her open palms.

Had she had it the whole time and Ash just hadn't seen? Hadn't been able to see the gift offered? Or hadn't been ready to accept it?

She'd been so sure the Goddess had betrayed her. The silent deity had betrayed everyone.

But she'd been wrong, and all of her anger had nowhere to go except out. Toward the Malady.

Ash surged upright and lunged for the statue. The Goddess's lips curved in a smile as her fingers closed around the familiar haft.

Lightning cracked, making her whole body seize, but she yanked the scythe free. It came without resistance.

The lightning shivered across her skin, stinging in a thousand tiny pinpricks, and she thought she could feel it like needles slipping under her skin, spreading the rot of the Malady within her.

Thunder rumbled a warning, and she swung around to meet the arc of lightning against the haft of her new blade. The movement felt awkward, the new weapon heavy, but it sent the streak of lightning crashing against an obsidian wall.

Ash panted, her heart pounding its rhythm through her body, but this time it wasn't panic.

The lightning surrounded her, flickering against the flagstones before striking at her. But she met the next blow with her weapon.

"You may have this much of me," she grated out between her teeth as she held back the Malady. "And no more."

The corruption in her veins was a tool. It was not her end. It would not take her over. And she would use it to fight the Malady in the world.

Ash held back the crash and flash of the Malady to a line just beyond her feet, keeping it from crossing over and sending any more needles of rot under her skin.

The moment her attention wasn't solely focused on the Malady, it was easy to slip back to see the world around her.

Somewhere behind her, Cass screamed.

That didn't bother her nearly as much as the fact that she heard nothing from Morlinna.

Sensation returned, and Ash blinked bleary eyes as pain speared through her. Her feet dangled above the ground, and a grip like steel circled her arms, keeping her aloft.

Ash looked up into the Malady creature's eyes. It held her, nails buried deep in her skin as the Malady surged into her.

And stopped.

Her barrier inside, the line she'd drawn and the battle some inner part of her still fought, was working.

With her hands still free, she grabbed threads of corrupted Nexum below them and wrapped them around the Malady creature's legs, winding them higher and higher until they circled its neck and shoulders.

And then she yanked.

The threads pulled taut and slammed the creature to the ground. Its hands spasmed, releasing Ashwyn.

The shock of the fall went through Ash, and she rolled away. She pushed to her hands and knees, an insistent tug somewhere deep inside, reminding her that she stood directly in the pool of Malady and the corruption in her veins was pushing past her defenses.

A distraction at best. An invasion at worst. She shook her head, staggering from the onslaught, trying to keep her focus here and there at the same time.

The Malady creature fought the strands holding it down, untangling itself with a shriek. It threw itself forward, and Ash rolled backward, coming up with her scythe.

The Malady creature shrank away from her next slash.

Behind, Ash made out Morlinna's form, huddled against the flagstones. The bonds still held her, but they were unnecessary now. Morlinna lay as if she had no more strength left.

Ash screamed and reached for the strands that held the other woman down. She snapped them with her hand, her strength augmented by the steel of her blade.

Morlinna sagged, free of the strands, her face turned toward the ceiling.

The Malady creature shrieked and drew to its full height, towering over Ashwyn.

Streams of Malady flowed from it, tracing through the flagstones, filling in the few spaces that had remained uncorrupted.

Cass cried out. "Ash!"

She and Deavita stood between the huddled villagers and the Malady creature, watching the corruption spread through the ground at their feet like oil across water. Felleron and Wraith snarled, herding them all deeper into the corner, out of the way. But it wouldn't be enough.

Ash turned from the Malady creature and grabbed a thread overhead. She pulled and sent herself spinning over them, weaving threads across the flagstones, creating a firebreak of corruption to keep it from spreading.

The stream heading for the villagers slowed to a trickle. But slow did not equal halted. Everywhere the creature set foot, it brought corruption. All it had to do was stumble forward, and the villagers would be in danger again. Cutting away the rot in the world wasn't going to be enough.

Morlinna had said to help Her. To strip it away.

Ash turned her eyes back to the Malady creature.

It shrieked and turned its head, and something in its movement spoke of pain. The narrowness in its eyes and the hurt in its voice told a story of confusion and agony. And rage.

The same rage Ashwyn had known as she'd fallen from the edge of the crater. The same confusion she'd felt when the Goddess hadn't spoken for her. The same pain Cass's words had driven deep into her heart as she'd stood in the rain and watched her world crumble.

Exiled. Banished. Carved out of her place. The words hit her one by one.

She was fighting the wrong thing.

Morlinna was right. The Death Goddess was still in there somewhere.

She threw herself at the Malady creature, her cry ringing from the walls, anger and hope churning into a mass of rage.

Ash slid between its legs and came up on the other side, slashing, her blade peeling away strips of Malady and cutting through their threads until they lay dead and shriveled.

She leaped out of the way as the Malady creature swiped for her, its nails slashing through the air where Ash had just been.

Wraith launched himself into the air with a howl, and Ash tossed an uncorrupted thread to him, attaching it to his flank long enough he could carry it around the Malady creature. Ash sent the heat and destruction of a flame through the strand before slicing it free from Wraith. The strand wrapped the

Malady creature and even as it went white with infection, it seared through the Malady at its surface, scorch marks sizzling in its wake.

Drips of burning Malady splashed Ash, and she raised her arm to catch them along the haft of her scythe. They burned into the wood, leaving pockmarks that smoked.

Ashwyn leaped, using the Nexum to sail over the Malady creature, and sliced through the scorch marks, cutting pieces of it away.

The Malady creature groaned and swiped, and Ash grabbed another strand to change directions. Her scythe whistled through the air, a whirling blur, slashing and burning as it went.

One by one, strips of Malady fell away from the creature, floating to the ground like withered leaves. And one by one they turned to ash and dust, coating the ground at the Malady creature's feet.

Ash peeled the layers back, tears streaming down her cheeks as the creature shrieked and fought. She pushed ahead, embracing the pain of its voice, knowing this was right. No matter how much it hurt them, she just had to keep going.

The Malady at her feet writhed, seeking a way forward. It stabbed through the firebreak, toward the life it could sense in the corner, and Ashwyn ruthlessly cut it back.

It sent twining strands of corrupted Nexum up Ash's legs, locking her in place. She slashed through them and tore herself free, blood streaming from the rents they left in her skin.

White streaks of corruption unfolded from the gap and shrouded the Malady creature in a new skin of infection.

But through the gaps, Ash caught glimpses of silver light.

And she fought harder.

Her own light had been buried by the Devastation, but it had still burned fiercely underneath.

She slashed and peeled away another strip, revealing a pulsing heart in the creature's chest.

The creature screamed and fell to its knees, clawing its way forward.

Her own heart had cracked in Edgefall, but it had not broken.

Ash sobbed and ran for the creature, wrapping her arms around its thin frame.

The skeletal head sank, and Ash drove her fingertips into the last layer of Malady that covered its back. She took her two handfuls and tore them away, like a cloth parting in two.

The tear traveled all the way up, and Ashwyn stumbled back, taking the severed blanket of Malady with her.

The figure in the center of the room collapsed, and Ash threw the Malady away from them both.

The last pieces of it disappeared into the gate, shredding like a threadbare cloak worn too long.

Leaving behind a woman. A tall, slim goddess who knelt against the flagstones, Her pale silver hair falling over Her shoulders in waves of moonlight.

Chapter 72
Concordim

Ash's arms ached, and the only thing that kept her scythe from falling to the floor was her numb fingers, so stiff she couldn't unlock them from around the shaft if she wanted to. Blood streamed down her arms from the places where the Malady creature's nails had cut deep into the skin and muscle.

And somewhere beneath the surface, a battle still raged. If she focused, she could just feel the smooth stone scythe in her hands and hear the crack of thunder as the Malady tried to gain ground within her veins.

But she had the hang of it now. She could keep it at bay.

She pushed herself upright, using her scythe as a crutch.

The sound of weeping was the only thing to disturb the silence of the ancient temple, and Ashwyn turned her head to find the villagers with her good side. They huddled together, shivering even now that it was all over, and Ash felt a twinge of frustration and a sort of horrified affection for the useless creatures.

Before them, the Life Goddess stood, hands clasped with Cass's. Ash couldn't tell who was clinging to whom, but at least Cass had kept her promise. And holding a goddess back couldn't have been easy.

Deavita's eyes locked on the figure in the middle of the room, waiting.

Ash finally turned to see what she'd wrought.

The Goddess of Death rose to Her feet and straightened, the last bits of Malady swirling away from Her feet like tattered wisps of smoke. She wore a thin, black stole, no more than two strips of fabric held together with a belt that draped Her bony form. But where the Malady creature had been skeletal, this woman was long and elegant.

Her straight silver hair fell over Her shoulders, not nearly as long as Deavita's but shining like moonlight against a still pond. Stark white wings stretched from Her temples, feathers blending into Her hair. Another set rose from Her waist, and they stretched and flapped once before they fell to settle around Her hips like a train. A few white feathers floated free, rising in the draft around Her to catch what little light there was this deep underground.

She raised Her chin, Her eyes opening to take in the temple, and Ash found herself pinned under that black gaze. Her eyes were the same color as the healthy black strands of the Nexum, shining with a sable glow.

For just that one second, Ash found herself the sole focus of a death goddess, and her hands went sweaty against the shaft of her scythe.

How much of the Malady was left in Her? Did this woman seek death above all else? How much was Ashwyn going to regret freeing Her?

She tried to swallow, but her throat had gone dry.

And then the moment was gone as the Goddess's eyes slid to Deavita.

Everything in Her changed in that instant, Her hair and eyes and wings gaining a lustrous silver light. And the Death Goddess lurched toward them at the same time Deavita let go of Cass and rushed forward.

They met under the temple dome, arms going around each other, and Ash's eyes watered at the searing brightness of it. Feelings came off of Them in waves, a surging, crushing tide of emotion too wide and too ancient to sort through.

Ash turned her face away, noting the way the Malady remained in its pool. It sat quiescent and still now. But it was still there.

And Morlinna lay beside the gap, face turned toward the ceiling.

Ash dropped to her knees beside her, heart in her throat.

Morlinna turned her head, white eyes just registering her presence.

"Ash," she whispered.

Ashwyn choked. "I'm here," she said, taking Morlinna's hand in hers and pressing her palm to her cheek.

She could do that now. Touch Morlinna without fear, even with the Malady rising high in her body, threatening to take her.

"I am so proud of you," Morlinna said through cracked lips. "I'm leaving the Devastation in good hands."

"No," Ash grated out. "Not yet, you aren't."

And she followed Morlinna's heart thread to her battleground. Hers looked like a flat black plane of obsidian with dark clouds crowding the horizon. A tracery of white covered the black stone at her feet as the lightning flickered over everything. A shrunken, exhausted form of Morlinna lay in the middle, hands over her head to protect herself from the lightning that swarmed every inch of her body.

And Ash swept them away, her throat choked with the futility of it. Morlinna was gone. She'd go Absent any moment. But she could at least give her clarity in the last moments.

She could give her what she'd always wanted. Safety. Acceptance.

She beat the Malady back, one pace, two. Enough that when she retreated, Morlinna breathed easier on the floor of the temple.

The Malady that Ash could see beneath the torn edge of her robe flickered, just a breath from her heart. But not consuming it. Not yet.

Morlinna took Ash's hand and used it to pull herself up to sitting, and she didn't relinquish it once she was stable.

Morlinna gazed at the destruction in the temple, the gap that still pulsed nearby, and the tattered edges of the Malady where Ash hadn't gotten to pushing it back.

"I expected it to be gone," Ashwyn said quietly. "Or retreat. Be weaker somehow."

Morlinna shook her head. "No. We have not defeated it. But you did separate the Malady from the Goddess it had corrupted."

Ash squinted and finally forced herself to look at the couple embracing in the center of the temple. "What happened to Them? Why is the world broken?"

"I don't know."

Ash gave her a look.

Morlinna's lip twitched. "She doesn't remember."

"She's the voice you've been hearing."

"Yes. All these years it has been Deamorta."

Ash blew out her breath. "Why didn't She just say who She was?"

"The Malady cuts Her off. Every word I've heard Her say, She's had to fight for. It wasn't until it brought me here that I could hear Her clearly."

"Clearly?" Ash asked with a snort. "I don't think it counts as clearly if She can't answer any questions."

Morlinna shook her head. "She has been exiled for however many hundreds of years, Ashwyn. She has had to pull pieces of Herself together and make sense of Herself like a puzzle with too many missing pieces. Think of how you felt when your whole life was stripped away and you had to create yourself anew without Cass."

Ash swallowed.

"From what we've learned here," Morlinna gestured to the city around them. "And the little She remembers, it is clear that She was cut from this world. Life and death both belong here. And without one, everything is thrown out of balance. Death's power ran amok, trying to restore the balance. And trying to tear a way for Her to come back. But without Her to control it..."

"It became the Malady."

"Exactly."

And the Malady was still killing Morlinna.

Ash stood, Morlinna clinging to her hand.

"What are you doing?" Morlinna asked.

"Figuring this out."

The Death Goddess had finally pulled back from Deavita, though They still held each other's hands, desperation in Their grip.

Ash gulped. How many hundreds of years had They gone without each other? It didn't change how Ash felt, but it did change the context. It softened the edges of her anger.

Deamorta met her gaze, black eyes latching onto hers. She released one of Deavita's hands and placed Her palm on Her heart.

"You are the one who freed me from the Malady."

Ash took a breath. "I am."

Deamorta bowed from the waist. "Thank you."

"You're welcome." Ash nodded, then she deliberately looked at the pool of the Malady and back to the Death Goddess. "Now fix it."

Morlinna choked behind her.

Deamorta's eyes squeezed shut, and a flicker of pain crossed Her expression. "I cannot," She whispered.

"Why not? You're a goddess. It's your power. You can control it."

Deamorta shook Her head. "I cannot. It is no longer a part of me."

"How?" Ash cried.

Deamorta opened Her eyes, the edges still creased with hurt. "I am still cut from this world. I don't belong here anymore. My power is a corrupted, nearly sentient thing. And it is now separate from me."

Right, Ash had done that. On purpose.

"But..." The fight was draining out of Ashwyn, and she held onto that feeling of anger if only to keep away the despair. "She's dying," she whispered.

"I know," Deamorta said, a smile coming into her voice. "But I am still the sovereign of that." She took a couple of deep breaths, like She'd been running flat out for hours. Then She held Her free hand out and touched Ashwyn's cheek. "Do not worry. This is only the first step on a long journey. We can move forward now."

The Death Goddess staggered, and Deavita lunged to catch Her.

"What's wrong?" Ash asked.

"I can't stay here." Her voice flickered strangely. "The world is pushing me out."

"How did this happen to you?" Ash said, desperate for answers that might lead them anywhere besides dying on the floor of an ancient temple.

Deamorta shook Her head. "I don't remember."

"Why can't you remember?"

"There are still pieces of myself missing. They still float out there." She threw out Her hand to indicate the gap, and Ash was struck with the realization that they'd been right. The gaps were gates to Obitullas. Realm of the dead.

Deavita flapped Her hands to get their attention, and when they looked at Her, She raised them over Her head and brought them down on either side.

Ash shook her head. "I don't know what that means."

Deamorta's lips thinned, and She took her wife's face in Her hands. "I am sorry, my life. I don't understand."

Deavita's eyes welled with tears that spilled over and down Her cheeks as She made fruitless noises in the back of Her throat.

"I can tell you one thing," Deamorta said. "This atrocity that has happened is not a *what*. But a *who*."

"How do you know?"

"Because they have maimed the one person who can tell us. They bound the one whose power could help bring back my own."

She pressed Her forehead to Deavita's, and Ash looked away, hiding from Their pain.

Until Deamorta cried out and fell to one knee.

The Life Goddess clutched frantically at Her shoulders and gestured to the gap, as if urging Her to save Herself.

"I don't want to leave you," Deamorta whispered.

Deavita pressed Her lips together and gestured again, indicating urgency. Then She held out Her hand to Ashwyn and Morlinna.

Finally, Deamorta nodded. "I know. I have survived it before. I will survive it again. For you. And this time, I have help."

The Death Goddess seemed to steel Herself and stood. She turned to Morlinna.

Morlinna knelt, eyes wide and filled with more emotion than Ash had ever seen.

"My lady," Morlinna whispered.

"My Saint," Deamorta said. "I can save you. But there is a cost."

"What is it?" Ash asked before Morlinna could respond.

"You must become mine," Deamorta said.

Morlinna sucked in a breath.

"You will no longer be my wife's Saint. You will be Obitusim. My realm is overrun with the Malady, and I need someone who can use it for me. Someone who can fight it for me."

Morlinna pressed her hand to her heart. "You know I am yours, my lady. I have been since the day I knelt before the throne and heard your voice."

Ash fought the lump in her throat. She was done interrupting, but mortis, it hurt to bite back the words that would turn Morlinna from this.

"I know," Deamorta said with a smile. "You listened and learned and trusted even without knowing my name. But you cannot take this next step without knowing what I am asking."

Morlinna fought to climb to her feet, and Ash rushed to support her. "I'm willing, my lady."

"Are you? Mine is a realm for the dead. Not the living."

Mortis.

"Then how...?" Morlinna whispered.

"Death does not work exactly the way it once did," Deamorta said with a tilt of her eyebrow. "Neither does the Malady. It is a corruption of my power, but it is still my power. Stop fighting it, and it will change you. As long as you know who you are, you will be able to hold yourself through the change."

"Just stop fighting it?" Ash said, incredulous.

"The conflict is what makes it vicious," Deamorta said. "With acceptance, it becomes what it was supposed to be. A key to Obitullas."

Deamorta was asking Morlinna to become the thing she'd spent her life fighting. It seemed like madness, but Ashwyn knew Morlinna's answer before she even said it.

"I will have to go with you," Morlinna murmured. "To fight the Malady."

Deamorta nodded. "Yes."

And, strangely enough, Morlinna hesitated.

Ash could guess why. Morlinna would be leaving the Devastation to the Malady. She would be leaving the villagers in danger. She would be leaving Ash in danger.

Morlinna's hand tightened on Ash's.

She was choosing between Ash and the Goddess. The Goddess who had been speaking in her ear her whole life. The Goddess who had given her purpose and a place and the truth when everyone else had lied.

Ash swallowed, her chest one fierce ache. "Morlinna," she whispered.

Everything in Ash fought it. Morlinna was her life now. Her purpose.

But every moment of Morlinna's life had been leading to this. While Ash had been drawn toward Morlinna, Morlinna had been drawn toward the

Goddess. One with a different name than they'd thought, but that hardly mattered to her.

Ashwyn had no claim on Morlinna's heart because her heart had always belonged to Deamorta.

"Go," Ash said through the ache in her throat. "Go with Her. You're not leaving the Devastation undefended. I'm here. And...and I will keep the part of you that you allowed me to have. And cherish it even if it's not the whole."

Morlinna leaned into her, resting her forehead on Ash's, her hand tightening on the back of her neck. "That part burns as bright as the rest," she said. But her voice was clear, like a weight had lifted free. "I know who and what I am because of you."

Ash pressed her lips to Morlinna's, ruthlessly shoving down the realization that this would be the last time.

And Morlinna stepped away from her, leaving her white porcelain mask in Ash's hands.

"I'm ready, my lady."

Deamorta bowed Her head. Then stepped forward and kissed Morlinna's brow. The way Deavita had done to Ash that day in the necropolis.

"Then you are my Saint in power as well as name. You will be my hands, and I will be your strength."

Deamorta stepped back, and Morlinna closed her eyes. Ash felt the change in her. The raging fight stilled, and peace settled over her shoulders. For the first time, Morlinna stopped pushing back the Malady.

It took every ounce of willpower for Ash to withdraw from her own place in that fight and let the white lightning sweep across the black plane of Morlinna's battleground.

Morlinna shivered, and the lines of white along her arms writhed and circled her heart, spiraling around and around until they formed a white knot.

But they did not become a gap.

Morlinna opened her eyes, and Ashwyn gasped. A halo of white surrounded the blue, and though the lines in her face had stilled, they streaked away from her eyes like rays of the sun.

"Felleron," Morlinna said, and the old wolf whined as he stopped at the edge of the pool of Malady.

Morlinna stepped to him. A moment passed, and some communication swept between them. Then the wolf bowed his head and pressed into her hands.

The Malady swept through the wolf's fur, streaking it with silver, and his eyes reflected the same change as in Morlinna.

Deamorta turned and swept the Life Goddess into a fierce embrace one last time. She whispered something in Her ear and then stepped back.

Morlinna walked to the edge of the gap and stared down into the lightning-streaked blackness. She looked back at Ashwyn.

"Make me one last promise," she said.

"Anything," Ash said without really thinking.

"Trust Her," Morlinna said. Then she swept her hand through the threads of Malady clustered at the edge of the gap and formed a set of stairs plunging down into Obitullas.

Ash's heart seized. Trust Her?

The Death Goddess bowed Her head to Ash once more. Then She kissed the tips of Her fingers and pressed them to Ash's forehead.

"A part of your power is mine now as well, magpie."

Then She disappeared down the stairs, into the gap. Morlinna followed with Felleron close at her side.

A promise or a threat, Ash wasn't sure.

But they'd left her standing here with the Life Goddess. A woman she'd distrusted and maligned. She'd believed the worst things of Deavita and still wasn't sure how she felt about the Goddess who seemed more victim than deity now.

She turned to Her.

And Deavita smiled, a sardonic quirk in Her lips telling Ash She knew much if not all of what was going on in her head.

Ash flushed. What was she supposed to do with Her now? Bring Her back to Morlinna's cloisters and put Her to bed? Introduce Her to Father Liman? How did you care for a goddess?

Deavita touched her on the forehead, where She had bestowed Her kiss years ago. Then She gave that same gesture from before, Her hands held out as if pleading.

Then She relaxed, as if She'd been fighting some sort of tether or leash this entire time, and Her form disappeared in a flurry of green sparks.

Ash huffed. After all this time, she shouldn't have been surprised.

But she could feel the stretch of a tiny connection. A strand from her forehead, stretching away to the north. Toward Vitamorn.

Chapter 73
Animatim

The throne stood empty, and V had to draw in a breath or risk passing out.

She sucked air into her lungs and dropped to her knees before the throne. She'd believed. She still believed.

Deavita would return. She'd choose to return. She had to. Or V had just doomed their entire world.

Her dry eyes burned, and her hands formed the words of the Saint's petition, the signs translating her belief, over and over.

"Deavita, keep us in goodness, gentleness, and joy. For your freedom we pray."

Inside the words changed to something simpler. Something desperate.

Please. Please. Forgive me. Come back to me.

She couldn't mouth the words, her body failing her in her grief until she fell back on the signs she'd had since childhood.

One thread stretched from the throne, flashing black in V's sight, thin and impossibly fragile. It wasn't enough. V would have to help.

She reached for it...

And let her hand drop. She collapsed against the seat of the throne, her heart clogging her throat until she couldn't breathe through the pain.

Her forehead touched something warm and soft, covered in a layer of green velvet, and her eyes snapped open.

V gasped and scrambled back from the knees she'd clutched.

Deavita sat enthroned, a shaft of green light fading around her.

V stifled a sob. She'd returned. She'd come back without V's help. She'd chosen to return. She chose to be here. With V.

Her heart twisted and released. Her father was wrong. V was right, and the relief and regret threatened to swamp her.

The Primarch Divine had told everyone the Goddess had chosen her, had returned for her. But She hadn't, really. Not until now.

"Thank you," V signed, fingers shaking. "Welcome home."

A familiar flash of guilt for using her hands swept through her, and V gritted her teeth against it. Her hands spoke the truest language of her heart, and she wasn't going to apologize for it anymore.

For so long the Abdicant had made her feel like any weakness was a flaw. That everyone who saw her sign would use it against her. But the only one who had tried to bring her down with it had been her father. And she wasn't going to let him control any part of her anymore.

The pain still hadn't faded, but she willed a numbness to cover it. A sweeping cooling wall protecting her from the scars of duty.

Her hands continued to move through it all. And when she raised her gaze, she found the Goddess's eyes were open. Just as they'd been the day she'd been gifted.

Deavita's pale gaze trained on V's face, then dropped to her hands.

And Deavita watched her sign.

Concordim

Ashwyn had no idea how long it took to transport the villagers back to Edgefall. She could only jump them two or three at a time to the edge of the village where the strand that had reformed in her chest wanted to take her. Just beside the necropolis.

Each trip blurred into the next until the only thing she remembered was the constant drop in her stomach and an army of frightened faces and clinging hands.

Cass insisted on going last, and night closed in deep and black around the village when she and Ash appeared on the flagstones beside the necropolis.

Cass raced back to the village through the stand of feverdusk trees while Ash staggered behind her, blood drying on her sleeves. She had to use her scythe as a crutch to stay upright.

It had taken hours at least to get them all back. Some, if not all of them, should have gone to sleep.

But they waited on the village green, arrayed in a crowd before the Lower Temple. Wraith lounged on a roof above them, keeping watch with a lazy eye, his tongue lolling out of his mouth. Ebonheart circled with the flock above. Some of the villagers eyed them warily, but no one dared raise a stick to frighten them away.

Cass went from person to person, checking in with each of them, assessing their cuts and bruises and murmuring reassurances.

But none of them paid attention to her. They all turned as Ash limped into Edgefall.

Ash's teeth clenched as she felt their eyes on her. Years of watching everything she said and did came crashing in on her, and she struggled to stand up straight under the onslaught of memory.

Had she ever been happy here? Maybe there had been moments here and there with Cass, but all of those had been drowned under the weight of her childhood and the horror of her exile.

As she passed, the Fairhand boys turned aside to make room for her. Selah gave her a smile and a nod. And finally, Bayna stood with Father Liman and Greta on the steps of the temple.

Father Liman beamed. "The Goddess has spoken," he said, and his smile faltered for one nervous second before he shook his head and laughed. "Both of them. Welcome home, Ashwyn."

Bayna grimaced as Greta pushed past her and clasped her bony arms around Ash's middle.

Ash froze as Father Liman gave them both an enthusiastic embrace. The rest of Edgefall surged forward, patting her on the back, calling their thanks, crowding her with their praise and goodwill.

And Ash shivered under it all, holding back the tide of rage and exhaustion if only so the Devastation wouldn't feed off of her feeling and overrun them all.

Perhaps Greta felt her stiffen under their touch because she backed away, pushing back the wall of villagers, shooing them away while she promised to visit them and tend their bruises in the morning.

In the shifting mass of humanity, Ash caught a glimpse of Bayna. The old woman sniffed, nose in the air.

"You've fooled them all," she hissed. "But not me. Apostate. Monster. Don't expect a warm welcome from me—"

"I expect nothing from you, Bayna."

This moment should have felt fierce and right, facing Bayna and forcing her to acknowledge every word, every slap, every hurt she'd ever dealt. But the brittle, aging woman held no power over her anymore.

"I expect nothing because you are nothing to me," she said, voice flat.

And all the vitriol drained from Bayna's face as her jowls went slack.

"Just out of curiosity..." Ash said. "Why do you hate me so much? Even as a child you hated me."

Bayna's throat worked. "You weren't one of us. Your mother was from the city."

Ash waited for more but Bayna's face tightened and she sniffed.

That was it. That one difference had been enough for Bayna to condemn a girl to misery and abuse. The imagined slight of feeling lesser than an orphaned child had turned Bayna into a taskmaster seeking control where she felt weak.

It was not understanding that made Ash step back. It was acceptance that she'd never know anything deeper than that. Because there wasn't anything deeper.

There were more important things in this world than one petty tyrant. All of those too big emotions Ash kept locked up inside, Bayna wasn't worth a single one of them anymore.

She stepped past the woman and didn't watch her leave.

Out of all of it, Bayna's disdain was easier to deal with than the praise. It was truer than the villagers' belated goodwill. Bayna at least didn't hide how she really felt or pretend that all of this was right. That everything would go back to the way it had been, and that was a good thing.

Ash let the rage shiver out of her veins and tasted its bitter edge on her tongue. She'd dreamed of this acceptance her entire life. She'd planned it all in her mind, from becoming a Saint to returning to Edgefall in triumph, but it should not have been like this.

She shouldn't have been exiled. She shouldn't have had to survive the Devastation or save the villagers from the Malady to prove that she was worthwhile. She shouldn't have had to earn her childhood at all.

She squeezed her eyes shut, angry at the way they stung and moisture pooled in the corners.

Morlinna shouldn't have had to go through what she did for them to not see her as a monster.

Ash sent a thought to Wraith to follow, and she rushed from the square, pushing past the last of the villagers who returned home, weary and laughing after their ordeal.

She got as far as the orphan house before a voice behind her made her legs seize.

"Ash."

Ashwyn stopped, free hand on the sagging railing where they'd stood and watched Selah stare into the Devastation. The other clenched the shaft of her scythe.

"Where are you going?" Cass asked.

Ash turned to face her, putting the Devastation behind her back. It felt better there. Like an old friend waiting.

"I'm going home," Ash said.

Cass licked her lips and glanced at the creeping roots of the forest. "I didn't think you'd want...I guess I thought you'd stay here."

Ash's brows drew down, and she raised her chin. "Why?"

"Because things will be different now." Cass took a step forward. "I'll make a place for you here. I'll make sure you never have to fight anyone for your right to exist again. We could...we could start over." Cass swallowed, and even in the dark Ash could see the movement in her throat. "Maybe this time we could be better for each other."

Cass reached for her hand and dropped her gaze to find it in the dark. Ash saw the moment Cass saw the Malady in her veins.

Ash unlocked her fingers from the railing and held them out in front of her. White streaked through the back of her hand, and she had to swallow, knowing what it meant. Death was creeping toward her heart, getting closer every minute.

But for now it barely reached her wrist.

Wraith flapped down and trotted to her side. She deliberately placed the hand on his head, burying her white-laced fingers into the fur between his horns.

"I'm not coming back," she said and realized that all the anger had drained out of her somewhere along the way. All that was left was an aching sadness for what could have been.

She could have held onto the hate, let it simmer in her blood alongside the Malady, but she couldn't help remembering Greta's rough voice teaching her at the edge of the Devastation, and Father Liman's wink as he manufactured reasons to help her. There were good memories mixed with the bad, and they couldn't be untangled from each other without losing something from each.

Cass's fingers clenched, and she drew her hand back toward her chest. "Are you...are you going to wait for her? Morlinna?"

Ash turned her face away. "No. She's where she was always supposed to be. I got what little sliver of her life I deserved, and that's it. She's not why I'm not coming back."

She gave Cass a pointed glance.

Cass flinched. "I thought after everything, you didn't hate us anymore."

"I don't hate you." And somehow that was true. "But that doesn't make me love you."

"Ash..."

"This was my home. I shouldn't have had to earn my place here. You shouldn't have to make sure I'm accepted. I shouldn't have had to forgive you because it never should have been a choice."

"People make mistakes," Cass said.

"I know. I've made plenty. But those mistakes change things. They changed me. And I can't be the person who goes back to that place. Something in me wishes I could. I wish I could see what we could have been. But I'm not that person anymore. And neither are you."

"No," Cass said, voice shaky. "I hope I'm better."

Ash laughed. "Me too."

She turned, and her gaze caught on the orphan house. "But now it's time to be better for them. Not me."

She stepped away from the railing, leaving Cass behind. She didn't look back to see if the other woman was watching.

Ash held her scythe to her chest as she walked, her thumb rubbing the pockmarks in the shaft.

Morlinna had given herself up for something far greater than any of them knew. Ash would spend the rest of her life honoring that, if she had to.

She would still protect Edgefall. Still keep wanderers out of the Devastation and away from the Malady. Not because they'd earned that from her, but because that was Ash's purpose. But Morlinna had left her much more than that. A task far greater.

And a home that accepted her.

A thin, fragile thread stretched from her chest, connecting her to Edgefall whether she wanted it or not.

She cut it free and held it in her hand for a moment. Then she tied it around her wrist, keeping it with her but not a part of her.

Ash lifted Morlinna's mask to cover her face. Then she stepped into the Devastation and let it consume her.

Chapter 74
Animatim

Vitania stood on the stone balcony above Vitamorn's necropolis, hands resting on the cold balustrade. Below, hundreds of Absent milled in the filtered sunshine, moving listlessly across the flagstones.

V fought to unfocus her gaze and let it skim the crowd without taking in any details or looking for a specific face.

"We don't get very many surprise inspections," the Keeper beside her said, his eyes darting between her and his charges below.

She forced a smile. "Yes. That's why they're called surprises."

His ears went red and he cleared his throat. "Of course."

A sharp pain zipped up her hand, and she realized she'd gripped the stone railing hard enough to tear a fingernail. V breathed and relaxed her fingers.

"Are they happy?" she asked abruptly.

"What?" The Keeper blinked watery eyes.

"The Absent." She jerked her chin toward them, deliberately not looking. "Are they comfortable? Do you think they're happy down there?"

She expected him to spout platitudes, but his lips flattened.

"I don't...I don't know, Your Serenity. I think only the Goddess can say. We try to take care of them, make sure they're clean and have a place to sit or lie down. They get fresh clothes every week and sometimes—" He stumbled to a stop and glanced at her, eyes wide.

She raised her eyebrows. "Sometimes?"

"Sometimes I...well, I sing to them. I like to think it calms them."

V's throat tightened until it ached and she stared out across the courtyard until she could school her expression.

"It sounds like you know them very well."

"I care for them every hour of every day. I know their faces if not their names. We received two new unknowns a couple of days ago."

"I'm aware," V said quietly.

"And they will be as treasured as the rest, even without names." The Keeper glanced at her sidelong. "If you don't mind me asking, Serenity, why the sudden interest in the Absent?"

V raised her chin. "The Abdicant is too busy to handle every duty within the city. I intend to take this burden from her from now on."

"That is admirable," the Keeper said. "But she usually performs her inspections in the winter."

"I'm leaving to hunt heretics along the front lines tomorrow," V said, pushing away from the railing and linking her hands behind her back. "I wanted to make sure everyone here was in good hands before I left."

The Keeper coughed uncertainly as V turned away from the Absent milling below, leaving before she could accidentally spot a familiar beard or soft eyes.

Her chest ached enough to make her gasp and she held her breath to hide it. Every step away sent a splinter of ice through her heart.

But she pasted a smile across her face, an easy expression designed to misdirect.

Judges did not show pain. Judges did not show anger. They did not bleed with their choices or their doubts. They did not worry or question or weep.

Judges reflected perfection. Always.

Concordim

Ash knelt on the thick vines, her black robe pooled around her, watching the strands of Malady twist and untwist in front of her.

Have you ever seen them do that before? Wraith asked.

"No," Ash said.

She reached out to take a strand in her hand, bolstering the battle within her to take the strain. But the thread felt just like a corrupted thread always did.

Something is changing, Wraith said.

Ash let go of the strand and stood, brushing off her robe. "I think it means that Morlinna and Deamorta are doing something on their end."

Curing the Malady, maybe?

"No, I've tried it. It doesn't work the way it did. I think now that it's separate from Deamorta, it's too different from a human to follow a human's template."

Then what is it?

"I have no idea. But I think it's going to take work here and in Obitullas to fix whatever is wrong with it. That's why She took Morlinna."

And Ash prayed every day that Morlinna wasn't actually dead. Just some sort of death Saint. Maybe when all this was over, she could come back.

Maybe that's why They needed someone who was both things.

Ash stopped to look at him. "What?"

You belong to both. If Morlinna is Death's Saint, then you are both Life and Death. The balance between them.

Ash snorted. "I thought Felleron was the one who was named after a poet. It's a lovely idea, but if there's supposed to be balance, then wouldn't there be three of us? Someone has to represent Life, too. And I don't see anyone else around."

She shook her head as she swung her scythe to cut the new threads of Malady. It whistled now as air moved over the pockmarks, a shrieking cry that reminded her of a dread. She should probably fix them, but there was something satisfying about the way the Devastation beasts scattered when they heard her coming.

So what are we going to do now? To fight it if we can't heal it.

"I'm going back to Mournefast as soon as I can. Now that I know what I'm looking for, I'm hoping I can still find answers there. Someone tore Deamorta out of this world. Someone cleaved Her from Her power and let it become the Malady. And we need to find out who."

Deamorta's words rang in her head most days now. "They have maimed the one person who can tell us. They bound the one whose power could help unbind my own."

Cass had described the Life Goddess as having grown into Her throne. Ash had just assumed it was another symbol of Her divinity, like the hair and the eyes.

But Deamorta made it sound like She was a prisoner. Perhaps that's what the gesture She'd kept using was. Perhaps the same person who had cut Deamorta out of the world had cut out Deavita's tongue so She couldn't give voice to their sins.

"I'm coming, Deavita," Ash whispered under her breath, not sure if it was a promise or a threat. "And I'll learn the truth, finally."

She no longer asked questions of the Goddess, knowing She couldn't answer. But it felt different to talk to Her now. There always seemed to be a sense of listening coming from the trees around her.

Morlinna had said to "trust Her." And Ashwyn was trying. For her own sake as well as Deavita's. It was very uncomfortable to be angry with a goddess.

She didn't understand why Deavita had chosen her in the first place. Didn't know exactly why She hadn't appeared to defend Ash from exile. But she was willing to see now that her whole life was more complicated than a single missing voice.

And she aimed to find the truth of it all by the time Morlinna needed her help again.

Ebonheart swooped overhead. *Intruders. Heading for the Heart.*

Wraith blew out a sigh and lurched to his feet.

Ash just chuckled. "There are always more."

She drew Morlinna's mask over her face and pulled a thread, launching herself into a higher layer of the canopy before she followed Ebonheart between branches.

A group of merchants argued at the edge of the Devastation, one gesticulating wildly back toward the Heart.

"It's that way. I swear."

Another scoffed. "You're full of it. The moss was on the other side of the trees when we came in."

Ash marked him as the smart one. She dropped to their layer, startling them.

"You cannot be here," she said, lifting her head. "The Devastation is forbidden."

They crowded back from her, stumbling over each other.

"It's the witch," the smart one said, eyes latched onto the mask. "Oh, mortis."

"We just wanted to cut through," another one said, voice shaking. "Make quicker time."

"The Devastation is forbidden," she repeated. "It's deadly. And you ventured in here for a shortcut?"

"We apologize," the smart one said. "It won't happen again. Er. If you could just point the way out..."

"Now hang on," the other said. "I never agreed to leave. We can shave three days off the trip by going straight through."

Ashwyn raised her scythe.

The smart one's eyes went wide, and the other started babbling, "No, no, no."

She brought the weapon down, and vines snaked out of the trees to wrap around the merchants' legs.

"Think hard about whether three days less is worth your lives," she said as they stared at her in terror. "If you return, you will get no second warning."

The vines yanked, and the merchants fell.

"The Devastation is mine," Ash said, over the sounds of their screams as the vines dragged them away to deposit them at the edge. "Do not trespass here again, or I will kill you."

She should have hidden, taken care to only show herself when there was no other course but to kill them. The way Morlinna had always done. Protecting her identity and her existence until the end.

But too much of Ashwyn wanted them to run away carrying tales of the new witch. She wanted them to tell the ones responsible for the ruination of the world that she was here. That she was coming for them.

She stood, knowing that the last thing the trespassers saw through the vines of the forest was a young woman with a white face and a double-headed scythe.

Who knew? Maybe it would keep them out.

The Devastation was the Life Goddess's place. And it had grown over Mournefast as if to hide it. Maybe Deavita really was hoping to keep people away from the place where the Malady had started. Or maybe She was holding a space where Deamorta could claw Her way back into the world.

Either way, Ash would guard the forest and the secrets that lay underneath. Because she now held the truth of the broken world, and she'd never let anyone bury it again.

Thank you so much for reading!

Morlinna's story began long before she met Ashwyn. Her experiences with Tavian and Illyra paved the way for her identity as Obitusim. Sign up here to read Morlinna's account of her accusation and exile.

If you're looking for more dark epic fantasy featuring kick-ass women, you'll love *The Pain Bearer*. This is more Indiana Jones meets Lord of the Rings and has lots of ancient ruins containing magical artifacts that really should have stayed buried...

And if you loved spending time with Ashwyn, Morlinna, and Vitania, consider leaving a review so other readers can find more stories about kick ass gals in kick ass worlds!

Acknowledgments

Mom and Dad, for so many years of support and encouragement.

Miranda and Lacey, for sharing your art and stories with me. It's an honor to be your sister.

Fiona McLaren, for copy edits and enthusiastic answers to "hey, you wanna read another book?"

Arielle Sigler from The Write Knight, for proofreading and an amazing eye for details. There would be a lot more missing commas if not for you.

Jenna Beacom, for sensitivity reading and insights into a lived experience I've only just brushed. Thank you for the challenges to V's story. She's so much more real with your input.

Lucy Lin, for an amazing cover. Your art brings these books alive in a way nothing else does. I always appreciate an excuse to work with you again.

Rio Burton, for beautiful illustrations that are perfect for the dark setting of this book.

Abby and Evie, for letting me fill our house with books and share this thing I love with you.

And Joselyn, for Morlinna and Deamorta and showing me that change can be divine. Thank you for this life we live.

About the Author

Books have been Kendra's escape for as long as she can remember. She used to hide fantasy novels behind her government textbook in high school, and she wrote most of her first novel during a semester of college algebra.

Kendra writes familiar stories from unfamiliar points of view, highlighting heroes with disabilities. Her own experience with partial paraplegia has shown her you don't have to be able to swing a sword to save the day.

When she's not writing she's reading, and when she's not reading she's playing video games.

She lives in Denver with her very tall wife, their book loving progeny, and an ever expanding library of new adventures.

Visit Kendra at
www.kendramerritt.com

facebook.com/kendramerrittauthor

goodreads.com/kendramerritt

instagram.com/kendramerrittauthor

tiktok.com/@kendramerrittauthor

www.ingramcontent.com/pod-product-compliance
Lightning Source LLC
Chambersburg PA
CBHW061531190726
48289CB00004B/998